What You Don't Know Now

To Kate
Thanks for such a
wonderful day!

Maria Diehl

What You Don't Know Now

Marci Diehl

MERGE PUBLISHING

SYRACUSE, NY

www.marcidiehl.com

Merge Publishing
Syracuse, New York

www.mergepublishing.com

"Questo O Quella" and "La Donna Mobile" from *Rigoletto* by Guiseppe Verdi
"Che Gelida Manina" from *La Boheme'* by Giacomo Puccini
"Torna a Sorrento" by Ernesto de Curtis

Publisher's Note: This is a work of fiction. Names, characters, places, and incidents are a product of the author's imagination. Locales and public names are sometimes used for atmospheric purposes. Any resemblance to actual people, living or dead, or to businesses, companies, events, institutions, or locales is completely coincidental.

Book design ©2014 Leslie Taylor, buffalocreativegroup.com

ISBN 978-0-9904432-0-9

Printed in the United States of America

For the MacDonald sisters

~ Marg, Mary, Kap, Bet and Fran (especially Fran)

Acknowledgements

I'd like to thank my parents for recognizing that they had a budding writer on their hands — a little girl who loved to put words together and continued to do so, in many forms, throughout their lifetime. They saved those words in their dressers drawers and never failed to encourage and sometimes tolerate my expressions. I thank my Aunt Bet, who was my first letter correspondent, and who saved every single letter I wrote to her for more than forty years — and then gave me the gift of having them back, so I could re-read them and hear the voice of the girl I used to be, grown into a woman, wife and mother.

Thank you to my friend and fellow writer, Kathy Johncox, who has been with this novel since it was a chapter or two in a fiction workshop at Nazareth College; and to the incomparable author, Zena Collier, who led the workshop and then created a writers group for those of us who stuck it out. Zena's encouragement, critiques and comments, and Kathy's unfailing enthusiasm for Alessandro, kept the story going even when I had to take time off to do the business of life and bill-paying. Thank you to the tenor Bruno Longharini for your help understanding the training of operatic tenors.

Thank you to Don Stevens for creating Merge Publishing and asking me to be a part of it. I'm so grateful to have Cynthia Kolko for an editor — her keen eye and ear helped put the polish on the book and I am now more aware than ever of my penchant for using way too many em-dashes.

Above all, I thank my darling family and friends who have believed in me and supported me at every turn. Thank you, Ellen and Cindy, for being two of my first readers and cheering me on. Most of all, I thank my "magic circle," my precious sons, Matt, John, Graham and Colin, for all of your unwavering belief, support, love and confidence in me.

"Travel is more than the seeing of sights; it is a change that goes on, deep and permanent, in the ideas of living."

~ Miriam Beard

In the Summer
1967

The grass was soft and she could smell the rich earth beneath her. Some voice of reason tried to struggle up inside her as she lay stretched out with him on the ground. You're in big trouble now, it tried to say, but her legs ignored it, they opened beneath him. The hem of her dress bunched in a creased crumple under her arms. Her bra stretched, deflated, along her neckline. She sensed the disarray, but it didn't matter. All that mattered was the feeling of her breasts against the warm skin of his chest, the soft tickling of hair that spread across his breastbone.

Her head was cradled in the grass and she slipped into his eyes, a swimmer walking into the warm surf of an ocean, poised to dive in. This was what she'd wished for at the beginning, wasn't it —? The unexpected? Something real? He was all of this, and so much more. She'd prayed for something to happen, something extraordinary from this trip, but even when she was praying, she doubted. She'd wanted to come to this city least of all. What could it hold for someone like her?

Now she knew. She closed her eyes and let him take her where she needed and wanted to go.

CHAPTER ONE

One

Being in Venice the day you turn eighteen shouldn't be the one of the worst days of your life. She wasn't supposed to be unhappy. She was supposed to be having the time of her life. Finding romance, maybe. She shouldn't be stuck following a fat guy around in the wind and pouring rain. Bridey McKenna wanted to love Europe, but so far, the relationship was hard going. This was not the Europe of the posters on her bedroom wall back home.

Bridey boarded a water taxi for Venice that morning along with two dozen others who were part of the Summer Vacation Pilgrimage Tour, and they were all handed over to a local guide, a huge Venetian with a bushy mustache and a booming voice, whose belly slid over his beltline like a cake that had fallen in the oven. He held his folded umbrella aloft like a sword and instructing them to follow it at all times, he led them into battle with other groups of tourists, who followed similar guides also holding umbrellas or little flags on whippy poles. He was a large man, but he had long legs. He strode swiftly, beginning a four-hour walking tour in the soaking rain. The Pilgrims, especially the elderly ones, were hard-pressed to keep up.

The itinerary for the tour had the Pilgrims visiting seven countries in twenty-one days. They had three countries left. They hadn't actually slept in or visited two of them — Switzerland and Austria were pretty much a drive-through; they brushed the outskirts of Innsbruck on their way into Italy.

Americans were trundling through the cities and countryside in Europe by the busload that summer. The tourists peered down at the natives from tinted bus windows, high above the everyday population. They poured out from the air-conditioned behemoth cruisers to catch the day's scheduled dose of history or culture; then it was back on the bus to the next meal or stop before arriving at the night's accommodation in the next city. They brought snobbery and a sense of entitlement along with their wallets. *Let's just see what we've saved in this world*, they seem to say.

Venice sat regally sunk to its ankles in seawater, bones cracked and bowed from the great flood the year before, a collection of jewels muddied by the driving rains that arrived in the middle of the night with a massive thunderstorm. The rains relieved the heat and oppressive humidity the Pilgrims suffered through the previous night at the Hotel Tritone in Mestre.

Bridey's sandals squished and slipped against the soles of her waterlogged feet. The temperature dropped steadily as the Pilgrims walked, clammy and chilled, more concerned with avoiding pneumonia than with the magnificence of the Ducal Palace. Bridey's mother and Aunt Corinne dropped to the back of the group where their daughters marched with unhappy faces.

Deep in resentment and irritation, Bridey felt treated like a child, led like a nursery school group by this man with the ridiculous umbrella staff, who persisted in giving them the complete tour, rather than allowing anyone to take rest in a sheltered chair somewhere, or better still, escape back to their warm, dry hotel.

If this had been five days earlier — the way she felt in Ulm, achy with cramps and sore from sunburn — she'd be ready to rip the guide's umbrella to shreds, instead of just wishing he'd fall into a canal and disappear. But an incident in Ulm had spent her.

By the time the tour group boarded another water launch en route to the glass blowing factory on the island of Murano, Bridey no longer tried to hide her dejection. When she returned home, what would she have to tell about her days on this journey? The creepy old hotel in Brussels where the wait staff sneered at them throughout their dinner, and the beds were concave? The drunk the guide pulled out of a bar in Mannheim to guide the bus to their hotel, where baby roaches scared them out of the only private bathroom they'd had? They were nearly half way through the itinerary and she was beginning to feel a sense of panic. So far, she'd managed to do nothing but lose weight and peel from sun poisoning she'd gotten on a boat tour down the Rhine.

At least the glass factory was warm. The group watched glassblowers create exquisite bowls and vases and decanters, and obliged their hosts by filing into the gift shop to shell out many thousands of lira for treasures. Bridey's mother Tilla bought a green decanter set with hand-painted flowers that would be on display, but never used, in her corner dining cabinet for the next thirty-five years.

The wind died at noon, the sun barged its way through a crowd of clouds, and the humidity moved back in to stay. By one o'clock, the Pilgrims had three hours to explore Venice on their own, to stroll like normal people down narrow streets, which they did tentatively, sticking to the St. Mark's perimeter, looking in shops but buying little. They were already laden with packages from the glass factory and those packages grew heavy in short order. Someone pinched Corinne's behind. Corinne whooped in surprise, but laughed it off. Tilla clutched her purse tight to her chest.

Bridey's soggy sandals chafed. Her mother's back hurt and

she was limping, so Bridey carried the shopping bags. The handles cut into her hands. Her eyes began to well with tears.

On their walk to St. Marks' Square, a man sidled up behind Tilla and whispered something in her ear. Tilla dug her fingers into her purse, clutching it tight. Before she could utter a sound, the man strode away with a smile, folding a knife plainly in her view. "That man!" Her voice was a hoarse croak.

"What man?" Corinne asked her sister.

There was no one to point out. The man was gone, absorbed into the crowd that clogged the little avenue. "There was a man," Tilla insisted. "He tried to cut my purse strap! I felt it."

"Where?" Bridey scanned the scene. The street was full of people emptying into the huge piazza at St. Mark's Cathedral.

Corinne stepped around to examine Tilla's back. There was a small cut in the back strap of Tilla's purse. "I'll be damned!" Corinne said. She rubbed her sister's shoulder, more for reassurance than in the belief that Tilla had been hurt.

It had only been a few days since the mess in Ulm. The four decided to ditch the group's tour of the Ulm Minster. They reached a small square, empty except for a fountain pool. Bridey plunged her bare arms shoulder-deep into the water, her forehead puffy with sun poisoning from their cruise on the Rhine the day before. She'd refused any sun lotion and sat on the open top deck. If she'd brought a bottle of the baby oil and iodine concoction she and her friends used to sauté themselves to a golden brown, she would have used that, too. Bridey trailed her hands back and forth through the fountain pool. Then she took off her sunglasses and submerged her face.

"Bridey, stop that," Tilla said. "You don't know what's in that water. And don't bend over like that. You're giving everyone a show." She tugged the back hem of Bridey's dress, trying to pull it lower down the backs of her daughter's thighs. "Besides, you'll get your dress wet."

"Oh, that felt good! I'm broiling. Aren't you all hot?" Bridey turned around and wiped the water from her face and chin. The ends of her hair stuck together like soaked tassels, creating tiny streams of water running down her shoulders. The top of her dress was saturated. Her best friend Dena made it for her to wear to the party after their Senior Ball — it was full of tropical flowers and colors, with a few parrots thrown into the print. It screamed American Tourist.

"We have to get a picture," Corinne said. "Stand in front of the fountain." She stepped back several paces, adjusting the f-stop of her camera.

"Look." Bridey's fourteen year old cousin Sara nodded toward a man who appeared to materialize out of nowhere. He settled himself against a streetlamp, watching Corinne. "That guy has on those leather shorts."

"Lederhosen," Bridey said. The man wore a white shirt with the lederhosen, flowered suspenders, and knee-length socks with embroidered garters. Bridey thought he might be a waiter. The only place she'd ever seen an outfit like that was in her German textbook at school, the covers and pages soft with years and use by decades of previous girl students.

"Guten Tag," Bridey said, because the man was staring at them.

Corinne hurried back to her sister and the girls. "Bridey," she said. "Ask him if he'll be in the picture."

"I can't," Bridey said. "I don't know how to say that." She had four years of high school German under her belt, yet could barely conjugate verbs. She couldn't carry on a conversation. The best she could do was to read the restaurant bill for her fellow travelers.

"Well, say what you do know and use sign language," Corinne said. "It'll make a darling shot."

"Wie gehts?" she said to the man. Corinne grinned and held

up her camera. "This is embarrassing," Bridey said to her mother and aunt.

"Ask," said Corinne.

"Um," Bridey began. "Sprechen Sie English?" The man frowned back. "Um... ich spreche Deutsch nicht so gut, aber... Bitte. Kommen Sie, bitte? Mit uns? ...uh... Fur Photographen?" She made a gesture toward the fountain and her family.

The man stared hard at her, so hard she felt herself take one step back, as if he'd pushed her. Then he switched on a smile and answered with a string of sentences she had no hope of understanding. He said something far beyond her small powers of translation, but she sensed a threat in it. *Geld*, he'd said. She knew that word. Money. He arranged Sara and Bridey beside him. He checked Corinne's f-stop and nodded in approval.

"Okay, everybody," Corinne said, focusing the camera. "Smile!"

"Corinne, it's too bad you can't be in this," Tilla said.

"Strike a pose," Corinne said from behind the camera.

Tilla draped her arm around Sara. Bridey put one hand on her hip and tossed her hair. She smiled her best silly cheesecake grin. The man slid his arm around her, high above Bridey's waist. He barred his teeth at the camera. They were all still. Except... Bridey felt a stroking pressure on the inside of her arm and breast, where it was damp. She flinched. Then his hand slipped behind her, coming to rest at the curve of her bottom cheek, his fingers creeping against the fabric. Bridey wrenched away from him and glared.

In the photo that would be developed, she's in profile, her narrowed eyes fixed on the man beside her.

Tilla slipped a look at the watch that hung like a bracelet off her bony, freckled wrist. No matter how many links her husband removed, watch bands never really fit her. "We'd better get to the cathedral," she said. "It's two-twenty. They'll be getting ready to leave."

The man watched them gather their totes and purses and bags of souvenirs. Bridey could still feel the ghost-like pressure of his fingers. Tilla, Corinne and Sara looked so vulnerable. She stepped pointedly between the man and her mother. The man crossed his arms.

"Let's just go," Bridey said. "Start walking."

"What's wrong?" Tilla asked. "What did we do?"

"Nothing," Bridey said. "It's what he did. I'll tell you later."

The man knew the direction they wanted to go and placed himself in their way. It's four against one, Bridey thought — what can he do? But sensing the bewildered paralysis of her mother and aunt, she knew they were not going anywhere, not without his permission.

He hissed at them. "The money, ladies."

"Money!" Tilla threw her hand over her heart in comprehension. She opened her purse. His eyes went from Tilla to Bridey with a smirk.

Later on the bus to Munich, Bridey would puzzle over the feeling that took hold of her, facing that menacing look, never mind his arrogance in touching her, and watching her mother scrambling through her purse, obedient. Something rose up in her. She heard herself say "NO." Loudly.

"You phony!" Bridey said. "Do you dress up and wait for people like us to wander here? Like a spider?"

"Bridey! For God's sake, be quiet. We'll pay," said Tilla.

"He's trying to rob you!"

"I would shut up, fraulein!" the man said. "Tourists." He spat the word out like a spoiled piece of meat. His hand shot out and clamped viciously onto Tilla's knobby wrist. "The money — all of it — and you can go."

"I have it," Corinne offered. She held out a wad of bills. Sara stood behind her mother, her eyes round with fright behind her glasses. The man made no move to release Tilla.

"Let go of my mother!" Bridey demanded. Her hand tightened

around the handle of her zippered tote. It was more like a little suitcase, heavy with her makeup case, sweater, wallet, a pair of sandals, a bag of candy… She lowered her head and turned away, then swung the tote with both hands, letting the weight of the loaded bag pull her arms up and across in an arc. She did it as fast and deliberately as she could, so that when the bag slammed into the side of the man's head, it knocked him over. Tilla fell hard with him, her wrist still tight in his grasp. He fell to the ground , releasing Tilla. He lay sprawled on the cobblestones, touching his cheek where the zipper had cut it.

"Bridey, my god —!" Corinne yelled.

"Run!" Bridey shouted. She was afraid the man would jump up and come after her. She pushed Corinne and Sara forward. "Go! Now! GO!" They began to run, Corinne's high heels clattering against the cobblestone. Tilla lay frozen on her back, trying to sit up. She held her open wallet in her hand. Her legs splayed and the hem of her shirtwaist dress and slip revealed pale, slender thighs. Bridey hoisted her mother to her feet, grabbing the same reddened wrist the man had held. She dragged her mother as fast as she could out of the square, leaving the man on the ground staring at them open-mouthed.

When they were safely on their bus, Sara turned to Bridey. "That was the coolest move I've ever seen," Sara said. "It was like television."

Bridey hugged her tote bag and sank against the bus seat. Where had that feeling come from? She didn't think it was bravery. Whatever it was, it was powerful — it felt better than boredom. It was the most exciting experience of her trip so far. There were castles but no romance. There were cute guys, but unless they were waiters or the border guards at Aachen who flirted with her, holding her up to pretend to check her passport — she'd never get near them. She rode hermetically sealed inside the bus away from any real experience. Was this why? Was it actually dangerous?

When they arrived in London, soldiers patrolled London's Heathrow Airport. Belgium and Germany weren't places the Pilgrims were especially welcome, either. Now and then, their bus would go through underpasses plastered with graffiti. *U.S get out of Vietnam. Johnson is assassin.* Swastikas equated with the letters U-S-A. There were spray-painted, graphic descriptions of sexual acts the States could perform on itself in English, French and German. But it was her combination birthday/graduation present, this tour. She was determined to make the best of it.

Bridey looked around the bus she'd already nicknamed "The Phantom" for its way of disappearing off known roads, off course, ending up in places not listed on their itinerary. The nuns and widows on the tour sat like lemmings behind the guide and the driver. Bridey's eyes shifted to the four-page itinerary sticking out from the inside of Sara's log, a three-subject spiral notebook. The log was a thorough chronicle of every hotel and mishap (and who knew what else) from the time they arrived at JFK in New York for the charter. Each scrap of evidence of their journey so far was meticulously taped into the log: tickets, sugar cube wrappers, postcards, even a growing collection of different toilet paper sheets, from waxy to so-rough-they-resembled-roofing-shingles. The glossy brochure from the travel agency tucked inside the log enumerated cities, churches and museums for days to come, full of promises not yet kept.

"I need to sit down," Tilla said when they reached St. Mark's, her skin pale beneath her freckles.

"I'm getting blisters on my toes. Can we find something to drink?" Bridey complained. The heat of the sun bouncing off the huge plaza baked the air, and the ground stones of the plaza were beginning to lose the massive reflective puddles left from the morning torrent. Sara spotted a table for four with a large umbrella providing just the right amount of shade. They collapsed into the café chairs like refugees from a march in the Sahara.

Bridey slipped her sandals off. The skin on her toes burned, as if someone was holding tiny coals to them. The footpads of the sandals revealed the damp imprint of each foot. *Happy Birthday to me*, she thought. At least her friends had thrown a bon voyage-birthday party for her before she left. Dena made a pair of flower earrings out of tissue papers, along with a funny home-made card. The clothes in Bridey's suitcase were early presents. The trip was the biggie. She was the only girl in her class that got a trip to Europe for graduation. Her Aunt Corinne — well, really her Uncle Garner — was footing the whole bill for her and her mother. Her mom wasn't even going to come at first. But her aunt said it would be a "sister trip," a chance to have girl-time with their daughters before Bridey left for Georgetown University in the fall. The next thing you knew, they were the Fearsome Foursome.

She was in Venice and eighteen. It should feel bigger than sitting with sore feet waiting for a Coke, she thought. The water in the puddles shimmered cool and inviting on the stones of the square. She stood up, barefoot. "C'mon, Sara," she said. "I've got an idea."

Tilla grabbed at her. "Where are you going? Bridey — stay here."

"I'm just going to the puddle," Bridey snapped.

Sara followed her to the miniature lake on the stones twenty feet away. They walked in the water, dodging the pigeons that swooped over them in hopes of breadcrumbs. At first, they didn't notice the small band of prepubescent boys that headed for the same puddle they waded in, until the band swooped in their own way, dashing in and out, nearer and near to the girls. They had the leering, conspiratorial air of boys up to no good. Bridey recognized it; she'd seen it plenty of times in her own brothers. She tried to figure out their game. Before she could guess, they struck.

In threesomes, they grabbed the edges of Bridey and Sara's skirts and hoisted them up. A flash for the crowds at St. Mark's. Sara let out a screech of fury and humiliation and ran back to the safety of their table. Bridey fended off another attack by the full force.

Bridey's A-line dress hung from her shoulders like a tent, loose and flowing and easier to grab, easier than Sara's straight cotton skirt. She swatted at the boys, little hornets swarming at her thighs. As suddenly as they descended, they retreated, scattering into the crowds, trailing high-pitched giggles as they escaped. Bridey planted her hands on her hips and watched them go, then realized she was the center of attention of a few bystanders. More than a few of the men smiled at the view they had of her legs and underwear. One of them whistled and kissed his fingertips.

Her indignation turned to embarrassment. She shaded her eyes to hide but then lifted her chin. "Sei una Modella?" one of the men called to her. For a second, she felt glamorous — barefoot, long-legged, standing in a puddle in St. Mark's Square in Venice with her sunglasses on. Her girlfriends told her she looked like Jean Shrimpton, the British model, but all she had in common with The Shrimp was her height. She stood out in her family, towering over her mother, aunt and cousin.

She threw out her hands to her observers: What was one to do? It didn't have to be embarrassing. She could imagine she really was The Shrimp, doing a photo shoot.

Back at their table, Bridey sat down with a thump and slipped her sandals back on her feet.

"Are you happy now?" said Tilla. "Half of Italy has just seen your underwear." Tilla's purse sat on her lap. The strap wound around her forearm like a tourniquet.

"Good thing I was wearing some, then." She looked to Corinne and Sara for a smile at the joke, but got none.

"They were just kids," Bridey said. As if she would ever, ever not wear underwear. She hadn't even been braless since she was ten.

"Well it wasn't kids that were staring at you. We're just fair game here." Tilla unzipped her purse a few inches and stuck her wrapped-up arm in to fish for her cigarettes. A waiter appeared and took their drink orders. They stuck to colas. Tilla gagged down some aspirin without any liquid while they waited for the drinks. She still had nasty reddish-purple bruises on her spine and hip where she'd hit the cobbles in Ulm. Tilla didn't think anyone should drink the water, even with all the shots she and Bridey got for the trip — smallpox boosters, tetanus, and the ones for typhoid that her doctor said weren't required, but you might as well be safe than sorry. ("Typhoid?" Corinne had said when her sister told her weeks before they left. "We're going to Europe, Tilla, not the Congo.")

"It's three-thirty," Sara announced, checking the watch on her mother's wrist. "I wonder where all the others are?" The Pilgrims were supposed to meet in front of the cathedral to return to the hotel in Mestre, taking a vaporetto to the mainland and then a regular bus to the Hotel Tritone. Most of the group was probably touring the inside of the cathedral. By now, the foursome had established their reputation as regular tour-skippers when it came to churches.

"I'm ready to put my feet up for awhile." Corinne yawned. "Oh, look. There's Father. I wonder if the group is finished with the cathedral? Ah. He sees us."

Father Clement was American, rented by the travel agency for his spiritual services. The priest was from Arkansas. Bridey couldn't figure how a travel agency in New York City got a-hold of him. He stood about six-four and bore a startling resemblance to President Johnson, glasses and all. Father Clement said daily Mass at 6 a.m.. for the group, an event Bridey tried to miss as often as possible. She wasn't about to follow some priest around every day of their tour, not if she could help it. She planned to find enlightenment in other ways.

Still, ingratitude pricked at her like a straight pin poking out of a corsage.

"Hello, ladies," the priest said when he reached them. He took off his straw fedora and fanned his face with it. He was dressed in a short- sleeved shirt and tan pants like every other American milling in the busy space. "How was your afternoon?"

Tilla unwound the purse strap from her arm and held the strap up to him. "I was nearly purse-snatched. Someone tried to cut it. See?" She pointed out the slit in the vinyl. "I was lucky I wasn't stabbed."

"My. Y'all do seem to be having a time with thieves. But you're okay?"

"We're fine," Corinne said. "Would you like to join us, if you can find a chair?"

"Bridey," the priest said, winking at her. "No acts of heroism in this latest criminal attempt?"

"Whoever did it disappeared too fast," Bridey said. Father had been the only one who didn't question her hitting the man in the square in Ulm when he heard about it.

"Sometimes even a lady has to pack a wallop," he'd said.

"How's the birthday going, then?"

Bridey stalled, taking a swallow of her soft drink. Out of one hundred, she'd give it a forty-five percent. "Well… I mean, how would anyone not like spending her birthday in Venice, Italy? I'm sure dinner and the gondola ride will be fun tonight."

Father Clement glanced at the sky over St. Mark's. The tip of a cumulonimbus cloud peeked out from behind the dome, as if the heavens had added globs of whipped cream and were about to put a cherry on top.

"Let's hope we get lucky with the weather," he said.

"I'm not sure it's a great idea to come back here at night," Tilla said. "If someone's bold enough to try to steal a purse in broad daylight, imagine what they might try in the dark."

"We'll be in a group," Corinne countered. She signaled to the waiter for the check.

"What we've seen today is only a small part of Venice," Father Clement offered. "You really can't get the feel for a place spending part of a day in it. Besides, today is a momentous occasion. You don't turn eighteen but once."

Tilla stubbed out her cigarette and re-wound the purse strap back on her arm. "I'm ready to get back to the hotel and lie down." She glanced over at her daughter. "I want to make sure I'm rested up for the festivities."

By the time they found seats on the bus at Mestre to their hotel, the sky was already dark with the grey-green undersides of thunderclouds. Heavy splats of raindrops chased them to the Hotel Tritone, keeping up a torrential assault for the rest of the evening.

There were, of course, no gondola rides for the Pilgrims that evening, and they ate dinner in the hotel dining room. Outside, rain mixed with occasional pellets of hail. Lightning lit the windows and the following booms of thunder made more than one Pilgrim startle.

Rose the tour guide, Father Clement, and three waiters stood around their table as Bridey made a wish on the candle in a piece of tiramisu in front of her. The waiters sang *Happy Birthday* in Italian and brought everyone, including Sara, a small glass of wine for a toast. Bridey closed her eyes and made her wish.

"Now for presents," Sara said. She nodded at her mother. Corinne snapped open her purse and extracted a little box wrapped in the most ornate paper Bridey had ever seen.

"Save that paper," Tilla said.

Bridey unwrapped the package. Inside the box was a gondola charm.

"It would have been cooler if you'd actually been on a gondola," Sara said.

"I love it," Bridey said. "I'll have to start a charm bracelet.

Thank you." The golden gondola charm, complete with a tiny gondolier, shone in the light on its bed of velvet. Beneath the tablecloth, Bridey ran her fingers over the smooth surface of the gold bangles she wore on her right arm. They were a present from her Aunt Maura and Uncle Hugh, sent from Jordan for Bridey's graduation. She hadn't taken them off since. She loved to hear them clink and jingle on her wrist. Aunt Maura wore a dozen gold bangles on one arm — she had for as long as Bridey could remember. When Bridey was little she loved to play with them, moving the lustrous circles up and down Maura's arm, listening to the music they made. When Bridey opened the box and saw the bracelets from Maura and Hugh, she wanted to cry. Maura and Hugh were often in some faraway part of the world — Pakistan when Bridey was born, London, Beirut — now Jordan. They were so worldly Bridey barely knew what to say to them when they visited. She never thought about them missing her, or thinking about her growing up, let alone what gift would touch her. But here was proof that they had.

Tilla picked up the wrapping paper and folded it carefully into a small square. Bridey showed her the charm.

"It's beautiful," Tilla agreed. "Let me put it in my purse so we don't lose it." The paper and box safely stowed, Tilla looked at her family and smiled. "This is my favorite part of this whole day. We're safe and sound together. Can you imagine getting caught out there on a boat?" As if for emphasis, a crack of thunder rattled the dining room windows. She jumped "Oh! Lord. I hope this doesn't keep up all night."

"Maybe we'll have better weather in Rome, if Maura is able to come," Corinne said.

Sara scraped at the last smudges of tiramisu on her plate. "Athens is only a two hour flight by jet from Rome. I asked Rose."

"Maura would never pass up the chance to see us," Tilla said.

Maura was with her five-year-old twins in Athens, evacuated from Amman with other British and American families because of the war between Israel and Jordan. Hugh remained in Amman the last they'd heard. There was a chance Maura could arrange to fly to Rome with the children for a quick visit. Tilla and Corinne tried not to count on it, but they were full of hope. Bridey's wish on the candle was for her aunt to come to Rome. Maura had been in Rome many times. They wouldn't need Rose the guide or have to trudge through sites with the Pilgrims. Surely, things would be so much more fun if Aunt Maura had anything to do with it.

CHAPTER TWO

There were times on the tour when Bridey wondered if her mother regretted coming along. Since she'd fallen in Ulm, Tilla wasn't her usual youthful, energetic self. Corinne figured Tilla might have cracked her tailbone. The bruise she had was impressive; she'd shown it to them in Munich, carefully hiking up her nightgown and the side of her panty to show just the deeply bruised skin. But her attitude had changed, too. She'd become negative and irritable.

They'd had two full days of touring back in Munich. One afternoon, Bridey stood, arm linked with Tilla's, in front of *The Rising of Christ* by Fra Angelico in the Alte Pinakothek, the venerable art museum of Munich. Tilla stood, her arm linked with her daughter. Sara and Corinne at the gift shop. It was the first chance Bridey and her mom had to be alone since they'd been on the flight to Heathrow.

"I saw a slide of this painting in Art History," Bridey told Tilla. "The projector lens had lint on it, so the painting looked like it was full of black snakes. I thought it made the image interesting.

Christ rising in a sort of whirlwind of serpents. Think of the inter-
pretations you could put on it. 'Fra Angelico paints on acid'...."

"Shhh. We're standing in front of a masterpiece," Tilla said.
"There's real gold in that paint. Think how lucky you are to see it
in person, rather than on a slide."

Bridey began to sing "Jesus-in-the-Sky-With-Gold-Paint"
into her mother's strawberry blonde hair. It smelled of shampoo
and cigarette smoke.

"I'm trying to enjoy this," Tilla whispered. She glanced to see
if the people in the huge room heard them. "Behave yourself."

"Mum," Bridey said as they strolled along in the hushed
room of a gallery, "Do you ever think that you're inventing reality as you go along? Like what's real is what's in front of you, and
if you turn around you'd see nothing, because the past instantly
disintegrates? So even if you have the evidence of time right in
front of you, like this painting, deep down you still can't really
accept that someone lived in the past to paint it?"

Her mother raised her eyebrows and paused in midstep. "Did
someone slip something into your soda at lunch?"

"Every day that I'm here is a little lifetime, kind of. We've only
been in Europe five days, but it's like a time warp. Everything
feels so much longer. Extended, I mean. Minutes, hours, days.
Nothing I do here has anything to do with home."

"That's what vacations are for," Tilla said. She stopped at a
painting and leaned in to read the title plaque.

"But this isn't a vacation to me. I can't explain it, exactly. Like
you and I and Dad and the boys exist in different dimensions,
not just different countries."

Tilla adjusted her purse strap higher on her shoulder. "I
guess most travelers feel that way sometimes," she said. Her
voice became soft with fatigue. "But, sweetie, you're always connected to your home. And you always will be. Your dad hasn't
forgotten you. Or your friends, or your brothers. Or anyone
who loves you. No matter where you go, home is always there.

That's your reality."

"I think reality is where you find it," Bridey said. "It isn't one place or certain people. For me, it's this painting, this museum — this very afternoon. You and me, standing here this instant."

Tilla turned and began walking down the gallery. "That's a pretty self-centered way of looking at things," she said.

"I'm only trying to tell you how I think," Bridey protested, following.

"Thinking is a new experience for you," Tilla said. She caught Bridey's look. "I don't mean that the way it sounds..." She sighed. "All mental gyrations boil down to simple truths. And once you know the simple truths, things are clearer, and you don't have to twist your thoughts into pretzels."

"I'm not twisting my thoughts," said Bridey. "I'm thinking them. They make sense to me, even if they don't to you." Mental gyrations?

"Your generation may be content to settle. But mine isn't. We don't want to be told what's real for us and what isn't. We want to discover the truth — find out for ourselves, instead of taking someone's word for it. Just because we're original..."

"Original!" Tilla stopped walking and turned on her daughter. Even though she had to look up at Bridey, she still could cut her down to size with her expression. "What makes you think you kids are original? People have been going around the same questions and ideas since time immemorial: 'What is life?' 'Who am I?' Well, my generation hasn't had time to spend on self-indulgence. We were going through the Depression and the war, and re-building the very good lives we've given to you. That's the trouble with 'your generation,' if you ask me. You confuse silly thoughts with originality. The hippies use drugs to counterfeit creativity."

"I've never used drugs!"

And she hadn't. Bridey knew kids who did and one had shown her a bag of marijuana, which she'd mistaken for oregano.

It was true she'd been hearing Grace Slick singing *White Rabbit* in her head all morning, probably because it was the last thing she listened to the day they left home. It wasn't even her album anyway; it was her brother Daniel's, and she'd stood in his room listening to the record on his stereo, waiting for the moment her dad would back the car down the gravel driveway to take them to the airport. That was as close to drugs as she got: a song. Thousands of kids were heading to San Francisco, the opposite direction from her that summer, looking for sex, drugs and rock and roll. She had no desire to become a stoned-out hippie .

"You kids think you invented existence. Like nothing ever happened before you were born. But I guess that's our fault. We hand you your lives on silver platters."

"We didn't ask for anything." Bridey thought about her purple bedroom at home, the hand-me-down furniture and the dressing table her dad had made himself, the view out her window of a very old, middle class street full of houses built after the Civil War. None of it said "silver platter."

"I could never have taken a trip like this when I was your age," said Tilla.

"What am I supposed to do about that? Never have anything good, because you didn't?"

Bridey sighed. She pretended to read about Goya in the museum pamphlet, hoping to de-escalate the conversation. "Why are you so cranky?" she asked.

Tilla shook her head. "I'm sorry, sweetheart," she said. "I'm still a little rattled from yesterday."

"That's behind us," Bridey said quickly. The fewer reminders about the less enjoyable parts of their trip, the better. "Just think about Aunt Maura. Rome is only a few days away."

"I'm sorry I let you down in that square," Tilla said. Her blue eyes glistened with imminent tears, emphasizing how young she really was. "I wasn't… I should have been the one protecting you. Instead, I stood there like a fool."

"You were surprised, that's all. You didn't expect him to be a creep."

"I always thought that if anyone ever threatened my children, I'd kill him. But all I could think about was paying him, so he'd let us go. I didn't want to make a scene. A scene! I didn't even want to scream, for God's sake. When I think of what he might have done, that he may have had a weapon..." She shuddered. "I'm so angry. Now! When it doesn't count. And taking it out on you."

Bridey wasn't used to her mother criticizing herself. Tilla always seemed in control at home, competent, and until now, fearless. But she was looking small and thin and doubtful, while Bridey felt taller, stronger and more heroic.

That night in Munich they feasted on roast turkey with raspberry torte for dessert. The food was exceptional — or at least not breaded veal cutlet, fried potatoes and peas, which kept showing up as their pre-ordered entree for lunch and dinner with puzzling regularity. The mood at the table was so relaxed and merry that Bridey thought she might have a chance of getting her mother and aunt to agree to walk down the block to the huge bierhaus. The music from the bierhaus drifted down the street and filtered through the walls of their hotel room the night before, harrumphing tubas and the thump of drums making their bare feet tap. They heard laughter and even the occasional clink of glassware. Into the early hours, voices passed beneath their windows, disembodied conversations landing on the sills like pigeons, perching long enough to penetrate dreams of the tourists inside the hotel.

The night was when life went on, Bridey imagined. She wanted to be a part of the laughter and conversation, not stuck in her room in the early evening giving her toenails another coat or writing postcards about things she didn't care she'd done.

Sara finished the last bite of her torte. She closed her eyes and breathed a contented sigh. "For the first time since we got here, I feel full," she said. "My stomach is dancing with glee."

"Tell it not to dance too hard," Corinne said. "I don't want to be cleaning any up-chuck in the middle of the night."

"What we need is a good walk," Bridey suggested.

"Let's find a mailbox," Corinne said. "Are your feet are up to it?" she asked Tilla. They'd tramped through the tours of the day with the rest of the Pilgrims, to the art gallery and Radio Free Europe, where they'd seen their first newspaper headlines there since leaving the States and it was more bad news of race riots and cities on fire. And yet, as Bridey had tried to say to her mother in the morning — it all seemed so very far away and removed, in that strange dimension called Home.

"Mine are ready, if yours are," Tilla said. She stubbed out her cigarette. On the way to Munich, the bus had stopped at a U.S. Army base. Young soldiers swarmed them, anxious to have a few minutes of conversation with people from home. Bridey had been a big attraction. Corinne and Tilla gave two of the soldiers some cash to buy them a couple of cartons of cigarettes from the PX. When the Phantom's engine started up again, it was hard to leave those soldiers, desperate as they seemed for any touch of home.

Find a mailbox. Whoopee, Bridey thought. "While we're out, why don't we go to the bierhaus next door and see what all the noise is about?"

"I don't think it would be wise," Tilla said. "Four females walking into a beer hall? And Sara is only fourteen."

"They're family kinds of places," Bridey said. "The drinking laws are different here anyway."

"We'll see what's out there," Corinne said. "No promises, but we'll see."

They couldn't find a mailbox but they found something better. They were standing on a corner near the Marienplatz, arguing whether to continue walking and mail their letters or turn back for the hotel and ask the desk clerk to mail them. Munich's center was brightly lit and bustling. Couples strolled by. Women walked arm in arm. Teenagers smoked on street corners and necked in front of stores.

"This is the first city we've come to," Corinne said, "that feels like New York."

"I wonder if all big cities are like that?" Sara said. "Except for the signs, you end up feeling like they're all imitations of New York?"

"All you New Yorkers think that way," Bridey said. "Maybe New York City is an imitation. Munich's been here for centuries." A young couple paused in the middle of making out to watch her go by. The girl whispered something to her boyfriend and he laughed.

"I think we're getting lost," Tilla said.

"We're not lost!" said Bridey, practically spitting with impatience. "All we did was walk in a straight line from the hotel."

"I'm in no hurry to talk to strangers, Madamoiselle," Corinne said. "The next thing you know, you'll be giving someone a jujitsu flip, and we'll be touring the inside of a German jail." The sound of a low, male laugh interrupted her.

A young man was waiting at the corner for the traffic light to change. Dressed in khaki slacks and a madras seersucker shirt under a navy blue blazer, he could have walked off any American campus. His hair was scalped "high and tight," as Bridey's dad would say. Once he made eye contact with Bridey, he smiled and walked over.

"Excuse me, ladies," he said. "Are ya'll in need of assistance?"

Tilla's face brightened. "You're American!"

"Yes, ma'am. It's awful nice to hear some friendly voices from home. When I do, I can't help but say hello." He looked again at Bridey. She smiled back at him.

"We're looking for a mailbox," Corinne explained.

"I believe I can help," he said. "My name is Brian Greene." Lieutenant Brian Greene USMC, from Atlanta, Georgia, on leave, doing a little traveling before his next assignment. Bridey studied him. Even in civilian clothes, he held himself as if in uniform. His oxblood leather tassel loafers were shined to perfection, far from the scuffed-up, worn-down penny loafers the boys at home wore as part of their school uniforms.

No question, he was All-American, apple-pie handsome. She mentally dressed him in Marine dress blues. Mmmm. Impressive. And he was wearing English Leather cologne. He smelled like home, like the boys at the dances that St. Theodore's, the all-boys high school, gave one Friday night a month. It would have been more exotic if he'd been German, but he'd do.

"Are you here on your own?" Tilla asked him.

"Yes, ma'am."

"Lieutenant, would you like to come back to our hotel and have a cup of coffee?" Tilla asked him.

Excellent, Mumma, Bridey thought. *Surprising. Good move.*

They sat in the tiny Edelweiss Cellar Bar of the Hotel Alpen. Lieutenant Greene sat next to Bridey. He told them he'd been commissioned out of Duke University two years ago and done a stint at the embassy in Austria. Now he had some time to see some of Europe before heading back to his family in Atlanta and leaving for his next tour of duty.

"Where to, next?" Corinne asked. She offered him sugar for his coffee. After he emptied three paper packets into his cup, he smiled apologetically.

"I developed an awful sweet tooth in Austria," he said.

"Your parents must miss you terribly," Tilla said. "How long will you have at home?"

"Just a couple weeks," he said. "It's better if I make it quick, I think. I don't have a girlfriend to say goodbye to." Bridey caught the message. "And my mother — well, she got pretty broken up when I left Quantico the first time, and this time…" He hesitated, stirring the melting sugar. Then he looked into Tilla's sympathetic eyes. "Well, it's going to be even harder on her, I expect."

Tilla imagined the pages of the calendar hanging on her kitchen wall flipping in fast-forward toward her son's eighteenth birthday — the day they'd drive him to the post office to register for the draft.

"Where are you going?" Bridey asked him. "This time."

He took a sip of coffee. "Southeast Asia."

"You mean Vietnam."

"In the neighborhood," he said, and kept stirring. It took him awhile, but the lieutenant asked Bridey if she might consider a walk to the Englischer Garten with him.

"I was on my way to dinner when I met y'all," he said. "I could really use some company. Have you been there?" He addressed the question to the commanding officers of the group, Tilla and Corinne.

Tilla tried to maintain a pleasant expression, but lines of worry began to creep across her brow.

"It's real pretty," he went on. "There's a bunch of nice beer gardens set up in the summer. The one by the Chinese Tower is famous. It's something you have to experience or you can't say you've really been to Munich. Plates of sausage and huge steins of beer, brass bands — you know — oompah bands? And a mess of people from all over the world, all singing loud and laughin.'" He looked young and sincere. "It's crazy, but a lot of fun. And very safe." He emphasized the last point. "I swear on the Corps, Bridey would be okay with me, and that oath is my sacred honor."

Bridey didn't doubt his word. An evening in the Englischer Garten with this Southern gentleman soldier sounded like just the right combination of excitement and propriety. Her first chance to venture on her own into everyday German life. And how better to do it than with her personal military guard? The vibes she got from Brian Greene were that he was exactly what he appeared to be, a polite Georgia boy, one of the military elite, a guy who loved his momma. Maybe he had a girlfriend back home, and maybe he didn't.

Tilla's face was regret overlaying reluctance. Bridey could see that her mother was about to reject his request. Tilla could not possibly allow her not-quite-eighteen-year-old to go off alone into a strange city with a guy they just met on the street — whether he was American, Marine, Rhett Butler, or whatever. No way. When it came to Bridey, Tilla could never be too careful. But Bridey could see that Aunt Corinne was for it. How could they turn down a bronzed god, a college graduate from the Southern Ivies, so clean-cut and Eagle Scout that a flag practically waved over his head?

Sara yawned. She could see where all this was going: none of it would be in her direction.

Tilla shook her head.

Lieutenant Greene made a salvaging move to include Tilla, Corinne and Sara. The arrival of Father Clement at their table interrupted him. Papa Joe, the oldest member of the tour and besides Father Clement, the only male, shuffled up behind the priest. The pair had been sitting at a corner table in the same bar, nursing beers.

"Good evening," Father said. He was dressed in gray slacks with a blue plaid, short-sleeved cotton shirt. Bridey thought he looked more like Lyndon Johnson than ever. His earlobes looked the size of saucers, and the lines on his face gave him the look of a bloodhound.

"Hello, Father," Corinne said to him. "Hi there, Papa Joe."

"There's a'my girl." Papa Joe smiled and reached for Corinne's hand, giving it a squeeze and a pat. Brian rose to his feet and gave each man a firm handshake.

"At ease, at ease." Father laughed. "I made it to corporal in the infantry," he explained. "But I figure I got a few years on this here boy, so I get to give the orders."

"No question, sir," Brian said, sitting.

Father put his hands in his pockets and tipped up on the balls of his feet. "Did I hear mention of somebody going to the English Garden?"

"Yes sir," Brian said. "I was hoping to take Bridey — well, all the ladies. I think it'd be a good time."

"Oh, yes," said Papa Joe, still clasping Corinne's hand. "I been to the beer gardens, long ago. It's lots'a fun."

"Joe and I were headed over there ourselves," Father Clement said. He took in Bridey and Brian's hopeful faces and turned to Tilla. "What do you say? Why don't you ladies come with us? We'll make it an unscheduled sightseeing trip."

Corinne crossed her legs. Papa Joe released her hand. "I'll have to pass," she said to the priest. "All I want to do is get my shoes off and go to bed early."

Everyone looked at Tilla. "Well," she began.

"Can I go?" Sara broke in.

"We're talking about beer gardens," Corinne said to her. "You'll have to sit this one out."

"That stinks," Sara complained under her breath.

"How about lending us these two young people, then?" Father said to Tilla. "We could do with some fresh faces. And we'll have Bridey back before the coach turns into a pumpkin."

C'mon, Bridey said silently to her mother. A priest, a soldier and an old man. How much safer does it have to be?

"I have to catch an early train tomorrow," Brian added. "I can't be out late."

Tilla drew in a deep breath, the kind you take before diving into cold water. "I suppose it would be all right."

"Wonderful," Father Clement said. "We'll guard Bridey like the Statue of Liberty herself. Won't we, lieutenant?"

Brian gave the priest a small salute. "Yes, sir!"

They found a table under a trio of enormous chestnut trees. The beer garden at the Chinesischer Turm was roaring with voices. People of every description sat at the green tables eating, and drinking from huge glass mugs of beer. The Chinese pagoda rose above them all, looking incongruous and beautiful in the setting of darkened trees. It was the biggest outdoor party Bridey had ever seen.

"I don't suppose they serve soda here," Bridey said to Brian. They were within sight of Father Clement and Papa Joe. It became apparent on their walk to the park that Father did not intend to play chaperone too seriously. He and Papa Joe walked together, ahead of them. Now they were sitting a few tables away, getting to know the people next to them, while Brian and Bridey sat beneath the trees.

"I think if you ordered a soda here, they might take serious offense." Brian laughed. "You have to drink beer at a beer garden! The more beer, the better. It's the only way to ingratiate yourself to the locals."

"I can't drink this!" Bridey protested when a mug the size of a pitcher was set in front of her.

"Fake it," Brian said and clinked his mug against hers. "Here's to the U.S.A."

"Cheers." She sipped the froth from her mug and licked her top lip.

"Your mom is pretty protective of you," Brian said as he dug into his food.

Bridey broke a piece of the salted, doughy pretzel and nibbled at it. "It's a drag," she said. "I'm turning eighteen within days. She treats me like I'm a kid."

Brian's eyebrows knit together at this. He covered his mouth with his napkin, settling his expression into politeness. Bridey told him about the man in Ulm. When she got to the part about hitting him with her tote bag, the lieutenant nodded, chewing his noodles and sausage.

"It can happen here. Tourists, women alone, y'all are easy pickin'," he said, swallowing. "But you have to be combat ready."

"Combat? I hope I don't have to fight my way through Europe."

He smiled. "Are all you Yankee girls so tough?"

"When we have to be."

He chewed another piece of sausage and leaned in toward her over the table. "Suppose I challenged you to a little hand-to-hand combat. What would you do with me?"

"That depends," Bridey said. The way he looked at her, there was no mistaking his meaning. Her guard went up.

"On what?"

"On whether you're a dirty fighter. If you are, I'd have to use all my girl tactics. You know — screaming, biting, scratching, kicking."

His smile was superior. An amused, tolerant smile. Silly female, it said. "I can assure you, your tactics would be completely ineffective."

"I'm trusting you're a gentleman and I won't have to find out."

"Now, why would you think you'd want to fight me off? Who says it wouldn't be fun? You might like it." He winked and speared another piece of sausage.

Bridey popped another piece of pretzel into her mouth and checked to make sure Father and Papa Joe were within sprinting distance, just in case he wasn't kidding.

"I apologize. When I saw you on the street, I was 'about knocked out. You're the prettiest thing I've seen since I left home. I couldn't walk by you without giving it a shot and seeing if I could spend some time with you. I swear I would not hurt one freckle on that perfect nose of yours. I was just bragging on myself. It was stupid. Did I scare you?"

"No," Bridey said. It didn't sound convincing. The pretzel had gone down drily, probably because of the small nut of anxiety she felt as a lump in her throat. It made her voice hoarse. She took a small swig of her beer, hoping to wash the nut down. "I guess 'action' means something else to me." She thought back to the few times she'd been alone with a boy in the front seat of cars, the interior heated with anticipation and expectation on one side, wariness on hers. There was no "action" to be had from her, but the boys she dated were decent enough to keep their disappointment and frustration to a minimum.

"I'm in the business of protecting our fair American ladies. If you can't depend on being safe with a Marine, you can't depend on anyone. That's my job."

"I know," Bridey said. "It's okay. You don't have to keep apologizing."

"Am I going on too much?"

"Kind of," she hedged.

"You better take another sip of that foam," he joked. "It's gonna take you most of the night to get to the liquid part."

Bridey picked up the stein with both hands and attempted to take a swallow of the beer. It fizzed around her nose and mouth, leaving a sudsy peak on her lip. Its bitter taste reminded her of her dad. He used to let her have a tiny sip of his beer when she was little, just a taste, because it always looked so good to her, bubbly and chilled. One taste was always enough. It wasn't as delicious as it looked. Like a lot of things, she suspected. She took a big swallow and set the mug down with a clunk. The effort felt silly. "I can't do it," she said.

He reached over and tried to pat her upper lip dry with his napkin. "You look cuter than a kitten in a yarn basket with that mustache," he said.

She dodged the napkin by wiping her lip with her finger. She was starting to feel too much like a kid with him, too inexperienced. "Where exactly are you going in Southeast Asia? Aren't you scared?"

"I can't say where," he told her. "And why should I be scared?"

"They're having a war over there. You know, with real bullets and bombs? Blood, guts, fire?"

"Exactly."

"But isn't that different from an embassy? What did you do there, help ladies out of limousines?"

His smiled faded. He wiped his mouth again and looked at her. "You have no idea what goes on at an embassy. Once in a while they have receptions and parties, but for the most part, a lot of sensitive work goes on every day."

"My uncle works in embassies," Bridey announced. "British embassies — he's in Jordan now. He's from England. So I do know a little about it."

"*Really.*" The word was loaded with sarcasm and pointed like a barrel at her. "What's he do there?"

"I don't know," Bridey said, dismissive. "Whatever they do. He doesn't talk about it much."

"I'll bet he doesn't," said Brian.

She shifted in her seat, tugging her skirt to cover at least a few more centimeters of the backs of her thighs, which were stuck to the wooden bench, making her more uncomfortable. No one ever articulated what her Uncle Hugh did. They would only say 'he works for the Foreign Office' or 'he's with the embassy.' She sensed that whatever he did, it was complicated and important. Just like her uncle himself. And even if she were to pluck up the courage to ask him — she knew he'd never really take her into his confidence.

Brian gave her a superior smile. "For my next tour of duty — I volunteered to go. I'll be doing recon. I've asked to be sent there."

"You volunteered?" Bridey said, incredulous. Every boy she knew at home was scared to death of going to Vietnam. Every single one. Most of them scrambled safely into college and a student deferment, but even then, you never knew. You could flunk out and once the draft got you, you were as good as dead. That's how the kids she knew thought of it. If you didn't die, you could end up like Peter Macchelli. He was two years older than Bridey. They dated for a semester when she was sixteen. He flunked out of his first year at Villanova and got drafted immediately. Before anyone knew it, he was gone to Vietnam and come back home already. But all he did now was drink and go to the racetrack. He never made sense anymore. He was drunk and angry and he looked too old to be barely twenty-one. He looked forty. He didn't shave or wash his long hair. Nobody knew whether to be sorry for him or scared of him. Bridey was both. It was like the old Peter died in Vietnam and an alien took his place.

She didn't tell Brian any of this.

"Damn right," Brian said. He balled up his paper napkin and dropped it on his empty plate. "I want to get there before it's over and help settle a score for my brother Marines."

"What score?"

"I doubt you'd understand," he said.

"I don't understand," Bridey agreed. "What's Recon?"

"Reconnaissance. We go ahead, check out the VC before they know we're coming. Take them out. Get them before they get us."

"You talk about it like it's a game." She stared at his tanned, handsome face and clear eyes. Saw him in combat gear, his face smudged and camouflaged. In the movies it seemed sexy. But this wasn't sexy.

"I guess, in a way, it is a game," he said. He took a long swallow of his beer.

But you could die, Bridey thought. *Is death real to you? Or did they cut a nerve so you can't feel anything about it? How does it work?* She wondered, but didn't ask. If his thinking/death/fear nerve was dead, he wouldn't have the answer she hoped for. Or wanted to hear. So she asked instead: "Do you have a girlfriend?"

"That's what I call a change of subject."

"I was just wondering."

"Oh, yeah? Just wondering, huh?" A moth flittered on to his plate. He squashed it with a flick of his finger. One wing stuck upright as if in surrender. "Nobody recent. I dated girls in Austria. The last time I had somebody serious was back at Duke. I was about engaged."

"About?" She felt sorry for the moth, just a powdery smudge on the plate and that one upright wing. He didn't have to kill it. Live ones flickered like snowflakes in the glow of lights above.

"We were pinned, looking at rings. Except then I signed up with the Marines and she broke things off. Being a military wife was not on her program. She should have taken the fact that I was in ROTC for a hint. She wasn't good at long-distance romance. I was pretty wrecked for a while. But I'm over it." He reached across and picked up a remainder of her pretzel, holding it up for permission to take it. She nodded. After another drink of beer, he stifled a belch politely. "What about you?" Brian asked. "Got a sweetheart writing love letters while you do the Grand Tour?"

"No. No one."

His brows lifted.

"I'm going to Georgetown in September. There'll be plenty of fish to fry there."

Brian smiled and shook his head slowly. "Oh, how you will fry those Hoyas, too! They'll be lining up at the door. I pity the poor old boys."

He leaned away from the table and stared off across the crowd. "You know, I'd actually like to get to know you better. Would you write to me? I may not be able to answer much, but it would be nice getting letters from you. Letters from home."

"I wouldn't know what to write," Bridey said. "Basketball games and parties? All the while knowing you're in a jungle somewhere, shooting somebody?"

"Those 'somebodies' are communists, and if they ever made it to your dorm, they'd have no problem doing slow, horrible, excruciatingly painful things."

"They're not going to invade Georgetown University. They're fighting in their own country, against the army of a world power from the other side of the earth."

"Spoken like a true leftist embryo! You've got no idea about what's really going on over there."

"Maybe I don't," she said. "But neither do people back home. Nobody can figure out what we're doing there, taking so many boys away to die. And it isn't just people at home — we saw graffiti all over Belgium and Germany. They don't like the United States for what we're doing."

"That graffiti you saw? It's all connected. There are subversives working in the interest of communist, genocidal regimes. Just like they're working in the U.S. with all the mobs and firing up stupid college kids. Then they come over here — the hippies — and spray paint their propaganda. We have to fight it, wherever it arises."

"Gee," Bridey said. "I feel like waving a flag." In the following summer, there would be blood on Chicago's streets. In three more springs, there would be gunfire on an American campus and students would die at the hands of the military. But on this summer evening, Bridey felt safe enough to be sarcastic.

"Listen. You're right about one thing. Nobody's going to invade your dorm unless it's a panty raid. Nobody's going to keep you from strolling around campus, safe and sound in your miniskirt. And you know why? Because guys like me will be in a jungle getting our fucking *asses* shot off, making sure you'll never have to worry. Pardon my French!"

She picked grains of salt from her plate and said nothing. She got into arguments like this at home, with her dad.

Brian Greene stared up into the trees for a moment and then blew out a long breath. "Again, I apologize. You got me going. It's just hard, you know?" he said.

She gave a conciliatory shrug. "Getting into a political argument wasn't what I thought about when I saw you, either."

"We keep heading in the wrong direction, don't we?" he said. "Look, if I gave you an address, would you write me once in a while? Even if it's only about parties and basketball."

"I might not be a good correspondent." Bridey braced her hands against the edge of the painted table, shoving off from this rocky shore. "I should leave," she said. "I'm really tired. All the sight-seeing."

"Sure," he said. "I'll walk you back to the hotel."

"No — you don't have to. I think I'll join Father over there. They're going back to my hotel anyway, and… I'm sorry."

"Hey, I didn't mean to offend you or scare you. Or whatever is wrong."

Bridey stood, tugging the skirt down to keep an illusion of modesty. "I …" She held out her hand. "I wish you luck. No, luck isn't enough. Keep safe. Be careful. Crawling through the jungle and all."

"It's okay," he said. He stood next to Bridey. They made a great looking couple, almost like an ad out of an American magazine. "I know what you mean. Sure I can't walk you home?"

"Goodbye, Lieutenant."

"Bridey, I'm not saying goodbye," he said. "Even if you won't write, I plan to look you up when I get back. Georgetown, right? Wait and see."

"Would it be okay if I sit with you?" Bridey asked Father Clement at his table. She looked back where she'd left Brian Greene. He was slowly walking backwards, looking at her, his hands shoved deep in the pockets of his knife-creased khakis. When she turned, he brought his hand up in a small wave. Then he turned around and walked out of the beer garden, into the night-shrouded park.

"You surely may sit with us," Father said to her. When she squeezed onto the end of the bench seat next to Papa Joe, Father asked, "What happened, Bridey? Did our soldier turn out to be less than a gentleman?"

"We just didn't have a lot in common," she said.

"I saw that," Father said. "Looked like you had a few words." He pulled a pack of Lucky Strikes out of his shirt pocket and offered one to her.

"No, thank you," she said. She never knew priests smoked or drank beer. She couldn't imagine nuns putting their feet up in their hotel rooms at night, lighting up. She'd been educated by nuns since she was five. There were different orders of nuns with different habits, not just in what they wore, but in their approaches to children and girls. The nuns at Providence, the all-girls high school where she'd graduated just three and a half weeks ago, were of an order that prided themselves on their elite levels of education. They were bright women with high expectations of the girls they taught. They practiced a special kind of discipline on their pupils. For those who didn't follow every minute rule, they could control and diminish with the drilling look and quiet, hissing words. It wasn't so much different, Bridey imagined, than being in the military.

"We thought you two made a fine pair," Father said. "Didn't we, Joe?"

Papa Joe twisted stiffly on the bench toward Bridey. His heavily lined face creased more deeply as he regarded her. "What's a'matter, Bridey? Why you don't have a good time? You look sad."

"We thought we were giving you a break," Father said. "Get you out among the living." He blew smoke away from the table and coughed noisily.

"Oh, I'm happy you did. I really wanted to come. If it hadn't been for you, I'd be stuck in my room at the hotel."

Papa Joe crossed his legs with some effort. His thighs were thin beneath the cloth of his trousers, but his knees were enlarged and rounded with arthritis. He wore a long-sleeved dress shirt and pale blue sweater vest, even in the humid warmth of the July night. He smelled of menthol and Vitalis hair tonic, and was scrupulously shaved and combed. John Lennon would have called him "a clean old man." When Papa Joe was thinking hard or paying close attention, she noticed he pushed out his lower lip and knit his heavy brows. He was doing that now.

"You don't look happy. You look like, maybe you gonna cry. This boy say something wrong? Not so nice as he looks? Why you sit with two old men instead of a good-looking boy who gots' the eye for you?"

Bridey sighed. She was beginning to regret bailing on the lieutenant. She could have sat there and been pleasant; made small talk and flirted. She could have stayed off the subject of where he was headed and why. It was only a couple of hours of one night. It could have been no big deal. Now she would think of him the rest of her life. She would think of him walking backwards out of the beer garden, waving that lonely way. She would think of him, and not want to. Every time she saw soldiers on the news being pulled half-dead out of villages and rice paddies, she'd look for him. And feel guilty, because in his last weeks or months on earth, she didn't like him, wished he hadn't picked her out on a street in Munich. "I was possibly the worst person in Munich for him to run into," she said.

"A bit of an overstatement, I'd guess," said Father.

"All he wanted was a nice meal and some company. And all I gave him were arguments."

"Sounds like y'all had some right lively discussions," Father said.

"They felt more like arguments," she said. Father was looking at her as she watched his smoke pass. She felt like Alice at the feet of the caterpillar in Wonderland. Father studied her face. There was something in his eyes that made Bridey feel she could step in, no threat of reprimand or rejection. Kindness. "I didn't want to be around him anymore. He asked me to write to him, and I said no. I told him I didn't want him to walk me back to the hotel. I dumped him, right in the middle of everything. I mean — here, after he gave me the chance to get out tonight. I've never done that to anyone before."

"Perfectly wise choice, not to walk back with him alone. That's what we're here for," Father said to her.

Bridey took a breath. "All I could think of was that he'd be dead soon. I saw him — dead. Like a premonition. And I wanted to get away. I didn't want to be with someone so close to ... Someone so close to being destroyed. He's young. He's ..."

"So close to your age," Father said.

"It's a stupid waste," she said. "Can't he see what a waste it all is?" Suddenly all she wanted was to be in her bed at the hotel. Papa Joe touched her shoulder gently with a silent pat of empathy. On her bare shoulder, his hand was dry and warm. "This isn't the good time I thought it would be," she said.

"There'll be other evenings ahead," Father said. He finished off his beer and stubbed out the last inch of his cigarette. "Don't give up the ship. Right, Joe?"

"I think many adventures are coming," Papa Joe told her. "Yesterday, you save your mama and her sister and little Sara from a robber. Tonight, you meet a soldier, going to war. Who knows what tomorrow brings, eh?"

CHAPTER THREE

 Three

The Pilgrims headed through the Apennines from Venice through Ravenna to Assisi, through green wilderness and ancient, bluish purple peaks. The roads were twisted and precarious, yet Roger the bus driver forged ahead at full tilt; his hairy, muscled forearms caressed the steering wheel like a lover confident of his woman's response. He seemed determined to get through mountain ranges as swiftly as possible, without a thought for the natural wonders racing past. Bridey and Sara balanced themselves on imaginary surfboards in the aisle between Tilla and Corinne's seats. The Phantom careened and bucked its way along the treacherous, narrow roads. The girls sat backwards on the long backseat to wave to the Italian men on motorbikes who followed them, blew kisses and threw their arms out to the girls in flamboyant invitations to leap from the window of the bus and come for a joyride.

Tilla checked her watch. It was one o'clock. The skies were growing darker, the roads more twisted. Roger never slowed down. Tilla held her breath and covered her eyes as they skirted cliffs a foot or two away from The Phantom's wheels. More than once, when they did come to a halt, it was to wait their turn for traffic to go by in the opposite direction, the road washed away or caved in or under construction on one side.

It was a little over a week since Tilla had left Rob and the boys at home. Bridey was right. Time seemed to stretch out here; it felt so much longer. Tilla thought about her husband, six hours behind, wondering how he was doing alone with the boys. Summer was his busiest time and she felt a stab of guilt for not being there to make his lunch, or sit with him at the picnic table in the backyard while he ate his supper. She kept her eyes closed, the better to imagine the swell of his biceps and the soft pattern of dark hair across his strong wrists, the small scabs and bruised nails on his hands, battle scars from days of hammering and handling lumber. They'd been married for nineteen years — half of her life — and he still looked at her with an expression that made her catch her breath with desire. Often at the picnic table, he'd reach out and hold her hand while he munched a hot dog still smoking from the charcoal grill. The sun would wash the sky in oranges, violets and mauves, and fireflies would start to appear across the lawn. Their Lab, Sheila, would sit drooling guiltily at Rob's side, hoping for the last morsel from Rob's plate. He always gave it to her. In those moments, no matter what the day had brought them, they were content.

Tilla stared out the windows at the contrast of three homes on the road they were following. It was either a shortcut or Roger was lost again. The second stories of two neighboring houses were completely missing, or partially there, the lower outside walls pocked-marked with what she realized were old bullet holes, scars of war. The women and children ran out of the houses to watch The Phantom go by in all its chrome and glass glory. The women waved aprons in greeting. The children skipped past preoccupied hens that scratched, unconcerned, through the scrubby front yards. The expressions of the women were a mixture of delight and consternation. Why was a tour bus going down their road?

The Phantom reached the end of the road and gained altitude with every shift of its gears. Tilla fought off a nauseating vision of the bus sailing off the next cliff, flying into infinity. Why had she said they would come on this trip? She could have been safe at home, hanging wash in the sun. But she knew why. It was her last chance to share some real time with Bridey. When Corinne invited them along, Tilla wrestled with the idea of having this trip — this indulgence. Maybe it was selfish, taking three weeks just for Bridey but the thought of leaving her only daughter on the doorstep of Georgetown soon, the sense that the winter days would be that much colder without Bridey's light coming in the door after school, the absence of her laughter, the energy and companionship she felt in her daughter — she had to be here. And maybe she would see Maura, know Maura was whole and safe in the life her sister led so far away.

Bridey slid into the seat beside Tilla. "Yee-ha!" Bridey said, smiling. "Some ride, huh?" She picked up Tilla's icy hand. "Scared, Mumma?" Tilla could only shake her head in false denial. Bridey gripped Tilla's hand in hers and gave her a peck on the cheek, her face alive with the novelty of the moment, uncluttered by fear.

Late in the afternoon, the light and clear mountain air began to take on a foggy look. At first, it seemed like another random, low-lying cloud, parked for a rest on the hairpin curves of the road. Roger downshifted as the cloud grew thicker. He braked slowly. Soon, they were consumed in a heavy, dark fog.

Not a cloud. Smoke.

Visibility vanished. The Pilgrims craned to look out of windows that no longer contained a view.

Tilla jammed her right foot forward under the seat in front of hers, reflexively braking. The roads were two lanes, no place to swerve, no shoulder to hug. Nowhere to go with a giant bus full of people. The Phantom slowed to a crawl. The air was thick with a sooty, acrid smoke. Three vehicles ahead of them, a vegetable truck stood at a forty-five degree angle to an overturned Volvo. The Volvo was in flames, wedged up against the rocky, wooded side of the mountain. The ignited gasoline created a river of fire that spread into the forest edge, burning fallen branches and dry grass. The truck's front end had hit the Volvo and crates of lettuce and smashed tomatoes littered the roadway. Some of the crates were on fire, too. The stench of diesel fuel and burning tomatoes mixed with the Phantom's recycled air. Roger ground the bus to a halt. Outside, a knot of men gestured and argued, surrounding a man who sat, his head in his hands, against the embankment.

"Now we're really stuck," Tilla said to Corinne and the girls. "How do you call the police or ambulances way up here? There's nowhere for anyone to go." Traffic lined up behind the tour bus.

Roger disembarked to check things out, followed by Rose the tour guide. They could see that one of the men on the road was in charge of the situation. After a brief consultation with the man, Roger brushed Rose aside and climbed back up the steps of the bus. Rose scurried right behind him. He sat in his seat and looked into his rearview mirror at his worried passengers.

"Not to worry," he said to their reflections. "All is fine." He shifted again and prepared to start up.

"You've got to be kidding me," Corinne said. "Don't tell me we're going to go around!"

"Go around where?" Tilla said. "We only have half of the lane to spare and it's a cliff with no guardrail."

The Phantom inched forward. There was a collective suspension of breath inside the bus, a silent cohesion of energy all directed at the back of the man whose driving skills held their lives in his hairy-backed hands. Those passengers seated on the left side of the bus — the cliff side — either riveted their eyes to the inches of roadway that stood between the bus wheels and a precipice, or averted them, unable to look. Sara, who normally sat on the left, slid over and jammed herself up against Bridey, who put a protective if powerless arm around her cousin's shoulder.

But maestro Roger guided the great vehicle deftly around the accident scene and out of the heavy smoke, away from the flames. Like one of Hannibal's elephants, the Phantom skirted the edges of the drop-off, its wheels gripping the narrow track. Light filtered into the bus dimly at first and then brilliantly as they cleared the area. The atmosphere among the Pilgrims relaxed, though the odor of burning vegetables, wood and fuel clung to the interior of the bus, long enough to give a few of them headaches. Soon Roger was back careening along the mountain curves at sixty miles per hour, but this no longer concerned the Pilgrims. Roger had proven himself.

They came through the mountains into the Umbrian valley. The shadows lengthened across fields of sunflowers and grape-vines as the sun turned the light to gold. They began the ascent on Mount Sugasio, upon which the city of Assisi perched, a pink and white crown ringed by medieval walls and eight gates. Sitting between the Porta San Francesco and the Porta San Giacomo was the crown jewel, the immense Basilica of St. Francis. Roger found the Hotel Windsor Savoia after only one wrong turn. At the hotel entrance the Pilgrims stumbled off the bus as if delivered out of hellfire into heaven itself. For Bridey, that was about to become truer than she could imagine.

Four

There was no private bathroom, just a sink and a bidet, but their room was pretty, with ornate moldings and gleaming wood floors. Bridey and Sara unlocked and opened the French doors on the opposite side of the room. They had a small balcony overlooking a hillside. It was the first real view they'd had yet from a hotel room. The Umbrian countryside spread in every direction, a quilt of gold, green, and brown. Beyond, hazy in the early evening, were the Apennines they had left.

"Wow," Bridey said to Sara. "Are you sure we have the right hotel?"

"This is right," Sara confirmed. "It's actually on the itinerary." Which was a switch, since most of the places mentioned in the itinerary weren't where they usually ended up staying.

Bridey and Sara washed the smoke and engine smells from their skin. Bridey fussed with her own hair, freeing it from the ponytail she'd been wearing all day in the hope that it would straighten out. She was always fighting with her hair, trying to make it as straight as the models' she saw on the covers of magazines, styles smooth and sleek, tucked behind their ears. She gave up. It fell in fat, zigzag waves and curls across her shoulders.

Tilla and Corinne 's room was a few doors down on the opposite side of the hall; they could see the top of the Basilica over the shade trees. Tilla was dressed for dinner in a nice turquoise sheath that played up her still-intact figure, tiny waist and thick, fair hair. She set her hair every night despite the discomfort of the little brush rollers making it harder for her to sleep. Corinne, who'd begun to color her coppery hair to hide the gray she found alarming at forty-three, was blessed — or cursed, depending on whose perspective — with naturally curly hair that she could just dampen to get to style itself. Rollerless, she slept soundly beside her sister. Corinne was a big fan of Pond's cold cream to keep her freckled Irish skin soft and relatively wrinkle-free.

In the dining room, the maître d' showed them to a large table already occupied in part by Father Clement, two of the nuns, and Papa Joe.

Oh, great, Bridey thought. *Another lively night.* Father and Papa Joe were okay, but she hadn't been required to dine with the nuns before.

"Ah!" Papa Joe said. "Here are my favorite dinner partners." He rose stiffly from his chair. His trousers hung like a bag from his bony hips, and the tie he'd put on encircled a collar that looked two sizes too large for his neck.

Their tablemates were discussing the afternoon's wild ride. "I had my rosary going a hundred miles an hour, let me tell you," Sr. Joan told them.

This is going to be a barrel of laughs. Rosaries and nun jokes. Bridey rested her chin on her hand and tuned out the conversation, staring out the dining room's doors to the rock-walled dining terrace beyond. Large pots of flowers stood along the ledge of the wall, flowers fidgeting and waving like schoolchildren in the soft breeze. Little puddles of rainwater, remnants of a late afternoon shower, pooled on the empty tables and the terrace's stone floor. A waiter arrived at their table for their drink orders. Lost in thoughts of outdoor suppers, Bridey paid no attention.

"Scusi. Signorina?"

Bridey's eyes widened before she could catch herself. The waiter stood, pen in hand. He was nearly as tall as Father Clement, and his shoulders were solid beneath his waiter's jacket. Little grooves framed his mouth, hinting at dimples if he were to smile. But he wasn't smiling. He stared back at her. Bridey saw something spark across his eyes, a reciprocal appraisal and approval of what he saw. It was an instantaneous connection that flickered electric between them. His eyes were topped by dark brows that arched at her: Well? A cola, she meant to say, but the words didn't form at first because her breath caught, causing her to stumble over her order.

He glanced down at his pad, writing; his eyes snapped back to hers. She watched him walk toward the kitchen. He looked back and saw her. Bridey dropped her head, embarrassed, and bugged her eyes out at the tabletop. *Wow.*

When he came back with the drinks, he set down Corinne's wine, colas for Tilla and Sara, but a beer for Bridey. She stared at the beer in front of her. *Hello*, it said — *here's your opening.*

"Excuse me," she said to him. Nearby, he was brushing invisible pieces of lint from a tablecloth at an empty table, straightening a napkin, picking up a glass to check for spots.

"Si, *signorina*?"

"I ordered a cola, not a beer." Oh, nice. Brilliant. Way to impress him.

His apology was too profuse. "So sorry, *signorina*...of course. A mistake." The beer was whisked up and away. When he came back with the soft drink, he made a ceremony of setting it in front of her. "For you, Miss America." He moved off to another table, but in between taking orders his eyes kept returning to hers.

The first course was served, a thick lentil soup. To everyone else, the waiter was polite, correct and efficient. Before Bridey could start to eat her soup, though, he swooped in and picked off the spoon from her hand. "*Mi scusi,*" he said. He turned the spoon carefully in his hand, scrutinizing it. "Is no clean. I bring another." The spoon disappeared with him.

Sr. Joan tittered from her end of the table. "I think he's playing tricks with you, Bridey." The nun was dressed in her new modern habit — a white blouse buttoned to her chin, a navy blue skirt that ended well below the knee and a navy blue vest. Her graying brown hair peeked out from under the white headband of her shoulder-length black veil. She may have only been in her late forties. The changes in religious habit to a more contemporary dress were not popular among all her order — her companion at the table, the much older Sister Evangelista, also wore the new habit, but only because she was forced to give up her full, long habit by her order. Sister Evangelista always looked embarrassed to have her white hair exposed, as if she was showing her underwear.

No kidding, Sister.

"We've developed a saying for Bridey," said Corinne. She winked at her niece. "She leaves a ticket agent, a border guard or a waiter in every port."

A new spoon arrived with the waiter. He carried it on his path through the tables as if carrying a piece of treasure through a royal court. "Better, yes?" he asked Bridey as he presented it to her.

She tilted her face up to him. "Thank you," she said, not shrinking from his eyes. Perhaps this called for a dash of sarcasm. Let him know she was on to him, but not angry. Shake out the welcome mat in front of him and leave the door ajar. "May I eat my soup now?"

"*Si.* Of course." She brought the spoon to her mouth while he stood over her. "You like another bread?" he asked, offering the bread to her before she could swallow the soup.

Bridey put the spoon down. A drop of soup splashed onto the pure white tablecloth. She glanced down to check whether any had spotted her dress. The top was cut straight across, with small straps at the shoulders. She realized that it gapped enough as she sat to have a line of sight to the tops of her breasts, down into the shadowed valley of her cleavage. She touched her hand to the top of the fabric, closing the gap. "No," she said. "Thank you."

The waiter gestured toward the napkin on her lap. "You allow me?" he asked and slipped it off her, leaning close. He patted the spot on the cloth. "I bring another, don' worry. You don' get soup on your most beautiful dress?"

"I'm fine, really."

"More butter?"

She bit the inside of her cheek to keep from smiling. He was playing with her, all right. Dinner was suddenly no longer a chore to get through, but a game to prolong. "By all means," Bridey said.

He glided around the table, picked up the small bowl of pats from in front of Father and Uncle Joe, and came back to Bridey. He stacked seven pats high on her plate, a boy with building blocks. Then he hustled off to the kitchen.

"I should be used to this by now," Tilla said to her, nodding toward the stack of butter pats. "Yet you continue to amaze me."

Bridey busied herself eating the soup. Her sense of taste seemed to have disappeared.

"I'm taking notes," Sara said. "Someday I'm going to write a book and call it: How to See Europe on Three Waiters a Day: The Bridey McKenna Way."

Tilla put her arm around Sara and gave her a squeeze. "You'll have your own method to write about," said Tilla. "I saw you get plenty of attention in Venice."

Sara's face darkened. "Yeah, from those brats in St. Mark's."

"Those were little criminals-in-training," Bridey said. The butter pats leaned like the Tower at Pisa on her bread plate, a monument to flirting. She picked off the top two and spread them on a piece of bread.

"That's not what I was talking about," Tilla said to Sara. "There were a lot of admiring glances coming your way. Everyone can see what a pretty girl you are."

Bridey was the last to be served at their table. There was only a small piece of fish on her plate, no roasted veal or potatoes or carrots like everyone else's dinners.

"Where's the rest of it?" Corinne asked her.

Tilla turned in the waiter's direction and signaled to him. "This is getting irritating," Tilla said. He nodded to her summons.

"*Si?*" he asked, when he arrived back at their table. He was looking at Bridey, not Tilla.

"She —."

But Bridey interrupted. This was her show. "I have no vegetables," she said. She pretended to be puzzled. The waiter — she dubbed him Romeo — crossed his arms.

"You ask, no vegetables," he said.

Vay-jay-tabuhls. She loved his accent. So sexy. As if she could eat anything at all, the way he made her stomach do back-flips. "I did not," she said. "It must have been someone else. Someone else's order. There must be a mistake." She left out the part about having fish instead of veal. Why ruin a good thing?

He blinked at her. "Is your order, Miss America," he insisted. "I don' think is mistake. You say it. No vegetables."

"No, I didn't," said Bridey. "I didn't *say it*. I'd like some vegetables and potatoes as well. I'm very hungry tonight." Maybe they could manage to argue the night away, parrying and feinting, stretching out their brief contact.

He capitulated. He shrugged to her tablemates. But behind his eyes Bridey saw a clear message of delight and pursuit. "If you say. I bring whatsoever you wish." He picked up her plate. Back to the kitchen.

"This could take all night, missy," Father Clement said, spearing a piece of veal. "If you play your cards right."

She tried to hide the smile that was spreading across her flushed face. "I'm just sitting here trying to eat," Bridey said. "I have no idea why he's being so difficult."

"The boy's downright ornery," Father agreed, smiling back at her. "Can't imagine why he'd pick on you that way."

Tilla turned in her chair to look for the offending waiter. "Your food will be ice-cold by the time he quits fooling around."

"He's really an excellent waiter, Tilla," Sister Joan said. "He's just trying to get Bridey's attention." Perhaps the modern habit had given her the insight of a contemporary woman, wise in the ways of romance and flirtation.

"He's cute as a button," the elderly Sister Evangelista piped in. "He reminds me of a boy I taught in seventh grade, years ago. Full of the devil, but oh how the girls loved to be teased by him. His name was Steven Cassidy, and he…"

Romeo came out of the kitchen with Bridey's plate. A fellow waiter passed him and they exchanged words. The other waiter peered at Bridey. She sat like a skyscraper among her table companions. Romeo placed her dinner in front of her with a flourish. He concerned himself with straightening out her silverware. Bridey was acutely aware of his hand on the back of her chair, of his jacket near her face as he leaned forward. She turned her face toward his, catching his eye. He glanced down at her. He was humming something pretty. "So." He straightened. "Is okay, Miss America?"

Her expression left no doubt between them just how okay it was. She knew he was watching her throughout their meal, and her mood soared. She glowed under his not-so-secret focus. She found Father Clement witty. She regarded Papa Joe with patient fondness. She even paid the nuns rapt attention. She ate daintily, sat straight instead of slumping (this didn't miss her mother's notice). And when she could sense his eyes on her from across the room, she swung her hair from her face and off her shoulders. *Here I am, Romeo. Come and get me.*

"We 'ave dessert," he announced, after the dinner was cleared.

"Dessert!" Corinne said. "We haven't had dessert in quite a while."

"We haven't had dessert, period," Sara said.

"We had a torte in Munich," Sister Evangelista offered. "It was lovely."

"That was weeks ago," said Corinne.

"We were in Munich three days ago," Sister Joan reminded her.

"You'll have to forgive my sister," said Tilla. "This trip is causing her to lose all sense of time and space."

"Breaded veal poisoning, I think," Corinne said.

Romeo tsked. "Too much seeing the sights? I give you gelato... ice cream," he said to them. "Okay?"

"Spumoni?" Papa Joe asked over the clinks and conversations of the room's other diners. Rose was holding forth at another table about the shopping opportunities the next day would provide.

"Chocolate...eh...vanilla. *Delicioso!*"

"You speak English very well," Sister Joan said to him. "You must have studied very hard somewhere."

For the first time he smiled broadly, as if enjoying a private joke. His smile creased into dimples, his teeth white against the dark hint of beard. "*Mille grazie,*" he thanked her, and left it at that. When it came Bridey's turn to order — last, again — she asked for chocolate.

"You don' want ice cream," Romeo told her, shaking his head.

"Yes, I do."

"Is true, beautiful girls wishing to be Miss America don' like to be —?" He puffed out his cheeks.

"Fat!" Sara guessed. She giggled and he turned his electric smile on her. In its light, she opened like a small bud, suddenly prettier, a preview of the beauty she would become. She looked at her cousin, safer in Bridey's gaze.

"I will have ice cream," Bridey said. She straightened, drawing herself up and in the process, making the most of her neckline and its assets. "Chocolate, please."

Romeo shook his head at her request: What was a poor waiter to do? Then he flashed his smile: Just kidding, Miss America.

"He's a flirt, isn't he?" Corinne said, watching his retreat to the kitchen. "Talk about bedroom eyes."

"He can park his order pad under my bed anytime," Bridey said to her.

"Mary Bridget!" Tilla fussed at her, shooting a glance at the nuns and priest. "Watch yourself."

"What?" Bridey said. "That's what you used to say about Clark Gable."

"That's different," Tilla said. "If you ask me, this guy is trouble."

Who's asking? Bridey thought.

The waiters stood in the hallway leading out of the dining room, leaning up against the wall, waiting for the last of the Pilgrims to straggle out of the room, giving Tilla, Corinne, Sara and Bridey the visual once-over. Sara blushed deeply. Romeo hid his hands behind his back, his eyes pinpointing Bridey.

"Buona sera!" Bridey said to the waiters. She had a pamphlet of Italian phrases. She resolved to study it immediately.

Buona sera, they chorused. *Ciao.*

"Miss America," Romeo called to her. He stood away from the wall, hands still behind his back.

She wished that everyone would go about their business and leave her alone with him. That Would Not Do, she could hear her mother say. But the thought didn't prevent her walking back to him. From behind his back he brought a deep blue flower, like those in the little vases at the tables. He held it out to Bridey, twirling it by the stem. The other waiters watched. They were young and old, tall and short, stocky and thin, all dressed in the same black and white outfits as Romeo. But not one had the kind of look that made her feel as if her blood had gone fizzy, the way he did.

"Thank you. Grazie," she said, accepting it. Their fingers brushed.

"Sleep well, eh?" Romeo said. His eyes flicked from her eyes to her lips and back.

Bridey knew he meant just the opposite.

"That was something to write home about," Corinne said.

"I don't know about that," Tilla said. "I think her dad would be on the next flight over to punch his lights out."

"It's just a flower, Mum!" Bridey said. "Geez. Don't get hyper." She wore the blossom tucked behind one ear. She wasn't sure her sandals were completely touching the ground. It was as if her body was suspended from balloons, skimming air, remembering the way he looked at her, the way he singled her out.

"He was so funny," Sara said. She pushed the elevator button. "I hope he waits on us again at breakfast."

Bridey could feel the butterflies still rearranging themselves in her gut. Tomorrow!

"I wish someone would tease me like that," said Sara. "I saw those long, burning looks you two kept giving each other." They all watched the old-fashioned dial indicating the floor numbers over the elevator door. It was only a three story hotel, but the way the arrow moved, it could have been sixty.

"Cool your jets, lady," Corinne said to Sara. "He's 'way too old for you."

"Look who's talking, Corinne," Tilla said. "Those waiters were eyeing you, too."

"Yes. Well." Corinne patted her hair and wiggled her tiny hip.

"I've still got it."

"Got what?" Sara asked. She pushed the elevator button again. That seemed to make it go back up, instead of down to the lobby.

The needle dropped. They could hear the gears and pulleys moving within the little elevator. There was a cube of a window in each door, and the floor of the elevator slid by inside. Finally on the elevator, Bridey sank against the wall. She felt jittery, buoyant. "I like Assisi. I think I'll stay here and take in the sites. Sight. You all go on to Rome without me."

"Slow down, 'Miss America,'" Tilla said. "He probably pulls that stuff with some girl every week."

Bridey's face fell. Tilla didn't want to hurt her daughter, but what did Bridey know about men? Bridey took them at face value, even here in another culture, where attention could mean something entirely different than what she might think. They often had other things in mind, things Bridey was in no way prepared for, in Tilla's estimation.

"Don't worry, sweetie," Corinne said to her niece. "I think you could be the one to give that young man a run for it."

CHAPTER FIVE

Five

Church bells woke Bridey. The room was illuminated in morning sun. For the first time since she'd arrived in Europe, she felt flooded with the sense that the day promised wonderful possibilities. She got out of bed quietly, not waking Sara, and padded to the French doors. She stepped onto the balcony into a new light, a new dimension of time. The mountain sunshine bathed her in warmth. The landscape of Umbria lay below, an embroidered cloak spread before her by some long-forgotten medieval prince. Birds flitted across a sky of delicate blue. Wildflowers spilled down the mountainside, pinks and yellows, white on green. The Apennines stretched along the horizon, an emerald necklace against the throat of the sky. And above her, behind her, within her, the little city of Assisi called with its bells. Bridey leaned out from the balcony, straining to take it in. Why hadn't anyone told her that Italy could be this beautiful? Why had they only warned her not to drink the water, watch her money, and not to get pinched? Here was light and air so rich, it possessed a color all its own, a color invisible to those without the soul to perceive it, invisible to her until this moment.

Standing in her thin summer nightgown, her hair moving in the breeze, she was Juliet on the balcony. She was every heroine of all the ages' romances, poised on the brink of her fate, lacking only an answering soul with whom to share her own. None of the days that had gone before mattered now.

Bridey nearly danced through the morning. She led the way through Assisi ahead of her mother and aunt and Sara, exploring the narrow cobbled streets that twisted uphill. There were flowers everywhere, crimson geraniums in pots, on balconies, lining ancient stairs. Blossoms tumbled from cracks in the walls, popped up in spaces between walks and buildings, dotted the far cliff sides. They were gathered in pots and vases surrounding mosaics and street shrines to the Madonna. The twisting streets held a treasure of shops — antiques and glassware, pottery, *objets d'art*, religious items. In Assisi, Christianity was more than a spiritual resource; it spun a wheel around which so many things revolved — tourism, street names, landmarks, history.

In any other place, this would have soured Bridey, but a spell was cast on the balcony. The image of St. Francis in his monk's robe, with a bird perched on his hand and animals nestled at his feet, was omnipresent. Once, doing research in the library at school, she'd come across a book on the life of St. Francis. Hadn't he been a party guy? She tried to remember. Yes. Like a medieval frat brother, she thought. He paid everyone's tab. He sang in the streets. He even chased girls. He was a rebel, the book said — well, not in those words. Francis was the son of a wealthy textile merchant. God gave him a message, a direction. He followed it and got beaten by his father, locked in a cellar for punishment. He left the constraints of his society, going against the expectations and ambitions of his family. He threw off one life to live another.

You must have been something! Bridey thought, staring up at the alabaster face of the saint's statue. The world's first hippie! You stripped naked in court, threw your rich-boy clothes at the feet of your father, and took off to live in the woods, alone and broke. For a while, there were only the birds and animals to preach to. They say wolves lay down at your feet when you spoke to them about God.

Bridey walked to the Piazza di Francesco, thinking of St. Francis entombed deep in the giant basilica. What did it take to live in a vision, apart from the rest of the world? Who was the God whom Francis fell in love with, the God he listened to, the God he saw in every creature of the earth? Was it easier to see Him from the top of this mountain, where birds flew above wild-flowers, where the sun lit the air into invisible color?

Bridey rested against the gritty wall beside the basilica, con-templating the view from the piazza, listening to bells chime the hours somewhere in Assisi.

Cool in the dim heart of the shrine, she thought about Romeo the waiter; she hoped he would be there to serve her at lunch. What her mother said to her last night about him pulling the same stunt with other girls had lost its barb. Bridey decided her mother was wrong. She knew mutual attraction when she saw it. There was radar in people, in men and women, Bridey believed. It sent red lights flashing and flags flying when it picked up cer-tain signals. She didn't analyze how it worked. It was enough that it did. In Romeo's eyes, in his voice, and his trying-not-to smile, she saw those lights, spotted flags being raised on both ships: Red Alert.

"I'm ready for lunch," Tilla said.

They were standing in front of a small outdoor market. The sight of fruits and vegetables made Tilla's stomach rumble. The noon sun beat down, making her hair glint with gold and red. The pedestrian traffic had increased on the streets and the men made their admiration for Tilla known in double-takes and smiles. She tried to let herself enjoy it a little, but she couldn't forget the man with the knife in Venice, the horrible smirk on his face as he looked back at her in the crowd.

"We'd better head back to the hotel," Bridey said.

"Look at those braids of garlic," said Corinne. "They're like something in a magazine picture. My mouth is watering."

Tilla set her shopping bag down. Her feet hurt. The pain in her back and legs was striping its way toward her knees. Two men in suits passed by, brushing her on the narrow curb. *Scusi.* She jumped. The men continued their conversation. One carried a thick folder of papers in his hand. Just two men on their lunch hour.

"We'd better get back," Bridey said. "Follow me."

"Why don't we eat around here?" Tilla said. She wanted to sit down. Immediately. The heat and pain were beginning to make her feel fuzzy-headed.

"Let's find a pizza place," said Sara.

"What about that trattoria back on the last block?" Corinne suggested. She pointed in the opposite direction from Bridey.

They turned to walk back toward the café, all except Bridey. She stood rooted to the sidewalk, looking confused.

"C'mon, Hon," Tilla said to her. "This way."

By the time they got back to the hotel, Bridey felt like screaming. The service in the café was like slow death. The proprietor wanted them to relax, enjoy, and spend the entire afternoon there. Anytime Bridey pointed this out, someone would say: "Where do you have to be in such a hurry?" The walk took forever because of her mother's back. They had to walk slowly, so slowly.

Bridey walked supporting her mother, feeling a mixture of resentment and guilt. She wanted to run down the street, into the kitchen of the hotel to find Romeo. *Take me somewhere!* she'd say to him. *Show me who you are!*

When they limped into the hotel, Bridey was rewarded with a glimmer of hope.

"I'm sorry," Tilla said to them. "I'm going to have to rest on the bed. I need to get off my feet." She appeared to be hunching her back, and her skin was chalky. In one walk, she seemed to have aged ten years.

Corinne put her arm around her sister. "Do you want me to get a doctor?"

"Oh, God no," Tilla said. She grimaced. "Ooo."

"Don't be silly," Corinne said.

Tilla shook her head. "Really. All I need is some aspirin and a nap. It'll pass."

"I could use a lie-down myself," Corinne said, after they had gotten Tilla on her bed. Bridey was particularly nurse-like, arranging pillows and taking Tilla's shoes off to rub her feet.

"What about you girls?" Tilla asked. "I'm ruining your afternoon."

"No, you're not," said Bridey. Despite the heat of the day, her mother's feet felt cold. She gave both of them a rub to warm them.

"They'll be fine," Corinne told her.

"Don't go traipsing off alone," Tilla warned the girls. "Don't leave the hotel."

"I'll probably write in my log for awhile," Sara said. She peered into the mirror, checking for any lunch remnants caught in her braces.

"I mean it. I can't rest if I think you're out wandering the streets."

"They're not orphaned, for Pete's sake," Corinne said. She kicked off her shoes and sat on her bed beside Tilla's, picking up the room phone. "I think I'll try to get us a cold drink. Do you girls want anything?"

Tilla folded her arms across her forehead and closed her eyes.

Bridey arranged a pillow under her mother's feet and stood. She put her hand on Sara's shoulder and guided her toward the door, trying to keep it from becoming a push. "If we get bored, we'll go down to the dining room and see if we can get some ice cream," said Bridey.

"That's fine," Tilla sighed. "Take some lire out of my purse."

Bridey went to Tilla's purse and extracted some lire from Tilla's wallet. Her mother's wallet was crammed full of all sorts of papers — emergency phone numbers; a list of the shots she'd insisted she and Bridey get before they took this trip. Inside was a picture of her dad and mom with their arms around each other on their honeymoon looking like the kids they were, self-consciously happy to be so intimate. There were the latest school pictures of her and her brothers.

"Do you think ten thousand lira will be enough?" Bridey joked. She bent down and kissed her mother on her forehead. Even though it smelled faintly of cigarette smoke, Tilla's skin was still sweet.

She followed Sara out of their mothers' room, closed the door, and chewed the inside of her lip to keep from looking too happy.

Bridey let Sara have an hour to write in her log. So far she'd resisted the urge to sneak a peek at Sara's account of their trip. Sometimes it amazed her that Sara found so much to record. She wondered how large a part she played in Sara's accounting.

"Aren't you going to write to anyone?" Sara asked her.

"Nope," Bridey said. "I sent postcards in Munich: 'Can't get out of mother's sight. Eating so much veal, I'm developing a moo. Otherwise, things are great.' When I have something better to say, I'll write."

"Um-hm," Sara said, absorbed in her writing. Her pen moved methodically over the page, her face inches from the paper, as if she might be pulled in and disappear.

Bridey played at arranging her suitcase. She took off her eye shadow and liner, put some back on. Her face had a healthy color, a soft tan now that her sunburn from the boat trip had healed. She thanked God that the swelling from the sun poisoning went down and she didn't look puffy-eyed or have a thick widening of fluid built up at the bridge of her nose, like she usually got. What if she'd turned her head to look at the waiter and all he saw was a Neanderthal? She teased her hair up a little and pulled it back off her face with a turquoise ribbon, added her daisy stud earrings, a spritz of cologne, and a slick of Peach Frost lipstick. All hands on deck. Battle stations.

"How about some ice cream?" she said to Sara.

CHAPTER SIX

Six

When Bridey and Sara reached the dining room, a few people were still lingering over late lunches. The doors of the dining room were so tall they came nearly to the ceiling; they were of beveled glass and constructed so that they folded flat when fully opened to the terrace. Outside, people sat at tables in the sunshine. White tablecloths rippled in a soft breeze. The girls were shown to a table for two beside the smooth, stacked rock wall of the terrace, overlooking the valley.

"A drink today?" the waiter asked. He was as young as Romeo. But he was not Romeo.

"*Due colas,* please. I mean, per favore," Bridey said. "This is perfect," she said to Sara after he left. "Just us, on our own." She looked out between large flower urns on the wall at the view of Umbria below. "Let's come back here someday, Sara."

"If we do, promise me we'll use a normal travel agency," Sara said.

"We won't use a travel agency. We'll do it on our own. No

tours, no schedules. No six o'clock wake up calls. We'll wander. We'll rent a car. We'll go where we want to go, get to know the real people. We'll blend in. People won't even know we're American."

"I don't know," Sara said. "I don't think I could quit shaving my armpits."

"Nobody's going to be checking out your armpits. I'm talking about being free. Not like a tourist."

Sara crossed her arms and sat back, slumping. Beneath her sleeveless cotton print blouse, two small breasts made dainty mounds. She wore a bra but didn't need one. In five years, she would need one but not wear one. Sara was at the awkward stage of braces and glasses. She had hair the color of a chestnut and the large hazel eyes of her father. When the braces were off and the glasses exchanged for contacts, she'd be a stunner. But that wouldn't be until college. "So. Speaking of getting to know the real people — where do you think he is?" she asked Bridey.

"Who?"

"You know who. That waiter? Mister-I-can't-get-your-order-straight?"

"Sara. I have no idea where he is. As if I care."

"Get off it, Bridey. You didn't bring me down here because you're dying for ice cream."

I'm dying for something, Bridey thought. "Look," she said. "If someone that good-looking waved a flag in front of your face, wouldn't you want to know what he was up to? I'd do the same for you."

Sara opened her mouth to say something, but shot a look behind Bridey and cleared her throat in warning.

Romeo set two colas in front of the girls. He wore simple black slacks and a pressed white dress shirt with a black tie. A small white apron was tied around his waist.

Bridey tilted her head and shaded her eyes from the sun. Her heart was fibrillating. "Where is our waiter? The one who took our order?" she asked.

"I don' know what you say, 'our waiter,'" he said, as if she had asked him if he were from Mars. "I am your waiter." He smiled at Sara. "*Buongiorno*," he said to her.

Sara beamed. "Hi."

"What is Miss America wishing today?"

"Excuse me?" Bridey said.

"To eat." He winked at Sara.

"Oh," said Bridey, flustered at the thought he might be reading her too clearly. "We'd like ice cream."

"You are sure?" he asked. "Again ice cream? No lunch? Dessert only?"

"We've already eaten lunch," Bridey said and immediately wanted to bite her tongue. Rats! A giveaway: She'd come to see him. He knew it. She could see in the way his brows lifted. The half-smile to himself. For a minute he seemed to study something far out in the Apennines. Bridey and Sara followed his stare. Nothing.

"No ice cream," he said finally.

"No ice cream: you don't have any? Or, no ice cream, you won't bring any?" Bridey said.

"I don' bring it," he said.

"You're very obstinate for a waiter," Bridey said. Her toes wiggled in delight beneath the table. "Haven't you ever heard of the saying 'The customer is always right?'"

"Is beautiful day, no?" he said to Sara. "You don' argue on beautiful day."

"We'll have chocolate," Bridey said.

Romeo jerked his head, indicating Bridey. "She is like the principessa, eh? 'We 'ave chocolate!'" he said, still to Sara.

Sara laughed in collusion. As an afterthought, she covered her braces with her hand.

"Maybe I should get another waiter." Bridey sat straight in her chair in mock indignation. Oh, this was going very well.

"You don' want another waiter," he said, turning his

high-voltage eyes on her. "I tell you. I am your waiter."

She ordered her eyes not to flinch from his. "I see," she said. On the S.S. Female, a semaphore signal was sent: MESSAGE RECEIVED. PREPARING TO COME ABOUT. "If I can't have ice cream, what can I have?"

A direct hit! The S.S. Male was in flames. Bridey blinked at him. In the mid-afternoon sunlight, his face haloed by the bright sky, he could have been a statue of a saint, a soldier or an ancient god. But he was not stone, not strange and cold. He was someone very much of flesh and blood. Someone scrambling a little inside, not sure of what his next move might be. It was just a peek, a few seconds of weather changing across his eyes. He smiled down on her, acknowledging her message.

"Maybe, I surprise you," he said.

He brought them lemon ices and cookies. "You like this," he predicted to Sara. The terrace had emptied of all but a couple of people and the staff was taking advantage of the lull, cleaning off tables and resetting them, moving others in preparation for dinner. Romeo stood waiting for them to taste the ices.

"Mmm," Sara said. "This is great. Thank you."

"And Miss America? You like?"

"Do I have a choice?" Bridey asked. He stood as he had done last night in the hallway, hands clasped behind his back. Then he shifted, putting his hands on his hips. In that slight fidget from one stance to another, Bridey sensed he was anxious. She hoped it was because he wanted to please her, not an impatience to get back to his work. The fidget also gave her another chance to appreciate the way his body filled out that white shirt, the strong shoulders and solid chest, the way his ribs narrowed to a flat belly… He looked like an athlete.

"You don' —? Ah! If you do, you don' say, eh? You are — what you say — obstinate!"

"I like it," Bridey conceded, after tasting a spoonful. "I'm not the least bit obstinate."

"So I am not bad, to bring this?"

"I haven't decided," she said. She took another dainty spoonful of ice, considering. She gave her lips a little lick. "You were full of tricks last night. At dinner."

Romeo struck his chest with the flat of his hand and shook his head. "I don' trick!" He held his hands out to Sara, seeking an ally.

"I believe you," said Sara.

"Now I have one friend, eh?" he said, smiling at Sara. One of the older waiters called across the terrace to him from the dining room doors. Romeo answered him rapid-fire.

"I come back," he said to the girls and half-jogged his way past the tables.

"Do you want me to leave?" Sara asked Bridey, after he'd gone.

Yes, Bridey thought. "No," she said. "You don't have to go anywhere. And it would look like a set-up if you did."

"But it is a set-up," Sara said.

"Okay," Bridey said. "Yes. But I don't want it to look that way."

"I hate to break it to you, Bridey, but I don't think he's fooled." She brushed a bee from the rim of her glass and gave a tiny shake of her head. "He's only being nice to me because I'm with you."

"Oh, I don't think so," said Bridey. *It hurts to be fourteen,* she thought. *Like always being on the wrong side of the fence.* "I think he's nice to you because he really is nice. And you're nice to him. But he pretends to be something else to me because — well, it's a game. A test. If one of us doesn't play along, the other would know there was no point. No interest in going any further."

"You don't have to explain it to me," Sara said. "I'm not six years old. Like the way he switched places with the other waiter. As if he's personally assigned to us. He really wants to be with you."

"I know." Bridey couldn't help smiling.

When he came back, he had his sleeves rolled up and his collar button undone under his loosened tie. He pulled a chair out from the next table and sat down on it, the chair backwards, his arms crossed over the top of the chair back, relaxed. He was obviously off-duty, though work continued around him. Sara looked from Bridey to Romeo and took a last large spoonful of ice, gulping it down. She winced at the brain-freeze it gave her.

"Now, you are better," he said to Bridey. "No so... er..." He searched for the word, made his thumbs and forefingers into pincers.

"Crabby?" Sara prompted.

"*Si,*" he agreed. "*Grazie.*"

"I am not crabby!" said Bridey.

"Si. Crabby." He mimicked a crab coming at her with pincers. "Fsst. Fsst. Fsst! You don' sleep good?"

"I slept very well, thank you," Bridey said.

He rested his chin on his arms, smiling at her. "Is funny... because I am today so tired. I don' sleep all the night for thinking."

Bridey held his gaze. A tiny wren of doubt hopped onto her shoulder, chirping in her ear: *Be careful. He's very smooth. Maybe Mumma's right.* And she wanted her to be so wrong. "Isn't the service here exceptional," she said to Sara. "Why, they have their waiters sit with you while you eat, and check up on your sleeping habits as well."

Romeo regarded Bridey. "You think I don' know what you say?" he asked. "You can' talk to me?"

"No," Bridey said. "I think you understand." She tried to gauge whether she had actually insulted him. Better pull back a little on the sarcasm. A change of subject.

"Where did you learn to speak English so well?" she asked.

"Little from school. From family." He shrugged. "And I learn from working, also. Many English come here. Is good, no? Or we don' talk. They don' teach much Italian in America, I think."

"Sure they do," Sara said. "In some schools. Well, not that

many, actually."

"What do you study, in your school?" he asked Sara.

She squirmed in her seat. "French." She'd studied French from Kindergarten at the private school she went to in New York. She'd even skipped a grade.

"*Est-ce que vous parlez le français couramment?*"

"Oui." Sara nodded. Her face brightened.

The young man beamed back and then looked to Bridey, asking Sara: "*Nous pouvons continuer notre conversation ainsi — ou bien est-ce que la princesse ne parle pas cette langue?*"

Sara giggled. "*Non, elle ne le parle pas du tout. Vous pourriez me dire n'importe quoi en français et elle comprendrait rien.*" No, Bridey doesn't speak a word of French, she told him. You could say anything and she wouldn't understand a word.

The way they smiled at each other, Bridey knew the joke was on her. She caught the word "conversation" and figured 'la princesse' referred to her. "That's not fair!" she complained.

"And you, Miss America? What do you study?"

"German and Latin," she began. "I —." Before she could go on, he fired off a question in German. She translated as loosely as she could. *Do you know how beautiful I think you are,* he asked. She swallowed with embarrassment at not being fast enough to form an answer. "Danke," she said. Oh no, she thought, please don't let him start conversing in German. He can speak one, two, four languages, to my one and a quarter. I look like a dolt.

"Show-off," she said, to head him off. "Do you know what that means?"

He shook his head, no.

Sara put her napkin down on the table. "Well, excuse me," she said, rising. "I'm way behind on my writing. Have to write home, you know." She avoided Bridey's eyes.

"I see you at dinner tonight, eh, my friend?" Romeo said to Sara. He held his hand out to shake, but then tilted Sara's hand and gave it a tiny kiss. Sara went crimson. She tripped over the chair in front of her and made a quick retreat.

Without Sara, Bridey sat in uncomfortable silence. She thought the S.S. Female was ready to take prisoners, but the gangplank suddenly fell in the water. Romeo unnerved her with his ability to switch from one language to the next, and flirt in all of them. What else could he do that she could not? Is this what foreign men were like? So far ahead of her, in so many ways? He sat quietly, watching her. Maybe she wasn't ready for this. She watched the bee that had landed on Sara's glass as it gathered pollen from the flowers in the pots on the wall. He never took his eyes off her, she knew. Her bravado was fading fast. Any moment he would figure out that she was just a barely-eighteen-year-old virgin who was so scared of guys getting too worked up that she was known as the Ice Princess back home.

"I should go, too," she said, sliding her chair back. The legs dragged across the stone with a screech.

"You don' want to talk to me?" He sounded a little hurt.

"It isn't that."

"You run to Mama?"

Bridey flinched. How did he know? She frowned at him. "Not at all."

"Where is Mama?"

"She's resting. Her back hurts."

"Ah," he said. "Is too bad. I am sorry to hear." He didn't look sorry.

"But that's not the point," she said, not meeting his eyes. "I can do what I want. I hardly need my mother's permission." Scared as she was, she definitely did not want to run to her mother.

"So, stay."

"Fine." She sat back in the chair and crossed her legs. Deliberately, pointedly, he took them in, the length of them, then her breasts, and her eyes. Her pulse thudded in her chest and ears.

"Are all Italian men so bold?"

"I see what I like, I look," he said. "Is like looking at piece of art. Like a Michaelangelo."

"What if I mind you looking that way?"

He propped his chin on his palm, his gaze steady on her face, direct and calm. "Do you?"

She did and she didn't. It wasn't as if men hadn't looked at her before. She'd caught them doing it. And it wasn't as if she didn't look at men as well. Secretly. But she'd been trained from birth, it seemed, never to let them know she did, and to pretend she didn't know they were. Never give them the satisfaction of acknowledging herself as a sexual creature. Ladies were above that and to be a lady was the ultimate goal. A lady was someone above reproach. Respectable. Unreachable. Un...touchable. Neuter, she thought. How depressing.

His voice grew soft. "What do you think of, Miss America?"

"Bridey," she said. "My name is Bridey. Bridey McKenna."

"And I am Alessandro," he said, with a gentleness that made Bridey let out the breath she'd been holding in.

She cleared her throat. "I think..." She stared at her lap, at her hands, where her ruby class ring from Providence shone. She thought of all the warnings and restrictions and rules that went along with it and slipped it off. It didn't matter that she was an honor student back home, or a class leader, or that she won medals for swim team. Her whole life to this point was dictated by the expectations and measurements and plans of other people. In taking off the ring, she slipped from the bonds of that scratchy mooring of others' pride and set sail on her own path. Then she smiled at Alessandro.

"I don't mind," she said.

"And?" He tapped his temple with two fingers. "There is more, no? I see it."

He didn't ask as part of a game. There is more. He said it simply, reading her. She sensed an intuition and recognition in him she'd only hoped for, but not expected. In three words, he changed her course. She might have walked the path of dishonesty, denying

what was real in her, for the sake of one-upmanship in a flirtatious swordplay. She could walk that path forever, only to find it
led nowhere. *There is more.* She knew it, felt it. Why not admit it,
if not to him, then at least to herself? And if she were to admit
it to him, where might it lead? Possibly nowhere. Possibly away
from the untouchable and neuter.

"I'm very glad you're my waiter," she said.

"And I, also," he agreed. He held out his hand to take hers. "I
am happy to meet you, Bridey McKenna." He didn't release her
hand. But she didn't pull it away either.

"Assisi is my favorite place in Europe," she said. His eyes were
the color of milk chocolate, his expression as sweet. "I think I've
come here for a reason. Not just to sightsee. I just hope I have
enough time to find out what it is."

He smiled at her, a smile of pure gladness. He held her hand
by the knuckles of her fingers, caressing them lightly.

"I think it's you. The reason." She hadn't meant to say this
aloud. But she did.

He pressed his lips together and nodded. The dark brows
knit together. "I see you tonight, at dinner," he said. "But is not
enough. I wan' —." He gave a sharp sigh and linked his fingers
with hers. "I wan' more. Not just to play tricks. More time to be
with you. To know you."

"I do, too." She responded to the squeeze he gave her fingers
and marveled at the delight of feeling the moistness of his palm,
the tiniest indication of nervousness, the satiny skin along the
sides of his fingers, the square shape of his nails. She liked the
strength of his wrist and the hair growing toward the backs of his
hands. She memorized the gentleness in his touch.

"Bridey," he said. "Is pretty name."

"Mary Bridget, actually. But Mary is too plain."

"Maria Brigitta. *Cosi bella.* So beautiful, your name. I like to
say it."

Bridey gave a quiet, self-conscious laugh. "Do you always say just the right thing?"

"I think I am no so good in English sometime. Maybe I don' say right."

"You say it perfectly," Bridey said. "I guess I meant that you're full of surprises. All of them good, so far."

"We see," he said. "I hope only good, for you."

They sat holding hands, alone on the terrace except for a lone waiter setting up tables. They held their conversation in their eyes and with their touch. The bees continued their mission with the flowers and the perfect Umbrian afternoon stretched across the landscape, the sun heating the rocks of the stone wall. Something had dropped Bridey into this magic place, something powerful and benevolent that understood the need of the young to believe in miracles. The miracle could be the slant of the sun on a young man's arms as he sat very near her, as near as he dared. Alessandro wasn't like any boy she'd ever known. He wasn't a boy at all, but a man; she knew she'd left boys behind her forever. It wasn't a case of geography. It was one of emotional physics.

In the small time they sat together, she began to comprehend the nature of miracles. They existed and appeared, not as events to be prayed for and bargained over, but as things random, hidden and unexpected, like the sudden flight of tiny birds from within ivied walls. They were there, around her. She had only to open her inner eyes, and wait.

CHAPTER SEVEN

Seven

Sara wasn't in their room when Bridey came back, and that made Bridey glad. She wanted to keep the feeling she'd carried in from the terrace, to savor it alone. Something wonderful was happening. To everyone else, it might seem she had only flirted with a young man waiting tables. That was all right with her. She didn't want to have to explain the difference in him, or herself. The first thing they would do would be to try to explain it away, or make fun of it. Then the miracle would veer away from her and disappear. She knew it was a delicate thing, the balance between magic and the willingness to see it.

The room dimmed as the late afternoon sun crossed the mountain. Bridey unlocked the doors to the balcony and opened them wide. She stretched out on her bed on her stomach, her feet on the pillow and her head at the end of the bed, and looked out through the doors at the ancient mountains, amethyst now against a deep blue sky. She drifted in a state between fulfillment and expectation. Then her eyes closed and she was asleep.

"Hey. Sleeping Beauty," she heard her mother say to her. "You'd better wake up, or you'll make us late for dinner."

Bridey opened her eyes, trying to focus. Her mother was sitting across from her on Sara's bed smoking a cigarette. Corinne was sitting out on the balcony with Sara. Bridey hadn't heard them come in.

"You were really zonked," Tilla said. "Must have been all that walking today."

Bridey sat up on the bed and stretched stiffly. "What time is it?"

"A little after six."

"When's dinner?" She jumped up from the bed and went to her suitcase, pulling out a clingy yellow mini with daisies splashed all over it. In the mirror on the wall above the dresser, she could see that her cheek was red from sleeping on the chenille bedspread. The pattern was etched on her skin. She pressed the backs of her fingers against it, the same fingers Alessandro held so tentatively on the terrace.

"Oh, yes. Dinner," Tilla said. "We wouldn't want to be late, would we? Wouldn't want to miss a minute."

"Darn right we don't want to miss it," Corinne said, coming in from the balcony. "Rose says we're dining al fresco this evening. It should be absolutely gorgeous outside. And guess what?"

"What?" Bridey asked, gathering her bath things. She headed for the door.

"Rose says we're going to have music with dinner," Corinne said.

"Sounds fantastic," Bridey said.

"Maybe Assisi is the turning point," Sara said. "Maybe here's where it starts getting good."

Music and the terrace, and Alessandro. And a hundred other people, all in the way. He didn't just want to play tricks with her. But what else was there for him to do? Bridey opened the door to the hallway and turned back to her mother.

"How's your back now, Mumma?"

"A little better," Tilla said. "My nap did me a lot of good."

"I'm glad," Bridey said. *Your nap did me a lot of good, too.*

"Did you tell her I was with him?" Bridey accused Sara in a whisper as they followed their mothers toward the dining room terrace doors.

Sara shot Bridey a resentful look. "I didn't tell her anything," she hissed. "She asked me where you were when I went to their room and I said you hadn't finished eating and you wanted to write some postcards out on the terrace. And then she said, was that waiter around, and I said yes. And she said, was he hanging around Bridey? And I said he was just joking and giving you a hard time, but he had a lot of work to do."

"Then why was she so edgy when I woke up?"

"I don't know," Sara said. "Maybe her back hurts a lot."

They walked onto the terrace to the strains of classical music. Tilla was limping noticeably. A quartet of musicians was set up in the corner of the terrace, three men and a woman. They were playing violin, harp, piano, and flute. A cello was propped against the wall.

The maitre d' greeted them. "Buona sera," he said. "You will enjoy this evening very much." He picked up four leather-bound menus and lead them to a table opposite the musicians. "The view, the music." He gestured toward the pale evening sky. "A perfect night."

Father and Rose already occupied their table for six. Bridey sat down and twisted in her seat, scanning over the view of the valley, scanning the crowd for Alessandro's face somewhere in it.

Sara held up her large menu. It was completely in Italian. "No subtitles," she said. "What's Italian for veal? I don't want to have any."

"*Il vitello*," said Rose. "I'd recommend the chicken and pasta dishes. Or the trout. It's sure to be fresh, right from the mountain streams. The cheeses are excellent, too."

Father Clement sipped his wine. " 'Long as I have the opportunity, I'm going to ask the waiter to recommend something," he said. "There's nothing like a local to know what the chef does best. Although..." He smiled down the table at Bridey. "If we get that same boy from last night, I'd be real careful taking his advice."

"Oh, believe me, Father," Bridey said. "I'll be watching out for him."

An older waiter took and delivered their drink orders. The same one, Bridey realized, who'd shouted to Alessandro on the terrace. She toyed with the gold bangles on her arm to keep her disappointment from showing.

The quartet played a piece from *Carmen*. Tilla sat back in her chair and sighed. "Aren't they wonderful? I haven't heard live music out-of-doors since I can't tell you when."

"It does have a completely different feel, I think," Rose said. "Something to do with blending nature and music."

Nature, Bridey sniffed. How can she shrink what's around us into a single word? Can't she see it? Can't she feel it? It's there. Color. Only one that can't be named, like blue or green. You feel it, instead. Like colors swirling on a bubble.

Bridey bent her head over her menu, her hair spilling forward, shielding her face in a veil. Please, God, where is he?

"Speak of the devil and up he pops," Corinne said. "Here comes your waiter, Bridey."

"He's not my waiter," Bridey said. But of course, the way her heart lifted and began to pound, she knew he was.

Alessandro seemed rushed. He was full of apology. "So sorry," he said to them. "I do two jobs tonight. Is very busy."

"Take it easy, young fella," Father said. "Catch a breath. We got all night. It's so pretty here, I doubt any of us feel like jumping up and going anywhere."

"I certainly don't," Rose said, raising her glass. Maybe it was

Bridey's imagination, but she thought she saw Rose flutter her eyelashes at Alessandro.

He nodded and poised his pen over his order pad. He stole a quick glance at Bridey and turned to Rose for her order, all business. He left Bridey for last again. "And for Miss America?"

"I'm not sure," she said. She pretended to study the menu. She didn't feel the least bit hungry.

"I think, this for you tonight," he said, coming to her seat and pointing to a line on her menu.

"It's not octopus or something, is it?"

"No, is not *octo'*pus," he said. "Is farfale. Pasta."

"How do I know you're not fooling me?"

"So pretty perfume," he said, inhaling the air near her hair. "Only Miss America can smell like the summer."

She'd given herself a couple of spritzes of Wind Song in the bath. "You're not answering my question," Bridey said, playing the game. "Is it really pasta? Or will it have eyes and tails in it?"

He stood tall. "I am wound," he said to the table's occupants. He pronounced the word 'wound' like a clock but made a stabbing motion at his chest. "No to be trust by Miss America!"

Corinne laughed. "Heavens, Bridey. Don't wound the poor boy."

Tilla concentrated pointedly on brushing tiny crumbs from her lap.

"Okay," Bridey said, trying to have the right amount of skepticism in her voice, instead of letting it slip into high excitement. She closed the heavy menu and handed it to Alessandro. "I'm going to have to trust you."

He smiled down on her. They were back in the afternoon, alone, with only the sun and church bells for company.

"You won' be sorry," he assured her.

But when the food was served, it was not done by Alessandro, but by the older waiter. Alessandro was nowhere to be seen. Bridey pushed the pasta around on her plate, miserable with disappointment.

"Cheer up, Sweetie," Tilla said. "It's a beautiful night."

The evening settled on the valley. The sun was only a narrow wash of orange and violets on the horizon and the few lights scattered across the valley floor mirrored the first stars in the sky. Candles were lit on the tables. Bridey felt sick. It was as if Alessandro had disappeared off the side of the cliff wall. He had not served any table that night. Once he had their orders, he was gone. Why?

The musicians finished a selection of traditional songs. The maitre d' walked out onto the open floor of the terrace. He held up his hands and looked at the diners, smiling, ready to make an announcement. Spoons stopped clinking against coffee cups and conversations died down.

"Ladies and gentlemen," he began. "*Signores e Signoras*. I am sure you have all been enjoying the very beautiful music of our quartet this glorious evening." The diners clapped appreciatively at this. "I must tell you, they are like a family to the Hotel Windsor Savoia. They are, in fact, a real family. May I present Signore Roberto de Luca, our violinist and cellist; his wife, Signora Celine de Luca, harpist; and Roberto's brothers: Alphonse de Luca, flute and clarinet, and Otto de Luca, piano." The de Luca family rose and bowed to more applause.

"Tonight," the maitre d' continued, "we have a special treat for you. We are most proud to employ Signore e Signora de Luca's son, Alessandro. We know him since he was little boy. He is not only one of our most excellent waiters, but!" He held up a finger for emphasis. "Alessandro won recently the very prestigious Achille Peri competition." He paused as a few people applauded in recognition. "Soon he will go to the Opera di Roma to study and perform! He is a gifted tenor. He brings great pride to Assisi and to us, his hotel family. Tonight, our Alessandro will do us the honor of singing, accompany by his family. May I present, with great pleasure, Alessandro de Luca!"

Alessandro. At the sound of his name, Bridey sat straight up in her chair. Alessandro. She loved classical music, even had a few albums of Tchaikovsky and one that was a sort of "greatest hits" of various composers but she knew little about opera. What she heard, she hadn't liked. All that crying and moaning, and never in English. It was something old people listened to. What if he sang and she didn't like it? What if it changed everything?

When he strode out onto the terrace to the excited applause and murmuring, everything did change. He walked on not as a waiter or an ordinary young man but as an artist with presence, one who knew he belonged in front of an audience, who knew he had much to give. He bowed, then flashed a wide smile to his family and nodded to them.

There were only a few notes of introduction. He began to sing. By the renewed applause, a great many people seemed to recognize the piece immediately. It was something quick and sparkling, full of playfulness and energy. For the first time, she heard his language in its most perfect form. He made it dance and spin, dive and soar. Bridey sat immobilized by the sheer force and power of his skill. The song ended abruptly with a flourish and the people on the terrace burst into a frenzy of clapping. She clapped, too, but through a fog of wonder. Her hands felt as if they were dragging through water to come together. Her whole body felt strange, altered, buzzing with an alien excitement. She had to sit on her hands to keep them from shaking.

"Oh, that was marvelous!" Rose said somewhere in Bridey's fog. "What a surprise."

"That was *Rigoletto,* wasn't it?" Corinne said. "*Questo o quella?*"

"Right," Rose said. "He's terribly good."

"Gosh," Sara said. "I thought he was a normal person. How does he have so much air in his lungs? He doesn't even have a microphone and I'll bet they can hear him sing all over the mountain."

"It's called talent," Corinne said. "It's training. That's not something you're going to hear from your average singer. It's

all about breath and control and knowing how to use it. But the
quality of his voice — it's — it's exceptional!"

"He's no Mario Lanza." Tilla snipped. Tilla was no fan of
opera either, but she did think the young Lanza was handsome
and he'd made a movie and been on television.

"He's got the looks and the voice," Father said. "He's the whole
shebang. Imagine, our waiter."

Bridey couldn't take her eyes off Alessandro; his being
seemed to alter before her. Alessandro's father struck up another
song on his violin. And this time, Bridey did recognize it. She
knew it — oh God, how humiliating to admit — from a Bugs
Bunny cartoon. Bugs dressed as a ballerina, waltzing, pirouet-
ting. Background music in a cartoon. And if Alessandro were
ever to find out, she would curl up and die with shame.

La donna mobile.

She shook Bugs Bunny from her head. Across the valley, the
sky was dark and specked with stars; the air sweet and clean with
the fragrance of pines. Whatever he was singing, it was beautiful. And so was he, transformed past mere handsomeness by his
intensity, by something perfect.

He changed from sparkling to passionate, from Verdi to Puccini, sweeping Bridey off the earth-bound terrace and away from
its tourists, into the heavens with his voice. He sang a song that
could only be about a terrible sadness. The words in Italian made
no sense to her. But it didn't matter that she couldn't understand
the words. In the music, she heard the breaking of a heart, so
poignant and full of hopelessness. It was a cry of a human being
to God. Alessandro gave the story life as he sang.

Bridey knew she was in the presence of something blessed.
His voice penetrated her, a vibration that woke her soul from
sleep, a chord only she could hear. She took in the way his lips
moved, the curve of his throat, the gleam of his teeth; the shape
of his shoulders moving beneath the material of his shirt as his
chest rose and fell with his breath. Desire filled her. She was lost

in his voice, leaving all she thought she knew, to enter a separate world. His was the voice of an angel, calling to her, a mere earthly being. The terrace was in absolute silence, the little audience frozen in admiration and pleasure. Knots of waiters stood on the periphery of the terrace and a crowd of listeners, people from the street outside, staff and guests, were drawn to the dining room doors. Some rose to their feet, applauding him when he finished the aria. They called out requests. The waiters nodded and smiled among themselves, clapping for one of their own; cheering him on like an athlete.

As his family accompanied him, Alessandro didn't seem to see Bridey, nor acknowledge her in any way. But as the last of the applause and bravos died down and violin and flute began a delicate phrase of his last aria, he lifted his eyes to lock with hers.

Che gelida manina, he began to sing. What a tiny, frozen hand.

He walked slowly toward her. He was singing to her, speaking in music just to her. Telling her of tenderness and strength. Of pride and elation. Of gentleness and passion. She could hear these things in his voice. He held his hands out to her, inviting her to stand with him. The buzzing that started in her veins earlier was now full trembling. She had to clench her teeth together to keep them from chattering. She had never wanted anything more in her life than for him to look at her, acknowledge her. And now he was taking her hands in his, so there could be no mistaking who was the object of his song.

La diro' con parole chi son, e che faccio, come vivo. I will tell you in a word who I am, what I do, and how I live.

She held tight to his hands for fear she would float up into the air, above the mountain, spin out of control among the stars.

She might never come back to earth again. These feelings were dangerous, like tasting a drug. He was drugging her ears and eyes and heart with his voice. She wanted more, and more.

Or che mi conoscete, parlate voi, deh! Chi siente?
Now that you know all about me, he sang, won't you please tell me who you are?

The final notes of the aria hung sweet, tender and full of hope, then drifted like smoke wisps out into the night and were gone. The terrace went from silent to ecstatic. *Bravo! Bravo!* There were whistles, and shouts of *More!* People rose again to their feet. Some threw flowers from the tables toward the quartet, euphoric from wine and music.

Alessandro held onto Bridey for a moment more, presenting her to the audience as if they were on stage; then he kissed her hands. He gave her a smile. Of pride? Mischief? She didn't know. He let go of her and threaded his way through the tables to his musician family, and took his bows.

Bridey was the only one not clapping. She sank down, buckling into her chair. The trembling in her stopped with the music. In its place was a blurry double vision and the sense that she might faint. *This will only happen once in my life, she thought. No one will ever sing to me that way again. Never. Not in candlelight on a mountain in Italy. Not anywhere else. Never. No one will ever give me a gift like this.*

Alessandro scooped up a few of the little pink carnations littering the stones of the terrace floor and held them above his head in thanks to his audience. He turned and bowed to his beaming family in acknowledgement of their playing. Then he kissed one of the carnations and presented it to his mother, who looked at him with an expression of adoration. His mother looked over at Bridey for a long minute, and then busied herself smelling the carnation.

Bridey watched Alessandro clapped on the back and hugged by his fellow waiters as if he were walking into the wings of La Scala, instead of disappearing beyond swinging kitchen doors.

"Lord, I have chills," Corinne said. "I'll bet ten years from now we'll see him at the Met."

"Wouldn't that be a lark?" Rose said. "Bridey!" She grasped the hand Alessandro had kissed. "What a thrill for all of us."

"Were you embarrassed?" Sara asked Bridey.

People were staring at her, Bridey realized. Some of them were smiling. Her head cleared. She was back at the table, not floating above the mountain.

Tilla was silent and unsmiling. She looked into her wine-glass, twirling it slowly between her thumb and forefinger. The wine spun in slow motion, creating a tiny vortex.

"A penny for your thoughts, Tilla," Rose said to her. "What do you think? Your girl has been made a star of the evening. Gave us all quite the romantic boost."

Tilla looked at Bridey. "I was just wondering," said Tilla, "how many times he puts on this act, with all the tourists who come through."

"Oh, surely not!" Rose said, turning to Bridey.

Bridey stared back at her mother. *Why do you have to do this to me? Why are you always holding me back, trying to take things away from me?* The flame of the table's candle burned, reflected in the pupils of Bridey's eyes.

Eight

Alessandro was waiting for Bridey when they came from dinner; waiting alone in the hall leading out of the dining room. "Signorina," he said. "May I speak one moment?" He was the picture of courtliness and respect. No teasing, no "Miss America."

Tilla tugged her purse strap higher on her shoulder, not looking at Alessandro.

Rose stepped forward, brushing Bridey aside, assuming her official tour leader capacity. She cranked her British accent up a notch. "May I introduce myself, Signore de Luca? I'm Rose Birch. I'm the guide for the group to which Miss McKenna belongs. So I feel pleased to make formal introductions." She wagged a spidery hand in Bridey's direction. Alessandro gave her a perfunctory smile, but his attention returned to Bridey. "And may I say," Rose went on, "on my own behalf, and of course, on the behalf of everyone here, how absolutely —."

"Signora Birch." Alessandro stuck out his hand to Rose. He raised his brows at her in an obvious message: Can we get on with this, please?

"Oh." Rose shook his hand. She took a step to the side, like someone directed behind a velvet rope.

"Signora," he said, offering his hand to Corinne, then to Tilla who didn't offer hers.

"Corinne LeDoux," Corinne said in return. She caught Tilla's arm and gave it a pinch. "And this is my sister, Tilla McKenna. My daughter, Sara."

His face softened as he held his hand out to Sara. "We are friends, no? *Bon soir, Mademoiselle.*"

Sara shook his hand. A blush crept its way up from her jaw line. "I think you're a good waiter, but you're a great singer."

A soft smile. "*Vous êtes très gentille, ma petite amie.*"

"And this," Rose interrupted, determined in her role, "is Mary Bridget McKenna."

"My daughter," Tilla emphasized.

Bridey's face was incandescent looking at Alessandro. She offered her hand to him, feeling as if she knew him well and as if she were meeting him for the first time, in the same instant.

"Well." Corinne observed the two, then turned to her sister and Rose. "Why don't we go for a little walk? Signore de Luca, you were superb tonight. I have no doubt you'll perform in New York someday and when you do, I'm going to invite you to dinner and say I knew you when. What do you say?"

"I say is a date!" He laughed. "*Mille grazie.*"

"We'll meet you in the lounge after our walk," Corinne said to Bridey.

"Shortly," Tilla said. She was propelled away by her sister. In the lobby, she muttered to Corinne. "What's in your head? What do you think you're doing, leaving her alone with him? He's on the make! He couldn't be plainer about what he wants than if he rented a billboard."

"Bridey can handle him," Corinne said.

Alessandro looked at Bridey intently, waiting for her to speak. More people were leaving the dining room, passing by, and some repeated their praise to him. *Bravo! Excellent!* He nodded and thanked them. Some smiled speculatively at Bridey. A few wanted to start conversations, but moved off, sensing Alessandro's reluctance. He led Bridey to an alcove behind the maitre d's desk, a place less visible.

"Thank you," Bridey said. "Thank you for singing to me tonight. I..." She shook her head. "I don't know what to say. Where to begin. It was so beautiful. So special. I'm... speechless."

"Speechless?"

"I don't know the words."

Something caught the corner of his eye, something over her shoulder. Two faces were peeking out at them from the kitchen doors, farther down. He took three long strides toward the faces and gave the wall near the doors a thwack with the flat of his hand, gesturing at them and speaking in rapid Italian. The faces disappeared. He came back to her. "You are saying?"

What am I saying? How do I tell him? Bridey thought. "You are full of surprises. I'm stunned. I don't know the words for it."

"I don' do it for words," he said. "I wan' to tell you, tonight was for you only." He was very close to her. "I wan' to take you to dance. Come with me tonight."

Bridey's eyes widened. "Tonight?"

"Si. I take you to discotheque."

"There's a discotheque? In Assisi?" It seemed impossible that Assisi would have any nightlife at all, as if it had been banned with Francis's departure from the material world.

He turned his head away, laughing. Then he drew even closer. "We dance in Assisi. We are not all of the time saints, eh?"

Thank God for that, she thought.

"So. You come? You ask Mama. Is very safe. I take good care for my Miss America." He brushed her hair back off her shoulder, his fingertips trailing along the nape of her neck. It gave her goosebumps.

I'd go with you to China, Bridey thought. *My prayers are answered. All those prayers I made, rattling around in the Phantom.* Then her heart dipped, remembering her mother's expression at the table. *Ask mama.* She knew there was no chance Tilla would agree to let her go anywhere with Alessandro, not even with St. Francis himself along as a chaperone. If Bridey asked, Tilla would ruin everything.

"Come with me." He whispered. "Soon, you go."

"Yes," she told him.

She was supposed to meet him at eleven, at the bottom of the terrace side. It was two stories down to the parking lot, at the end of a long series of stone steps. He didn't say so, but Bridey figured it wasn't hotel policy for their waiters to openly date guests. That was okay, she thought; it wasn't her mother's policy for Bridey to date this waiter. Except that he wasn't simply a waiter. Didn't her mother see that? He was brilliantly talented. Bridey didn't know what this competition he won was all about, but it must be something pretty extraordinary. He was going to Rome soon, going places in his life. And opera. How could you get more cultural? How could her mother object to someone like this?

He's European, that's how, Bridey thought. More specifically, he's Italian. This put him in the category with sharks and wolves, as far as her mother was concerned. Her mother was a sweet person but she also had a suspicious nature. Some people rated more suspicion than others. It was silly and stupid, Bridey thought. Under her mother's rules, if you were Irish, you were okay. Anything outside of that was subject to reservation. But Bridey realized, from the day they'd run into the man in the square in Ulm, that her mother had been seeing everything through a hazy cloud of fear. The thief with the knife in Venice clinched it. Unless she wanted to experience Europe and everyone in it in the same way,

Bridey knew she had to take her chances where she found them. It was going to be tricky. Deceitful. And deceit hadn't been in her vocabulary much, before now. The pale realm of little white lies was more her territory. This would require a very big, black lie.

It came as some surprise to Bridey how cool and calculating she was able to be, rejoining her family in the lobby, acting as if there was no more to her talk with Alessandro than a chance to thank him and enjoy more of his teasing flattery. While at that very minute, she was deciding how soon she could claim fatigue, or maybe stomach cramps would be more convincing, so that she could end the evening in her room soon enough. But not too early; that would seem odd, and oddness would generate curiosity, then suspicion on her mother's part. Tilla possessed an uncanny psychic sense. It was hard to keep anything from her. Why did suspicion follow so closely behind over-protection?

I'll wear my black dress, she thought, while Rose and Tilla and Corinne talked. She'd brought a sleeveless black linen sheath she was saving for Rome or Paris. Tonight was special enough. The dress was simple and fitted, the most sophisticated one she owned, with a deep, square neckline. When she tried it on at home, her dad had grown almost teary.

I didn't think you'd be gone so fast, he had said to her.

I'm still here, Daddo, she had replied. But later, in her room, she looked at herself in the mirror, smoothing the dress over her waist and hips, observing how the neckline gave a peek of cleavage. She knew her father was right. She was pretty much gone.

The real hurdle would be Sara, Bridey thought, glancing at her cousin. How to sneak out of their room? Unless Bridey could slip her a mickey, Sara would be wide-awake at eleven. Sara would have to know.

Bridey wondered just how far Sara would go in the name of hero-worship.

Sara trotted behind Bridey after they said their goodnights to Tilla and Corinne. She followed so closely that she stepped on the back of Bridey's heel. Once they were in their own room, Sara stood with her arms crossed and watched Bridey.

"What?" Bridey asked. *Uh-oh.*

Sara walked across the room and unlocked the doors to the balcony. She stepped outside and peered down the balcony rail.

Bridey followed her out onto the balcony and looked out into the darkness shrouding the hillside. The moon rose over the valley, set in a clear, black velvet sky. She leaned on the rail. *Okay... How to do this? Beat around the bush? Flattery? Or just out with it, and hope for the best. If she won't go along with it, will I leave anyway?*

"Have you ever seen anything so beautiful as this night?" she asked Sara. "I feel like I've walked inside a painting."

"A painting?"

"It's more beautiful than a painting, because it's so alive."

Sara sighed heavily. "I guess."

"Sara..."

Sara sat down in one of the chairs and hugged her knees to her chin. "Let me guess," she said. "He wants you to meet him somewhere."

"Jesus!" Bridey hushed. "Keep your voice down." She was afraid Sara's words would carry away on the breeze, around to the front side of the hotel and into her mother's room. They could hear bits and pieces of conversations from open doors below, and one or two other occupied balconies. "How did you know?"

"A wild guess. The way he looks at you! It's pretty amazing. I've never actually watched anyone fall in love before, in person. He's so sweet, but cool at the same time. Talk about him wanting to impress you!"

"He wants me to go out dancing with him."

"Out? Like, away from the hotel?"

"There's a discotheque he wants to take me to. I know," Bridey said, acknowledging Sara's look. "I didn't think there was any-thing like that in Assisi. But that's kind of the point. There are a lot of things in these places we never see. I want to go and see it with him. Sara, nothing like this has ever happened to me, and it might be the only time it ever will. I don't want to leave without having it to remember."

Sara cast her eyes toward the floor and the corners of her mouth tugged downward.

Of course, Bridey thought. There would be nothing like this for Sara to remember. But Sara was fourteen. She could return to Europe again. She could afford to wait.

"Do you blame me for wanting to go?"

A shoulder lifted in a half-shrug. No comment.

"If he had a younger friend, I'd take you. If you wanted to go."

"You would?"

"Sure," Bridey lied.

"But what about your mom?"

"If I'm lucky, and you keep this secret, she won't ever know. We'll just get up in the morning and have breakfast, like usual. They'll never know I was gone." Bridey crossed her fingers behind her back. *Please, please, Sara.*

Sara glanced back into their room. "I don't want to sleep here alone. I think it would be scary."

Bridey dragged a chair close to Sara and sat at the edge of the seat. "All you have to do is keep the door locked. I'll only be gone a little while. This place is so safe. It's practically next door to the Basilica. Who's going to try anything with all these saints watch-ing over you?"

Sara looked less doubtful.

Bridey decided to go for broke. "If you get really scared, you

can call your mom or run to their room. You can tell them everything, and I'll face them when I get back. I'll take all the blame."

"No," Sara said.

Bridey's hopes sank. Disappointment stabbed her. "You won't
help me?"

"I mean no, I wouldn't do that. I won't tell."

"Oh my God." In a heartbeat, the disappointment shot up
to become hope. The speed of it felt like a G-force ride. "Sara,"
Bridey whispered. "You're the best. I mean it. You're better than a
sister." It was not a lie to tell her that. Even if Bridey knew it was
what Sara wanted to hear.

Sara's eyes shone. Her braces glittered. "You owe me, though,"
she said. "You have to tell me everything that happens."

"Every detail," she lied again.

Bridey strode quickly through the lobby and out a side door,
her heart pounding with fear and a flush running through her so
fiercely she felt heat radiating from her scalp. Only three people
gave her a second glance. One was the night clerk, who stared at
the tall young signorina with the length of slim leg going by in a
black sheath mini.

The other two were Father Clement and Roger, coming out of
the bar lounge.

Nine

Bridey descended the stone stairs that hugged the two-story wall of the terrace side. Alessandro stood at the bottom of the stairs in the shadow of thick vines of wisteria that clung to the wall, his hands shoved into his pants pockets. The vines obscured his eyes and she saw only the white of his smile, the strong curve of one shoulder and the moonlight shining across the hollow of his throat. He was dressed in his normal clothes, his collar open and shirtsleeves rolled, looking casual and elegant, as if he'd stepped out of an Italian fashion magazine. She stopped at the last step. Her voice was soft with secrecy.

"Hi."

They stood facing each other in a moment of silence, hesitant in the realization that, for the first time, they were truly alone. There was only the sound of rustling leaves in the mammoth oaks and pines around the lot.

"I am so happy you come," he said.

"Did you think I wouldn't?"

"I don' know. Maybe no. Maybe you think is not right, is not safe. Maybe Mama, she say no." He shrugged. "Maybe you don' come for many reasons."

Gone was the teasing flirt from the afternoon, gone the self-possessed performer. Here in the night shadows, someone else peeked out.

"Maybe I'm here for all the right reasons," she said.

"And Mama?" he asked. "All is right with her?"

"Absolutely," she said.

He stepped out from the leaf-patterned dark and searched her face with an undecipherable smile. He held out his hand. "So, we go."

She took his hand and moved toward the Vespa he had parked nearby, but he caught her short and pulled her gently to him. If she were home and following her old rules, she would have resisted subtly, he would have backed off, and they would not kiss right away. But she was not home. All bets were off. She drew against him and met his kiss. It was soft at first, almost chaste and formal, but there was something unchaste and promising about the way her body fit to his. It sent a current through her and she let him kiss her deeply. The boys she'd dated tried French kissing her and it always felt like someone trying to force a small fish into her mouth, wiggling and too wet. She never liked it. Until now. *This is how it's supposed to be*, Bridey thought, like an invitation, soft and private. He whispered something to her in Italian as he slid his hand along the top of her arm and down her hip. She supposed she should be afraid to go too fast with him. What did she know of him, really? But she was not scared.

They got on the motorbike. Bridey tucked her dress beneath her bottom. She pulled her hair back from her face and wrapped her arms around Alessandro. They rode slowly and quietly out of the parking lot and turned onto a cobbled street. He sped up and they roared off through the city.

As they left the hotel farther and farther behind, Bridey felt a spreading sickness in the pit of her stomach. It was not fear of Alessandro. In vivid detail, she imagined her mother discovering her gone, the hotel turned upside down in a search. There might even be police involved. The anger she would face! And Alessandro. What would they do to him? Could he lose his job? She'd take all the blame she could. She'd lied to him, too.

In the middle of her panicked imagining, he reached down and touched her knee. It was as if he read her mind and was reassuring her. With that gesture, Bridey felt her fear melt and a feeling of safety envelope her. No. What she'd felt all day was real. The miracle had landed on her shoulder. It was with her. The night became beautiful and benign again. She leaned in and held him closer on the Vespa.

They turned down a narrow street no larger than an alley-way. It was a maze of cars and motorbikes. A group of young people stood smoking outside a doorway with an awning, the door framed in pink neon lights, incongruous with the age of the thirteenth century building. LEONE, the neon read. Music boomed from inside the building. When Alessandro pulled the Vespa into a space by the tiny curb, they were greeted by some of the men. There were whistles and comments directed to Bridey. The eyes of the girls were curious, somewhat unfriendly. Their dresses were at least a decade behind in fashion, almost doo-wop. All of the girls were smoking cigarettes. Their conversations stopped as they watched Bridey, who swung off the back of the bike and stretched to stand as tall as she could. She pretended she'd arrived this way a thousand times before. She pretended she was The Shrimp, at home in the jet set. Alessandro laughed off whatever comments were coming his way, leading her by the hand to the door of the club.

"Is too bad you don' speak Italian," he said to her inside the doorway. He eased his arm around her waist and pulled her to his side. "They say, they are crazy for you," he said, above the music. "They say, 'do you fall out of the sky, like the angel?' Where do I find you?'"

Bridey laughed. She cupped her hand around his ear and spoke into it. "Somehow I don't think they were that poetic."

"Is how I say it," he said. His voice and breath against her ear traveled through her like a heated path.

They inched their way through the crowd, toward the bar. The small club was jammed with people. The walls pulsated with multi-colored lights and Bridey could feel the floor vibrate with the bass of the music. Alessandro asked her if she'd like a drink, but she said no. She wanted to dance.

They squeezed through to the little dance floor, dodging elbows and gyrating hips, and found a miniscule space. Dancing always made Bridey smile. Always one of the last to leave the dance floor, she could dance for hours. But most of the guys back home couldn't, or wouldn't, keep up with her. They wanted to take her away from the dance floor, head off to a dark corner or stairwell and try to reap the benefit of the wild energy rushing through them. They weren't successful. Bridey the Ice Princess.

Alessandro was much more physical and had better rhythm than the boys at home, dancing nearer, touching her, more possessive. She found herself mirroring him, responding in a way she'd never done.

Songs changed from one to another without pause. The room was hot and opaque with humidity and smoke. It smelled of cigarettes and perfume and sweat. Bridey turned, dancing with her back to Alessandro. The heavy hair at the back of her neck was wet with perspiration. She lifted her hair up off her neck and shoulders, piling it on top of her head. It was so good to be free, to be young and pretty, good to feel him slip his arms around her from behind, moving with her. Perhaps she'd pay dearly for this, but at that moment, she didn't care. She didn't care about anything outside that room. She was exactly where she wanted to be. A door had opened within her and she was stepping through. Everything was new. She could be anyone, from anywhere. She could create herself right here, in ways she'd never dared. When Alessandro pressed his lips to her neck, she closed her eyes and moved against him in a dance as primal and ritualistic as any in the world.

She didn't escape the notice of the patrons inside the dance club. A tall thin man around Alessandro's age worked his way over to them through the crowd. He gestured to Alessandro: May I? Without waiting for an answer, he began dancing next to Bridey. Alessandro jerked his chin in a message that clearly indicated the man should shove off. No chance. The man smiled and shook a finger at him, but moved on. It got so hot on the dance floor that Bridey fanned her face with her hands. Tiny droplets formed on her upper lip and dampened her temples. Alessandro tugged her through the crowd, up near the bar. He pantomimed: A drink?

She shouted toward him, over the music and conversation. "A cola."

He wrinkled his nose and held up a hand: Wait for me. Then he disappeared between two men, on his way to the crowded bar. She wasn't more than a dozen feet away from him, but felt alone and vulnerable. Some of the men were looking at her, a stranger, a prize palomino mare at an auction. She felt conspicuously American. Two of the men signaled to her from tables: Come. Sit down.

Alessandro, she pleaded. *Come back now.*

The tall, thin man from the dance floor appeared at her elbow, accompanied by a friend, a man with sandy hair and cheeks pocked with acne scars. The tall one began making conversation.

She threw her hands up in a helpless gesture. "I'm sorry," she said. Damn. What was that phrase from the hotel book? "Scusi. Non parlo...um..l'Italiano." This didn't appear to deter them. "Do-you-know-Alessandro-De Luca?" she said, in slow motion. "I am with Alessandro."

At the mention of his name, the men looked at each other. And burst out laughing.

Oh, my God, she thought. *What does that mean?*

Alessandro was back before she could let the thought go further. He handed her something clear and fizzy. Definitely not a cola. He put his free arm around her shoulders and took a sip from his glass, unperturbed by the presence of the two men. He leaned close to her.

"Is my brother, Gianni," he said, waving his glass at the tall one. "Also, his friend, Piero."

She felt better. Much better. "Hi," she said to Gianni. "Nice to meet you."

"*Buona sera*," Gianni said. He shook her hand. She could see the resemblance now. The eyes. The finely-shaped nose of their mother.

"Miss America," Piero said and was immediately elbowed by Gianni.

Bridey looked at Alessandro. She didn't like this at all. Why should this stranger call her something that only Alessandro knew? "Is that supposed to be funny?" she said to Alessandro.

Alessandro took this in. "No," he said. "Is no to be funny. I tell my family I see Miss America. I tell them, I think I am in love at first seeing, eh? But Gianni say I won' ever see you again. You are American tourist... em... just going by."

"Passing through?" Bridey said.

"Si. But you are with me, no? I don't give it up."

"No," Bridey said. "You don't." His efforts on her behalf, in not giving up, in the arrangements he'd made to be with her here and now, made her smile.

"Don' be angry with me," he said.

She clinked her glass against his. "I'm not angry. Here's to not giving up."

"*Bene*," he said, and kissed her damp forehead. "Is okay to speak with Gianni and Piero for one moment? Gianni, he speaks no much English and Piero can speak nothing."

"Sure," Bridey said. He launched into his high-speed Italian. The sound of it amazed her. When he spoke his language, he seemed so apart from her. He was no longer hesitant, as he was in English, but in command, intelligent, mysterious; his expressions changed and shaped his face in ever more appealing ways. She felt she was seeing him as the person he was every day, before she knew of his existence. It was pure sexual allure.

She busied herself by sipping her drink. It was cold and sweet and very alcoholic. The glass dripped with condensation. She took a long swallow and wiped the cold wetness from her hand across the back of her neck. She was so thirsty. She took another gulp. A brain-numbing wave hit her head and made her knees rubbery at the same time. What was this stuff?

Gianni was watching her, asking questions of his brother. She smiled politely. *Well*, she thought, *do I pass inspection*? She giggled to herself and took another sip. The three men looked at her.

Piero said something that made Gianni laugh loudly. Alessandro glared at them and took the drink from Bridey's hand. Gianni seemed to apologize to him; whatever he said sounded contrite and was accompanied by Gianni cupping and patting Alessandro's cheek.

"Did I do something?" she asked Alessandro. The wave spread slowly through her limbs to her elbows and ankles. Then it seemed to lift her feet slightly off the floor. She was glad he'd taken the drink from her. She really wished she could have a soft drink or even a glass of the forbidden water to quench her thirst. Did her reaction show on the outside? Could you be drunk just from a couple of sips?

He shook his head. "Piero is like the monkey, you know? He says stupid thing."

The music changed, slowed to a ballad. It was the Rolling Stones.

Alessandro handed their glasses to his brother. "Dai! Come," he said to Bridey. He led her back to the dance floor. They danced holding each other close in a tender rocking, their feet barely moving. The rocking turned to a sway that started at their knees and moved to their hips. His hands moved to the small of her back, then lower. They were forehead to forehead. Nose to nose. Mouth to mouth. She placed her hands on his chest, feeling the dampness of his shirt, the warm muscle beneath it, the beating of a heart that made her palm tingle with its force. The Stones faded into another song. It was in Italian. Alessandro sang the words to her, his lips brushing her ear. His voice. Only for her now. It made her dizzy with happiness and intimacy. She could feel him against her, hard with wanting. The song ended. They stood still, looking at each other, then wound their way off the dance floor, away from Giannni and Piero, past the people at the bar, out into the night. They got on the Vespa. Alessandro made a sharp U-turn in the narrow little street and took off. He was taking her somewhere, and Bridey knew it wasn't home.

Ten

The night air, almost chilly as they rode along, began to dry Bridey's dress and hair, both damp with perspiration. It raised goosebumps on her arms but it was anticipation that made her shiver. Bridey rested her chin on Alessandro's shoulder. It couldn't be that late. There were still lights on in a few of the apartments they passed and she counted that as a good sign. She shut out thoughts of her mother and aunt and Sara as firmly as if she were shutting a door.

They rode uphill through the steep winding streets and out the Porta Nuova, to a road that led along an old wall on the mountain. Bridey could see the dark valley below them, specked with lights. If she looked hard enough, she was able to blur the horizon with the sky, so that it became one endless, star-spotted space. Alessandro followed the wall as it curved down and around a large building set in an olive grove. He slowed the bike and drove off the pavement and over grass, into the trees. When the engine cut off, there was a surprising stillness.

Bridey got off the Vespa. "Where are we?"

He pushed the kickstand. "San Damiano," he said. "My church. Is like you say. I am full of the surprise." He crossed his arms and leaned in against the gnarled trunk of an olive tree. Then, seeing her genuine bewilderment, he smiled and reached out for her. "Is okay. I don' bring you here to pray, eh?"

The dark shapes of the trees were a bit discomfiting. Once again, she marveled at her sense of safety with him. She took the few steps through the soft undergrowth to where he stood, the grass tickling her painted toes. Leaning against him at the tree, she scanned the orchard. The trees were in full leaf and heavy with clumps of olives, full of shadows.

She looked at him narrowly, in the near dark. "What do you have in mind, Signore DeLuca?"

"To be with you." He hesitated. "In Assisi, in many place of Italy, there are no ways for the man and woman to be alone, if they are no married. Not much place for, eh..."

"Privacy?"

"Si."

"You don't have your own apartment?"

"No. I live with family. My mother. My father. Gianni."

"I live with my family, too. With three brothers and my parents."

"I love my mama and papa. But I have no apartment in Assisi. When I go to Rome, *si*. But here, no. I can no bring you to my home to be with you."

"Kind of a problem everywhere you go, I guess."

Not that Bridey would know. The only place she'd ever parked was in her own driveway. So far there hadn't been anyone she was dying to be alone with. Until tonight.

"Here, is my church. I sing here, since I was little boy. So I bring you to this place. Very quiet. So much peace." He drew a strand of her hair between his fingers. In the humidity of the club and the heat of her dancing, it had reverted back to its natural state, waving in wisps around her face. "When I ask you to come tonight, I pray you don' make fun to me. All I can think, when I see you at the table, is to be with you."

"I was so upset at first not to see you after you took our orders. I kept looking for you. And then we had some other waiter. I didn't know what to think."

"Si, Mario. He is like papa to me. He knows to take care of you, for favor. You are special to me."

"But I was miserable! I thought — well, I didn't know what to think. Not seeing you. And when I did, you were in a hurry."

"Because I prepare to sing for you."

"Yes, but I didn't know that. And my mother..." She might as well say it. "She's been saying that you put on an act for every tourist girl that comes to the hotel. Like I'm just one of many. And it hurts to think that maybe I'm just another Miss America to you."

He looked puzzled. Then realization spread across his face. He laughed, short and flat, and threw his head back, closing his eyes. He looked at her again. She had turned her face, embarrassed to say her fears out loud. He turned it back to his.

"Bridey, I think you make mistake. You don' know my life. I do nothing. I go no place." He was emphatic. "Since I am small boy, I sing. Sing and study. In my family, music is most important to be the artist. Is my dream to sing for my career. To sing in the opera, you don' have time for many things, you know? I must sing every day. I work with maestro, to prepare for competition. And to have money for the maestro, I work at the hotel. So, I am working all the time, eh? Maestro or hotel. Gianni, sometime he take me to the discotheque. He say I forget to be young."

Bridey softened with sympathy. She remembered the affection Gianni had shown to Alessandro in the club.

"But," he went on, "is no good for my..." He touched his throat. "La Voce. The voice. Too many cigarettes there, no?"

Oh no, she thought. *Not his beautiful voice.* She thought about the air in the club, thick with smoke; the way it stung her eyes and made her want to choke. The chill of riding in the night, damp with perspiration. That couldn't be good. Wasn't he supposed to wear a scarf or something around his neck? She always thought it was just a movie thing, an affectation.

"Maybe we shouldn't have gone there," she said.

"No, no... I want to dance with you. Is what I ask. I love to do it." He wrapped his arms around her. "I tell you what I do, so you know me. So you know, for me, is only one Miss America. You are this one. I don' sing at the hotel. Only I serve the food. But this night, I ask to sing. Is first time I ask. I don' tell why, but I think they know."

"Everyone seems to love you there."

"Si," he admitted. "I am blessed. But, they know me from time I was..." He held out his hand, indicating someone very small. "I wan' to tell you, my singing. Is my...is not the act. Is too important to me. Is what I give to you. You understand?"

She nodded. Tears of relief gathered at the back of her eyes. She was not part of a show. He had tendered himself to her, and she had rightly seen the intimacy of it and the trust that she would understand it. Respond to it. Want him for it.

"Is like the aria, no? The one I sing to you tonight?"

What was the aria? What did the words he sang mean? Here was another pothole to avoid: admitting she'd never heard that music before in her life.

"Is from *La Boheme*. Now, you are like Mimi. You tell me, what is your life?"

"My life? You mean my life story?"

"Where you go. What you do. In America. Who is Maria Brigitta in America?"

In America, I'm plain old Bridey McKenna, she thought. *But here, with you, I'm someone I haven't even met yet.* "I suppose you could say my life is school, for the next four years," she said. "Georgetown University, in Washington, D.C.?"

It seemed so foreign, so far away from this little orchard, the brick and spires of Georgetown, high on the banks of the Potomac. She'd only been there once, for her interview and tour. And now it was going to be her life. It felt like she was talking about Mars.

"So. You go to study. We are the same. Soon?"

"September."

"And what to study?" He was looking at her lips.

"Liberal Arts. I'll probably minor in History, because… I might want to… go… into the School of Foreign Service." She looked at his mouth, the slightly thin, well-shaped top lip over the fuller bottom one. Her eyes followed the line of his neck as it disappeared into his shirt collar.

"And then?" His arms tightened on her waist. He was still looking at her mouth.

"And then. I don't know. Maybe law school, or …"

His fingers brushed lightly up and down the little rise of her belly. "To marry? To have many bambinos?" Bridey felt something inside her, beneath his touch, burst into a strange kind of bloom.

"You have a lover, in America?"

"No," she whispered. His hand was still on her stomach, a patch of heat through her dress.

He knit his brows and bit his bottom lip. "No? How can this be? Somebody so beautiful?"

"Very easily," she said. Her face was close to his. "There are no good waiters in America."

His dimples creased in a deep grin. He gave her a teasing little shake and she laughed. His eyes followed his hand up to her breasts. He brushed his fingertips across them.

She swallowed. It felt hard to breathe. Her heart was beating rapidly, much too eagerly. She squeaked out what sounded like a laugh.

He was looking at her with that same hooded expression, the

one he gave her when he said they weren't all saints in Assisi. Bedroom eyes for sure. If they were anywhere near a bedroom at this moment, Bridey knew she would be following him into it with the sort of huge, hypnotized, spinning-spiral eyes characters had in cartoons.

His mouth was on hers, his tongue touching her own in the barest of meeting.

"Oh, my God," she said.

It was more a plea than exclamation.

He kissed her. Little playful kisses. Long, sensual kisses. Kisses for her forehead, for her neck and behind her ear. He found the zipper of her dress and slid it down, found the hooks of her bra and snapped them apart. It was the first time she'd let anyone do that. She guarded her body like a fort. It was hers and she never had any intention of admitting anyone into it without her invitation. It was the only thing that really belonged to her and to her alone. She froze for an instant and he held her still.

"Shh," he said. "Shh."

She wanted his touch. For the first time, she invited his, welcomed it. It was the right touch, the right man. So she relaxed and closed her eyes and pressed her forehead to his cheek, feeling her breasts fall free from the bra cups. His hand slipped between her skin and the material, pushing the bra up and away, tracing his fingers over her nipples. His other hand supported her thigh, pulled up on his own. Her skirt was hiked near her waist and he toyed with the edge of her panty line. She slid her thigh up a little more, wanting him to touch her, but when he did, she jumped. She was very wet and suddenly embarrassed by it. When Alessandro felt her, he sucked his breath in sharply and spoke to her in Italian. He didn't take his hand away from her, but took her hand with his other, and slid it between them so that she could feel him, too.

She thought: If I unzip him, it's all over. I won't go back.
Except it already was over, because she was sliding down onto
the grass with Alessandro.

He reached through the waistband of her bikini underpants
to slide them down. She lifted her hips and then kicked off the
panties to somewhere near the base of the olive tree. She could
hear her breath rushing in her ears, the sound of her own blood
coursing through her. Alessandro slid his hand from her breast
to her belly, over the soft hair between her legs to the place where
all the feeling in the world now was centered. It was as if this
place was magnetized, pulling his touch to it, expanding toward
it, drawing his finger into her as she clamped his hand to her, not
out of protest, but in assent.

Bridey closed her eyes. She heard him make a movement and
then he was over her, his opened shirt tenting them both. He
paused. She looked up into his eyes and felt him guide himself
to her. Above him, in the sky, the stars winked down at them,
silent conspiring witnesses. She could smell the olives in the trees
around her. He buried his face in her neck and pushed into her.
Though she was slick with desire, she didn't know how it would
feel. She didn't expect it to hurt so much. She sucked her breath
in and groaned a tiny moan.

"Ow."

He stopped moving, now within her.

"I've never..." There was a stinging burn. But only for a
moment. Mostly there was a feeling of being filled and stretched
beyond anything her body could bear.

He moved slightly. Out and in again. Carefully. She ran her
hands down the smooth muscles of his back. "It's better now,"
she whispered. And it was. Very quickly better. He moved again.
Deep beyond the sting there was an ache that was relieved by his
pressing. She began moving against it, and in their rhythm the

pain she felt dissolved, it became something that felt natural and then something she wanted beyond reason. She wanted to gather him up as if she had wings to enfold him and for it never to stop, this blending, this night. He pulled away from her. He cried out and she could feel him, stiff against her belly. She felt incomplete without him inside her.

He lay still on top of her, gasping. Her heart was banging, as if it were driving stakes to the ground beneath her. Alessandro lifted his head and kissed her, over and over. He touched his nose to hers. Then he rolled onto his side and pulled her with him, holding her close. The grasses pricked her bare hip. She could feel something trickle from between her thighs, down the crease of her right bottom cheek. A deep, dull ache centered itself inside of her.

Did she think that she could do this and then leave him? Get on her tour bus the next afternoon and never see him again? Go on to more hotels, more sightseeing, like nothing momentous had ever happened to her? Everything changed for her in just this one night. *I'm not a virgin anymore*, Bridey thought, and it surprised her to realize how indifferent she felt about it, how little it mattered to her now, this event of loss, crossing the unspoken boundary that had dominated her adolescent life. She could make out the silhouette of a bell tower on the church. The olive tree spread its branches over them, as if shielding them from judgment. They lay together in silence, regaining breath, retreating to their own inner sanctuaries to recover. For a while, there was only the sound of their breathing and the tiny whirs of nocturnal summer insects in the grove.

"Forgive me," Alessandro said. The sound of his voice surprised her.

"What?"

"I hurt you. Forgive me. You are thinking something unhappy. I feel it, you push from my arms."

"No. I'm not pushing away." Bridey sat up anyway, pulled

her bra on and tugged her dress down to her waist. She finger-combed a piece of grass from her hair. She crawled on her knees to where her panties were, and then wondered what she would do about the sticky wetness drying on her stomach. Alessandro sat up and pulled a handkerchief from his pants pocket and held it out to her. He pulled his pants up.

"Thank you," she said, taking the handkerchief. While she put herself back together, she had her back to him. She heard him lay back with a thud and when she turned, he lay on his back with his arms across his face. His chest was heaving in ragged breaths. She realized he was crying.

"Oh! Oh, no." She scrambled to him on hands and knees. "I'm sorry, I swear to God. Please. Alessandro." She knelt over him, rubbing his arms tentatively, hoping he wouldn't jerk away. His hand settled on hers. He rolled toward her and buried his face in her lap. Hesitantly, she cradled his head and smoothed his hair. "You didn't hurt me. Really, it wasn't bad. I wanted this, too. It's just that it's cool out here and the ground is hard, you know? It isn't that I don't want to hold you."

"I don' wan' you to go." His voice came up stifled, and Bridey's heart ached with its appeal. "What do I do?" he said to her. "Is only two days and I am in love with you. Now you go. Is not possible. Is not right."

In love! Bridey thought: *He's in love with me.* Can you love someone so quickly? She wiped the tear on his cheek. How strange to wipe tears from a face rough with a beard. How powerful and tender it felt to do that. It felt like love. Maybe when you love someone, it doesn't matter if it's two days or two years. Maybe it's just meant to happen and you just know, like having a shaft of sunlight beam down through heavy clouds, to shine on that one piece of earth.

"I have to go," she said. She said it aloud to herself, in argument. "There isn't any other way. I can't stay here. I want to. There's so much I wish. So much more that I want to know about you."

He raised himself on one elbow, looking into her face. His hair was disheveled from passion and her comforting, his eyes moist.

"I wan' to marry you," he said.

"What?" Her voice seemed to hit the far wall of the church and bounce back through the trees. He looked dead serious. But he couldn't be. He was joking. Of course. Playing with her. Wasn't he?

"I ask you to marry me."

"That's —. You're teasing me."

"No," he said. "I don' think so."

"But no one gets married after seeing each other three times."

He stared down at his bare chest; then he swept his eyes over her as she sat rumpled and barefoot in the weeds. "I think we do more than see."

She hid her eyes with one hand. A wave of embarrassment swept through her.

"You're right. Much more. More than I've ever done. I've never done this with anyone. Not even close. But it doesn't mean I expect you to marry me."

He remained propped on one elbow.

"And why you do it with me?"

She looked away. Why, indeed? For so many reasons. "Because I think you're..." *Magnificent,* was the word she wanted to say. Handsome, yes. And sexy. Funny and sweet. But what she witnessed on the terrace was magnificent. A talent, a gift so powerful and exquisite, so filled with glory it could only come from heaven itself. Something so moving that it constricted her throat with feeling, remembering it. He possessed this. There was a world of hurt her family tried to protect her from. But they'd never told her that what was beautiful could pierce her in its own way. It was just as painful to brush against the magnificent, because once you had, you'd be afraid you'd never be touched by it again.

Alessandro was watching her, his eyes full and vulnerable.

"When you sang nothing has ever made me feel that way. As if I saw everything in a new way, in an instant. Saw you. Who you are. What you are. Like I could see into your soul. I loved what I saw and what I heard. What I felt... I want that to go on forever. I don't know anyone like you. If I'm going to give myself to some-one, I want it to be with you."

"Then, you must marry me if you feel this thing."

"This is a very big deal to me. I'll be getting on the bus tomor-row in the afternoon. Leaving Assisi. This time tomorrow, I'll be sleeping in Rome. Then Florence and the next thing you know, I'll be in France. I'll be so far away."

He sat up and stared off into the grove. After a moment, he began carefully picking away grass pieces from his pant legs, his eyes avoiding hers. "What must I do, Miss America?"

He picked a long blade of grass and traced letters across the wrinkled skirt of her dress. "You don' know what I think to do."

Could it be possible, she wondered, that this miracle would not raise its wings and lift off with the dawn, climbing up and above her, to disappear? What if this is exactly as it's meant to be and her life, in this one night, is swept up and beyond any-thing she could allow herself to imagine? She reached out and ran her fingers through the soft, tousled hair at his forehead. Hers was the prayer of all lovers, the prayer to stop time, a way to make a moment freeze, so that the clock would not tick another second toward change, toward parting, toward obstacles and impossibility.

"I wish for a night of the wedding," he said. His voice was forced into half-hearted teasing. "I can see the newspapers: Miss America marries with Alessandro DeLuca, the famous opera tenor. We make love, we don' worry for leaving, ever."

"It sounds like a dream." Out across the grove, fireflies twin-kled their way through the dark.

"All my life, I dream. I dream to sing in Rome. In Vienna,

Paris, London. New York. Soon one dream, it comes true. Why no more?"

"I don't know," Bridey said. "I guess I've always thought if even one dream came true, you'd be lucky. Like you've won a contest with God. 'One prize to a contestant' and then you have to go back to the end of the line. A very long, long line. That's the way my family thinks. Dream, but dream small; you have a better chance of getting it, that way."

It was the first time she'd ever given thought to her family's unspoken messages. Before they left home, her mother kept referring to this as their 'trip of a lifetime.' Bridey didn't want to think that this was the only time she'd ever live outside her own world, but the future seemed mapped out pretty well for her, what she was supposed to do and be. Even her idea of the Foreign Service was gently pooh-poohed. Getting into Georgetown was a big dream, and she'd made it. To her family, and to her, until this point, it was big enough for now.

"No, Bridey! Not so long line. I win the prize again tonight, eh? If you have many dreams, some… they happen. God has many to give, if they bring good to us. And to marry for love is only good, no?"

"I can't argue with that," Bridey said.

Her face had grown sad thinking about her family. She turned back, or maybe she was going forward, to Alessandro and smiled. "You are the most persuasive man! Maybe you missed your calling. You'd make a good lawyer. Or a priest."

He slipped his hand up her thigh. "I make very bad priest."

"Yes. I take that back. The priesthood is out."

"We dream together, eh?" he said. "You say you love me. Say you wish to be my wife. God can' say no to so much good. Look." He turned his head toward the looming shape of the church beyond them. "He hears."

She looked at the church as if the ear of God was pressed to its wall. She could feel the wings of the miracle stir its silken feathers against her, as it arranged itself upon her shoulder.

"To San Damiano, Francesco is very close," he said. "God speaks to him, here. He sends St. Clara to this church, when she ask to join him. He is dying and alone, and he comes to this church. I know it has great power, my church, to be so close to our Francesco. The prayers we say, they hear. I pray tonight. I tell you, I sweep your feet. You don' leave me for good tomorrow. I find the way."

It could happen, she thought. If I can be here with him now, anything is possible.

"Off my feet," she said.

"*Che?*"

"You'll sweep me off my feet. You have. You do."

"Si. I find the way to be together. Maybe no tomorrow, but soon." He kissed her. A kiss that said, if she were willing, they could be back on the grass in a heartbeat. "I think when we are together, you don' be on your feet much, eh?" He was full of play at this, tickling her so that she giggled, grabbing her wrists and pulling her hands around his neck so he could hold her. "What does Miss America say for that?"

It was her turn to kiss him.

CHAPTER ELEVEN
Eleven

In the parking lot of the hotel, kissing goodnight was taking a very long time. Bridey was grateful that there was no soft grass around. Her body was a magnet pulled toward a southern pole and she might have sailed back into its uncharted waters without hesitation, she wanted him that much. They were caught in that strange sense of time, when it's neither day nor night and the shadows have lost their edges, when the heart lives a lifetime in twenty-four hours.

"Don' go," Alessandro said. His breath warmed the hollow at her shoulder, his voice whispery and hoarse.

She kissed his hair and the top of his ear. "I don't want to."

"Come with me."

"Where?"

"Away. Someplace. I don' know. Don' leave me to go crazy like this." His hands cupped her bottom and pressed her against him. "I don' sleep, or eat. How do I work? How to think?"

"If there was any way, I would," she said. She slipped her

arms around his shoulders and hugged him close. "My beautiful Alessandro."

They stood holding each other for a long, quiet time, until their hearts slowed and a tired peace came over them.

"We find the way," Alessandro whispered.

"Yes," Bridey said, though she saw no hope for it.

He held her out from him, his eyes intense.

"I make promise for this," he said.

"I believe you," she said. Maybe he could see her again. Some day.

In the draping clumps of wisteria on the stone wall, a bird chirped. A tentative, waking chirp.

"Alessandro, what time is it?"

He moved his arm with his wristwatch behind his back, hiding it from her.

"No." He groaned.

"I have to know."

His shoulders slumped and he twisted his wrist to show her the face of the watch.

Four forty-three.

She gasped. "Jesus, Mary and Joseph!" Somewhere above her in the dark hotel was her room. Somewhere above, her mother and aunt. *God*, she begged. *God, let them be asleep!* She covered her face with her hands, trying to block out the vision of them waiting in her room, the lights on, the manager there, or worse, the police.

"Bridey?"

"Alessandro, I'm scared."

"You don' tell nobody where you go tonight?"

She shook her head.

"I know this." He sighed heavily and took her hands away from her face. "I come with you to see Mama. You don' be alone."

"No," Bridey said. "It's better if I'm alone. I won't tell anyone who I was with."

"You think they don' know? Bridey, don' be crazy. I don' make secret what I feel to anybody."

"I don't want to get you in trouble. I'm afraid you'll be fired. Or arrested. You don't know my mother, Alessandro. She thinks I'm a child. Like I don't know what I'm doing. She's afraid for me to be out of her sight. If I told her even half the things I want to do, I'd never get to do anything at all. So it's my fault no one knows where I am. It's got nothing to do with you and you shouldn't be blamed for it." She hung her head. "I just wanted to be with you for as long as I could."

"You tell Mama, I marry you tomorrow," he said, lifting her chin. "You are a woman. No a child."

"Don't joke about this — it is tomorrow."

"I don' joke," he said. "I don' be fired. You are afraid for nothing. If I do, so? Soon I go to Rome. I am not afraid of the *polizia*, eh? Is crime for two lovers to dance? To kiss? To be together? We are not children. The *polizia*, they don' worry about dancing and kissing. What can Mama do?"

"It's about more than dancing and kissing. I lied. I've been out all night. She'd know I've been with you. It would flip her out. She could get mad enough to take me back home, right away," Bridey said. "That's what scares me most. Leaving. Leaving now."

"If this happen, I come to you," he told her. He took her face in his hands and kissed her. "I think you don' believe this, but is true. Come." He stifled a yawn. "You leave in the afternoon, no? I serve you lunch. We say *ciao* tomorrow."

If I'm still in one piece, Bridey thought.

He led her to a door on the bottom level of the hotel. They were in a service area. Bridey could smell laundry soap and steam and beneath that, the clinging smells of garlic and cooked meat. She and Alessandro passed two older men in work clothes sitting on a bench, drinking coffee. They greeted Alessandro with some surprise. One laid his finger alongside his nose and gave Bridey a conspiratorial wink. Finally they reached a stairwell.

"This take you to your room, in the hall," Alessandro explained.

"Don't come with me," she warned. There was a brassy taste in her mouth. Panic. She swallowed.

He looked worried, reluctant to leave her. "I say a prayer to the Virgin, you don' see Mama."

"Thanks," she said.

He opened his mouth to say something but she quickly kissed him quiet and began running up the stairs barefoot.

The stairway came out three doors down from her room. The hall was deserted and still. She clutched her room key in her hand so hard she could feel the edges of it digging into her fingers. She steadied her hand to keep it from trembling as she fit the key slowly into the lock, each tiny click seeming to reverberate in the hall. The door pushed open a fraction.

There was blackness around the frame. No lights. Her stomach twisted. She eased the thick door open enough to slide through and closed it gingerly behind her without a sound. Her pulse hammered in her temples. Sara had the curtains pulled tightly closed, but she could make out Sara's sleeping form on her single bed.

Thank you, thank you, thank you, God! She felt like dancing with relief. Instead she moved with stealth, carefully unzipping her dress and pulling it over her head. She unhooked her bra and felt for her nightgown, slipped it on and then pulled off her underpants. The crotch felt dried and stiff. She crossed the room in her bare feet and pulled the curtains at the balcony doors open in a crack, still holding the dress and underpants in her hand. In the sliver of light, she could see a watery bloodstain on the pants and her dress was a mass of wrinkles. It smelled of cigarettes and perfume and grass. Of him.

I have to get rid of it, she decided. She felt a momentary stab of sadness. It was the best thing she owned and it reminded her of Alessandro. But it was evidence, and she was already planning any future defense. She folded it and the underpants into a small roll and lifted the mattress of her bed. She pushed it as far as she could beneath the mattress.

In the morning she would wash herself, wash away Alessando's traces from her body. She slid into bed and looked at Sara's travel alarm. Five minutes after five a.m. Dawn was sifting into the room through the drapes. The birds in the ivy were fully awake, cheeping and taking to the sky. She lay back on the pillow and was nearly faint with exhaustion. When she closed her eyes, Alessandro began singing her to sleep in her dream.

Sara woke her two hours later.

"Bridey. Hey."

Bridey's eyes flew open. In her dream, her mother had found her sleeping on the hotel lobby floor, still dressed in her black sheath, with grass hanging from her hair and her drink from the discotheque sitting on the floor beside her. She reached for her hair, afraid to find grass there.

"You've got to wake up," Sara said. "You'll miss breakfast."

Bridey blinked. Morning. The heavy brocade drapes were pulled back, spilling light across the room.

"What time did you get back last night?" Sara asked. She was already dressed for the day. Little smudges of blue circled the bottom of Sara's eyes, but otherwise she was bright with anticipation.

Bridey yawned, numb with too little sleep. "Not late," she said. Her head and limbs felt as if they were full of concrete.

"It must have been pretty late, because I didn't go to sleep until after one-thirty."

Bridey pushed herself up on her pillow. She'd skip over the time question. "What happened last night? Was everything okay? Were you all right?"

Sara nodded. "I wasn't worried. I just felt weird being alone. But Bridey — your mom came to the room last night."

Bridey sat bolt upright.

Sara waved her hands in front of her. "No, no. Don't worry."

"Don't worry? I'm screwed! Oh, God, I'm screwed, Sara."

Sara grasped Bridey's forearm. "She brought some Kaopectate because she thought you might need some for your stomach."

Bridey groaned. Kaopectate! Why hadn't she thought of that before she made up the stomach cramps? Of course her mother would have a remedy on hand, ready to bring to her. She had it all in her bag: aspirin, Rolaids, Band-Aids, a tiny jar of Vicks Vaporub. She would have brought splints and crutches if she'd been able. "What happened then?"

"Well, I had the lights off, because I was in bed. I went to the door and told her you were already asleep." She let go of Bridey, clearly ready to tell her story.

"Did she buy it?"

"I told her I had some Pepto-Bismol and you took some of that. But the best part," Sara said, lowering her voice and glancing back at the door, "was that I had your bed already fixed up. I put my raincoat and sweater under the spread, and your rollers in a scarf on the pillow for your head, just like in the movies. I figured she might come to check on you. She doesn't seem to like Alessandro very much." She added, "My mom does, though."

"But did it work? You don't have any Pepto-Bismol."

"Yes I do. My mom got it at that Army base commissary, remember? I just never gave it back to her. Your mom peeked inside the door. She didn't come in. She told me to be sure to lock our door and she'd see us in the morning."

"Honest to God?" Bridey threw her arms around her cousin and hugged her tightly. "Sara, you are a genius! You're fabulous.

I will owe you forever, I swear. Thank you. Thank you for doing this for me."

Sara allowed herself to be hugged. Her glasses got knocked askew and she wrinkled her nose and poked them back into place. As a little girl, she wasn't crazy about affection, offering her forehead for the kisses Bridey and her brothers took for granted from their parents and aunts. Now she gave Bridey an awkward hug back.

"You saved my life," Bridey said. She hung on like a drowning person to her rescuer. Sara smelled sweet, freshly washed, innocent and clean in contrast to the stale smell of smoke and sex Bridey felt must still cling to her like a badge.

"You smell like cigarettes." Sara said when Bridey let her go. "How was it? Was he worth it?"

Bridey slumped against the headboard and closed her eyes. Worth it. "Oh, Sara." She sighed. "Sara, I am so in love. It was... perfect. Like a dream. We went dancing at this discotheque, and I met Alessandro's brother, Gianni." Sara's interest peaked. Her eyes lit like a puppy waiting for a treat. "He's way too old for you, though."

Sara grimaced.

"We danced for hours," Bridey said. "Then we went... for a ride around the city on his Vespa."

"Cool," Sara said. "And?"

"And you'll never guess where he took me." Her cousin registered a small amount of alarm and even greater curiosity. Bridey could almost feel Sara itching to start writing it in her spiral notebook. "His church!"

"Weird," Sara said. She slumped back. "What a drag. I thought he'd be more romantic."

"No, it really was! It was incredibly romantic. I mean, at first I didn't know what to think, but it was so, so special. He told me how he used to sing there, and how he grew up, and about his work and the maestro, and his dreams —. He's wonderful, Sara.

He's everything."

"Everything what?"

"Everything I could want. Forever."

Sara's face pinched with doubt. "Forever? Bridey, you've only known him a couple of days. And we're leaving today."

"I know that. But so what?" She adjusted her nightgown beneath the sheet; it had ridden up around her waist. The secreted dress and underwear beneath the mattress were squashed flat, but she thought she could feel them, like the Princess and the Pea. She pushed off the covers and sat on the edge of the bed, ready to get up. It was like leaving the night behind, stepping firmly into the reality of this day, whatever it brought. That it would bring her to leave Assisi there was no doubt. But Alessandro?

"So, you're never going to see him again, probably. Forever's just not going to happen. Not with him. There's no way."

"You don't know that," Bridey said, starting to get annoyed. "No one can say that. Things happen. There are such things as miracles."

Sara got up off the bed. She walked over to her suitcase and picked it up, ready to place it outside their door to be loaded onto the Phantom.

"That's about what you're going to need," she said to Bridey. "A miracle."

Twelve

Bridey held a teapot made of brass. She was in a shop on one of Assisi's little streets, a shop filled with glassware and pottery. Rose recommended it, assuring them the place had excellent buys if you were willing to dicker. The teapot had tiny etchings on it in an exotic design, with a hinged top. Bridey had never seen anything like it. Not that she wanted it, really. All she could think about was Alessandro. She was woozy from lack of sleep and barely able to drag herself through the streets for which she'd had so much energy yesterday. She was sore inside and every step was a reminder of the intimacy she and Alessandro shared in the night. She hoped she wasn't walking strangely. Well, she could take some aspirin and sleep on the Phantom all the way to Rome. She could sleep for the rest of the tour, for that matter. Nothing could match what she'd found in Assisi.

She turned the teapot over. *Made in India*, the bottom read.

"We'd better get a move on," Corinne said to the girls. They came out of the shop squinting into bright sun. Corinne checked her watch. "We've been gone over an hour. Your mother's going to think we've been kidnapped."

Tilla had begged off shopping. The pain in her back was worse and she had a sick feeling in her gut, she told Corinne. Like something wasn't right. Something wasn't good.

You worry too much, Corinne had told her. Think pleasant thoughts. Think about maybe seeing Maura soon.

Bridey shifted the package with the teapot in her arms.

They walked single-file down the paved sidewalk that hugged the old wall of shops and turned a corner onto a main street. Bridey drifted behind them, yawning.

"Are you going to make it, lady?' Corinne said. "That teapot dragging you down?"

Bridey shook her head. "I'm fine. I don't know why I should feel so tired this morning, with all the sleep I got last night."

Behind her aunt, she weaved and listed toward the side of a building wall, steadying herself with one hand against it. Anyone would think she was hung-over, though she'd only had about three sips of her drink last night. She was hung-over with the sensations and feelings of her night with Alessandro flowing in her veins. He had penetrated her in every way, right through to her cells. She felt drunk with him.

Corinne continued her march up the street. "Well, sometimes you can get too much sleep, and you end up all headachy and tired the next day."

Sara turned and raised her eyebrows at Bridey, giddy and energized with conspiracy. But Bridey just frowned back at her.

"That's probably it," Bridey said.

The puttery whine of a Vespa engine came from behind them. It cut to an idle as the driver drew alongside.

"*Buongiorno*, Miss America," Alessandro called. She would remember the sight of him on the street for the rest of her life — his hair gleaming under the sun, his dimples in deep curves around his smile, his shirt-sleeved arms leaning on the handlebars of the motorbike. Sunglasses hid his eyes. She was jelly-kneed with longing.

"*Buongiorno*, Signora," Alessandro said to Corinne. "Miss Sara, hello."

"Well, for heaven's sake," Corinne said, at the curb. "Signore de Luca. How nice to see you this morning. Fancy running into you! How are you today? All rested from your performance last night?"

"Now, I am much better," he said to Corinne. Barely visible behind his black lenses, his eyes stayed on Bridey. "This morning, I am sad for you to leave Assisi. And now I see you on the street. So lucky for me."

"What a coincidence," Sara said. She looked at Bridey.

"We've been doing some last minute shopping," Corinne said. She, too, glanced at Bridey, who had not greeted him and appeared to be in some kind of trance. They were blocking the narrow sidewalk, so the pedestrians walked around them. Bridey took no notice, as if they were invisible.

Alessandro dipped his head and peered over his dark glasses at Bridey. "And Miss America? What do you find in Assisi? Something to remember?"

Bridey clutched her package, looking back into his eyes. "A teapot," she said.

"From India, no less," Corinne added.

"Maybe it's a magic lamp," Bridey said. Her words were measured, meant to sound casual. It had the opposite effect. "With a genie inside. Maybe I'll get three wishes."

Corinne observed the look that passed between her niece and Alessandro.

"Where is Signora McKenna?" Alessandro asked, breaking his gaze from Bridey to focus on Corinne. Someone on another motorbike whizzed past and called out his name. He gave a small distracted wave back.

"Not feeling well, I'm afraid," said Corinne. "Back problems.

If things don't improve by this evening, I'm going to insist she see a doctor in Rome."

Alessandro frowned over his glasses. "I am so sorry to hear this. *Si*, she must see the doctor. I bring one, if you wish. Maybe, she is no good for travel, eh?" he ventured. "No before the doctor, he give the okay?"

Bridey bit her lip to keep from smiling. A most persuasive man, her Alessandro.

"I'll wait for Rome," Corinne said. "We'll be meeting our sister there, I think. She's living in the Middle East, but she's quite familiar with Rome and her husband has connections with the American Embassy there. He's British," she went on. "He's with the British embassy in Amman. But he could get an American doctor. Or a British one. Not that the doctors in Rome aren't good, I'm sure. The language barrier, that's all. And who knows, maybe seeing our sister will do Mrs. McKenna more good than anything."

He gave no reaction to her unintended slight to his countrymen. "Family is most important."

"But thank you," Corinne said. "You're quite a nice fellow. My offer of last night still stands, by the way, about having you to dinner when you come to sing at the Met in New York. Sara and I live there. Bridey will come, too. Won't you, Bridey? To celebrate how we knew you when."

"You can count on me," Bridey said. "Just let me know when and where."

Alessandro shifted on the Vespa, a look of discomfort crossing his face. His fingers tapped against the handlebars.

"Well," Corinne said. "We don't want to hold you up."

"*Si*," he said. He rocked back and forth on his seat, staring down at the pavement. Then: "Signora, I know is no polite, but I ask one favor."

The dark glasses came off and he leaned forward toward Corinne so she could see the begging in his eyes. "I ask to give

Bridey a ride to the hotel."

"Oh," said Corinne.

"Forgive me," he said. "I don' wish to be uncaring for you or Sara, to walk. But ..."

"I don't know." Corinne looked at her niece, whose eyes were openly pleading. "It's just that we have to get on the bus very soon and Bridey couldn't be late for that." She tapped her long, glossy nails against the side of her purse.

"I don' be late. I must serve you lunch, no? We are at the hotel for same time. I only wish to talk before she goes." He smiled at Corinne, turning up the charm a notch. "You know, the artist, he must have the muse. My muse, she is American."

Bridey broke out of her silence and touched Corinne's thin, heavily freckled arm. "Aunt Corinne, please? I'll be fine. I'm perfectly capable of getting where I need to be."

"Okay," Corinne said. "Go. But Bridey..." She grabbed her niece's hand as Bridey started toward the Vespa. "Don't make things complicated, with your mother. Don't give her any reason for concern. Or we'll both regret it." She let go of Bridey and turned to Alessandro. "I'm depending on you, young man. I believe you're a gentleman. Don't disappoint me."

Bridey straddled the motorbike's seat behind him. She steadied herself with her arm around his waist and blew a kiss to her aunt.

Alessandro called his thanks over the sound of the gunning engine. "Someday, I sing in your honor."

"Just get her to the hotel," Corinne answered loudly as they buzzed away.

As the Vespa roared off into the street traffic, Corinne turned to Sara, who stood holding Bridey's teapot package and watching the backs of her cousin and the waiter disappear. "I did the right thing, don't you think? I don't think there'll be a problem letting her go."

"No," said Sara. "Not unless you mean Aunt Tilla."

"Oh, I'm not concerned about Tilla."

As Corinne walked, her high heels click-clacked against the cobblestones. Her feet were made of iron. They'd held up through several miles of tours through museums, and shopping, always in heels. Without high heels, she was barely five feet tall. But she had a way of carrying herself that gave the impression she was much taller. She attributed her towering attitude to the fact that she was a redhead, or was until the gray started taking over and she reinstated the red with a bottle.

"They looked right together, didn't they?" said Corinne. "Like something out of a movie. I believe those two are just plain love struck. It happens. And not always in the most convenient way. But when it does, it feels like life or death. Be together or die of wanting to. It was like that for your father and me. We met, and he had to go off to war. There's nothing worse than that."

Corinne brushed a mist of perspiration from her upper lip and continued. "Now Bridey's destined to go her separate way. They'll never know what might have been. Sometimes I think it's not fair, falling in love and having nowhere to go with it. The least we can do is give them a few moments together to remember."

Sara shifted the packages in her arms. She hid a smile from her mother.

Alessandro steered the motorbike in and out of the late morning traffic. They passed near the hotel once. Twice. Bridey rode with her arms around his chest, her cheek pressed to the back of his shoulder, her eyes closed, feeling the air lift her hair, the warm sun on her back. She could smell his crisply pressed shirt and the scent of sandalwood soap on his skin as he steered the Vespa. He lifted her hand to his lips, kissing it, holding her palm against his cheek. They rode past basilicas and churches, past the

Temple of Minerva and streetside shrines to the Madonna, past graveyards, past offices and stores and apartments, past children playing in cobbled courtyards, through medieval arches and past cheerful pots of bright flowers under awnings. They rode in the company of the present and through the brilliance of centuries past and were aware of none of it, only each other.

Finally, they drove down the tree-lined lane that led into the parking lot of the hotel and pulled into a spot near a few other motorbikes and small cars. He led her by the hand up the stone stairs, with Bridey silent and wondering . There was a little path just off the viney, treed growth before the landing leading to the upper terrace. It was a path the employees sometimes used to cut around from the street entrance of the hotel, not ideal or romantic, but all there was. All there was time for. When the saplings and overgrown flowering shrubs concealed them, he scooped her into his arms and kissed her. For a moment they were joyous at having these too-few minutes together. But side-by-side was the queasy feeling that it was nearly time for her to leave.

They stood kissing, ankle-deep in grassy weeds and wild-flowers, while honeybees drifting across their shadows gathered pollen from old roses grown tangled and wild.

"You are okay?" Alessandro asked. "You don' see Mama, at the hotel? I worry so much I don' sleep. All the night, I am thinking of you. To see you today. To touch you." He dissolved into a stream of Italian, holding her close.

"I'm okay. Nothing happened. Your prayer to Mary must have worked." She still couldn't believe her luck. She smiled up at him. "I even slept a couple of hours. I dreamt about you singing to me. And being with you at the church." She could see her face distorted in the lenses of his sunglasses. She slipped the glasses from his face. His eyes were puffy and shadowed with circles. He looked exhausted. He looked sick.

"Oh my God," Bridey said. "You need to get rest."

His shoulders dropped and he sighed. He let go of her and

pulled at a bush beside them, shredding a flat, green leaf between his fingers.

"What's wrong?" said Bridey.

He was silent. Shredding.

"What is it? Something bad? Did you get fired?"

"No, I don' get fired. I..." Anger mixed with embarrassment. "This morning I have... *argomentazione*. With my mama and papa. They are very angry with me."

"An argument? What about?" Seeing his half-shamed, half-guilty frown, she guessed. "About me?"

"*Si*." He raked his hand through his hair. "They say to me... is okay to play love for fun, you know? For the days you are here in Assisi is okay, to sing to you last night. They play the music for me. Is okay. Even is okay to dance." He ripped another leaf from its stem. "But they say I am stupid to stay all the night with you. Stupid not to sleep, to rest my voice. My practice this morning is no good. They say, do I no think, for my art? They say, what does this girl care for it? She is here to play with you, only play. She know nothing of your work, how you must take care for your voice. They say, I live in their home; they help me to train. Why I worry them? They say there can be no room for love now, for nothing, only for my work if I dream to be a great tenor. Many years to train, because I am more young than most tenors who do this. My voice is more... what do I say... grown. To win the Achille Peri with my age is rare. I am *ventuno anni*. Twenty-one. This is why they say no room for love now."

"But that's unfair!" Bridey said. "I'm not playing with you! I love your voice. I would never want anything to hurt it. Or hurt you. You said last night, all you ever do is work. Even your brother says so."

"Gianni has much fun," Alessandro said with some bitterness. "He works for bank. He sleeps with girls. He is not home at many times. But Gianni can do this, because he has no art."

"But you're an adult," Bridey said. "You said last night we're not children. You can make your own decisions. Can't you tell them that? What did you say? It's your life, not theirs. No one can say when you can and can't love someone."

She wanted to say, I'm leaving. How can I hurt you now? If I were an Italian girl from Assisi, would they say the same thing?

"I think they are afraid for me," said Alessandro. "Like you say, your mama is afraid? I decide my life. But in my country, *la familia es tutto quanto*. All things, eh? We are angry, but we love much. This way, we are strong in the world."

So what does that mean for me? Bridey thought. *I'm not family.* She blinked back tears. A bee landed on her foot and crawled unnoticed across her instep. If it stung her now, she wouldn't feel the pain over what she was feeling in her heart. What was he saying to her? She felt angry and frantic. This wasn't how she wanted to leave.

"I'm sorry," she said.

His eyes were rimmed with red. She knew there was more there than fatigue. There had been tears, as well. All last night, fearing her own family, she'd never given a thought to his. Now she saw how much weight they held, how much power their words of reprimand and guilt affected him. She was only a ripple in Alessandro's ocean, as far as his family was concerned. But how did he see her? As a ripple, or as a riptide, pulling him out to sea?

"I won't cause you any more trouble," she said. "Your parents don't have to worry. I'll be long gone. But I wouldn't take back last night for anything. Would you?"

He stood frowning, staring into space. Anger and sadness played alternately across his face. His eyes searched the ground, as if looking for some answer in the weeds.

"Would you?" she asked again.

He looked up out of his thoughts and met her eyes.

"Would you take back last night?" she repeated. She held her breath, knowing that his answer would either carry them on to whatever was meant for them, or send the miracle flying from her.

"Take back?"

"Do you wish you hadn't been with me last night? Do you think your mother and father are right? About me. About your life?" Anger melted into fear, choking off her voice.

Alarm flooded his face. "No," he said. "No! *Mater Deo* — Bridey, don' think this! I am happy to be with you. Last night. Today. What I say to you is true. Everything I say. I wan' to sing... But how do I sing if my heart, it feel nothing — no love, no tears, no life in it? How to be great tenor if I sing only the notes of music and I don' live? I must love. I can' tell God 'no', when he send you to me, eh? The first time I see you at the table, is like for me the sky open. I don' care who believe this. I don' care you are from America. I don' care you go home, so far." He took her by the arms. "You don' leave me. *Capisce?* I go with you, in your heart. You stay in mine. I pray to Francesco, something bring us together again. This I promise."

Yes, she nodded. She had no voice because she was crying. She was crying because he hadn't failed her, not once. Because he was so full of faith; because he held enough hope for both of them. She knew she wasn't gifted like him. But maybe it was possible that in his gifts, she would discover her own. The ability to love, for example. The gift to see life as he did — full of light and potential, full of joy.

She didn't know how this would happen. She only knew, as they stood with their arms around each other on the hillside path, that the miracle had decided to roost, and they were sheltered beneath its wing.

Thirteen

"She's what?" said Tilla.

"Oh, for Pete's sake, Tilla," said Corinne. "It's only a ride on a motorbike."

"Corinne, are you out of your mind? What possessed you to allow such a thing?"

Corinne threw up her hands in exasperation. "What is the problem? He asked — in a very humble way, I might add — to give her a ride back here. All of, what? A half-mile?"

"He could take her anywhere! Where are they? You're back. She's not."

"Come on, Tilla. They just wanted a few minutes alone to say goodbye. I think it's sweet."

Corinne pushed her shopping bag and her purse away from her legs and eased her small white patent leather pumps off her feet under the table. They were seated on the upper terrace, shaded by a substantial pergola covered in thick, roping vines and a ceiling of leaves.

"I'll 'sweet' him!" Tilla said. "You can't tell me he just happened to be passing by on that particular street. He was out looking for her. On the prowl. And you fell hook, line, and sinker for it."

"On the prowl? You're making out like he's Jack the Ripper. Tilla, you're overreacting beyond belief. So he's flirtatious. He's also good- looking, charming, hard working, and you have to at least agree on this — extraordinarily talented."

Corinne sat forward in her chair. "What's wrong with Bridey having a little romance with someone like that? We're leaving in less than three hours and he's got to spend most of that time working. What do you think they're going to do, run off and have a quickie in the bushes?"

"Corinne!" Tilla rolled her eyes in Sara's direction.

Sara sat beside her aunt, toying with her soft drink.

"It's okay, Aunt Tilla," Sara said. "I know what a quickie is."

"Oh, wonderful. Fourteen years old," Tilla said, throwing up her hands. "I can't believe we're having this conversation." She rubbed at her back. "My point, Corinne, is that I trusted you. I thought you would ensure that the girls would be safe out shopping and you come back and tell me you don't know where my daughter is. That you let her ride off on the back of a motorbike with some foreign waiter in a strange city. If I did that with Sara, you'd be just as upset as I am."

Corinne lit a cigarette and put the match out with a snap. "And my point is that, first, I resent your implication that I can't be trusted with my own niece, especially in view of all the times I've had her alone with me in New York. And second, I also resent the idea that my instincts are poor about people and I can't tell a Lothario from a decent young man. I'm not an idiot, Tilla. No one is pulling the wool over my eyes."

"If I weren't along on this trip, what would you allow Bridey to do?" said Tilla. "Run off with every Tom, Dick, and Harry who came along?"

Sara looked up from her drink. "Tomas, Ricardo and Heinrich, you mean." Tilla flashed a look of annoyance. "Sorry, Aunt Tilla."

"We're not arguing," Tilla snapped. "We're discussing the situation."

"What are you going to do when Bridey goes to Georgetown?" asked Corinne, poking her index finger into the oiled checkered tablecloth for emphasis. "Move into the room across the hall? I'm telling you, Tilla, you've got to give that girl some breathing space, or she's going to break free one of these days and do something completely rash, just for the hell of it."

"She can have all the freedom in the world when she's ready for it." Tilla rummaged through her purse for her cigarette pack, avoiding looking her sister in the eye.

"Who's to say she's not ready for it now?" said Corinne.

The pack was empty. Tilla shut the purse with a snap and faced her older sister. "I say. I'm her mother. Not you."

"Here's Bridey," Sara said. When Tilla turned to look, Sara made a slicing motion across her own throat at her cousin.

Bridey acknowledged Sara's warning with a bright and artificial smile. She pulled out a chair beside Corinne and sat down.

"Here I am," Bridey said. "All in one piece. Am I on time, Aunt Corinne? I was under pain of death if I didn't get back before lunch."

Tilla stared at her daughter. Seeing Bridey before her, calm and chatty, took the wind out of her sails. Bridey was fine. Nothing had happened. Corinne was probably right. Tilla had over-reacted. She'd read too much into this fellow. Considering it rationally, Bridey seemed relatively unaffected by him. Still, who wouldn't be irrational with this pain building and the way the whole trip was going? *I need a vacation from this vacation,* Tilla thought. But she didn't want Bridey to think this was the way it was going to be from now on, that she was free to do whatever she wanted. She, Tilla, was in control.

"Did you say your goodbyes?" she said to Bridey.

"Yes, we said goodbye," said Bridey. "He's very sweet."

Below the tabletop, Bridey gripped her hands together in her lap. She hoped her face showed no traces of the tears she'd shed a short while ago. Her mother was an expert at detecting tears.

"Anyway," Bridey said. "That's that. My Assisi adventure."

"Well, it's one to write home about," said Tilla. "But I wouldn't. I don't think your dad would want to know about this particular anecdote."

Corinne is right, Tilla thought. It wasn't worth worrying about. Bridey just said it herself: That's that. On to Rome. End of story.

Alessandro stood in Bridey's line of vision all through lunch. His eyes were always on her. She tried not to stare back. She tried to be witty and entertaining to everyone at the table, but it fell flat. He looked ill with sadness. She felt nauseous with it. He stood apart, subdued, as if he were already thousands of miles away.

Maybe it would have been better, Bridey thought, *if we'd left early this morning, if we'd kissed goodbye once and for all last night, instead of enduring this meal.*

Aunt Corinne watched her with sympathetic and curious eyes. Tilla talked excitedly about getting to Rome, hoping Maura would be there as a surprise.

Then it was time to go. Rose counted heads as the Pilgrims straggled toward the exit for the parking lot. Bridey gave Alessandro a look of helplessness. He bowed his head and stared at the floor.

Tilla put her arm around Bridey.

"Off we go, my angel," said Tilla.

Bridey slumped in her seat at the back of the Phantom and stared up at the Hotel Windsor Savoia. The Pilgrims settled into their customary seats, ready for the drive to Rome.

Sara curled up on her end of the back seat. She gave Bridey a sign of inquiry, but Bridey simply turned her head and stared out her window.

Bridey closed her eyes and placed her hand over the top of her left breast. Tucked inside her bra, a folded piece of paper crackled against her fingers and a corner of it pricked her skin: Alessandro's address. All the sensations of the night before, and the hour before lunch, came flooding through her. For the first time on the trip, she was grateful for the hours that stretched ahead of her in the bus, time to replay the last two days in her head: how he looked, what he said. The way he touched her. The way he felt over her. The feeling of completion within her.

The bus began rolling forward. Bridey looked up to see three waiters leaning over the wall, watching the bus pull out. None of them was Alessandro. She thought about the way he had sung on the terrace last night. Tears pooled on her lower lids and began to slide toward her chin.

I would give anything to hear him again, she thought. *Anything, God.* She closed her eyes and might have drifted to sleep, but she heard someone — Mrs. Wadely? say: "Would you look at that!" Papa Joe called Bridey's name.

"Oh, for God's sake!" Tilla spat.

Sara knelt on the back seat, sitting on her heels like a prairie dog popping out of its hole.

"What's going on?" she asked no one.

Bridey pressed her face to the window, looking at the long, zigzagging set of stairs at the end of the parking lot. Alessandro was bounding down, two stairs at a time. He ran into the parking lot toward the Phantom, holding up his arms, asking Roger to stop.

Bridey stood. "Wait!" she called to Roger.

"Bridey, sit down!" Tilla said from the seat ahead.

"Stop the bus!" Father Clement called out. He had to hunch his shoulders to keep from hitting his head on the rack above him as he stood.

Roger braked gradually, until the hulking Phantom stood still, its engine thrumming. Father turned back and looked at Bridey.

"Well? Get out there, gal, before that young fella busts a leg."

Bridey dove up the aisle of the bus without looking back. Roger winked at her and threw the bus door open. She tripped down the wide metal steps and stumbled into Alessandro's arms. He caught her up and kissed her, a long, deep, fierce kiss, guaranteed to give the Pilgrims their money's worth in the cheap seats. What difference did it make who saw them now? She was on her way to Rome. She'd never be back here again; never see any of these people again after this trip. She was young and in love and they were not. Romance was not on their itinerary. She'd carved it into hers. She didn't care what her mother thought.

Above them on the dining terrace, the three waiters leaned over the stone wall, whistling and clapping, waving their white linen towels in salute.

Alessandro covered Bridey's face with kisses.

"Goodbye," she said to him. "I'll write as soon as I get to Rome."

He shook his head. "We don' say goodbye. For today, we say ciao. Don' forget. I see you again. Is all I think, how to find the way." He kissed her again. "Ciao, my Miss America."

She let him go, climbed back onto the bus, and walked down the aisle back to her seat, past the amused and the wistful and the judgmental. Past the surprised Corinne, past gawking Sara. Past the stinging gaze of her mother. Alessandro followed alongside the bus, following Bridey's form through the high, tinted windows. She knelt on the back seat, looking out the rear bus window, and waved to him. Roger shifted into gear and gathered forward speed out of the parking lot.

Alessandro stood alone in the gravel expanse, waving and throwing kisses until the Phantom was out of sight.

Fourteen

Okay, Tilla thought. Okay.

She gripped the arms of her seat, digging her fingernails into the maroon corded upholstery. She was rigid with the pain burning through her right buttock and down the back of her thigh. Rigid, too, with anger.

Calm down, she told herself. *Get it together.* The scene replayed in her mind. Him: bounding down those steps, like a man possessed. Waving and shouting. Her daughter: leaping out of her seat. Flinging herself at a guy she barely knew. That kiss! In front of everyone. There were different ways to look at it. That it was showmanship. A crazy Italian gesture. They were famous for being over-dramatic. And Bridey loved drama. She loved getting attention. After all, nothing between them could continue, could it? Bridey was young. She'd be going to college. So Bridey had broken a heart and could take that memory with her. A little self-confidence under her belt wouldn't be such a terrible thing. She'd need it in a city like Washington. Tilla relaxed her grip on the seat arms a little and tried to shift her weight to her left side. She couldn't walk to the bus today without limping. The last thing she needed was to be hampered by pain, just in time to see Maura.

Maura would get a kick out of hearing about Bridey and this waiter. It was just the kind of stunt she enjoyed. She'd love the melodramatics, probably laugh and launch into one of her own stories. It wouldn't faze Maura a bit. She'd be the last person to come down on Bridey for making a spectacle — having made a few spectacles of her own...

Maura was a pistol in her day, Tilla recalled. Gorgeous and smart. Full of energy and fun. When Maura walked into a room it was like someone flipped on klieg lights. And Bridey's so like Maura. All that life and beauty. Even the smile and her height — the same. Both women demanding more from things than might be wise. Except, Tilla thought, Bridey had never been defiant, the way Maura was. Raising Bridey was a piece of cake compared to what Mam went through with Maura. From watching the fights and struggle between Maura and their mother, Tilla learned it was better to keep your head down and fly under the radar. But things are different when you're a mother. It was fascinating to be Maura's little sister. All of the fun and none of the work. *God, I followed her around like a puppy. Anything to feel part of her world,* Tilla thought. *To be in on her escapades. I see that same look in Sara's eyes around Bridey,* Tilla thought, *and I —*.

Sara.

Last night, at the door of the girls' room: Bridey's asleep already, Aunt Tilla. The room so dark. Impossible to really see. And Sara, so chatty. But in just a bit too much of a hurry to close the door and go to bed.

Tilla struggled up from her seat, groaning at the white-hot wire of pain in her back and legs. She pulled herself into the aisle of the bus and launched herself at the long back seat.

Her mother's voice was a low hum of fury vibrating in Bridey's ears, the sound of hornets massing over an intruder at the nest. She sat with her back pressed hard against the corner of the window and back seat, braced against her mother's words. Bridey had known she'd have to pay, of course.

Jammed in the corner of the back seat, she didn't see the other Pilgrims craning to look down the aisle from their seats in the front, hoping to catch the gist of whatever scolding they assumed Tilla was delivering to her daughter.

"You snuck out." Tilla hissed.

"Yes."

"For how long?"

"A while."

"How long is a 'while,' Bridey? An hour? Two? All night?"

"What difference does it make?"

"Don't get smart with me!" Tilla's voice rose. Corinne, one seat ahead to their left, looked back at them, then turned away. Sara scuttled out of her seat near Bridey to the protection of her own mother.

Bridey stared back at Tilla without expression. It was a pose she was good at, the kind of non-reactive mask she'd learned to don in her years at Providence, where nuns had rights to anger and indignation and mere girls did not.

"Where did you go?"

"We..." Bridey considered lying. *We stayed at the hotel. We talked out on the terrace.* It would be easy to say. Would that balance things out with her mom? She didn't care if it did.

"He took me out to dance," she told Tilla.

"A dance? — Where?"

"It was a discotheque. We went dancing, that's all." There. It was simple, wasn't it? Telling part of the truth wasn't hard at all.

"Judas' priests, Bridey!" Tilla said. "Do you have a brain in your head? Do you know what could have happened? Do you have *any conception* at all? We're not home, for God's sake."

"Would that have made it okay? If he were some boring preppy at home and not Italian? You liked that Marine in Munich. You let me go off with him. He's trained to kill people — he told me he's looking forward to it. But you assumed he was an ideal American boy, protecting me in the biergarten. Alessandro is an artist and you don't want him anywhere near me."

Tilla leaned forward until her head was inches from Bridey's. She lowered her voice. "It has nothing to do with American versus foreign boys. You snuck out. That is forbidden anywhere. But it's worse here. It's dangerous. He could have taken you any-where. You wouldn't have been able to find your way home, you don't speak the language. He barely speaks English!"

Bridey flared. "His English is wonderful," she said. "You don't know anything! He speaks four languages. Really speaks them, as opposed to me, who can hardly put a sentence together in the one foreign language I studied for four years. You should have heard him talking to Sara in French! He studies music all the time — when he isn't working at the hotel, that is. All he does is work, trying to make something of himself."

"This is a different culture," Tilla argued. "You don't under-stand about that. You don't know."

"I know what you're saying," Bridey insisted. "He could have raped me. But he didn't. He didn't do anything wrong. He was wonderful. He was sweet, and fun, and romantic." *The way it's supposed to be, she thought, the first time you make love.* "He didn't even know I hadn't told anyone I was going out. He thought it was okay. It wasn't his fault!"

"Baloney. He planned the whole thing."

"Yeah." Bridey's voice was cold with sarcasm. "How rotten of him. He made me laugh. He talked to me. He made me feel beautiful and special. He took care of me at the discotheque. He told me about his singing, and what it means to him." Her throat began to clench. She swiped at the tears forming in her eyes. "He..."

Tilla's voice lost its edge. "Sweetie, you don't know —."

"I do know!" Bridey said. "I know what I want to feel. He makes me feel those things. I just wanted to have some fun. Some real fun. I'm so tired of grinding along on this tour, trying to make the best of it. I wanted something to happen. But you don't ever want me to do anything."

"Don't be absurd. Of course I do. But not lying. Not disappearing with a stranger in the middle of the night."

"He's not a stranger to me."

"We're not talking about him."

"*Alessandro*. He has a name. You don't want to say his name, because that will make him a real person in this conversation."

"I don't care if his name is Porky Pig. I'm talking about your behavior."

Bridey sighed and stared down at her lap. She felt exhausted. So little sleep. So much emotion. She wanted to fold her white sweater up and prop it on her tote bag, slide down and rest her head on it and fall away into sleep, where she could be with Alessandro. She wanted to be riding on the back of his Vespa, having another day in Assisi, losing herself in its spell. Now every mile the Phantom put beneath its wheels would be one more away from him and away from the best time of her life.

Her mother took her look for downcast. "Look," Tilla said. "If you say — Alessandro — is a nice guy, I'm willing to believe it. But the real issue is trust. And what would your dad think of what you did? I don't even want to think about it! You're his princess, his baby girl. You've broken our trust. Do you see that? I'm crushed that you would do that to us."

Crushed, Bridey thought. *Why? What does it have to do with you?* She wanted to say: Leave me alone. I'm here on the bus with you, aren't I? I'm not running off anywhere.

"It makes me wonder if you're the girl I've always thought

you were," her mother said. She'd pulled out the big javelin for the throw to the heart, or the conscience. But it missed its mark.

Here comes the guilt trip, Bridey thought. *Except I don't feel guilty. Not at all. If I had a chance, I'd do it again. And again.*

"There's something I'm not hearing, Bridey."

"What is that?" she asked, already knowing.

"I'm not hearing you say you're sorry, and that you'll never do anything like that again."

Bridey stared stone-faced at the back of the bus seat.

"Well?" Tilla asked.

She looked at her mother, imagining what her days would be like, if she didn't reach the limits of apology for herself. Tilla looked expectant. Bridey turned her back, pressing her forehead to the cold glass of the window without speaking.

That time is over.

Fifteen

Corinne slid into the seat next to Tilla's. "You're chain smoking," Corinne said to her.

Tilla blew smoke down toward the ashtray in the arm of her seat and picked a tiny flake of tobacco from the end of her tongue. "Do you blame me?" She brushed absent ashes from her seersucker skirt, like an animal shaking its fur after a skirmish.

"I don't know," said Corinne. "What did she say?"

Tilla twisted to look through the crack of space between her seat and Corinne's. She could see Bridey's hips and her long, tanned legs tucked up. Bridey's hand rested limp, curled in her lap. She guessed that Bridey was napping. When Tilla turned to face front, her back shot her a warning of pain.

The pain squeezed the breath out of her. She'd had backaches before; it seemed natural for a woman who'd toted three kids on her hip, not to mention the cleaning, the loads of laundry, the grocery bags... But this pain was different. "She says they went dancing. At some discotheque. I don't know if I believe her."

"Sounds plausible," said Corinne.

"A discotheque? In Assisi?"

"It's nineteen-sixty-seven, Tilla. Not the sixteen hundreds."

Tilla flicked her cigarette hard against the side of the ashtray. "She lied, Corinne. And forced Sara to lie." Her heart was still racing. She wasn't sure she'd won the argument. She'd had her say and in the past, her say always was the last word. She and Bridey would retreat to separate parts of the house for an hour or two. They'd calm down, approach each other, and their desire to kick anger out the door and let hugs back in would always win out. And Bridey would accept whatever point or rule Tilla and Rob had made. They really didn't have much trouble out of their daughter.

Corinne stretched out her small fingers and examined the diamond rings on them. She pressed each cuticle back with the edge of her opposite thumbnail. She needed to repaint her nails. "At this point, I guess I'd have to say — so what?"

Tilla stared at her in disbelief.

"So what?" Corinne repeated. "Is it the first time an eighteen-year-old has ever lied?"

"It's the first time my eighteen-year-old has lied to me."

"What is she, an alien from space? All teenagers lie at some point. Otherwise, how would we learn to do it so well as adults?"

"Are you saying my daughter lies to me on a regular basis?"

"Oh, stop it," Corinne said. "You are ridiculously defensive about her, you know that? No one is perfect, Tilla. Not even Bridey. And she shouldn't have to be perfect. Especially now."

"I've never said she was," Tilla said. "And what do you mean 'especially now'?"

"Just what I've been saying all along," Said Corinne. "She's eighteen, she's a knockout, and she's here in some romantic places. She's been a marvelous sport about things. Think of the hours we spend, cooped up on this bus."

Tilla fell silent for a moment. The Phantom was making its

way with the Pilgrims across the Apennines south toward Rome. But Tilla was not interested in the scenery outside the window, not interested in the tumbling waterfalls and strange green waters full of lime from the rocks, or the pine forests or gravel pits or pizzerias and souvenir shops in the middle of nowhere. What sort of memories did she want her daughter to have? Memories of family, not some Italian waiter.

"She's so susceptible," she said finally.

"Of course she is," Corinne said. "So was I, at her age. So were you. We're all dewy rosebuds, at the beginning. You put them in a vase and wait for them to unfold, more and more beautiful every day, until they're in full bloom."

Tilla paused mid-drag on her cigarette to look at her sister. "What in Sam Hill are you talking about?"

"Bridey is like a rose, opening up, and this trip is the vase."

Who adored her daughter more than Tilla did? Who cherished her and dreaded the day when she wouldn't be at home? Who told her she could come on this trip in the first place and then went completely out of character and left her husband — whom she missed terribly — and her boys, just to be a part of the trip with her?

"You're not any help," said Tilla.

"I'm trying to be."

"Well, you're not. Always taking Bridey's side. Taking a waiter's side, for that matter. Against your own sister. I need you on my side, Corinne. We need to keep control of things." Tilla turned her face away abruptly and jammed the burning cigarette into the fold-out ashtray. It poked up in a broken z-shape, trailing a wisp of smoke. "We're not even half way through this trip."

"Just don't punish her for the rest of it," Corinne said.

Tilla forced herself against her seat, eyes squeezed shut, mouth compressed in pain. She wrapped her hands around the ends of the seat arms, knuckles whitening, and stretched her leg out beneath the seat in front of her.

"Tilla?" Corinne said.

Tilla's voice was a rasp. "My back. My legs." She moaned, high-pitched, soft — private. Only Corinne could hear. "I can't, I can't breathe."

The sun was hot on the Via Veneto, bright through the windshield of the Phantom. Roger was sweating. His expression was far grimmer and more determined than when he was wheeling pell-mell through the Dolomites. There he had appeared limber and confident. The Mario Andretti of bus drivers. Here, crawling through Roman traffic, buzzed by lesser vehicles, picking his way through darting pedestrians, he frowned with concentration. Rose crouched over him. She held a small piece of notepaper with an address, and a map. For the last hour and a half, the Phantom had been making ominous shudders and clunks with every shift of gears. There was a faint, oily, burning odor filtering through the bus's overworked air conditioning unit at the front.

Out on the boulevard, people sipped drinks at tables under large umbrellas, or strolled in pairs and threesomes, watching the passing street life. Rome was vivid and beautiful, noisy and hurried with traffic, languorous in its cafés, world-weary and voluptuous in its architecture and sculptures streaked with grime.

Bridey slipped on her oversized sunglasses. Her eyes were puffy, burning with fatigue and tears. She was stiff from being cramped in the corner, asleep for most of the bus ride. But the ache went deeper. It seemed to center in her pelvis and spread upward into her heart.

I miss you, Alessandro, she thought. *As soon as we get settled, I'll write to you. I have so much to say. So many questions to ask. Have you ever been to Rome before? Do you know what to expect? Wherever I go here, I'll try to see it as if you were here. Maybe, if Aunt Maura comes, we can find the Opera di Roma. That will be my pilgrimage.*

Raised voices came from the front of the bus. Roger and Rose had been arguing ever since the tour bus entered the city. Arguing as always over directions. The Pilgrims were used to their squabbles. They'd been lost in other cities. They'd been left at the dock in a thunderstorm after their river cruise down the Rhein when Roger didn't meet them for a half-hour. Rose and Roger had arguments at the roadside in front of signs. It was like the bickering of an old married couple; but their shared abysmal sense of direction continued to be worrisome.

Now the Phantom was spewing black exhaust. As Roger came to a stoplight, it gave a massive shimmy. The sound of metal grating on metal filled the interior with a shriek, like the death scream of a huge, mechanical beast.

Suddenly, they weren't going anywhere.

If I live to be one hundred, Bridey thought, *I will never forget how it feels to be this humiliated.*

The Pilgrims were gathered around Rose on the sidewalk. The Phantom sat silent and forlorn in the middle of the street, surrounded by cars full of Italians in varying states of irritation. A small crowd of onlookers gathered, some were called out of shops by their friends to see this latest happening. Roger paced by the bus door, the top of his balding head glowing pink with agitation as two uniformed officers harangued him.

Rose held up her umbrella.

Please, no! Bridey thought. *Not the umbrella.* She ducked her head, hitching her tote bag and trench coat onto her hip, and pushed her sunglasses up the bridge of her nose. It was time to abandon ship.

"We will have to make the walk to the hotel on foot," Rose told them.

The group snarled. They'd run out of patience, run out of fortitude and endurance. Run out of humor. All of them, at the same time.

"The good news is," Rose continued — her long, large teeth exposed in an unconvincing smile, "It's only about three or four blocks. Or six."

"What about our luggage?" Mrs. Wadely spoke up. The heavy powder on her face was streaked with perspiration. It looked a bit like clown makeup. "Are we to leave our property here on some street?" She looked over at the bystanders, who were smiling and laughing at them, highly entertained. "How do we know they won't be pillaged?"

"Your luggage will be quite safe. Roger will have it delivered by taxi as soon as possible." Rose hoisted the umbrella higher. "Please follow me."

"Wait just a damn minute," said Corinne. She was standing with her arm around Tilla's waist as Tilla leaned, slightly bent, against Bridey, who supported her mother with her free arm. "My sister is not able to walk three or four blocks. Not even one! She's in pain. She's having a problem with her back and legs. We're going to need a taxi."

"Yes," Sister Joan agreed. "Not everyone here is able to walk a long way. They should be taken to the hotel by car."

"The difficulty is," Rose said, false cheer draining from her voice, "that the bus is, unfortunately, blocking traffic, as you can see. Including taxis. So we will have to do our best."

"We've done our best!" Corinne snapped. Her voice was full of heat. "We've been doing our best since we landed in London. Of course, you wouldn't know that, because you weren't there. I don't care if you have to hire someone to carry her piggy-back, Rose."

Yes, the group nodded. The scent of mutiny grew strong in the air.

Rose looked up the street, as if looking less for a taxi than an escape route for herself.

"I tell you what," Father Clement said. He set his black

carry-all bag on the sidewalk. "If one of you can add my bag to your pack, I will carry Mrs. McKenna myself."

"No, Father." Tilla's voice was thin with pain. She could barely breathe. Spasms enveloped her from her ankles right up to her upper back. "You can't do that."

"Bridey?" Father said, indicating his bag. "Can we make a trade and I'll take your mother?"

He unhooked his white priest's collar and stuck the stiff, semi-circular band in his back pocket. He unbuttoned the collar of his black clerical shirt and blotted his high forehead with his hankie, before scooping Tilla up into his arms.

"Nonsense I can't do it," he told Tilla. "Why, you are a piece of fluff. Light as a feather. I'll have you know, I was once a tailback on the University of Arkansas football team. Went there on a scholarship, in fact." He began to carry her down the street with the group. "Compared to bull-dozing those big ole boys, this is a walk in the park. Even at my age. You just hold on."

They followed Rose down the street to the laughter and commentary of their Roman witnesses. Bridey thanked God Alessandro wasn't there to see her, reduced to a pathetic tourist shuffling down the street like a refugee. An American taken down a peg. She burned with resentment. Why did it have to be this way? Why was she following a woman holding an umbrella like a parade flag in full view of everyone, as if she were in nursery school? *Who knows where we might end up this time,* she thought. *Certainly nowhere as wonderful as the Hotel Windsor Savoia.*

In front of her, Father carried Tilla like a small child. Seeing her mother so helpless, Bridey almost regretted being so cross on the bus. She perched precariously on the edge of the guilt pit.

I suppose I should be kind to her, Bridey thought. *She's still caught up in the old rules. After last night, I'm in a whole new game. I don't even know what the rules are for that.* As she followed the group down the avenue, Bridey was suddenly swept by the feeling that something had taken hold of her. It was a dizzying sense of premonition, a split-second of knowing. Stars were spinning out of alignment in her heavens, and however they realigned themselves, something was about to crack open in her universe.

She scratched the back of her head, thinking that something had crawled or flown into her hair. Then she realized: It was the hair standing up on the nape of her neck.

Sixteen

It wasn't the Hotel Windsor Savoia. That was for sure. It wasn't the hotel on the itinerary, either. It was some sort of third-rate pensione. Bridey and Sara hoisted their suitcases onto their beds and stood on opposite sides, facing each other. Their eyes lingered over the cracked walls, the yellowed lampshades, the dingy blue woven bedspreads spotted with their anonymous stains. The phone on the stand between the beds had a short, frayed cord that connected to thin air, like a tail. A large window was shuttered against the sun, casting thin bars of light on the dusty floor. Bridey walked over and forced the latch to open them. She and Sara peered out. The window overlooked a tiny courtyard that contained a small stone bench, a stubby palm, and a monk. The monk was reading on the stone bench. He looked up at them and nodded: Yes. He continued to read.

"Yes what?" Sara whispered to Bridey.

"Yes, now we're stuck, I guess," Bridey said.

"This place is awful, Bridey. I don't think we should be staying here." Sara's eyes were huge, magnified by her glasses.

Bridey put her arm around Sara. *Poor kid,* she thought. *This is not exactly the adventure of a lifetime for her. I have Alessandro. But she only has me to keep things interesting.* "C'mon," Bridey said. "Let's get out of here."

"I'm glad you've come," Corinne said to the girls when they walked into Tilla and Corinne's room. The room was identical to Sara and Bridey's. The spreads were just as faded and suspect.

Tilla, looking worn and pale, lay flat on her back on one bed. Whatever anger she felt on the bus was drained with the effort of dealing with physical pain. For the first time, Bridey realized how much thinner her mother appeared than when they left home.

Corinne sat on her own bed with several pieces of papers spread on the pillow.

"I called the Hotel Lunetta, the one listed on our itinerary here," she told them. "Our reservations were cancelled three weeks ago. They wouldn't say why. What do you think of that?" She asked no one in particular. "But Aunt Maura did call there looking for us. She left a message with them that we were to call her in Athens when we arrived. She insisted that they make note of any contact with us. She told them it had to do with the British Embassy, so they wouldn't forget."

Bridey couldn't keep the disappointment out of her voice. "She's not coming?"

"I don't know. I'm trying to get a call through to her. In the meantime, I'm going to get a doctor to come take care of your mother."

"Corinne, I wish you'd wait," Tilla said from her pillow. Her face was chalky; even the freckles on it had faded away in her pain. "At least until we talk to Maura. She can tell us who to call."

"Who knows when or if we'll even reach Maura," Corinne said. "You need a doctor now."

"But ..." Tilla was ready to burst into tears. "I don't want to see an Italian doctor, Corinne. I don't know what kind of credentials they have..."

"The Italians were studying medicine when the British were wearing bearskins and living in sod huts," said Corinne. "Besides, a doctor's a doctor. You had to be carried up here, for pity's sake. You can hardly move. You might need to go to a hospital."

"No!" Tilla cried. "No hospital. Not here." She struggled to sit up. "I'm not that bad." But the pain flattened her down again. It almost made her hyperventilate. "Oh God. Oh Jesus. What's happening to me? All right. I'll see whatever doctor you can find. No hospital."

"That's more like it," Corinne said, picking up the phone. "Bridey, see if you can find Rose or someone. Tell her I'm trying to find a doctor and if she values her life, she'll help me."

Sara eyed Tilla with an expression that bordered on fright.

Bridey moved toward the door. "I'll be back in a few minutes. Do you want to come with me, Sara?"

Sara sat down at the foot of her mother's bed and shook her head.

"Father, have you seen Rose?" The lady at the little desk in the pensione was no help. There wasn't a sign of a Pilgrim anywhere. Then Bridey spotted Father Clement.

Bridey walked into the small, sparsely furnished parlor that served as the pensione's lobby. Father Clement sat on an old sofa that sagged at the other end. His head rested back against a lace doily ochre with age and nicotine. His eyes were closed, and as Bridey approached him, he opened them to slits. He was sweating. He looked nearly as pale as her mother.

"Bridey." He smiled a little. "Fancy that. I was just thinking about you." He patted the cushion beside him. "Sit down a minute, missy."

"Have you seen Rose anywhere?" Bridey asked again. She sat down. Beneath her, some spring in the sofa gave a musical groan and collapsed. In the room there were four other chairs, fashioned in the kind of Danish-modern style that gave Bridey a chill, all straight wood with icy vinyl cushions that had cracks on the seats, exposing sharp edges of plastic. Three tall potted plants were grouped together in front of a pair of large windows. The plants were in graduating states of dehydration, like withered, disheveled old men in a police line-up.

Father hadn't answered her question. A trickle of sweat traced its way from his gray sideburn, along the path of his beard stubble to his jaw. One heavy, blunt hand rested atop his shirt-front. The hand rose and fell with his breath.

Rose can wait, Bridey thought. She wanted to thank him for stopping the bus in Assisi. She wanted him to know she was grateful, more grateful than he could imagine. She owed him, at the very least, a few minutes of talk in this depressing room.

"You were terrific to carry my mom all that way," she said. "I don't know what we would have done." She began to perspire, too. " It's so hot here."

A flicker of amusement crossed Father's eyes.

Bridey continued, "Everyone was dying of the heat, carrying stuff to the hotel. I can't imagine what it must have been like to carry another person."

"Well," he said mildly. "If Saint Christopher can do it, so can I. Took more out of me than I thought, though. The vanity of an old man, thinking I could do what I did when I was twenty."

"I could get you a cold drink." She made a move to get up from the sofa.

"No," Father said. He rested his hand on her forearm. "Just sit here with me a spell." He closed his eyes. "I'll be all right soon as I get my wind back."

"Father."

He opened his eyes and looked at her sideways.

"Thanks for helping me in Assisi. Making Roger stop the bus. It was really important to me."

"So it seemed. To our young friend as well, looked like."

"Yes," Bridey said. "To both of us." At the sound of the word *us*, she smiled again. *Us* was like acknowledging that they were really a couple, however tentatively joined.

He folded his hands across his chest, as if holding it in place. "Of course, your mama was mighty upset."

"Yeah, well, she was upset about how it looked. You know, to everyone on the bus."

"More than that, I think." New beads of perspiration popped out on Father's broad forehead. His shirt collar was even blacker than normal with sweat; splotches of wetness dotted his shirt front.

Bridey swallowed. How much had he heard? How much had they all heard in the bus?

"Such a guilty look," he said. "Don't waste it on me."

"I don't know what you mean." She stared at the potted plants. The leaves, the ones that were still green, were pale with accumulated dust. Someone had used one of the pots to dump cigarette butts.

"I know you went out last night. Late. Roger and I had a drink in the bar. He was sittin' there all by his lonesome, and I figured we could both use the company, even if we don't speak each other's language. Turns out we got along just fine. We saw you going through the lobby all alone and looking skittery. Dressed to kill." He gritted his teeth and squeezed his eyes shut momentarily. "It didn't take Albert Einstein to figure out what you were up to. And who you were up to it with."

Bridey was motionless with alarm. What did he know, and what was he guessing at? Did some kind of priestly ESP go along with ordination? What should she do? Make up an excuse? Lie to a priest? Or confess the whole thing? Then he couldn't tell anyone anything. But then she'd have to say she was sorry for loving Alessandro, for loving him with all of herself, mind, heart and body. And for letting him love her with his. She wasn't sorry.

"Got anything you want to talk about?" he asked. He pulled out a folded white square and wiped the deep furrows of his forehead and alongside the bridge of his nose.

He asked in such a normal way, Bridey thought. Like he just wanted to talk, not wrench contrition from her.

"Alessandro asked me to go out with him. It shouldn't have been a big deal," she said. "I'm eighteen, Father. I'll be in college soon. I do go out on dates back home, after all. And he'd just sung to me, and — it was the most incredible, beautiful thing. I can't describe how I felt. Like I was hearing and seeing something from another world. Like he laid something at my feet, something I would never dream of asking for."

"I know," Father said. "I saw your face." The way he said it made her think of her dad, who would listen to her like that. Gentle. Understanding.

"So all I wanted was to be with him." She warmed, free to speak of Alessandro. "He's a beautiful person, Father. I mean, he's very handsome, of course, but it's as if he doesn't even know that. —Well, he does, when he's flirting. — But he has a good heart. He has this joy in him. And he's strong inside. You'd have to be, to do what he does. To have a dream, and focus on making it happen."

Father's eyes stayed soft as he looked at her.

"And he made me feel loved."

"You seem to have three people right with you who love you."

"I know my family loves me." It came out sounding impatient. "Sometimes I think they love me too much. They're so busy worrying about me being safe and not getting hurt. I meant a different kind, with Alessandro."

"Ah. Not the kind you figure a priest would know about."

"Oh, I know you do," Bridey said, not meaning it.

"So he sounds pretty special. I think we all got that impression. And you decided to go for broke. So to speak."

Bridey sat up straight. "Yes. And I'm glad. Maybe I'll be with Alessandro again, as soon as we can. That's what we both want.

It isn't over. But my mother is furious. Telling me how I've disappointed her and broken her trust, and what would my dad say, and on and on." Bridey hit her thigh with her fist. "I'm so sick of living inside everyone else's rules! That's all I've ever heard, all my life from my parents, and from school, the nuns — and priests! It's always: don't. Don't think, don't breathe, don't ask. Don't live." She smoothed her palms against her skirt and slumped. Father stared at the dusty front windows.

"Well, a trust was broken," Father said. "And is 'don't' what God says, or what we hear?" Father Clement said. He shifted on the sofa, sitting more upright. "I'll let you in on a secret, Bridey. It's what got me here on this trip. I do a lot of thinking. Wonderin' what I hear, a foolhardy human, as opposed to what God might be tryin' to say to me. Fifty-six years old, and I'm still wondering where I go from here." His face furrowed even more deeply. "I can see you're surprised."

"I'm sorry," Bridey said. "I can't believe I said that."

"You got to quit apologizing for being yourself. I figured out this much: God doesn't want that kind of apology. You do something evil, you destroy something or hurt someone, you cut yourself off from love — then you got an apology to make to Him. But not for being a creation of His. Not ever. Not for loving, or dreaming, or thinking, or wanting to explore the world and the soul God gave you. God is not about 'don't', Bridey. God is about 'yes.'"

"What if I told you," Bridey said, her heart thudding, "that last night, Alessandro... asked me to... make love? And I said 'yes.'"

"I'd have to ask if this a formal confession. Are you asking for absolution?"

"No." Even if she were tucked away in the claustrophobic cubicle of the confessional, whispering to him through the grate, she wouldn't ask for forgiveness. Or promise never to sin again. In a life lived young and confined, there were sins you could avoid pretty easily. But now, the idea of sin —could love be a sin?

"Okay," he said. "Then what did you feel about it? What feeling were you left with, after you said yes?"

"Happy," Bridey said. "I thought I'd feel awful and guilty, but all I felt was free… and glad, and full of love. Alessandro didn't want me to leave. He even cried, and I didn't realize, well, that a guy could get emotional. He feels like I do, that we were meant to be together. He asked me to marry him. Of course that isn't reality, at least not right now but who knows? Alessandro says God only wants good for us, and marrying for love is only good. He says God will find a way, if it's meant to be."

Father took off his glasses and pinched the bridge of his nose. "Be careful, Bridey. Don't think you don't need God involved in whatever you do. Or who you choose to love. He sees into the heart of all things. We need Him to show us what's truly good and what's only posing as good. That's the trick. You'll know what's right and true in your soul, because that's where God holds our conversations. His is a quiet, loving voice. That's the one to listen for. If you keep in touch with God, keep talking to Him, He'll make it clear — about this boy, or another, or other things in your life." He sat up, prepared to leave.

"But you said you're still wondering."

"Yes. But I'm still listening."

Relief flooded Bridey. It made her want to hug him. So she gave him a hug and Father hugged her back. It felt just like her dad's hug — the safest place in the world.

"Thank you, Father. For everything."

He let her go and stood up slowly. "You're welcome. And listen, Bridey. God never said risk was a bad thing. He took the greatest risk of all, in giving us free will. He could have just played it safe and not given us the opportunity to make a choice. In fact, He said there's no life without risk. Remember the parable? Our gifts are like a sack of gold, remember. The object is not to keep them in the bag. He wants us to use them, risk them on what's worthwhile about ourselves, so that when we go back to God, we bring more of ourselves." He took a deep breath. A watery cough came out. "We're what God loves most of all. We're His treasure. —You're full of gifts. So go out there and live. Take your risks. Say yes. But always do it out of love... And forgive your mama for loving you so much. She's just doin' the best she can." He winked at her. Then he pointed his hand and made a small sign of the cross over her. She watched him walk to the little front desk in the hallway still mopping his face with his hanky.

Seventeen

Sara found Bridey in the dining room on the lowest floor of the hotel. No one had seen Rose. The lady at the desk shook her head when Sara asked after Bridey's whereabouts.

Tall? Sara signed to her. Long hair? She wiggled her hands through the air: Shapely?

Ah! Si! Downstairs, the woman pointed.

Bridey was going through her own manual gyrations to the cook, who looked by turns sympathetic, worried, and accommodating.

"Oh, Sara," Bridey said, spotting her. "I can't find Rose anywhere."

"You've been gone a long time," Sara said, ignoring the cook. "My mother found a doctor for your mom."

"Ah, *doctore*." The cook nodded vigorously in approval.

"At least something is going right," Bridey said. "It hasn't been easy finding anyone around here."

Sara didn't look in the mood for conversation. "Bridey," she said. "Come with me to the bathroom? I only found one, and it's not even on our floor. Plus, the lady at the desk says you have to pay five hundred lire for the faucet handles to the sink and the tub."

"Charming," Bridey said. "Pay for the handles to use the sink. How hospitable."

Sara tugged at Bridey's wrist. It was unlike her to be so physically insistent. "Come with me, okay?" Sara asked.

The two girls climbed the narrow, angled steps to the lobby.

"I guess it's just as well we go now," Bridey said. "Depending on what we find here, we may want to ration all bodily functions for the duration."

Sara didn't laugh. "I hope there isn't a duration," she said. "I hope we get out of here as soon as possible."

The bathroom door wouldn't budge. Sara held two heavy brass faucet handles, which were olive green with use and age. Bridey pushed again at the door. It didn't move.

"Is it stuck?"

"I don't think so." Bridey braced her arm on the door and turned sideways. She gave it a sharp bang with her hip.

"Want me to try?"

"It's not jammed. More like, blocked."

Sara knocked hard on the door. "Anybody in there? Hello? Scusi?"

There was only silence within.

"Let me ram it again." Bridey swung her hip harder. The edge of the door bounced inside its jamb. "Ow!" she said, rubbing the spot where her upper thigh hit the door. "That hurt." The door had moved open a fraction, though. "Something's in front of it, I think."

"What are we going to do?" Sara lowered her voice, though there was no one in the long hall. "I have to go, bad."

Bridey braced her back against the door and tried to push

with her feet. Her sandals slipped on the smooth wooden floor. "Now I'm getting mad. Something's definitely in the way. Something heavy."

The doctor was hugely fat but dressed in a finely tailored suit and starched white shirt with French cuffs. His tie was discreet and held in place by a tie bar — more gold — with a small ruby. He had a silver cloud of curly hair and a neat, salt-and-pepper moustache. His protruding eyes were large, and ringed in darkly pigmented skin, like a raccoon. A prosperous doctor, no doubt, Tilla thought. But he still had terrible perspiration odor.

Corinne moved to the window, to inhale the evening air. She had no stomach for certain smells, and this was one of them.

Tilla was having no such luck, however. She lay helpless, not only assailed by the doctor's armpits, but also unhappily aware of his strong garlic breath. He probed her back and legs with practiced and surprisingly tender fingers.

He stretched Tilla's leg.

She cried out with pain. Tears leaked from the corners of her eyes.

The doctor straightened her loose, seersucker skirt and gave her a sympathetic pat on her knee.

"I am finish my examination," he said. He sat down heavily on the side of Corinne's bed, causing the mattress to sag nearly to the floor, and then did a double-take at the condition of the bedspread. The bed frame made a minor splintering sound. He pulled out a syringe and small vial from his black medical bag. "I think, is a myalgia. Acuto. The disc, also: *ernia del disco*. This combine with strain of the muscles. You say you fall the last week? For now, I give you morphine. This take the pain away for tonight," he said, setting up the needle. "You sleep. You rest in the bed. Is best. Also, I give you hydromorphone and diazepam, for pills. This you take, one for each four hours. You must stay very quiet. Very relax. If you do no feel better in five days, please, call me. I come, and we decide what next."

"We don't usually stay in a place like this," Tilla said to him as he gave her the injection. She was distracting herself from the needle's sting and the anxiety over what was in it. "Our bus broke down, five blocks from here. We don't even know what happened to it, or if it can be fixed, or... We're trying to contact our sister in Athens, to let her know what's happened. We're waiting for her call." She felt the cold rub of the cotton swab after the needle was through, rubbing away the hurt.

"Si, si," the doctor crooned. "But now, you rest."

Tilla's head swirled. There was a windy sound in her ears. "Wow," she said. "What a rush. I feel dizzy."

"Close the eyes," the doctor advised. He fished out bottles of tablets and gave them to Corinne. "Soon, she sleep," he said to her.

"Tante grazie," Corinne said, showing him out the door. When the doctor had left, she waved her arms to stir the air.

"Ooo," Tilla said. Her voice was heavy and slowed. "I feel so 'better already." Her eyes were closed. One pale arm hung, out-stretched, over the side of the bed. Blue veins ran like a roadmap along its inside, beneath her white skin.

The phone gave a sudden, shrill double ring. Corinne startled at the sound of it.

"Bridey?" she said into the receiver. A strange and heavily accented voice, crackling and far away, said something she didn't catch. She strained to hear. "Hello?"

Then, from somewhere over land and sea, a familiar voice shouted on the other end.

"Corinne? Corinne! It's Maura."

Bridey and Sara stood behind the hotel clerk as he strained to push open the bathroom door. He seemed a little annoyed at first, not really believing they needed his help. But now he was taking them very seriously, pushing hard and grunting, making progress by inches.

They could have found some other bathroom to use, but they were hooked with curiosity and an undercurrent of urgency that had nothing to do with their need to use the facilities.

"Let me help you," Bridey said. She wedged herself against the door beside him. She was taller by a good six inches. Together, they pushed steadily until the door yielded another few inches, making enough space for the clerk to poke his head in.

Bridey turned to Sara and said: "There's something on the floor" just before the clerk started shouting. He withdrew his head and barked at Bridey, "*Spinge!*" "Push!" as he pushed frantically on the door with all his might. They made enough progress for him to squeeze into the bathroom.

Bridey and Sara crowded at the barely opened doorway. They could see an arm in a black, rolled-up shirtsleeve flung back on the tiled bath floor. Bridey poked her head inside.

Father Clement's frozen, open eyes stared up in amazement at the underside of the toilet bowl from his final resting place on the bathroom floor.

Eighteen

There were several final straws in Rome, so many reasons to leave the tour. Tilla's back, of course. And Father dropping dead that way, on the floor of a shabby bathroom. The capper was finding out the truth about the tour itself. The nervous proprietor of the hotel filled Corinne in on the real story. The tour never had reservations most of the time. Rose was sneaking off to phone ahead for rooms, making Roger stall by driving around until she knew where they could stay. They were lucky to get any meals at all. The Ave Maria Travel agency in Manhattan hadn't paid their bills.

God was watching over them for sure, with Maura so near in Athens. Corinne raised her champagne glass in salute to the ceiling of the aircraft, to the heavens beyond.

Poor Father. He never made it to the Vatican. If he even wanted to get there. Instead, three sweating ambulance attendants carried him down the narrow service stairs. The stretcher wouldn't fit in the little birdcage of an elevator, so they parked it by the service door. Then they hoisted Father's body onto it at the bottom of the stairs and pulled a blanket over his face. The Pilgrims wept and shook as he went out the door.

Corinne hadn't gotten the girls quieted until after midnight. Sara curled up against her while she tried to comfort Bridey. Bridey took it worst of all. She'd cried for hours. Which was understandable, Corinne thought, since Bridey had been the one to find Father.

Her niece had really run the gamut: from love and romance in the morning in Assisi, to being berated in the afternoon by Tilla, to finding a dead man by night. Corinne glanced over at Bridey and Sara in their seats across the jet's aisle. They were collapsed in exhaustion, asleep, tucked in with pillows and blankets by the stewardesses. Tilla slept as well beside Corinne, breathing in that peculiar way people do when they are heavily medicated.

Corinne stared out the window at the silver Mediterranean thousands of feet below, replaying the morning's scene in her mind. She woke the girls just after dawn, having spent a few hours dozing in a chair, since Bridey and Sara shared her bed and Tilla slept through the commotion in the other. Once the reality hit the girls, that they were flying to Greece immediately, they were models of strength and efficiency. They packed, washed and changed, then woke and dressed Tilla, who was so woozy and out of it that the girls had to suspend her between them and walk her out of the hotel like a beatific drunk. Corinne dealt with the proprietor's cousin, a travel agent, who raced over with their plane tickets.

They caused quite a stir leaving the Pilgrims and the hotel. Mrs. Wadely made it her final point to tell Corinne that in her estimation, Bridey and Sara were utterly spoiled. Papa Joe sobbed his goodbyes. He'd ridden to the hospital to accompany Father's body, and returned in the morning to find them on their way out the door. The nuns looked disapproving. The rest of the lady Pilgrims looked confused, or shell-shocked.

As the girls mashed Tilla into the waiting taxi, Rose chased out of the hotel after Corinne.

"You can't do this!" she shrieked. "How will we explain four missing passports at every border, when we're supposed to have twenty-six? You just cannot leave this tour!"

Corinne squashed into the back seat of the tiny taxi beside the girls and slammed the door shut.

"This isn't a tour!" Corinne shouted out the open window. "It's a goddamn endurance test. We can't leave? Watch us!"

The taxi tore off into Roman traffic with a squeal of tires. They would miss seeing the Villa Borghese and the Church of Trinita die Monti; the Triton Fountain and the Quirinale Palace. They wouldn't toss coins into the Trevi Fountain or see the Pantheon, the Imperial Forums or the Palatine Hill -— or the dozens of sites the itinerary listed to be crammed into one marathon day.

They raced through Da Vinci Airport. Bridey pushed Tilla in a wheelchair at breakneck speed.

"Whee," Tilla said.

The airline held the jet at the gate until the door closed behind them with a reassuring thud. The engines whined as the aircraft taxied to the runway and they were barely settled in their seats before lifting off to Athens.

Corinne sipped her champagne, savoring the taste. First class. A lovely piece of salmon for lunch. Fresh fruit and Greek pastry. Hot, steaming cloths before and after their meal. She pressed the cloth to her face as if to blot away the fatigue and sadness left in Rome. Never had anything felt so wonderful on her skin.

Yes, she'd made the right decision.

"Rinnie, you'd be insane not to come," Maura told her on the phone. "I'm a simple flight away. Bring Tilla to us. We can have her seen to properly, and it sounds as if you can all use some R&R. This is just the place to do it. We'll take care of everything. Think of it --— a suite at the Hilton. Wonderful food. The pool. The girls will adore it, and I know the twins would be beside themselves with excitement." If there was anyone who could cajole, it was Maura. "When will we ever get to do this again?" Maura said. "The three of us together in Greece! It's been two years since our home leave, Rin. Please come. I'll make the arrangements."

Tilla stirred beside Corinne. Her eyes lolled open. With effort, she focused them on Corinne.

"C'rinne," she said. "I've been sleeping."

"Yes."

"I'm so tired. But I don't hurt. Not since Jackie Gleason was at my house."

"Jackie Gleason?"

"He's very nice." Tilla's words slurred slightly. "D'ja know he was a doctor? I thought he was only on T.V. I wasn't sure about the shot, but I have t'tell you, it's done me a lot of good."

The doctor. Corinne laughed to herself. She tucked the blue and white blanket with the Greek design around Tilla's shoulders.

"Where are we going, again?" Tilla knit her brow.

"To Athens, remember? I'm taking you to Maura."

"Oh. I remember. Do Rob and Garner know? Is ev…everything okay with them? Where' the girls?"

"Everything is fine." She avoided the question of their husbands. She thought Rob would probably lose it if he knew how bad a shape Tilla was in. "See over there? The girls are napping, too. We've all had a long night. But it's going to be wonderful from now on, I promise. You won't have to worry about a thing. It'll be just what the doctor ordered."

Tilla's eyes rolled and her lids closed. "Sounds t'riffic."

Corinne cradled her sister's head on her shoulder. Tilla slid back into untroubled dreams.

PART TWO
Greece

CHAPTER NINETEEN

Nineteen

Dear Alessandro. How can I begin to tell you everything that's hap-pened since I left you in Assisi? So much has changed in just three days. Father Clement is dead. Remember him? The nice priest at our table? I think I was the one who killed him. I told him about us and...

No, Bridey thought. *I won't write about that. I'll save it for later. I'll just tell him where I am for now.*

She stared up into the sky over Athens. Through the polar-ized lenses of her sunglasses, the color of the sky was so intensely blue it was almost psychedelic. There was nothing to obscure the expanse. Not even a bird. Lying flat on an inflatable raft, floating in the crystal, pale water of the Hilton's pool, she half-dreamed she was upright, being pulled into space. She stepped into the void, and let herself fall free...

"Oh!" She startled, jerking out of the dream in a reflex. The raft rocked beneath her.

Dearest Alessandro, she began again. *So much has changed.*

What hasn't changed is the way I feel about you. My heart still speeds up every time I think of you. And I think of you all the time, so my heart is always racing. I wish you were here with me. I wish we could lie in this sun together.

The heat of the sun in Athens was liked nothing she'd ever felt. It was over one hundred degrees at the pool. Around the perimeter, people lay on cushioned lounges, some motionless in the heat, some sipping iced drinks, others oiling themselves, their fingers sliding methodically over browned skin the color of walnut wood. Bridey and her family were the palest people there, and so looked the most obviously foreign. Everyone else — men, women and children — seemed uniformly dark-haired and brown-eyed. Men and women of all ages strutted around the pool area in the briefest of bikini wear. There were pot- bellies and sagging breasts, stretch marks and appendectomy scars, birthmarks, rolls of flesh. None of the sun worshippers appeared to be the least bit concerned about any of it.

Bridey, on the other hand, was still getting used to having so much of her body exposed by the new French bikini she wore, a present from Aunt Maura, since they hadn't brought bathing suits with them for the tour. The bikini was hot pink and lime green, with an under-wired top that hooked in the front between her breasts. A small pink bow disguised the hook. The bottom cut across the lowest part of her pelvis. She kept tugging at it. It barely covered her.

"It's perfect," she said to her aunt, as she modeled it for Maura in the hotel boutique.

"You look like you just stepped off the cover of Vogue," Maura said. "We could send you to St. Tropez and they'd drop like flies at your feet on the beach. Don't slouch, darling. That's it. Stretch tall. You've got it, Bridey, so flaunt it."

And Maura still had it. Most of it, anyway. She'd lost weight, so that her hipbone jutted through the linen skirt of her dress. But she still had a nice bust and smashing, long legs.

Bridey posed with her. She put her hands on her hips and bent one knee in, pointing her toes. "How's this?" she asked her aunt, but she already knew how it was. She could see herself in the mirror with Maura. She wanted to pose like that for Alessandro, just to see what he'd do.

Maura dropped her pose and appraised her niece. "Now I'm inspired," she said. "What sort of things have you brought for dinner?"

"Dinner?"

"To wear at dinner. Do you have anything appropriate? I don't suppose your mother bought you anything that would approach a cocktail dress."

"Well, most of our dinners haven't exactly been formal," Bridey said. "We usually just got off the bus and went right into the dining room."

"What a horror story." Maura began picking through a group of dresses on a nearby rack. "So, I take it you're in need of a few things."

Bridey vacillated between excitement at being outfitted in such a sophisticated boutique — there were labels of French and Italian designs: Courreges, Chanel, Cassini — and guilt that her aunt was buying.

"I had a nice black linen sheath for special occasions, but... there weren't any. Occasions. And then I, sort of lost that dress."

Maura held a white crepe mini against Bridey. "Lost?" She checked the dress for size.

"I left it at the hotel," Bridey said. "By accident." She thought of the black mini dress, stuffed under the mattress in Assisi, crumpled and stained. She almost wished she'd kept it. It would be a reminder, something tangible from her night with Alessandro in Assisi. She looked at her aunt, debating about saying more. Maybe she'd understand about how Bridey felt. After all, Aunt Maura had met and married someone from another country, and look at how her life turned out. But it didn't seem like the right time to discuss Alessandro, so Bridey shelved the idea. It was too complicated to get into in the middle of shopping.

"One dress would certainly not be enough," Maura said. She plucked six dresses from one rack and two from another, and thrust them at the Greek saleswoman who waited at her side. "We'll try these," she said to the woman.

"Give me a fashion show and we'll decide," she told Bridey. "If you're to have dinner with us, you should look like an adult. Besides, you'll need things for school in Washington. Call it school shopping, from me to you."

Everything is different here, Bridey thought. She slid her right leg off the side of the raft, up to her knee, into the cool water to act as a thermostat. Her arms trailed at her sides and she scooped a palm full of water, letting it drop onto where her skin stretched up over her ribs and sloped to her navel. A small rivulet traced a path down her torso. The water felt so good, she rolled off the raft and submerged, feeling the cold creep through her hair. She stroked down to the pool floor, watching the surface sparkling in a ceiling of white above her.

What are you doing right now, Alessandro? Working? Singing? Are you thinking of me? When will you get the post card I sent? How will I ever see you again?

Whether it was the floating sensation in her body, imagination, or pure physical memory, she felt his touch throughout her. She broke through the water's surface, clasping the raft as if it were Alessandro. A small voice called to her from the side of the pool, breaking the hard breaths she took.

"Bridey! Bridey! Over here."

She turned to face the little boy who stood with hands on hips, his feet planted firmly apart in a stance of command. His dark hair was tight with springy curls that glistened, still wet from his swimming lesson. The waistband of his swim trunks hung low on narrow hips, emphasizing his slight belly and protruding navel. Material ballooned over his legs. Bridey swam the few strokes to the poolside, towing the raft with one hand. She reached out and tweaked one of his toes. "What is it, Sir Ian?"

Ian scrambled down on his bottom until his legs dangled in the water in front of Bridey. "Can we play the dolphin game?"

"Again?" Bridey said. "Francesca hasn't even had her turn."

"We didn't play it so very much," he said. "And Francesca isn't keen to play. She doesn't like getting her face wet, actually."

Bridey glanced over at Ian's twin. Francesca sat crossed-legged on a lounge, her back to Sara, who was pulling a comb carefully through Francesca's thick blonde hair.

Ian followed Bridey's glance. "See? She's quite happy."

Bridey smiled up at Ian. "Oh, all right." She held out her arms and Ian leaned forward into them, his hands reaching to circle her neck. She pulled him into the water and up against her. Beneath the surface, he clamped his thin legs around her waist.

His arms were firmly round her neck. "Don't let go of me," he said.

Bridey stepped through the water, cradling his feather-light frame. "I've got you. Tell me when you're ready."

"Nearly ready," he said. His body relaxed. He let go of her neck and leaned back into the water. "After we play dolphins, will you tell me a story?"

"Maybe."

"Please."

"It will be time for lunch." She swirled him in a circle through the water.

"You could tell it to me during lunch."

"We'll see. A story about what?"

"Aeneas," he said. "Tell what happened next."

Thank God for Latin IV, Bridey thought. She had no end of stories for him, stories he listened to with entranced eyes as if he were lost in time, shipwrecked on the shores of Carthage.

"Okay," she said. "More about Aeneas, but after lunch. Are you ready?"

"Ready."

"I'm the mother dolphin," she began her prologue. "And you're my baby. We're far out in the sea. I'm teaching you how to swim and come to the surface for air."

Ian took a large breath.

Bridey glided beneath the surface, the little boy holding fast to her. With her eyes closed and the world suddenly silent to them, she was a dolphin, sleek and strong and graceful in the depths, conscious only of her young and his safety. She pushed hard with her legs and arms upward back to the surface and heard Ian's excited gasp of air.

He spit water onto the back of her neck and laughed.

"Again!" he cried.

"Don't you want some lunch?" Corinne asked Maura.

They were stretched out on lounges side by side at the pool, shaded by large orange and white stationary umbrellas. Corinne wore her new sun hat pulled low on her forehead, so low she had to tip her head back to see from beneath the brim. She was lathered with suntan lotion and smelled of coconut. She tucked her legs up against her, keeping her feet out of the slice of sun at the foot of the lounge.

Maura stretched full length, feet crossed at the ankles. She flexed her pedicured toes, smoothed her dark pageboy from her face and lifted a gin and tonic to her lips. "I suppose it's time." She took a sip of her drink and trailed the cold glass across the top of her breastbone. "When it's this hot, it's a temptation to lie here and not move."

"Take a dip and cool off," Corinne suggested.

Maura gave her a doubtful look. "You know I haven't set foot in the water in years. Not even when we're at the beach in Aqaba."

"You used to be a marvelous swimmer. I still have some of your medals from school in a box somewhere."

"As they should be." Maura took another sip from this, her second drink of the day. A dozen gold bangles on her arm tinkled in harmony with the ice cubes. She watched Bridey surface once more with Ian.

"My god, she's grown up," Maura said. "I couldn't believe it when she got off the plane. I thought: who is that woman helping Tilla? Before I realized it was Bridey." She paused. "But then, in this part of the world, she is a woman."

"Tell Tilla that," Corinne said. "See how she reacts. She's been herding her like a sheepdog through Europe. Maybe being here will give Bridey a breather. Tilla's certainly in no shape to do much of anything. Has Bridey told you about her romance yet?"

"What romance? A boyfriend at home?"

"Oh no. Something much more intriguing."

"Don't be so mysterious."

"She'd want to tell you about it herself. But I can tell you that he is a waiter at our hotel in Assisi. Absolutely darling, and he's won a scholarship, or competition or something, to sing opera in Rome. The two of them could not have been more love-struck than if a meteor hit them. But that's all I'm going to say." She made a zippering motion across her mouth.

Maura smiled. "I'll make sure I get details."

"Tilla is fit to be tied about it," said Corinne.

"Tilla is so high right now I doubt she'll remember last week when she snaps to," said Maura. "Greek men can be just as charming, so she may as well prepare herself."

Maura was silent for a moment, focused on the water. "You know, it sounds like such a cliché, but I really do remember when Bridey was Francesca's age."

"Kids tend to make large leaps when you only see them once every few years."

Maura took a swallow of her drink. The remaining ice cubes

bumped against her plump lips. It was no secret that Maura's long absences from the States were a bone of contention between the two sisters. Hugh and Maura had been stationed in other countries for such long periods of time.

"It's the same for us, with Ian and Francesca. Ian and Francesca were just toddlers when you were home last and now look at them."

Maura watched Ian climb unsteadily onto Bridey's sunburned shoulders. Bridey had hold of his calves as he inched his way to a standing position.

"Watch this, Mummy!" he called. Bridey dipped into the water until she was submerged and Ian stood hip-deep. She rose quickly and propelled him through the air. He landed with a whoop and disappeared in a splash.

Corinne and Maura held secret breaths until the small mop of his curls appeared at the surface. Ian dog-paddled back to Bridey with a triumphant, watery grin.

"Today it's jumping into the water," said Corinne. "The next time we see him, he'll be sprouting chest hairs."

"I think we'll make it to the States before then. Good Lord, Corinne."

"I'll never understand how you do it."

"Do what?"

"Live this way."

Over the speaker system, a Frank Sinatra recording sang "Come Fly With Me."

"It's not terribly hard," said Maura.

But her elder sister was not to be waved off her point. "You know what I'm talking about. The last months, for example. Having no contact with Hugh. Only hearing from him by some secret message system."

"You've been reading too many spy novels. People simply told me what they knew, when they were able. Hugh got word through to me."

"That couldn't have been very comforting."

"All right," Maura admitted. "I was worried. I was scared to death. But now Hugh's here. I got all my family as a surprise, in one swoop. Who would have imagined he would get leave, twenty-four hours before you flew in? I can hardly complain."

Corinne swung her legs around to the side of her lounge and sat up, facing Maura. "You don't have to play such a cool cucumber," said Corinne. "You left your house behind. Everything you own. You don't even know if it's still standing."

"Of course it's still standing."

Maura traced her thumb through the condensation on her glass. She could have told Corinne about the time she spent on the floor under the dining table of their home in Amman, trying to make it seem like a game to the children, while shelling rocked the neighborhood and rattled the dishes in her cupboards. But Corinne was already aware of the dangers they'd left. Otherwise they wouldn't be sitting in Athens together.

"Sit there and tell me that it's a walk in the park," said Corinne.

"Did I say that? I'm not saying it is," Maura said. She lowered her voice. "All right, we live in a dangerous place. I doubt anyone in the States has the least notion of what's happening in this part of the world. You're all too busy focusing on the situation in Asia. But Corinne, I'm telling you, what happens in the Middle East can have immense impact. Immense. King Hussein is a decent man, but wolves are always at his door. It's Hugh's job to know who the wolves are. We can't afford to lose Hussein. Not the British or the U.S." She looked at her older sister. "Hugh knew a long time ago what he was getting into. And so did I. Some times are worse, or better, than others. But it's our life. You know that."

"It sounds lonely," Corinne said. Her voice was full of sympathy. Her sister and brother-in-law had always lived in places of unrest. But perhaps it was being so close to the latest piece of it, physically, geographically, and chronologically, that stirred Corinne's feelings. She added: "And frightening."

Maura sat up. She raised her empty glass in a toast. "Here's to me. I'm a brick." Maura's laugh was genuine. Her smile brought back the youthfulness and beauty she was known for. She stretched her hand out to Corinne's, giving it a squeeze. "As soon as Tilla's better, we'll get her settled by the pool and put some roses in her cheeks. And you deserve a rest as well." She gathered her cigarette case and the white linen cover-up to her bathing suit. "This has worked out so perfectly! We're going to have the most marvelous time."

"I could pass on the sight-seeing," Corinne said.

"Not a sight shall be seen, unless you want to see it. Nothing but sybaritic pleasure. Ah! Here's Hugh, back already."

Hugh Nowell made his way down the line of lounges toward Maura and Corinne, followed by a younger man. At six foot three, with a paunch that threatened to spread toward his hips and make him pear-shaped, Hugh did not look like anyone's movie image of his true occupation. His sandy hair was thinning in the front and he had large, basset hound pouches beneath his eyes. He looked more like a rumpled schoolmaster.

The official line to his family was that he worked for the British Foreign Office in whatever country to which he was assigned. Worked at what, no one said. Only his wife knew his real work. It was his eyes and carriage that gave hint to the observant. Even walking through the crowded area of the hotel pool, hands in pockets, he had an aura of power. It was the power of those with access to secrets the world might never know: who was trading weapons to whom; who could be deposed; where the armies might be sent; who could be persuaded to betray, and why. Large, bushy brows growing wild hung over his eyes, eyes that could be as flat as a shark's, then light with amusement and irony. They were calculating eyes. Preoccupied. They made women wary, as if they were being measured to some unattainable standard. They made children self-conscious. Men felt guarded.

Now, his gaze took in his family, his wife and sister-in-law, his tiny blonde daughter playing hairdresser with his niece, his own crown prince being hoisted from the pool by Bridey. He smiled.

"Hello, hello." He bent under the tall orange and white umbrella to kiss Maura on the cheek.

Ian struggled free of the towel Bridey wrapped around him as she attempted to dry him off. He ran to his father. "Dad!"

"How was your lesson, Ian?" Hugh asked.

"We pretended to be dead," said Ian.

"The Dead Man's Float," Francesca corrected him.

Ian slid his eyes in her direction. "Francesca couldn't do it."

"I don't see why I should," Francesca complained. "I'm not dead."

Hugh ruffled his son's hair, turning his attention to Sara and Bridey. Bridey was standing apart, conscious of her uncle's companion, who watched her drying herself with Ian's towel.

"How are the bathing beauties?" Hugh asked.

Sara ducked her head and averted her eyes. Bridey knew Sara wasn't ready for her uncle's scrutiny. She felt the prospect of his measurement. Sara was still a child in his eyes, Bridey knew, in the same category with Ian and Francesca. Children were out of the scope of his concern, in the care of women and nannies. They were interesting in their place, an hour or two before dinner. If you were to share dinner with them, they would sit at their own table, to have their own childish conversations, so that the adults might have theirs in peace.

Tonight, Bridey was determined to dine, literally and symbolically, with the adults. Her uncle always intimidated her as a child. She'd been afraid of his voice and his size, his condescension. Now she did not want his mental pat on the head. She wanted him, and men like him, to look at her and not through her. The way they looked at Aunt Maura: someone beautiful and intelligent. Someone whose company they sought.

"How nice to see you back, Uncle Hugh," said Bridey. "I hope you'll join us this afternoon." It came out sounding more like a hostess in a restaurant than a grown-up niece speaking.

He seemed to remember that he hadn't arrived alone. "Mm! I'm sorry. Corinne, ladies: I'd like you to meet a colleague of mine from the embassy, Riordan Clarke. Riordan, this is my sister-in-law, Corinne Ledoux."

Corinne extended a hand to Riordan . "Hello," they said, in unison. He shook Corinne's hand and then lifted a hand in greeting to Maura, who returned a small wave with her fingers.

"You know Ian and Francesca, of course," Hugh said. "Ian?"

Ian, cued, shook the man's hand. "Hello, Mr. Clarke. Are you going swimming today?"

"Perhaps," Riordan Clarke said. "Are you up for a race?"

Ian sized the man with a serious look. "That would hardly be fair," he said, matter-of-fact. "Do you know how to do the Dead Man's Float?"

"Expertly." He took off the dark glasses he wore and looked over at Bridey.

Hugh steered attention toward Sara. "This is my niece, Sara. Corinne's daughter."

Riordan inclined his head to Sara. "How do you do?" He looked back at Bridey before Sara could answer.

"Hi." Sara's voice was barely above a whisper. She watched him watching Bridey, then lowered her head and fidgeted with the hairbrush in her hands, opting out of the pleasantries.

"Maura's other sister is upstairs," Hugh said to Riordan. "The one I told you about."

"I hope to meet her when she's up to things," Riordan said. He turned, smiling in a way Bridey was sure was insincere. "So, by my enormous powers of deduction, this can only be your other niece, Bridey."

I don't like him, Bridey thought. *Alessandro is much more beautiful. I wish he were here.*

Tilla stared at the dresser top across the room from her hotel bed, first in mild confusion. Where was she? What hotel was this? Then, remembering where she was, she stared in a trance that approached happiness. The room was dark and cool; the only sound was the low hum of the air conditioner. A brilliant pencil line of sunlight divided the drawn, floor length drapes.

It was good to rest deeply. Good to lie in clean sheets, free of pain. She sighed. Floating. This was better than any hospital. So good of Hugh to bring that nice British doctor to see her. The pills he prescribed sat atop the dresser, a beacon of reassurance in an ocean of pain.

Twenty

"Here, Bridey, wear these."

The earrings lay sparkling in the palm of Maura's hand. They were diamonds set in gold, in a design of three leaves.

"Aunt Maura... are you sure?" asked Bridey.

Real diamonds. They would be perfect. She'd chosen the white crepe dress to wear to dinner. It bore a label from Rome and she was wearing it in Alessandro's honor.

Bridey fastened the earrings, her hair swept up into a chignon, setting off the planes of her face.

Sara wore a stripe of zinc oxide on the red bridge of her nose. Her hair was scooped back into a loose ponytail and she was barefoot, in new shorts and a sleeveless top. A small pimple bloomed on her chin. She looked younger than fourteen. Sara had volunteered to babysit with Ian and Francesca, and to keep an eye on Tilla in their suite. It was much more appealing to play card games and color pictures with the twins, she confided to Bridey, than sit at a table with Uncle Hugh and be ignored.

Besides, she said, Aunt Maura ordered room service for them for dinner, complete with squid appetizers. She'd never eaten squid before and felt it was her journalistic obligation to at least try it. Ian particularly loved squid and he assured Sara she would love it, too. If she didn't, he told her, he would simply eat her share.

Maura placed the cool backs of her fingers to Sara's deeply crimson forehead. "You scorched yourself today. The sun is exceptionally intense in this part of the world, girls. You must be careful. It's not a place for unprotected Yankee skin."

Sara pulled on the neckline of her shirt to reveal the white outline of her bathing suit strap over her shoulder. She poked a careful finger at the burn.

"I think I can still hear you sizzling," said Bridey.

"Don't cook yourselves in the first few days," their aunt warned. "I mean it. The sun here can make you ill if you're not used to it."

Corinne appeared at the doorway to the dressing area. "Maura, is this dress too casual?" she said, holding her hands out, indicating the floral polished cotton sheath she was wearing, a mélange of pastels that blended together like an Impressionist painting. Several hundred more freckles had popped out across her face from the sun.

"Quite pretty. You look like Doris Day."

Corinne waved a hand in dismissal of Maura's comment. She noticed Bridey and took a step backward, pretending shock. "Good God, girl."

"Is that all you have to say?" Maura asked. "What do you think of my creation?"

Bridey put her hands on her hips and lifted her chin. She did a half-turn to show off the chignon.

"Sensational. But since when is she your creation?"

"She is tonight."

Wrong, Bridey thought. *No one is in charge of creating anything. I'll do that myself, thank you.*

"Room service just came," Corinne said to Sara. "Everything is taken care of. You can leave the table in the room when you're finished and we'll put it out in the hall when we get back. Keep the door locked."

"I'll be fine." The corners of Sara's mouth ticked ever so slightly downward.

"I could stay here," Corinne said, picking up on it. "I don't have to go."

"Go." There was ambivalence in Sara's voice, but not enough to seriously concern her mother. The room's desk was full of stationery from the Hilton. She'd write a letter to her father. She'd catch up on her log. In the end, she would sacrifice a few blank lined pages to the twins, allowing them to draw pictures. She was already into the last tabbed subject portion of the spiral notebook.

In the living room of the suite, Francesca and Ian were uncovering plates of food, leaving stainless steel covers, like capsized turtles, on the floor.

"Here's the squid!" Ian announced. He picked up a small tubular portion between his thumb and forefinger and thrust it toward Sara as the women entered the room. "Go on, Sara. It's lovely. Taste it."

Maura snatched up a bread plate and clamped her other hand over Ian's wrist. "Ian Nowell, what have you been taught about china and utensils? Drop that immediately."

The piece of squid dropped onto the plate. Ian wrenched his hand from his mother's grip. "When I eat with Hadji and Kalil at home, we always eat with our fingers."

"We are not in Amman, and you are not eating in the kitchen with servants. I expect you to learn proper manners like the little English gentleman you are."

Ian licked garlic sauce from his fingers, unperturbed. "When I'm grown up, I shall eat with my fingers all the time. And I won't live in England. I'll live in Amman."

"If you expect to eat in anyone's house, you will eat with utensils," Maura said. She turned to Corinne. "This is an old conversation. He's just doing it for your benefit."

Francesca stepped over one of the plate covers on the floor and clung to Bridey's hand. "Bridey, must you go with Mummy and Aunt Corinne? Can't you stay? Sara is going to play Fish, and War." She stared up at Bridey with her round, deep blue eyes.

"Maybe another night," Bridey said.

"I don't like to play Fish," Ian said. He wiped his fingers on the back of his shorts. "I'm going to teach Sara how to play Bomb."

"What is that game, Ian?" Corinne asked "Is it like War?"

Francesca set up a wail. "Mummy! Tell Ian he mustn't! He's always making up stupid games and ruining things."

"Bomb isn't stupid," Ian insisted. "It's a real game."

"No, it isn't!" Francesca cried. "Once you played it with me and all you did was smash the cards with your hand."

"Because I won. That's a rule. The one with the most bombs wins."

"Ian has his own rules," Maura told Sara. "Beware." She caught her son just as he was lining up to do a cartwheel across the carpet. "Into the bathroom," she told him. "And wash those hands. I expect you to do everything Sara tells you. Or no card games."

"I'm just going to say goodnight to my mom," Bridey said to them.

Tilla lay flat on her back in bed. Bridey picked her way across the carpet as if she were crossing a floor of glass. She bent over her mother and kissed her on the forehead. Tilla stroked Bridey's cheek in return.

"I just came in to say good night," Bridey said. "I'm going to dinner with Aunt Maura and Uncle Hugh, and Aunt Corinne. Sara will be in the other room with the twins, if you need anything. She can call us up in the restaurant."

"Where are you going?" asked Tilla.

"To dinner," Bridey repeated. "They have a restaurant on the roof. You can see all over Athens from there."

Tilla nodded. Her eyes seemed to focus a little. "You look beautiful. Where did you get that dress?"

"Aunt Maura bought it for me, yesterday. Remember? I showed everything to you. She's loaned me her earrings to wear tonight, too." She turned her head and touched the back of her ear to show her. "Do you recognize them? She's had them forever."

"She shouldn't have done that. They're very val'able." Tilla sighed, blinking with the effort of conversation. "Don't lose them."

Her mother's hand felt bony and cool in her own. How funny it felt to be the one sitting over the bed, and not the sick little one in it, thought Bridey. Tilla's presence, her voice and touch were magic medicine when Bridey was sick — calm, strong, gentle. There had never been a demon Tilla couldn't banish, no symptom she couldn't relieve, no pain she couldn't soothe.

The doctor Maura and Hugh had brought in said Tilla's pain was the kind that immobilized people. She needed powerful pain killers and rest... and time. She was definitely not in any shape for a long plane ride back to the States. There didn't seem to be any telling how long it might go on.

Bridey stood up. She smoothed the wrinkles from the front of the dress and tugged automatically at the back hem.

"Goodnight, Mumma."

Tilla closed her eyes and blocked the light with her forearm across her brow.

"G'night, Maura," she said.

The three women stood inside the entrance to the rooftop restaurant waiting to be led to the table where Hugh was already seated. They made a striking trio, and eyes followed them. Bridey felt glamorous and elite. Affluence clung to her like a perfume to the observers in the dining room. She didn't realize any of this, in her gifted clothes and borrowed jewelry. But she did have a very different feeling in this different world, with its unique concerns and interests. No one mentioned the cities burning at home with race riots or the war protesters at the White House gates. Greece had its own problems. Turkey threatened to the east. The Middle East was a tinderbox. But on this night, everyone was enjoying summer on the roof of the Hilton.

Two other couples, the Sloanes and the Devoes, who were friends from Amman, were already seated with Hugh. And there was one other guest, who set his cigar in an ashtray and rose with the other men to greet the ladies as they approached.

Maura put her arms around her sister and niece. "Everyone," she said to the party, "I want you to meet two very special people."

While her aunt made introductions, Bridey concentrated on not paying attention to Riordan Clarke. He stood with his hand resting on the back of the chair next to his own, watching her. Bridey had to sit beside him.

Riordan drew on his cigar, listening to Hugh. The ash tip glowed red, then went gray again as he exhaled. He wore a tropical weight tan suit and a starched white shirt without a tie. Beneath the aroma of cigar tobacco, Bridey caught the scent of his aftershave. She could see where he'd nicked himself shaving and she examined him in a sidelong glance, checking for gray hairs. There were none. It was hard to tell how old he was.

She took a sip of the ice water sitting in front of her. She felt uncomfortable and equally determined not to show it. What on earth should she talk about with these people? It was probably best to sit quietly and listen for a while, anyway. You could learn all sorts of things.

Riordan's voice jolted her. "Can we get you something better to drink?"

"Oh. A cola would be fine."

He raised a brow. "Plain? Wouldn't you like a little rum to

dress it up?"

"No, thanks. I like my soda straight up." She didn't want to talk to this man. And she wished she'd developed a taste for wine. Asking for a soda was like admitting she still belonged at the children's table.

The cigar jutted from his teeth. "I suppose you don't smoke cigarettes or say dirty words, either."

I knew he'd be a pain, Bridey thought. She'd seen guys like him before, college guys, who carried themselves with a confidence borne out of the fact that they were male and dominant, the pick of the litter, grown to have first choice of everything.

"Sorry," he said, seeing her expression. "I'm taken aback in the presence of such wholesomeness. Truly. I believe you're the first bona fide American goddess I've ever met." He tipped his head near hers, his voice very low, flying in under the cover of the table's conversation. Under the radar. "You are a goddess. Surely you know that. Without question, the most stunning female at this hotel, though probably the least interesting."

Bridey shot him a look of surprise that transformed to indignation at warp speed. She gritted her teeth. She could feel heat creeping through her neck and face. She wanted to sink beneath the table and out of sight. How dare he! Why was he being so mean to her? He didn't even know her. And she was his boss' niece! She assumed Uncle Hugh was his boss. Not that she could get him fired or anything. She willed tears not to sting at the corners of her eyes. The truth hurt; she was the least interesting person at the table. She took a long sip of ice water, cooling the burn in her chest, and pretended she hadn't heard him.

Eventually Corinne and Maura steered the conversation toward her, with talk about college.

"I've always had a dream to go to the School of Foreign Service," Bridey told Peter Devoe.

"I thought you wanted to be a Navy nurse and go on submarines," Maura said. "That was the last dream I heard."

"That was when I was ten," Bridey said. Embarrassment crept up her cheekbones.

"The Foreign Service?" Devoe said. "Rather a lonely life for a woman. All career and no family. More suited to a spinster-type, I should think. Don't you agree?" He asked Hugh.

"Ask Clarke. He'd be the expert on what type of women make the grade. I think some of our secretaries would say he's been making a study of it."

Riordan tolerated the other men's laughter. "Better she should serve on a more personal level, I think," he said of Bridey, turning to her. "Marry and have babies. With a foreigner, if that will fit the bill."

The dismissal in his tone lit a fuse in her. She hated being underestimated. He'd thrown the gauntlet and she was ready now to pick it up, ready to risk and take his challenge. He chose the battle. She drew herself up in her chair beside him.

"With an attitude like that," she said to him, "it's no wonder you're not married."

"How do you know I'm not?"

"It's just obvious."

Alice Sloane laughed a high whinny. "You've got him pegged, Bridey!"

"I wouldn't say Bridey is averse to the idea of marriage and a family," said Corinne. "I agree somewhat with Riordan. Women do serve in life, generally. The important question is: what or who are they serving? If it's worthwhile and fulfilling, does it matter if it's on a worldwide scale, or intimately, in a home? Either way, the effect is important."

Tom Sloane nodded. "I consider my wife to be as much in the service of the British government as I. The very fact that she has traipsed over the globe with me and been a damn good sport about it is a tremendously valuable service. She allows me to do my job."

"My point exactly," Riordan said. "That's foreign service of the best kind. Free us fellows up to do what we do best." He leaned slightly away from Bridey, scrutinizing her. "Bridey seems well-fitted for that sort of role. A better use of natural talent than to be burrowed away in some outpost, typing reports and letters."

She wanted to kick Riordan in the shins. Hit him with her bread plate. Natural talent!

"I don't believe she's terribly interested in that opinion," Hugh spoke up. He too was studying his niece, observing her as she glared at Riordan. "Is that correct, Bridey?"

For a moment she froze. All eyes were on her. This was her audition at the grownup table. She took a breath. "What I'm interested in is forming my own opinions. And making my own decisions. All I want is the freedom to do that."

"Ah, the hope of everyone in a free society," Peter Devoe said. He picked up his glass. "Here's to the next generation. May they carry on the fight!"

"Bridey just celebrated her eighteenth birthday in Venice," Maura said. 'We should toast to that, too."

"I wouldn't say celebrated, exactly," Bridey said.

"No?" Maura asked. "Why not?"

"It rained buckets the whole time," Corinne explained. "And we never did get to do the gondola ride. It wasn't much of a celebration at the hotel. The waiters brought out a dessert with a candle."

Hugh raised his glass. "To Bridey. For many reasons."

The group raised their glasses to the toast. Bridey met Maura's eyes. *Am I doing all right?* She asked silently.

Maura winked in answer.

"I'm sorry." She apologized to her Uncle Hugh for what seemed the twentieth time. She couldn't follow, had never learned how, and Hugh was a very good dancer. Her size ten feet kept knocking against his toes, or stepping on them. She felt like a giraffe, all legs and knock-knees.

"You're doing fine," Hugh reassured her. He turned in a little circle, let Bridey twirl out at arm's length, and spun her back to him. "See? Lovely."

There was a French band with two singers, performing a lot of the English arrangements of songs popular in the States, a lot of Burt Bacharach and Sinatra. The music reminded her of the club in Assisi, of Alessandro. The most perfect night of her life.

"You have grown up so," her uncle was saying to her. "I give great credit to your mother and father for producing such a fine young lady."

"Thank you."

"What does Rob think of you and Tilla traversing the continent?"

Bridey's face softened at the mention of her father. "Dad's fine. Summer's always his busy time. But he was super about this trip. He said he was looking forward to being bachelors with the boys."

"Ah." They two-stepped across the floor. "Well, it's awfully generous of him to share you with us here. Your Aunt Maura is over the moon about it, I can tell you. Not to mention Ian and Francesca. Pity about your tour, but perhaps you wouldn't be here now if things had gone well."

"I wouldn't change anything about the way things happened. Except what happened to Father."

"Father?" His caterpillar brows came together in a crease.

"Father Clement. The one who..."

"Oh, yes. Died. I heard about that. Nasty business, you and Sara finding him that way."

Father's face came back to Bridey, but it wasn't the frozen-eyed, dead face on the lavatory floor. It was his face smiling at her from the table on the terrace in Assisi. It was his face as he watched her run from the bus and into Alessandro's arms. She saw him blessing her as he left the dusty little lobby room of the hotel in Rome.

"He was a good priest," said Bridey. "A good friend. We had a special talk, right before he died. There's someone I met in Assisi that I… I think I'm in love with. Father really understood."

"Mm. Heard something about that, too. You're a beautiful girl. Very much like your Aunt Maura. And men will notice you. But love takes a bit more than forty-eight hours. Italians are particularly adept at letting their emotions run away with them on a regular basis."

"Alessandro isn't like that."

"I'll take your word for it, then." His tone was tinged with skepticism. "But if you need my opinion at any point, feel free to ask."

"Thank you, Uncle Hugh. Being here means more than I can tell you. It would have been awful to leave Rome and go home early. Things are just beginning for me here."

Hugh drew back and studied her face. His unreadable eyes caught her up, a rabbit in a snare, a curious little trinket he'd forgotten, hadn't looked at in a while, and now discovered had some interesting detail.

"Then we'll have to see to it that you stay, until you've seen or done whatever is meant to be." The band wound down their song. "Ready?" he asked. "Dip."

When they returned to their table, Riordan stood and pushed Bridey's chair into the table. "Your uncle has been known to monopolize ladies on the dance floor," he said. "I have to leap at my chance." He held his hand out to Bridey. "May I?"

Bridey turned back toward the dance floor. *I'll dance with him once*, she thought. *Then I'll ignore him.*

He wasn't as elegant a dancer as Hugh, he kept his step simple and Bridey had less trouble following.

"Are you always this stiff when you dance?" he asked.

"Am I being stiff?" She was rigid with tension, she knew. She wanted to keep several inches of space between them, partly to maneuver her feet, and partly— mostly—to keep from touching him. Negative energy vibrated between them like an electrified fence.

His hand ran down the clenched muscles of her lower back. "If you don't relax, you'll end up with a nasty strain. You wouldn't want to end up like your mother, would you?"

"What do you know about my mother?"

"I know your aunt and uncle are very concerned about her. I know a lot of things happened on that tour that weren't pleasant, for any of you."

Bridey willed her back and shoulders to loosen, if only to keep him from stroking her again.

"There's a girl! Now try looking at my face, and not our feet."

She lifted her eyes as far as the cleft in his chin. It was more of a dent than a cleft, she decided. A scar. She wondered if someone had punched him in the mouth hard enough to split it. If so, he probably deserved it, she thought.

"I wasn't looking at my feet," she said to the scar.

"I've given you a bit of a burn, have I? I get the impression I'm not top of your list."

"I just met you. How could you be on any list of mine? Unless it was the Get Lost List."

He laughed. "I apologize. I didn't realize you're so prickly." His hand caressed the small of her back. "There you go again. Very tense. Tell you what. Let's start out fresh. We'll talk about something pleasant. Your Aunt Corinne has been entertaining us with tales of your conquests across Europe. I'm curious to hear more about the -— what was it? The singing waiter."

She could see the derision in his eyes. She narrowed hers.

"He's on his way to Rome to sing at the Opera. They've awarded him a contract to perform. He's an artist. And what's wrong with working hard to support yourself and your dream?"

"This kind of artistic nobility appeals to you?"

"Very much."

"I see." He nodded. "And this was a serious romance."

"Is. Very."

"So. You have your very own Caruso waiting for you in Rome. How romantic. One piece of advice, though: Italians don't wait long."

She sighed with annoyance, studying the musicians in the band. The drummer looked over at her and winked. He looked old enough to be her father. *The Italians don't wait long.*

"I assume you made love with him," Riordan said. Her attention snapped back. "How else to explain this protective indignation, this steadfastness in the face of such odds of ever seeing him again? I sense an investment."

Bridey stopped dancing. "None of it is your business! It's obvious I'm some kind of joke to you, but I take my life seriously. And I don't care if you are a friend of my aunt and uncle's, you have no right to be so rude." She tried to turn away, but he held onto her. "I want to sit down!"

"Wonderful!" he said. "There really is someone alive inside that goddess face and body. That's the first fire I've seen all evening. I was beginning to wonder if I was sitting next to a nun. Let me recall. You've just been sprung from convent school. They don't tolerate fire in convent school, I imagine."

They stood at the far edge of the dance floor, near the wall that overlooked the city and Mount Lycabettos. "It was a Catholic high school, not a convent school. Big difference."

"All girls?"

"Yes."

"Taught by nuns?"

"Yes, but ..."

"A convent school," he reiterated. "All the more reason to relax and enjoy yourself, then. Look where you are! This city can be a lot of fun."

She hated admitting how right he was. He might be rude and conceited and arrogant, but he was right. He wasn't afraid to say the truth.

"You don't really want to run back to that table, do you?" he said. "Isn't it far more interesting here?"

Alessandro had asked her nearly the identical question that afternoon on the terrace: Did she want to run from him, to safety, and miss whatever was next? She'd chosen to stay, to risk it, and look what happened.

He pulled her close to him and resumed dancing. "I thought as much."

She tried to think of something cutting to say. She wanted to fight on equal ground, but she was out-gunned.

"You're a much better dancer when you're furious. You forget to be rigid." He said this against her hair. She could smell the cigar on his breath and the spicy scent of aftershave on his skin. Then she realized: They were on equal ground. He was compelled by his physical attraction to her. There wasn't anything he could do about that, and therein lay her power. If he wanted to skewer her with words and attitude, she could torture him with her own devices. She drew her head back from his.

"I'm not angry," she said.

He gave a little sniff of a laugh. "The hell you're not."

"I'm indifferent. I'm only waiting for the music to end, so this dance will be over. I don't want to make a scene, that's all."

"Indifference. Very good. So much more effective. Anger would indicate an emotional response. That would mean you'd have to care."

"Which I don't. Care."

"Now you've slipped. Redundancy. You've already cut me with indifference. Repeating it is overstating the case. The lady doth protest."

"I'm not a lady, I'm a goddess, remember? If I really wanted to wound you, I'd hit you with a lightning bolt. You'd be a little pile of ashes at my feet. We goddesses don't waste our time with trifling human emotion. We have bigger gods to fry."

"Ah, now you've lost." He twirled her around. Bridey tripped and nearly bumped into a portly couple jig-jogging around the dance floor. He steadied her. "Once you've let humor in, you've shown softness toward the enemy. It could mean defeat."

"My father says a sense of humor can be the strongest weapon in self-defense."

At least he was trying to be funny. He was British, so maybe his sense of humor was more sarcastic. John Lennon was sarcastic and Bridey thought he was hilarious.

"A wise man. It can also lead the way to... negotiation."

The music ended and Riordan let Bridey go. She didn't move. People were clapping for the band, so she joined in politely. She was not going to run back to any table.

"Who taught you to dance, by the way?" Riordan asked.

"No one."

"Apparently. You're really awful."

"I usually don't have to dance with people from an older generation."

"We aren't quite as separated by an ocean of age as you may think," he said. "Nevertheless, let me offer my services and give you a few lessons." The music began again. Blue Moon. He held out his arms. "I could be a hell of a tutor."

Twenty-One

That night, Bridey slipped from her bed, took the hotel stationery and pen from the suite's desk and padded barefoot to the bathroom. She closed the door and turned on the bright lights above the sink, then sat cross-legged on the thick cotton floor mat, her back braced against the marble tub. It was after two o'clock in the morning, and only she and Aunt Corinne had left the party up on the roof. The rest of them moved into the lounge area of the bar, showing no signs of ending after-dinner cocktails. She wanted to share her evening with Alessandro, to tell him how she missed him, thought of him every day, fell asleep dreaming of him each night. She'd sent a post card to him the very first day they arrived. How long did it take for a post card to get to Assisi?

I'm in Greece, she wrote. *It seems so far away from you, Alessandro.*

She filled in the details about their sudden departure from the tour in Rome. She stared at the blank space on the stationery page, thinking about Father Clement. Alessandro didn't know how much of an ally Father had been to the two of them, keeping her secret after he saw her sneak out of the hotel that night, and then stopping the Phantom for Alessandro to say goodbye. To Alessandro, Father was probably just another nice person at their table. What should she say about his death? About telling Father the truth that afternoon, that she wasn't a virgin anymore, and didn't regret it?

She'd leave all that for another letter, after she heard back from Alessandro. She described the reasons why her aunt and uncle were in Athens in the first place, and about being included in their circle. And she wrote how her mother was out of commission, which Bridey told herself wasn't a bit upsetting. It opened up a whole new vista of freedom.

Finally, she compared her evening dancing on the rooftop to their own time dancing at the club in Assisi. She described the way she told Riordan Clarke off, proud of herself for not turning tail in the face of his abrasive persona. It had helped matters, she told Alessandro, because he finally became a bit nicer, most likely because he saw that she wasn't to be insulted and made fun of, she asserted. He even offered to take her to see some of the sights of Athens in the next few days. Much as she didn't like this man, she did want to see what Athens had to offer.

I'd much rather be doing these things with you, she wrote. *I want to tell you that I love you and miss you. All I could think about tonight was how much I wished I were back in Assisi at your hotel, listening to your family make music, high above your land.*

Her eyes teared. What kind of hope was there that they'd ever have a night like that again? Or even be in the same place again?

Most of all, I wish I were dancing with you, or listening to you sing, or doing anything at all with you. Please write to me, Alessandro.

She told him to address his letter to her in care of her uncle at the Athens Hilton.

Tell me you haven't forgotten me, she wrote. *That you will not*

forget. Everyone says you will.
She signed it: *Your own Miss America, Bridey.*

For the next few days, they lay by the pool, stretched out like a pride of lions, satiated after feasting and sleepy with sun and heat. Bridey envisioned them this way: Her uncle was the huge, craggy old male, the King of Beasts, accompanied by a younger lion slightly lower in status. That would be Riordan, of course. He was obviously part of the royal group. Hugh and Riordan lay groggy with relaxation, tolerating the presence of lionesses and cubs. Ian and Francesca climbed on them, tugging manes and tails, while the men responded with half-open lids, and rolled on their bellies to avoid the play.

Bridey the Lioness stretched her arms and flexed her toes, giving a mighty yawn. She ran her hand over the length of her ribcage and down to the concave of her pelvis, trying to gauge whether or not she'd added any extra flesh from the steady diet of steak and butterscotch sundaes she'd been eating since she arrived in Greece. Sara lay on a lounge with a towel covering her head and chest, hiding from the relentless sun. On the other side of Sara, Maura and Corinne flanked Tilla, who was experiencing her first day out of bed. Whether it was the effects of the medication or happiness at finally being able to enjoy her sisters, Tilla was calm and agreeable. She hadn't said a word about Bridey's bikini and the extraordinary amount of skin she exposed. In fact, she barely spoke at all.

Bridey skimmed a line of sweat from her hairline and roused. Time for another dip in the watering hole to cool off. She walked the length of the pool toward the higher diving board, past her mother and aunts. The lifeguard gave her an appreciative smile from his chair. Bridey climbed to the diving board and paused at the edge. She smiled back at the lifeguard and glanced over toward where Riordan lay by the pool. He was stretched out on the tiles of the pool apron with his head resting on his folded arms. It was hard to tell whether his eyes were closed behind his sunglasses, and if they were open, whether they focused on her. Just in case they were, she held her arms above her head and took two strong bounces on the board, before sailing into a high, perfect jackknife. She pierced through the water without causing much of a disturbance to its surface. The disturbance was meant to take place in Riordan.

Since their first dinner together, Riordan made himself a regular part of Bridey's evenings. If he didn't join her family at dinner, he showed up for drinks later. He took her dancing at the hotel club, "for badly needed instruction," he joked, though he was game to try the dances she brought from home in the States : the swim, the frug, the mashed potato, the dog. It was a chance to laugh at him for a change. He wasn't a natural like Alessandro, but he gave it a go. Riodan was sometimes at the pool, and always with Uncle Hugh. At times he was distant, with the same preoccupied air as Hugh. Present, but not there.

True to Maura's word, there was no sightseeing, no trips outside the hotel. Every whim could be catered, right at the Hilton. The Parthenon and Acropolis were on display to them from their balcony, spot lit in the evening, hanging like a bright, surreal dream with the moon rising in the black sky over Athens. An itch was building in Bridey to explore this new territory. There was only one person offering to guide her in it. She wanted to walk the docks of Piraeus, smell the sea and the fish. She wanted to bury her feet in the sand and let the Aegean wash over her. There were streets and flavors and music strange to her ears, just beyond the walls of her American hotel.

Bridey swam a streamlined crawl the length of the pool, reached the shallow end and made the turn. Lap after lap, she glided by Riordan. She turned to float on her back, closing her eyes, tipping her head chin-up, arching her back so that her breasts and the small curves below her navel rose from the water like an island chain.

To everyone else, Riordan appeared to be sleeping at the pool edge, one arm now hanging into the water. But Bridey could feel he was watching her. By now she knew what that felt like: A scorch on her flesh as intense as the Greek sun. A kind of hunger.

It made her feel full of power, and out of his reach.

"What did you do with that letter of Bridey's I gave you?" Maura asked Hugh. They were seated at a small round table in a taverna, alone for the first time since her family arrived.

"Gave it to Sloane," said Hugh. "He'll be in Rome for a week or so. Said he'd pass it on north. No sense relying on the post over there, if one needn't." He drew on his large Cuban cigar and exhaled a puff of opaque smoke. Before the smoke could drift in Maura's direction, he swatted the air, breaking it up. "What was in that urgent missive, anyway?"

"A letter to that young man in Assisi. A love letter, I imagine."

Hugh tapped the cigar firmly against the side of their shared ashtray and a round chunk of ash fell. "Think it's wise? To encourage it?"

"Why not?" Maura frowned. "You sound like Tilla. She took a dislike to the boy from the start."

"Perhaps with reason?"

"She thinks of Bridey as a seven-year-old."

Hugh smiled. "Tilla's a peach. Thought so when she was Bridey's age."

"And she thought you were the oddest man she'd ever met."

"How right she was."

Maura played with the string of pearls and emeralds that rested just at the top of her pale breasts. "Well, I'm not sure Tilla's right about this Italian boy. Corinne sees him in an entirely different light. A perfect gentleman."

Hugh gazed back at her, expressionless. He drew on his cigar.

Then his eyes shifted a few centimeters, watching two men who entered the taverna.

"And there is the music," Maura went on. She was used to her husband's watchfulness. "Corinne said he's most extraordinarily talented. She described him as 'a raw nugget of gold in a mountain stream.' Can you imagine?"

"Quite the poetess."

"I understand Bridey and he had quite the goodbye kiss when they left Assisi. He chased the bus down to do it."

Hugh turned his attention back to Maura.

"Bridey mentioned the word 'love.' I wrote it off to youthful hyperbole." Hugh drained the last of his drink and caught the eye of the waiter.

"Another for me, too, darling."

"What's the verdict, then? Think Bridey is a virgin or not?"

"That information will be on a need-to-know basis."

The waiter set their drinks before them and removed the empty glasses in one fluid motion.

"Bridey seems capable enough of handling her own affairs," said Hugh. "She's done well enough with Clarke, from what I can see."

At the mention of Riordan Clarke's name, Maura's eyes lifted to search her husband's face.

"He's part of the package this trip, I'm afraid," Hugh said. "London's a bit nervous about the number of unfriendly visitors in Athens these days, not to mention the Greeks' suspicions toward us and the Americans since the coup in April. Some people have no respect for a fellow's holiday." Maura's face remained tense. "Clarke's just a bit of added protection, that's all. Part of his on-the-job experience."

He leaned forward and took her hand across the table. "If anyone seriously thought you or the children were in any jeopardy, I wouldn't be anywhere in the vicinity. I am on holiday. There are simply a few extra people added to the bargain. As long as we stick to the Hilton, we really have no worries."

Maura stroked the back of his hand with her fingers. He squeezed her hand in return. "Don't worry," he assured her. "The only one who might not be safe is Bridey."

"Why?"

"I meant with Clarke. He's taken something of a fancy to Bridey, I suspect."

"Yes," Maura said. "He has been attentive."

"Fact is he's inquired about taking her out into the city. She'd certainly be safe enough with him. A pity to come all this way and not experience much more than hotel life. She's a bright girl, Bridey. A romance in Italy and a few go 'rounds with Clarke here might be just the thing to put the polish on her."

Maura considered this. "I suppose it would be all right. As long as they didn't attract any attention. If you think there wouldn't be any harm."

"It's not Bridey anyone is interested in. It wouldn't cause any blips on the radar screen, if that's what your concern is about. I'd arrange for one of our drivers, of course. I just wanted to clear it with you first. After all, you are an impeccable judge of men's character."

"So I am." She raised her glass to him.

"Then I leave it to you to run it by Tilla and Corinne. Assure them she would be in excellent hands."

"I don't think I'd want to put it quite that way to Tilla."

"You know what I mean. Educational experience of a lifetime, etc., etc. It might take the sting out, should the Italian chap not respond… He's unlikely to, I expect."

Maura crossed her arms and leaned them on their table. The pearls and emeralds swung forward. "Oh, you spooks are that, all right. A definite education. But sometimes we learn things we don't want to know."

Hugh glanced down the neckline of his wife's dress and met her eyes with a wink. "That's what happens to women who are too smart for their own good."

Alberto Scaasi gave thanks to the Virgin, to St. Clara, and to each saint whose bones he passed on his postal route in Assisi. He was hurrying: it was near lunch and he was hungry. His balding head was coated in perspiration and his glasses slid forward on his long nose. He pulled two pieces of mail from his pouch in preparation for his next stop — a letter from the Athens Hilton, posted in Rome, and a postcard also stamped from Athens — as he listened to the whistled tune coming from the top of the steps around the corner.

The tall, dark-haired young man was nearly to the street level when Alberto greeted him.

Good morning, Alessandro! Where are you off to, in such a hurry? At least, you're happy about it, whatever it is.

I'm late for my lesson, Alessandro told him. But it's too pretty a day not to be happy.

Alberto handed him the mail. Here's something for you, all the way from Greece. I hope it is only good news and makes your day happier.

Alessandro studied the front of the postcard, frowning. He turned it over and read the script on the message side. It was written in the smallest handwriting possible, in order to fit the maximum amount of space.

Good news? Alberto prompted.

But Alessandro said nothing. He reread the postcard and checked the face of the envelope, then sank down to sit on the steps.

Alessandro, are you all right? What news could be so upsetting from such a beautiful place?

Alessandro's answer was to rip the envelope open at one end and pull out sheets of hotel stationery.

Alberto did not often deliver mail in Assisi from Greece. He rested his mail pouch against the bottom step and tried to read over Alessandro's shoulder. But the letter was written in English, in a loopy, feminine hand. So he contented himself with watching Alessandro's face.

Twenty-Two

"You can put me down now," Ian told Bridey.

She carried him on her hip from the time they climbed out of the cramped taxi that pulled to a screeching halt on the dockside street in a marina at Piraeus. She carried him because he'd insisted and because she needed to reassure herself that they arrived safely, after speeding through the city of Athens at ninety-five miles per hour, careening around corners, dodging small carts pulled by donkeys led by wizened men. The taxi driver tore through traffic as if he were out for a Sunday drive, one arm braced casually on the open window. He kept up a running commentary to Riordan on the scenery. Bridey guessed this, since he spoke Greek scattered with a few recognizable English words.

Ian sat in the backseat of the taxi with her, relaxed and happy, the wind from the open window stiffly ruffling his curls. Riordan sat in the front with the driver, equally nonchalant. Only Bridey was frightened, gripping the armrest and gasping sharply each time it seemed they were about to crash. She could see Riordan smile when she inhaled audibly.

Two taxis disgorged the six of them at the docks — Hugh and Riordan, Bridey, Sara, and the twins. Hugh proposed the trip as a break for everyone, a day trip to the nearby island of Egina on board a two-mast trawler the British embassy had made available. Maura and her sisters would have a day to themselves at the hotel. Tilla wasn't up to a boat trip, of course, and Corinne was not one to leave dry land if she could help it.

Bridey let Ian slide from her hip to stand on the wooden planks of the dock. Riordan went aboard, instructing them to stay put until he talked with the crew. But Ian ran up the small gangway and jumped onto the side deck before she could stop him.

"Ian!" She called after him. Behind her, Sara and Francesca struggled with large woven bags full of towels and accessories for the day's cruise. Hugh strolled down the dock finishing the last of his cigar, following them.

Sara looked hot and resentful.

"I told Ian to wait for us, but he's on board," Bridey explained. Sara arched her brows in reply.

"Ian always does what he wants. He gives Mummy fits." Francesca's small voice chirped up below them. She shouldered her bag in imitation of Sara, a section of her long, fair curls squashed between the heavy rope handle of the bag and her delicate shoulder. The handle bit through hair and skin.

"Here, Francesca, let me have that." Bridey reached for the bag, relieving the little girl of her burden.

Francesca's pert doll-face tilted heavenward, regarding Bridey and Sara. "Are we waiting for Daddy?"

"Yes," Bridey said. She felt foolish for standing on the dock, obeying Riordan's orders, while her small charge explored the deck.

Hugh flicked the butt of his cigar into the alley of dark water between the boat and dock. It landed with a small watery plunk and floated to the surface, bumping against the carcass of a fish.

The water didn't appear to be anything Bridey would want to swim in. It was deep green, an opaque broth of algae, fish remnants, cigarette butts, and oily rainbows from fuel. But around them, the port was exotic and timeless. Sun-bleached pastel buildings with red-tiled roofs climbed the hill around the harbor, perched like spectators at an amphitheater watching the pageant of generations of fishermen come and go. Sea birds circled and called for handouts. The air smelled of sea life, windblown from places beyond the horizon. All around Bridey, there was the musical cacophony of Greeks speaking to each other.

Her foolishness vanished. She took a deep breath of happiness and walked up the gangway.

"Sara, you're not helping!" Francesca complained. "We don't go anywhere if we don't both paddle."

The two girls balanced on something called a husky. It reminded Sara of a squat surfboard and came equipped with paddles, one of which Francesca was dipping furiously, going nowhere, while Sara knelt on the husky with her paddle dragging.

They were at anchor near a beach taverna on Egina. The water was crystal clear, creating the illusion that the bottom was near enough for Francesca to stand on. But it was at least twelve feet deep where they paddled. Francesca wore a miniature life jacket.

Uncle Hugh and Ian glided by them, propelled by Hugh's strong stroke of the paddle. Ian held his across his knees, shaking his fist in gleeful triumph as they passed the girls.

"Daddy, it's not fair!" Francesca called. "We're not racing!"

"Yes, we are!" Ian called back. He pushed his paddle through the water in imitation of his father's stroke, but only succeeded in giving Hugh's kneecap a painful bang.

"Ow!" Hugh yelped.

It's not fair, Sara echoed silently. She wasn't thinking about the race. She was watching Bridey aboard the boat, standing near the rail. Riordan smoothed sun oil across Bridey's shoulders and spine as she held her hair off her neck. His hands moved in firm, long strokes over Bridey's skin. He said something to Bridey that made her shrug him off with one shoulder. He laughed, and poured another dollop of oil onto his palm.

Ever since they'd gotten to Athens, things had changed, thought Sara. Sara mostly spent time with Francesca, hardly ever with Bridey. The hotel was beautiful. Yet she found herself reminiscing a lot about the tour, the Pilgrims, the Phantom. It had been better when it was just the four of them —- Sara and her mom, Aunt Tilla, and Bridey.

She continued to paddle through the sparkling, aquamarine water. Francesca giggled in front of her, trying to splash Hugh. But Sara was thinking about the morning in Assisi when she'd wakened Bridey and heard about her night with Alessandro. She'd felt so close to Bridey then.

I wonder what Alessandro would think now, Sara thought, *if he knew how much time Riordan Clarke spends with Bridey.*

Sara liked Alessandro. He treated her like a friend. Like she wasn't fourteen. Riordan Clarke was nice, but he treated her as if she were Francesca's age. She and Bridey slept in the same room at the Hilton, but she never had talks with Bridey now. It was as if Bridey lived in another dimension, or had crossed a border of a secret country for which Sara had no passport.

Riordan and Bridey jumped from the side of the boat in masks and snorkels. They surfaced long enough for him to give Bridey some instructions, and then the pair dove toward the bottom, leaving a swirl of sea in their place.

You're such a traitor, Sara thought, as she watched Bridey's form disappear as a wavy, distorted shadow. *You don't care if all I do is babysit, while you dance all night. You don't care about your mom's back. You probably don't care about Alessandro anymore.*

She smacked at the surface with her paddle, sending up a

spray of water.

Francesca squealed and smacked her paddle, too.

The three sisters sat finishing lunch in the Hilton's large coffee shop, savoring the air conditioning and an afternoon free of children. A large piece of baklava sat half-finished in front of Corinne. She gathered flakes of phyllo crust and nut fragments with the tines of her fork, mashing them together, and swiped through a pool of honey glaze.

Maura smoked for dessert. She'd eaten nothing more than a small salad. Corinne was alarmed at how little her sister actually ate on any given day, but she'd stopped commenting on it, since that did nothing more than irritate Maura. Maura irritable was daunting, she had a way of sniping at the least little personality quirk that crossed her line of fire.

Tilla attempted another experimental drag on her Pall Mall. She made a face and tamped it out. There was something about the medication she was on that made everything taste odd. Consequently she'd hardly touched her lunch, either. She existed now on broth, vanilla milkshakes, and toast, with an occasional craving for olives and artichoke hearts. Despite being almost immobile for a week and a half, she'd lost more weight. The sharpness of her elbows seemed exaggerated to her. The curve of her collarbone was a bas relief beneath her blouse. She touched her hand to her jaw and wondered if it looked as bony as it felt.

Her perception of what was real versus how it felt was very off. *She* was very off. Her hair was a flattened heap and it didn't bother her. Nothing did. She could feel her attention slide. Concentration was a muddy track.

The medication kept her in a dream state, where the dream was real life going on around her, while she slept with or without her eyes open. It was a happy dream, either way. She was with her sisters and the children, with nothing to worry about. Even Hugh was there, a great reassuring presence, and he was solicitous and gentle with her. She knew he had cabled Rob and explained the situation, told him he would send everyone home when she'd had time to regroup from the pain. The medicine made her not care if there was pain or there wasn't.

Maura set her cigarette in the ashtray they shared and leaned across the table to Tilla. "Come here, darling," she said. "Bend toward me if you can."

Tilla braced her hands against the back of the booth seat near her hips and pushed herself in slow-motion toward Maura. Corinne placed an automatic arm around Tilla at mid-back, in support.

"You're really not moving well at all," said Corinne.

"I'm better," said Tilla.

"Better than what? Just say the word, and we'll get you back up in bed for the afternoon," said Maura. "You don't have to sit here for our sakes." Maura reached across to run her fingers through the top and sides of Tilla's soft, gold hair. She brushed the hair gently behind Tilla's ears, away from her face.

"You look horrid, Babe," Maura said. "We should take you to the salon and get something done with your hair."

"Would they send someone up to the room?" Corinne asked. She eased Tilla backwards. Maura's negative assessment hadn't fazed Tilla.

"Why didn't I think of that?" Maura said. "Of course it could be done. We could wash her hair in the shower, and the beautician could take it from there. I think it would make a world of difference to have your hair done, Till. It always feels so good. Remember how Mam used to wash our hair and put us in clean nightgowns when we had mumps or measles, and it felt so good to get cleaned up?"

"I remember her mustard plasters," Corinne said. "And the cod liver oil and the milk of magnesia… I remember burning my cheeks over pots of boiling water."

"But you always felt better for them," Maura reminded her.

Tilla sighed. "I miss Mam." Her mother was long gone, dead for twenty-six of Tilla's thirty-eight years. Bridey didn't know what it was like to grow up without a mother, to only have older sisters to fill the gap.

"We could do it after you have a nap," said Maura. "While everyone is gone. It's just us girls." Maura picked up her cigarette and resumed smoking. "We have to take advantage of this moment in time. We'll get our Babe here back in shape and have a ball. But first —..." She eyed Tilla, who looked exhausted. "We'll get you some rest."

"I think it's time for my next pill." Tilla turned to Corinne. "Isn't it?"

Corinne checked her watch. Technically, Tilla still had another hour or more to go. "It's not quite time yet," Corinne said.

"If it keeps her more comfortable, what's it hurt to have it now?" Maura said. She studied Tilla's hair. "Something short and gamine, I think. Something cool, yet sophisticated."

"Tilla's worn her hair this way for ages," Corinne objected. "What's Rob going to do if she goes home with her hair all chopped off?"

Maura stamped out her cigarette and signed the tab. "He'll love it. She'll be a new person when she leaves here. The last thing a man wants is monotony. They love it when they don't know what to expect from a woman."

"Oh, really?" Corinne said. "My husband loves nothing more than knowing exactly what to expect every day, from everyone." Garner was not a man who would have bumped around on a tour bus and shared bathrooms on a hotel floor. He was a man who wore a shirt and tie five days a week right up until bedtime. The news that his wife and daughter would not come home on the expected date had thrown him momentarily, but since he was commuting back and forth between New York City and Washington working on some legislation, it worked out okay for him.

"What do you think, Till?" said Maura. "Want to bring home a new woman to Rob?"

"Who?" Tilla asked.

"You, silly!"

"Oh," said Tilla. "Sure."

Twenty-Three

Riordan and Bridey treaded water together fifteen yards from the stern of the boat. They moved lazily, buoyant in the cool sea, resting from several dives to the bottom. Bridey's diving mask sat like a rubber crown on her head, skinning her hair tightly back from her face. Riordan's hair lay flat and lashes around his deep-set eyes clumped with wet droplets. It made him look younger, somehow vulnerable. Bridey liked him much better as teacher and guide, or with his mouth shut and occupied by a snorkel.

In the silence of the water, he was relaxed and encouraging, patient with her first attempts to dive and not inadvertently suck in water through the tube. When they pulled their way down through the water again to the bright sandy bottom, Riordan pointed out a hidden bottom-feeder. The fish was shy and sought to bury itself as soon as possible. Only when they got back to the surface for the last time did Riordan inform her it was a type of shark.

The water was peridot green and as sparkling as a swimming

pool. Bridey watched the legs of her family dangle above them on the huskies, alien extensions into the world below the surface. The boat's shadowed bottom loomed over her.

She followed Riordan underwater, staying close. Her experience with diving extended only to dunks in lakes at home, opening her eyes to watch sunfish guard their nests under wooden docks, or games with her friends in swimming pools. The unlimited expanse of the Aegean unnerved her, but she had Riordan as a reference point below. When a small ray glided into their range, she whirled to find Riodan. She was glad to grab his hand, to kick back to the surface, to feel safe in his competence.

On the surface, Bridey stretched out in a back float, while Riordan described the merits of scuba diving in deeper water, the sound of his voice muffled by the water over her ears. The sun seemed to shine directly over her. Nothing could be more perfect than this moment, unless she were on the terrace in Umbria, and the voice was Alessandro's. Her hair floated like fine seaweed around her head. The fabric of her white bikini clung semi-transparent to her wet skin. Suddenly, Riordan's face was close to hers. She let herself drop out of her float and was caught in Riordan's hands.

"Careful. It's a dangerous thing to offer up one's self to Zeus so carelessly. He has a very bad record with young goddesses." The volume of his voice was turned down, as if he didn't want it broadcast over the water.

"Don't be ridiculous," Bridey said. She could feel her breasts nearly floating out of the demi-cups of her bikini top. The fact that they were very near the dark mat of hair on Riordan's chest excited and embarrassed her.

"Didn't they teach you about the gods and goddesses at that little convent school?"

"Roman ones. I studied Latin."

"Upstarts. I'm talking about the real stuff. Zeus and Hera. Aphrodite. Eros. Priapus."

Her heart was pounding. The muscles in his shoulders and

arms looked like smooth stone glazed by the water. She had a
vision of Alessandro braced over her on the grass, in the dark.

"Of course I know them," she said to Riordan.

"Not well, I'll wager. Not the real stories. I'm sure the good
nuns gave you the hygienic version, all dolled up and neutered.
The fact is, the gods were a lusty bunch. Particularly Zeus. Amazing he had time to rule gods and men, with his appetites."

"What are you talking about?" A lap of seawater hit her
mouth. She could taste the bitter salt.

"You. Don't think I don't know what you're doing. Striking
poses. Parading at the pool. Stretching out on the altar. I think
you get my meaning. I certainly get yours."

"If you mean floating in the sun, then leave it to you to turn
it into some double meaning."

She kicked her fins and accidentally brushed his thigh with
hers. He held her arm. The strap of her suit top slipped off her
shoulder and she reached quickly to pull it back in place, before
her breast spilled from the cup. Too late. It bobbed up, a flash
of white flesh, like the underbelly of a fish. He glanced down as
she hiked at the cup to cover herself. There was so little between
them beneath the surface of the water. Just a few inches of fabric.
He stared hard at her and she knew he was thinking the same
thing. She was eye to eye with him, their mouths just above the
rim of the water. The salt taste made her cough.

"Let go of me. I can't swim like this."

"You're not in your world anymore," he said. "You're in Zeus'
world. So new rules apply. If you think you can keep pretending
innocence and naiveté here, you're wrong. Zeus didn't give a shit
for innocence. It was an aphrodisiac to him."

"I don't know what you're talking about. Let go."

He let go. "Don't play games, little goddess. You know damn
well what I mean." He turned and started swimming for the boat.

Bridey didn't follow Riordan back to the boat. Not while her throat felt tight, not with tears welling. God, she hated him. He was the nastiest, the most conceited... She pulled on her mask, fitted the snorkel into her mouth, and plunged her burning face into the water. She saw nothing of the life below. Her eyes blurred with tears. They dropped inside the faceplate of her mask. What had she done to deserve him ruining a perfect day? He was the one who suggested snorkeling. Why was he with them in the first place? There was never a way to be free of his presence. Every day, she thought he might leave and go back to Jordan, or wherever it was that he belonged, and leave her in peace. But he was stuck like glue to her uncle. He reminded her of a Doberman Pinscher, trained and intense, sleek at his master's side. No matter how you might wish to play with it, you dared not forget it could bare its fangs at any moment. But why would Uncle Hugh need someone like that around? Who would he be guarding Uncle Hugh from? Her? Uncle Hugh's own family? Who else was around him?

A bodyguard.

Of course. It made sense, with Uncle Hugh in the government, though she still had no idea what exactly her uncle did. Or if he might need protection. He wasn't an Ambassador. But it would explain some things. A bodyguard can't leave. He would have no choice but to stay, even if it meant hanging around women and children.

He must be so bored.

Good.

She stopped crying. She had to admit, she knew exactly what she was doing, floating in front of him, and why she wore this particular bikini today. It was difficult to cry and breathe with the snorkel. She wiped her nose under water. At least we have that much in common, she told herself. I'm not here to be bored, either. She swam in lazy circles, thinking. The sun burned her back and shoulders. The thing that was hardest to swallow was the truth, something he never had trouble bringing up to her. There were no allowances made for her age or inexperience. Each time he challenged her, he expected things from her she didn't always understand. If she met the challenge, she was rewarded with his estimation. If she didn't, she failed in her own.

I *like teasing him. I like knowing I'm putting him through something. It's a game I like winning.*

She'd lost just now, though. Lost this round. She wasn't thinking anything in particular when she was floating beside him, only thinking about Assisi. Not deliberately, at least. Just feeling confident. Feeling happy and alive.

What to do now? She still wanted to get to the Plaka, to the beach, places Riordan could take her, places he'd practically promised. He was her ticket out of the hotel.

I can do this, she thought. *I can handle him.*

His apology came as a surprise.

It came when she was curled up with Ian on the raised midsection of the boat, which formed the roof of the galley below. The roof was fitted with thick canvas mats, shaded by the second mast and an orange tarp awning. It made a perfect spot to rest out of the sun. She and the children were not allowed to go below for any reason other than to use the head. Below decks was the province of the silent, dark crewmen.

Hugh ordered a rest time for Ian, who was becoming sunburned over his already substantial tan, and planned to take Francesca and Sara back to the island's beach at Agia Marina to find some treats. This caused a massive meltdown in Ian, who despite his exhaustion and raging tears, couldn't understand why he needed to be left behind. Ian would only stay down for Bridey.

The two cousins curled toward each other. Bridey was in the process of singing him to sleep. Her choice of lullabies was unorthodox, but effective: Beatles songs. Sung softly and slowly, you could turn nearly any one into a ballad. Ian liked "No Reply" and "The Night Before" particularly.

Bridey could smell the sun and salt on Ian's skin, a faded scent of lotion and the perspire-y caramel fragrance of his hair. As she sang, she stroked her fingers lightly through the tangle of his curls, the way Tilla would do in Bridey's weepier moments. He sighed deeply, melting toward the edge of sleep.

"Bridey," he whispered. "Do you want to have babies when you grow up?"

"I think so."

"Which would you rather have, boy babies, or girls?"

"Well, I don't know."

"You're a girl, of course, so it's natural you should like them."

"Yes, but I like boys, too."

"You should have boy babies. I think boy babies would very much like you to be their mother."

His seriousness and sincerity swept her, an undertow in the surf of a new maternal ocean. She stroked the velvet of his cheek with her fingertips. "Thank you, Ian."

He closed his eyes. "Sing No Reply again."

She did, humming toward the end because he'd fallen asleep. She was still humming, almost inaudibly, when she realized Riordan was standing at the far end of the platform, watching. She acknowledged his presence with her eyes, but said nothing. He came to sit on the edge of the canvas mattress on Ian's side. Bridey braced herself. Instead, his voice was soft.

"You're very good with him," said Riordan.

She nodded. A compliment. An olive branch.

They didn't speak for several minutes. The boat rocked gently in a developing breeze. The sounds of sea birds and the rhythmic, strange music from the tavernas' loudspeakers on the shore filled the space between them.

"What kind of name is Riordan?" she asked, to break the silence.

"What kind of name does it sound like?"

"Irish?"

"Right you are, Miss McKenna. A gift from my mother. Or a curse, depending how you look at it."

"How can anything Irish be a curse?" There he goes again, she thought. More insults. But she realized quickly he wasn't referring to her own heritage.

"My mother was a romantic. She died when I was five. Just Ian's age. She was American." He caught Bridey's look of amazement. "Born in Boston, one generation off the boat from Ireland. She met my father there when he was over from Britain on business, and they eloped and came to live in England. She was disinherited for it. The British are the devil, you see. I'm sure your own family has said so."

"Not really," Bridey said.

"She died in a car accident. I remember crying so much when they told me. I tossed up on the nursery floor. I must have puked out all my tears, because I haven't shed one since. Two years later, I was sent off to boarding school and a lifetime of insults and worse. I had tainted blood, according to my schoolmates, on both counts. Being part Irish and part American. So I developed a hard shell, because it seemed like the only way to get through. But it stood me well in the Army, that shell." Ian stirred and rolled over in his sleep. His face relaxed into the angelic beauty of sleeping little boys. Riordan looked down on him. "My father got remarried to a proper English lady and I've been able to overcome the mongrel tag in the bargain. I may have Irish American blood in my veins, but it's not so noticeable now. So I suppose you could say it all worked out."

Bridey mulled over this new information. So he wasn't quite as superior as he acted. It would almost be sad, if he weren't so determined to be blasé about it.

"Look," Riordan said finally. "I'm telling you this because I'm sorry. I've been rough on you. It's uncharacteristic of me." He looked over at her to see if she believed that. "You were being a good sport in the water, and I misread..."

Silence was more effective than anything she could think to say. It was gratifying to see him flounder. The great Mr. Clarke.

"I enjoy our skirmishes, make no mistake. I'm sure we'll have more. Don't think I've gone completely soft. I just didn't mean to come down so hard on you."

He changed tack. "You make a lovely picture, gathered around a little one. Quite natural. Funny choice of lullabies, though."

"I don't know any real ones."

"Perhaps you should learn some. Lullabies, I mean. No doubt they'll come in handy in the near future."

She sat up, taking care not to disturb Ian. Talking to Riordan prone and nestled around the little boy was suddenly too intimate a position.

"What do you mean, near future?" said Bridey.

"Nothing. I only expect someone someday will be inspired to help you fill a nursery, is all."

"I have a lot of plans before anything like that happens."

"I'm sure you do. There is no question in my mind that you have plans." He glanced at her, half-smiling. "But that's the beauty of being your age, isn't it? Plans can change quickly. You're not locked into any one thing."

"I feel pretty locked in, sometimes," she admitted. "Parents. School."

He gazed out over the water, away from her. "Yes. It's easy to feel locked in sometimes."

Bridey hugged her knees and rested her chin on them. She thought of Alessandro and the feelings he stirred in her, back in the churchyard, in the dark. It was a frightening thought, how fast you'd change plans when you felt certain things.

"I'm not an easy person," Riordan said. "I tend to be sharp and I have no patience for foolishness. But I did think, out there in the water... Well. I was wrong."

You lost control, Bridey thought. *Just the tiniest bit. It didn't feel good, did it? Losing something to me. Someone you don't think is in your league.* Realizing this, she felt she could afford to be generous. This little conversation, this peek into his softer side, might be her bargaining chip. After all, though he was difficult, he was the only game in town. "I'll let you make it up to me," she said.

"Will you?" There was a pinch of sarcasm in his voice. "How might I do that?"

She shifted, tucking her legs beneath her, straightening her spine. His eyes slipped over her but it was a covert glance, she knew. Very unlike Alessandro, whose eyes went anywhere and stayed for as long as he liked.

"You promised to take me out to see Athens."

"Was it a promise?"

"Can we go?"

He arched his brows, teasing. "Are you asking me out on a date?"

"No. I'm holding you to your promise."

"I would argue semantics. But all right." He shook his head and laughed. "What have I gotten into?"

She grew prim. "I'd rather not go with someone who thinks of it as a drag, if that's the case. Like it's a reason for dread."

"That's a bit melodramatic."

"Well, what are you saying?"

"I'm saying I'll do it, if that would make you happy, oh Princess." He gave a semblance of a bow.

Despite herself, Bridey broke into a grin. "Great!" she said.

Riordan stood up. He gripped the edge of the awning and leaned in toward her. "When I get back to Amman, I'm going to have my head examined."

Twenty-Four

There is an art to painting toenails and Sara was an artist. She had a steady hand and a delicate touch, pulling solid little lines of polish across the smooth, neat tops of Bridey's toenails. Bridey sat at the end of her bed with her foot cradled in Sara's lap. Sara sat on the floor facing her, bent over her work, lips pressed together in concentration. Beside her, Francesca leaned over the process, absorbed, apprentice to the master. They were using Maura's polish. The color was called Flame of Desire — Sara translated from the French label, and it was a pure, deep red. This was something brazen, far from the pearly pink or pale peach colors Bridey experimented with the previous summer.

"Francesca!" Sara sighed with exasperation. A strand of the little girl's hair brushed over Bridey's freshly painted middle toe, leaving a thin red line outward from the cuticle, and a trace of polish in Francesca's hair.

"I'm sorry," Francesca said. She pulled her fingers through her hair, wiping the polish, and held her smeared fingers for her own inspection.

"You're making a bigger mess," Sara said, irritated with Francesca's presence. She wanted to talk to Bridey, really talk, but that was impossible to do with a five-year-old hanging on every word.

The painting was ceremonial. Bridey was going on a date with Riordan. Of course, no one was allowed to call it a date. Bridey was vehement on this point.

"I really want to see some things in Athens," Bridey had explained to Sara earlier. "I can't go by myself, so Riordan said he'd take me."

"I want to see things, too," Sara said. "Can't I go?"

"Not sight-seeing. I'm talking about neighborhoods and how people live normally. Places where they play music and dance at night. You have to be older."

Sara's mouth screwed with disappointment. What made everyone think she wasn't old enough to appreciate things or have fun? And yet she was old enough to be Ian and Francesca's nursemaid.

"He said he'd take you?" Sara said. "Does that mean you asked him out?"

"It isn't that kind of thing." But it must have been that kind of thing, because Bridey had her false eyelashes on.

"Your mom would have a fit if she knew you were going out with an older guy," Sara pointed out, though she figured Aunt Tilla would have a fit no matter who it was.

"My mom knows. And she's not upset because she knows it isn't any kind of date."

Tilla didn't get upset about much these days. She existed in a state of chemical mellowness. It was like an alien spaceship had come down and taken Tilla away and left a pod in her place. If it kept her out of pain and relatively numb, both Sara and Bridey assumed Tilla would get back to being herself when they got home. In the meantime, Tilla's acquiescence suited Bridey's purposes.

"I thought you didn't like him. You've been saying what a

stuck-up jerk he is."

"Who's a stuck up jerk?" Francesca asked.

"No one you know," Sara told her.

"He can be." Bridey watched Francesca examine her own toes, touching each one ceremoniously.

"Then why do you spend so much time around him?" Sara hoped her voice didn't betray the hurt that stabbed through her stomach.

"Well, he's hard to get away from, isn't he? He's not hanging around just because he's Uncle Hugh's friend. I think it's much more than that."

"Like what?"

"Like he's some kind of connection officially. He's from the Embassy, too. Otherwise, why would someone like him hang around every day and night with our family?"

Sara hadn't given it much thought. Uncle Hugh and Aunt Maura lived a strange life with unusual friends and she'd always accepted them that way.

"I think he's some kind of bodyguard," said Bridey.

"A bodyguard?" Sara considered this. "Then, if he's a bodyguard, wouldn't he have to be with Uncle Hugh every second? Why would he be able to leave and go out with you?"

"I don't know! I haven't figured it out yet. I just know he's not hanging around on vacation, that's all."

This new slant on Riordan Clarke intrigued Sara. She thought it was kind of weird that he wanted to come along on the boat with them. She thought it was because he wanted to hang around Bridey.

"So Uncle Hugh could have told him to take you out," Sara speculated. "And dance with you and make sure you had a good time."

"I doubt Uncle Hugh would do that." Bridey's voice was sharp. Very sharp.

Sara dotted the last of the first coat of polish on Bridey's little toe.

They both admired the effect, ten rubies adorning Bridey's feet.

"Don't move now," Sara warned. "They have to dry for the next coat."

"They look nice," Bridey said. "You do a good job, Sare."

"I have good hands," Sara said. She screwed the cap and brush back into the bottle of polish temporarily. "Probably comes from playing the piano." Francesca snatched up the polish and began to shake the bottle. "Put that down, Francesca. You don't have to shake it now."

"You're cross." Francesca pouted. She placed the polish back on the floor next to the remover and crossed her arms.

Corinne appeared in their doorway. She walked over to the bed and Bridey held her feet up to be inspected. Corinne whistled. "Don't they look sexy!" She spotted Francesca's protruding lip. "What's this? Look at that lip stick out!" she teased. "Can I have a ride on it?"

Francesca shook her head.

"Come here, Sweetpea," Corinne said. She held her hands out to her niece. Francesca sprang to her feet and let Corinne lift her into her arms. Corinne groaned with the effort. Francesca's legs dangled nearly past Corinne's knees. She slumped against Corinne, who wobbled slightly, carrying her off.

Bridey fanned her toes with a magazine, urging them to dry.

Sara rolled onto her back and stared at the ceiling.

"I'm sorry, Sare, " said Bridey. "You aren't having much fun around here, are you?"

"Oh, yeah. It's a ball baby-sitting night and day."

"Why don't you say something? Let them know you'd like to come to dinner, or go somewhere."

"Sure. Sit at dinner and get picked on for manners, or have Uncle Hugh ask me a zillion questions I can't answer? Or just sit there with no one to talk to."

"You could talk to me," Bridey said.

"When would we do that? In between your dances with

Riordan?" Sara sighed. She took the magazine from Bridey, and touched a tentative fingertip to Bridey's big toe. "I think they're ready for the second coat."

Bridey's hair was still set in giant rollers when Maura and Hugh came to their suite, dressed down for the evening. Bridey had picked the black and white Courreges dress for her evening in the city.

Tilla sat on the loveseat, staring into space. She had progressed to spending most of the day out of bed, but only with the aid of her pills. By the late evening, she was already asleep for the night. She'd taken a dose a half hour ago, to help her through dinner. She looked so relaxed that it made her appear much younger. Her hair was cut in a gamine style, very short, in layers framing her face. Bridey thought her mother looked a little like Twiggy. What would Rob say when he saw his wife again, a world traveler and looking very chic? Surely by that time she'd look chic, not just completely stoned.

Corinne and the children came in from the balcony. It was another perfect, balmy evening in Athens, if still somewhat hot. Below their balcony, the pool area had emptied out, except for a lone swimmer doing laps.

"Sara!" Corinne called toward the bathroom, where Sara was getting out of the shower. Sara appeared, wrapped in one of the hotel's terry robes and sat on the arm of an upholstered chair.

"We have a surprise for you all," Hugh said, lifting Francesca into his arms.

Bridey was only mildly curious at this announcement. She checked her rollers for dryness. Done. She began to unfasten them, one by one.

"We're all going to be leaving the hotel," Hugh began.

Bridey dropped a roller in her lap and stopped moving. She had two left on her crown. It looked like strange headdress.

"Leaving?" Corinne said.

"I have a friend who has offered the use of his villa to us," said Hugh. "It's on a little island, far south of here. I recommend everyone get packed tonight. I'm sorry you'll have to cut your evening a bit short tonight, Bridey. Riordan knows about this, so he'll have you back to pack and get some sleep."

"How are we getting there?" Corinne asked. She looked at Tilla.

"Does it have a beach?" Ian asked.

"It's an island, Ian," Maura said. She pulled the boy onto her lap and smoothed his hair. "It has beaches everywhere."

"How big is this villa?" Corinne asked. "We're quite a group."

"Five bedrooms; plenty of room for all of us. One of the bedrooms is smaller, but it will do for Riordan."

Sara shot Bridey a look, but Bridey was staring up at her uncle with her mouth half open.

"This is kind of sudden, isn't it?" Corinne asked. Her eyes narrowed a fraction.

"It's only just come up," Hugh said. He exchanged glances with his wife.

"Sit back and enjoy the ride," Maura told her. "You're in the best of hands."

Bridey removed the last of her rollers. She shook out her smoothed hair and scratched at the roller marks on her scalp. It all just kept getting better.

"Did you get that?" Sara said to her as Bridey brushed out her hair in their bathroom. "He's coming with us to the island. I think you're right. Why else would he be going, unless he was a bodyguard?"

"If he is, that means that Uncle Hugh needs protection. And if he needs protection, so do we, because we're with him." Bridey slipped on her dress and turned her back to Sara. "Zip me, will you?"

Sara pulled the zipper up. "Ask him tonight," she said to Bridey. "While you have him alone."

"I don't know if I want to know," Bridey said.

They were still sitting in the suite when the room phone rang. Hugh took the phone . "I see," he said to the caller, and left without any further explanation.

A half hour passed. Her Aunt Maura didn't seem the least perturbed with the delay, or the absence of her husband. It was probably a normal thing for her, Bridey figured. Maybe something had come up about Uncle Hugh's work. Who knew? Even here in Athens, on his holiday, Uncle Hugh often was gone for part of the day, off to who knows where, or with whom. He didn't live a regular life. He wasn't a regular man.

Hugh had a story he told all the kids in her family. It was her brother Daniel's favorite, about the time when Hugh was living in Kashmir and he found a snake on his doorstep. He said it was a cobra, but Bridey didn't know if that was just an embellishment on the story to make it scarier. Uncle Hugh would do a trick with a matchbook hidden in his hand, where he flicked a match out and lit it with his thumb so fast, it was like magic. This was at the point in the story when he said he grabbed the snake with his other hand — 'like lightning!' — and burned the snake's face, tossing it a hundred feet. If any other man had told this story, she probably would have grown up to disbelieve. But it wasn't just any man. Uncle Hugh seemed to have no fear in him. There was no telling what he could do. Whenever he told the story in front of her dad, her father would sit and listen with a skeptical smile, as if in conspiracy with his brother-in-law. But Bridey didn't think her dad really believed it was true.

Bridey wasn't confident that this call wouldn't turn into some kind of kink in her plans, or mean that her night was canceled. But if it did, at least she had the trip to the island tomorrow to think about.

The phone rang again. Maura picked it up. Maura listened, a tiny crease appearing between her brows. She glanced at Bridey.

That can't be good, Bridey thought, twirling a strand of hair at the back of her head.

"Corinne," Maura called, hanging up the receiver. "Could you come downstairs with me?"

"Is everything okay?" Corinne asked, hesitating.

"Something has come up unexpectedly, and Hugh would like us to come down," said Maura. "Bridey, can you take care of things up here for the time being?"

Tilla rested her head on the wall in back of the sofa and closed her eyes, in the middle of a pain killer float. If left to it, the float would take her downstream to a still pool of light sleep.

"Sure," Bridey said. "Is Uncle Hugh with Riordan? He was supposed to be here about twenty minutes ago."

"Yes," Maura said. And that was all. She and Corinne were out the door and gone.

Twenty-Five

Maura and Corinne didn't come back immediately, so Bridey, trying to hide her growing disappointment and irritation, pulled out a few sheets of Hilton stationery to entertain the twins with drawing.

Sara started her packing. She was looking forward to a change of scene. This hotel had become a monotony of days hanging around five-year-olds and her dazed, ailing aunt. She tried to imagine what the island would be like and how their routine would change. Maybe they'd go to the beach, or the market, or whatever was on this little island. Maybe she'd get to ride a donkey. That would be something to write about. She flopped down on her bed amid neat piles of clothing and pulled out her log. She was several days behind in it, so this might be a good opportunity to catch up.

The room phone in the suite rang for the third time.

Now what? Sara thought. "I can answer it!" she heard Francesca say. Before Bridey could protest, the little girl snatched up the phone.

"Hello, Mummy," Francesca said. She nodded to her mother's voice. "Yes, she's right here. Francesca held the phone out to Bridey. "She wants to speak with you."

Sara got up and walked to the doorway of her room to watch Bridey. This could only mean one thing : that she was doomed to spend this evening exactly as she had done, with the twins and Aunt Tilla.

"Yes?" Bridey answered. She looked over at Sara with a half-frown, half-question. What could be going on now? "I'll be right down."

"Does she want to speak to me?" Ian asked. He looked up from drawing a monster with five horns and a lion's mane.

Bridey hung up the phone. "I have to go to the lobby," she said to Ian. "But your dad is coming back up. Sara, Riordan is waiting down there, so I'm going to take my purse and I might be leaving."

"What's the big mystery?" Sara asked.

"No idea." Bridey dashed into their bathroom and checked her face, then applied some lipstick. She had a deep tan and was wearing her false eyelashes, which she'd cut up and applied in tiny sections. The dress hit her mid-thigh and jeweled sandals sparkled on her crimson-toed feet. Sara thought Bridey really did look more like The Shrimp than ever. For someone who wasn't going out on a date, she thought, her cousin sure had pulled out the stops.

Aunt Maura had told Bridey to meet them in the bar lounge, off the marble main lobby. Bridey assumed Riordan would be there too, waiting for her. Her step was full of optimistic bounce as she exited the elevator and strode happily through the lobby. When she entered the lounge, her step slowed and she squinted myopically through the dimmed light looking for her relatives.

She saw Aunt Maura wave at her at the back of the lounge. Relieved, she wended her way through the room, heading for the table where her two aunts and Hugh sat, along with two men who had their backs to her. One of them was Riordan, she could see.

So that's the hold up, she thought. *Someone showed up and they had to entertain him. Maybe it's the person who owns the villa.* She smiled at the little cluster. Corinne's eyes were riveted on Bridey.

Riordan and the other man pushed their chairs back to stand. Riordan's expression, a mixture of annoyance and hostility, caught Bridey by surprise. She feared that it meant she'd done something to wreck his mood. She barely noticed the other man until Riordan turned his face and looked at him.

It's strange, Bridey would muse years later, how the brain doesn't register recognition of someone out of context. That's why it took her a few suspended moments to take in the face of the young man beside Riordan, who drank Bridey in with eyes full with hope and expectation.

"I believe you know this young man," her uncle said.

The man stepped forward, held his hand out as if to shake hers, and then put it down.

"*Buona sera,* Bridey," he said.

Bridey's breath rushed in and came out in a strangled, high-pitched squeal of shock and joy. She held her arms out.

"Oh my God," she said, throwing herself into his arms. "Alessandro," she said, into the warm flesh of his throat. They stood for a moment, hugging each other tightly.

"I tell you, I come," he whispered to her.

It was excruciating to sit with Alessandro by her side. It felt alien, formal, and surreal as she tried to act polite and not rocket off her chair into hyperspace. Bridey held his hand, stealing glances at him as they sat, listening to the recounting of how Alessandro had come to the front desk to ask for her at precisely the time that Riordan was informing the clerk of his check-out for the next day.

Riordan sat on Bridey's other side like a guard dog. He toyed with the remnants of his drink in his glass, tilting the scotch from one side to another, looking uninterested.

"But, how did you get here?" Bridey asked Alessandro. She still couldn't believe her eyes. He was really there beside her, flesh and blood. Her heart was thudding in her chest. Her face felt hot.

"I know from your letter, the hotel," he said. "So, I take the train from Assisi, to Rome. And from Rome, the plane. I go this morning." Beneath the table, his thumb traced a nervous path back and forth across her hand.

"He's barely had time to check into his hotel," Corinne said.

"You're not staying here?" Bridey asked him.

Beside her, Riordan gave a contemptuous snort. "Hardly."

"I am in little hotel, only small walk from here," Alessandro said.

"We've been visiting with Alessandro," Hugh interjected. "Any young man who travels all the way from Assisi to Athens to see you deserves getting to know a bit."

"Who called you in the hotel room?" Bridey asked her uncle. But she knew already. She turned to Riordan. "You?"

"Yes, of course," Riordan said. "I thought it best to alert your family." He looked past her at Alessandro. "He might have been any unsavory character from the street, asking for our Bridey."

Our Bridey?

Alessandro stared back at him, unsmiling. "But I am not from street," he said to Riordan. "I am her friend, and the friend to Signora LeDoux, and to little Sara." He looked to Corinne for confirmation.

"It's fantastic to see him again," Corinne said. "Alessandro is a man of his word and an artist. I've already extended an invitation to come to my home for dinner when he comes to New York, which I'm sure he will, someday."

"We've been grilling him like a trout," Maura announced. "Asking all sorts of questions. Alessandro has been marvelous to put up with us, when he's probably ready to drop with fatigue from his trip."

"No," Alessandro said, gazing at Bridey. "I am no tired, now I see Bridey."

He looks wonderful, Bridey thought. She'd been with him in Assisi only a little more than two weeks ago, and yet it seemed longer. She'd been thinking and dreaming about him all those days and nights. The physical reality of having him beside her was almost too much.

"All that way for so little time," Riordan said. He picked a cigarette from the pack in his suit coat pocket and snapped a lighter open, flicking it into flame. The cigarette lit and Riordan took a long drag, letting the smoke stream from his nose like a dragon. "Really bad timing, sadly."

Riordan was clean shaven and wore the same light colored suit he'd had at the first dinner on the roof. It had been cleaned and pressed, his shirt white and starched, emphasizing the tan he'd gotten. He certainly looked like a man ready for a date.

Bridey's gut twisted. The trip tomorrow. The shock of seeing Alessandro wiped the fact that she was scheduled to leave in the morning right out of her mind.

Alessandro said nothing. He simply looked at Bridey as if he couldn't see anyone else in the room.

"Is there any reason Alessandro couldn't go with you tonight?" Corinne asked.

There was dead silence at the table. Maura and Hugh exchanged glances. Bridey could feel the tension between Riordan and Alessandro. If they were dogs, they would sniff each other with hackles raised, peeing on bushes to claim their territory. Bridey wanted Alessandro to herself, but she didn't see how they could be alone. Another chance to be with him, and the clock was her enemy once again.

Hugh rose from his chair. "I'm going up to the suite," he announced. "Alessandro, it's good to meet you. Perhaps we'll see you later this evening?"

Alessandro stood up, shaking hands. "*Si*. I hope. I am sorry," he said to Hugh. "I don' wish to make problem for your plans tonight."

"Nonsense," Hugh said. "You've just made it more interesting. Have you ever been to Athens before?"

"No, *Signore*."

Hugh came around to the other side of the table and gave Riordan's shoulder a clap. "The three of you should have a wonderful time, then."

Bridey, Alessandro, Corinne and Riordan walked north to Kolonaki Square. Bridey and Alessandro trailed behind, holding hands, while Bridey made every effort to keep Alessandro from voicing the question she sensed he was gnawing on, about how she came to be ready for an evening out with Riordan.

They found a taverna and sat through an awkward dinner of stilted conversation, sticking to comments on the grilled fish and Bridey and Corinne's aversion to eating anything with the head still attached. Corinne asked Alessandro why he'd never been to Greece; it was so close to Italy. But Siena, Padova — those were more in Alessandro's range of travel and experience.

Riordan sat chain smoking cigarettes and looking periodically at his watch. He ordered a bottle of ouzo and the one smile he cracked for the evening was when Bridey nearly choked on the small sip she took, coughing red-faced and teary-eyed for several minutes. Alessandro and Riordan toasted the ladies, and Bridey took pleasure in the fact that Alessandro kept pace with Riordan, two card players matching hands.

Corinne acted as chaperone. She knit the conversation

together and filled gaps. With years of experience as a corporate wife, she knew how to keep the attention even-handed, putting Alessandro at ease while acknowledging Riordan's generosity and hospitality. Riordan insisted on paying for all their dinners. A power move, Bridey thought, done to keep Alessandro on the lower end of the totem pole.

For Bridey below the surface swam a dark form, a creature of anxiety, reminding her of the hours slipping past.

If only he'd come sooner.

On the walk back to the hotel, Bridey tried to think of how she could spend time alone with Alessandro. She still had to pack, too. But when they arrived in the lobby, the concierge was waiting with instructions. She and Alessandro were to meet Maura and Hugh on the pool deck.

"Riordan, thank you for a lovely dinner," Corinne said. "I hope I wasn't too much of an imposition, horning in on your plans."

"On the contrary," Riordan said to her, "you saved me from being — what do you Yanks call it? A third wheel. I should have been enormously bored, otherwise." He said this loud enough for Bridey to hear.

"You didn't have to come," Bridey snapped. "No one twisted your arm."

"No, I suppose not," he said, his eyes contracting with annoyance. "But then you would have ended up at the hotel once again, wouldn't you? You did pester to see some of Athens. I remember a specific conversation on a boat. We could have gone to one of those places that cater to tourists, I suppose, with the Greeks dancing and smashing plates all over the place, but since we'll be on an authentic Greek island tomorrow, I think there'll be a better chance there of really experiencing the culture. I'm not one to shirk a duty. Or ignore an order."

His message was clear: don't think I looked forward to this, even before the Singing Waiter showed up. Riordan held out his hand to grip Alessandro's in a subtle wrestle meant to be painful.

"Nice to meet you, if I should never see you again," said Riordan.

"Don't pay any attention to him," Bridey told Alessandro as they made their way outside to the pool area. Alessandro flexed his crushed hand. "I told you he's been a thorn in my side since we've been here," said Bridey.

Alessandro took in Bridey's dress, the eye makeup, and her hair curled and poofed out with hair spray.

"He is no too much thorn for you, for dinner alone? Is what you plan, no?"

"It's not what you think," Bridey said.

"I think, maybe is crazy for me to be here." His step slowed to a halt.

Bridey stopped and faced him. "No, it's a miracle! It's like God answered my prayers. It's the wildest, most romantic thing ever. Riordan Clarke is an employee of my uncle. He's the least romantic thing I can think of. Most of the time he's a royal pain. I haven't left this hotel in over two weeks, except for one day on a boat. In all those days, I've thought about you a million times. And I just found out we're leaving tomorrow. Nothing has gone as I expected, or wanted."

Alessandro touched Bridey's face, as if verifying she was real. Her little flash of temper seemed to reassure him.

"If I have one night only, I do the right thing to come here," he said. "I think in Assisi: Do I love her? Do I dream this? To know, I must go to her. I must talk to your face. I must see in your eyes. So, I come."

Bridey head ached, maybe from ouzo, maybe from tension.

"I wish we could be alone somewhere!" She frowned with frustration. "Come on," she said. "We'd better go see what my aunt and uncle want."

Hugh, Maura, Bridey and Alessandro sat at the deserted pool bar. Bridey felt a cluster of knots developing in her stomach. She was sure it was nerves and not the fish she'd eaten at the taverna. Either way, it made her more nervous, generating more knots. A candle glowed in its small globe on the table, creating a sense of intimacy. A waiter stood at a discreet distance, ready to bring them anything they might want. Still, it felt as if she and Alessandro had been called to the principal's office and they weren't sure for what offense.

"Uncle Hugh and I have been talking," Maura said.

Hugh lit up one of his cigars and settled back. He didn't look upset. In fact, Bridey thought, he looked very relaxed, like he was at one of his meetings at the embassy. She imagined that, anyway.

"I am very sorry," Alessandro began, for the third time that evening. "I see, was very... eh... no good for me to come in a surprise, to come to Athens so quickly, to give no warnings. I receive Bridey's letters only three days ago. I don' know if she is in Athens today. I hope to find her."

Hugh shifted in his chair and leaned forward on the table, a man obviously ready to deal.

"Alessandro... my work is such that I am able to learn a great deal about people, through my own insight, and by way of information to which I have access. So I already know things about you, things that tell me you are who you say you are. Those things, coupled with the personal experiences and observations of my family members with regard to you, prompt me to consider the dilemma that's been created by your showing up at this particular point in time.

"We're scheduled to leave Athens in the morning, as you know. We have the opportunity to enjoy some time in the islands before we all have to head back to our homes."

The little candle flickered in its holder. Bridey saw it as a votive. *Father Clement, if you're up there, help us out*, thought Bridey. Minutes seemed to tick by.

"Alessandro, we are inviting you to come with us. Would you be able to do that?" Maura asked.

Bridey watched Alessandro's perfect profile. She counted the heartbeats beneath her breast. One. Two. Three. Four. Five.

"I don' understand," Alessandro said finally. "Come with your family?"

"Yes. We have room," Hugh said. "We'll be staying on the island of Santorini. An earthquake damaged a great deal of the towns, about twelve years ago. But it's still quite beautiful. Unless you want to kiss Bridey goodbye tonight and take your chances, it's your best bet to keep from wasting your trip here to see her." His hooded eyes watched Alessandro like a man watching a novice at a poker table.

Bridey recognized the expression that settled on Alessandro's face. She'd seen it in the olive garden at San Damiano and especially on the path at the hotel the next day, when he'd told her about the quarrel he'd had with his parents. It was torn, worried, and elated all at once. As for her, she was stupefied.

"I can no impose myself," he said, hesitant.

"If it were an imposition," Maura said gently, "we wouldn't invite you. Obviously, you have real feelings for Bridey or you wouldn't have gone to so much trouble to see her again."

"Where would he stay?" Bridey asked. The knots tightened.

"With Riordan," said Hugh. "Or if that doesn't suit, I'm sure we can find Alessandro a small room nearby."

"I 'ave money," Alessandro started. "What will be the expense for it?" He looked uncomfortable.

Alessandro and Riordan in the same room? Bridey cringed at the thought. If Riordan tormented her, what would he do to Alessandro? He was barely civil to him at dinner, not the least bit welcoming.

"You're going to Rome soon, are you not?" Hugh asked. Somehow in the conversation, his cigar had gone out. He re-lit it, puffing out a few clouds of smoke.

"*Si*. In one month." Beneath the table, against her thigh, Bridey could feel his leg bouncing as his foot jiggled on the concrete.

"Save your money for that," Hugh said. "We're being given a flight in a private plane and staying at a friend's villa, so there is no great expense involved. This island is somewhat of a backwater, really. Lots of fishermen and farmers. You'd only need spending money."

Alessandro looked into Bridey's eyes. Here was the man she sat with on the terrace in the sun of Assisi, holding hands and becoming aware of miracles. But, Bridey thought, maybe this was more than he bargained for when he decided to fly to Greece.

"Alessandro, you don't have to come," said Bridey. She would die of disappointment if he didn't. Yet she was scared to death that he would.

"I come, if is what you want," he said.

"Of course I do!"

Alessandro took a deep breath. "Yes! I love to come with you." He said this to Hugh and Maura, but he squeezed Bridey to him. She could feel him shaking.

"All right, then," Hugh said.

Alessandro jumped from his seat and came around to Hugh and Maura's side of the table. He kissed both Maura's cheeks, showering thanks in Italian. Bridey went to her uncle with an awkward hug.

"Thank you, Uncle Hugh," she whispered.

"Thank your aunts," Hugh said to her. "They've got much more of a romantic bent than I."

Alessandro shook Hugh's hand with unrestrained enthusiasm. "*Grazie mille!* How do I thank you for your generosity? I am so happy to know Bridey's most special family!"

Hugh shook back lightly, clamping the cigar out the side of his mouth. "Let's call it a night, shall we? Exchange your lire and meet us here at the hotel by ten a.m. If you should change your mind, call here before nine."

"I don' change it!" Alessandro assured him, still pumping Hugh's hand.

Bridey circled her aunt in a hug, bending over her. "Aunt Maura, I don't know what to say. Everything just keeps getting more and more amazing."

Maura reached up, the tinkling of her gold bangles filling the night air like fairy music. Their heads bent together. "I wanted your mother to send you over to us last year for a few weeks and she wouldn't hear of it," said Maura. "I know she never told you about the invitation. So consider this my revenge. Life has a way of finding its course, even if a few boulders block the stream. Now say goodnight to your Alessandro, and get packing."

Bridey hesitated. "What's Mumma going to say about this?"

"I don't think she'll put up much of a fight," said Maura.

Twenty Six

The sea passed beneath them as they flew at a lower altitude. The Cyclades islands rose like gems set into the silvery Aegean. Pockets of air sent the plane bumping and dipping. Alessandro looked queasy. Bridey's tried to be as nurse-like as she could, all the while praying that he wouldn't actually get sick.

The plane began to descend. Santorini was in sight. After a spectacularly hair-raising view of a giant cliff jutting into the sea, shadowing the stony black beach at Kamari, the plane skimmed past the ancient mountainside, so close it seemed they could open the window and scrape their fingers along the rock. Below them, whitecaps washed up on the shore as the plane turned inland to set down at the landing strip that overlooked the beach.

The propellers wound down with a comforting whine and Riordan, who spent most of the ride in the pilot's cabin (missing the sight of Alessandro's inner gastric turbulence, Bridey thanked God) cranked open the exit and lowered the steps. Ian and Francesca jumped down the stairs with glee, waiting for the grownups. Riordan,with uncharacteristic gentleness, helped Tilla navigate the stairs. Corinne and Maura managed shoulder bags and purses. Hugh stepped off with the lightened air of a man truly on holiday, and began to deal with the two drivers of the tiny, dusty cars that came to fetch the group.

Alessandro helped her off the stairs as if she were the newly arrived princess of this exotic land.

It was baking hot, but a cool sea wind blew away the fuel smell that clung to their clothes. It became clear that there would have to be two trips made with the cars, if everything and everyone was to make it to the villa. Two men with tired, resigned donkeys appeared and a deal was made to tote some of the luggage that way, though it would be a slow transport.

Bridey approached one of the donkeys. "May I pet him?" she signed to the driver. He nodded and laid his hand on the donkey's flank to steady it.

Meanwhile, Ian tried to negotiate a swap with his father: He would ride on a donkey with the luggage, saving space in the car. "I've ridden them before you know," he reminded whoever he hoped was listening. "I'd fit with no problem. I shouldn't mind riding a long way. The donkey's strong enough." But the deal was no go and Ian was stowed safely in the car with his Aunt Tilla, his sister, his mother and father.

Bridey stroked the smooth hide of the donkey's cheek and looked into its black, long-lashed eyes. The donkey had a faraway look, as if even the hand of a princess couldn't erase his fate to plod the island, laden with too many suitcases.

By the afternoon, Tilla was stretched out on a lounge in the villa's garden. A grove of fig trees and some olive trees stood behind the villa. The trees were short, with gnarled, low branches — easy for Ian or Francesca to climb. The villa, surrounded by a white stucco wall, sat on a piece of land that faced over the sea. In the wall, a gate painted a brilliant blue led into a courtyard with palms and bougainvillea planted artfully against the white walls of the villa. The villa was two stories high, with small balconies off the upper rooms. The balcony railings, windows, grates, and large shutters were all blue. In the garden grew lilies and geraniums, roses, trumpet vine and petunias. Tilla never expected to see such common flowers in this exotic place. Here, where there was so little green, they stood out, vivid and perfect like details in a piece of art.

Tilla's lounge was situated beneath a loggia shaded by pink bougainvillea. It reminded her of the upper terrace at the hotel in Assisi. It seemed ages ago. She gazed into the dappled sunlight filtering down through the vines above her.

There was something about the arid, cooking heat of Santorini that leached the pain from Tilla's back and legs almost from the moment she edged her way down the steps from the plane. Beyond the loggia was a swimming pool. She considered putting on her bathing suit later, maybe doing some little exercises in the water to get her strength back. She hadn't been swimming the whole time they'd been in Greece, save for the fog of her drugged dreams.

Maura and Hugh were inside unpacking; Corinne, resting in the room she and Tilla would share, had a headache and was still nauseous from the flight. The donkeys arrived and deposited the load of suitcases, along with some of their own piles, in the front courtyard. The kids, including Alessandro, went off to explore the beach below the villa.

Tilla closed her eyes and listened to birds chattering in the group of trees.

A shadow fell across her and she opened her eyes. It was Riordan.

"I see you've found the best spot in the place," he said.

"Oh, I don't know. It's all pretty beautiful. Like an oasis."

Riordan sat down on a lounge beside hers.

Tilla gave him an awkward smile. She barely knew this young man. She knew he was Hugh's associate from the Embassy, but they'd had very little interaction personally.

"How are you feeling?" he asked.

"A lot better. I'm surprised how much, really."

"The dry heat, I expect." A heavy-breasted older woman came out to the terrace with a silver tray. She was one half of the couple who were caretakers of the villa. She spoke to Riordan in a different language, looking at Tilla.

"Rula says that she'll bring you anything you'd like," said Riordan. "She's heard you've been ill."

"Not ill, exactly," Tilla said to Rula. "But tell her I appreciate it."

He translated to Rula in the same language. Tilla wasn't sure if it was Greek. She'd heard relatively little Greek since she'd arrived in Greece, staying in an American hotel, and speaking only with her family.

"What language was she speaking?" she asked after Rula departed.

"She's Greek, but she also speaks some English, and the language of the owner as well. "

"Who is that?"

"He's Saudi businessman," Riordan said. "He's a friend of Hugh and Maura's."

Tilla thought Riordan was handsome. His eyes were somewhat sharp, but he was reaching that mature masculinity of men around age thirty, that made them their most attractive. How old was he? Alessandro was almost pretty, he was so good-looking. He'd need it for the stage, she supposed. Riordan was more rugged, less perfect.

"The owner rarely comes here at all," said Riordan. "Just a few times in all the time he's had it. Mind you, it's well taken care of. You see that end of the building?" He pointed to the farthest corner. "It's completely rebuilt. It collapsed in the earthquake. The rest of the house sustained some damage, cracks and fallen ceilings, but the prince had it all restored."

"The prince?"

"A prince of his tribe. Mostly he's a businessman. He owns places all over the world but he doesn't get to many of them. He lets his friends and family use them. But Rula and her husband have the place to themselves ninety-nine percent of the time."

"It's strange," Tilla said. "When we were in Bonn on our tour, Corinne made a joke about Bridey meeting a prince along the way. I thought she was being ridiculous. And now here we are, staying in a villa owned by a prince."

"I suspect Bridey thinks she's found her prince," he said.

Tilla sighed. Bridey's feet had barely touched the ground since last evening. She seemed lit up, completely focused on Alessandro the waiter now.

"So much has happened. And almost none of it was supposed to."

"Surely this is a better outcome?" Riordan settled back on his lounge and put his feet up. A pair of aviator sunglasses perched on top of his head and he pulled them down to cover his eyes. He wore Italian shoes and thin silk socks. Even on a holiday, in an open collared shirt and slacks, he looked like a man dressed for work. Back in Athens at the pool, Tilla saw him in his swim trunks. He was built like a prizefighter, she thought.

"I just wish I hadn't missed so much of it. Being dr… Being in the midst of a back problem. I feel like I'm just waking up from a dream inside a dream. I still don't know how it came about that Bridey now has a boy she barely knows staying here. How in the world did it happen?"

"The famous Alessandro. Quite a determined lad."

"That's what worries me," said Tilla. "He's been after her since the day we arrived in Assisi. And Bridey's so naive." She didn't notice Riordan look askance at her. "She has no experience with someone like that. He's all charm and show."

"Hugh and Maura don't think he'll cause any harm," he said.

"And Corinne is mad about him. We had him checked out after Bridey told them she was…" his tone took a mocking edge, "in love."

Tilla winced behind her sunglasses. "I'm sure Hugh wouldn't have him here if he wasn't honest."

"Quite a cultured family," said Riordan. "And well-known in Assisi. Still, until he achieves whatever real success he's after in Rome eventually — or if — he's really just a waiter, isn't he?" When she didn't respond, he added: "For now, one can only hope he'll burn out all this Italian romantic nonsense with his impetuous decision to throw caution to the wind and chase Bridey to Greece. That he'll realize what an idiot he's being, showing up uninvited, and go back home."

Tilla regarded the lacy pattern of the bougainvillea trailing over the edge of the loggia. She looked over at Riordan.

"How old are you?" she asked.

"I'm twenty-six. Nearly twenty- seven."

"Really? You seem much older."

"It's the job, I suppose. And I was in the Army. That'll age you quick."

"My husband was in the Navy during the second World War. We were married three years after. He was only twenty-four, but he was already a man." She frowned. "How old do you think Alessandro is?"

"Know. He's twenty-one. If you want, I can tell you when he got his first tooth. Don't worry. Half the reason we brought him along here was so we could keep an eye on him. He'll mind his manners. Or he'll have me to answer to."

Tilla covered her mouth and yawned. Well, at least Bridey was surrounded by her family and had this young man looking out for trouble as well. How much harm could come under so many watchful eyes?

Twenty-Seven

A dusty path led downhill to the smooth black volcanic stones that made up the beach below the villa. Close up, the Aegean looked more greenish than blue, and so clear that one could see small fish huddling in little tidal bowls. Along the beach were four tiny white fishing huts — boathouses — and two unoccupied, one-room cottages with big pieces of multi-colored fabric serving as front doors or awnings. At the end of the line, there was a minuscule store with a few beach items, and a cooler full of soft drinks. The store had two café tables outside its door. Smoke wafted from a wood-fired grill where fish and baby octopus waited to be cooked.

Bridey sat on one of the straw mats Alessandro purchased from the little store. She was grateful for it; the black stones were burning hot. It was clear that if they were going to come to this beach, they'd need to stock up on the items for sale, especially flip-flops. It was impossible to wade into the water without them. And then there were the sea urchins that Rula warned them all about.

Sara sat beside Bridey. Alessandro swung Ian and Francesca

in turn, holding them under the arms, dipping them in the waves breaking against the stones. They were screaming with giggles.

"What do you think it's going to be like, having Alessandro stay with us?" Sara asked Bridey. "Are you excited?"

Alessandro scooped Ian up in his arms and slung the little one over his shoulder. The rolled cuffs of his pant legs were soaked, his shirttail untucked. The sea breeze ruffled his hair. Bridey couldn't take her eyes off him. He still seemed like a mirage to her, tantalizing and capable of disappearing in a blink.

"I think it's going to be weird," she said. "Being around each other constantly. Seeing each other in the morning. What if I don't have makeup on? What about my hair?"

Sara picked through the stones and found a red one among the black. She put it in her pocket. They watched Francesca hold up her arms to Alessandro. He stooped and lifted her up with one arm, carrying Ian like a sack of grain.

"This is the perfect place to forget all that stuff," said Sara. "You could just be you. Alessandro thinks you're beautiful anyway. Besides, you can't worry about fake eyelashes and stuff when you're at the beach."

"I'm ecstatic that he showed up," Bridey said, "and at the same time, I'm scared."

"Scared of what? Your mom?"

"No. It's too late for my mom to do anything about this."

"And she's pretty high most of the time," Sara pointed out.

Bridey frowned. "It's beginning to worry me, actually. I'm afraid she might get hooked."

"Might?" Sara said.

Bridey didn't want to think that Tilla might be more than a little dependent on the pills.

"I'm afraid of two things," Bridey said, returning to the subject of Alessandro. "I'm afraid we'll fall completely in love, and it will be worse than ever to leave each other. And I'm afraid we'll be sick of each other. That's usually what happens to me at home.

If a guy wants to get serious, I can't run away fast enough. Not that Alessandro's like anyone back home."

Another thought occurred. "And I'm afraid Riordan will be a creep to Alessandro," said Bridey, "and he'll ruin our time together."

"That's three things."

Alessandro let the twins down and the three of them raced for the girls. When he reached Bridey, he dropped down over her like an eagle hitting its prey in mid-air, and she squealed with laughter as she fell backward onto the beach stones with Alessandro on top of her. His face was framed above her in the brilliant blue sky, the sun outlining his hair like a halo.

"I am so happy!" he said, before he kissed her.

Her heart responded with a leap, while she lay tensed with what modesty she could muster in view of her cousins. She wouldn't get sick of this.

Ian climbed onto Alessandro's back with a growl, innocently rough-housing. He loomed beyond Alessandro's neck, grinning down at Bridey.

"We got you!" he cried.

On the way back to the villa, Alessandro burst into song. They were walking uphill, four abreast. Alessandro and Bridey were in the middle, holding hands, while Ian rode on Alessandro's shoulders. Sara walked with her arm linked in Alessandro's, as he held Ian's ankle. Francesca clamped Bridey's other hand, her little legs scurrying to keep up. They had no idea what Alessandro was singing, but it felt as natural as the air around them. Bridey would remember it as one of the happiest moments of her life, hearing his miraculous voice, feeling linked to him, as they walked in this strange landscape. She wondered, if anyone were to come across them on the path, whether they'd look like a family to the observer. A jolt of desire shot through her, just from the physical nearness of Alessandro and the possibility that at some point, very soon, maybe tonight, they'd be alone.

In mid-song, Alessandro looked at Bridey, as if reading her mind.

The cliché was true, Bridey thought. The look in his eyes could make her knees turn to jelly. She stumbled and stubbed her toe on a stone. It hurt so bad she nearly cried, but it was worth it to have Alessandro set Ian down and put his arm around her to help her limp the rest of the way against him.

After dinner, everyone drifted out to sit on the terrace beneath the loggia except Tilla, who excused herself to turn in for bed.

Ian, struck with the instant hero-worship of five-year-olds, positioned himself at Alessandro's side to be lifted onto his lap. Alessandro had no problem with Ian's attachment and although Bridey felt somewhat abandoned by Ian, she was proud that Alessandro was the kind of person who took so easily to children. It looked good to her family, she thought, and was a point in his favor over Riordan, who had a tendency to either dismiss the little ones much like Hugh did, or tease them in a way they didn't understand.

At the moment, Hugh was holding Francesca, who was reveling in his company. She snuggled against his shoulder and rubbed her eye with fatigue.

"Well, this is a bit different from our typical evenings in Athens," said Riordan. He directed his comments to Alessandro. "You missed it, I'm afraid. It was all one could do to keep Bridey from wearing out the dance floor, night after night. I could have used a break."

Shut up, Bridey thought.

"You don' have to worry no longer," Alessandro said, his glare piercing Riordan. "I make sure Bridey get what she wishes. Is my pleasure. I don' get tired of this."

"It's heaven here," Corinne said. She breathed in deeply. "And I haven't even seen the island yet."

The sky was spread so thickly with stars, it looked like navy blue satin encrusted with diamonds. Bridey had never seen a sky like it. She felt she could stretch her arm up and gather a fistful of celestial sparklers.

"A night like this requires some special entertainment," Riordan said. He polished off his wine and poured another. "Alessandro — why not sing for your supper? I've heard nothing but what a sensation you are. How can we pass up this golden opportunity to have a sneak preview of the next great tenor?"

Bridey couldn't believe her ears. How dare Riordan treat Alessandro like some kind of servant, an employee. Sing for his supper!

Riordan crossed his arms, his smile supercilious. No one said anything. Bridey's heart sank in her stomach. Either everyone else was just as shocked as she was with Riordan's nastiness, or they all secretly viewed Alessandro the same way.

"Alessandro can't sing here," Bridey said, beginning her argument. "Why should he have to?" But Alessandro interrupted her with a hand on her arm.

"I am happy to sing for the family," he said. His voice was even, calm on the surface, but underneath there was a glint of hardness that Bridey had never heard before. "Is little thing to do, for the generosity of Signore and Signora Nowell."

"How can you?" Bridey objected. "There are no instruments here, no one to play for you. Alessandro, you don't have to."

He lifted Ian and set him on Bridey's lap, then stood. "I can do it."

"Really not necessary," Hugh said finally. He looked half asleep.

"Oh, I'd so like to hear him sing!" Maura said, looking from Riordan to Hugh. "It's not about paying us back. It would be a privilege to hear someone who's won such a famous competition.

Accompanied or not."

Alessandro stepped to where he could give attention to his impromptu audience. The light from the interior of the villa served as stage lighting. "I must tell you, my voice is no perfect, because I eat only little time ago," he explained. He patted his belt with a smile. "Is no much room for the breath."

"Oh, please," Corinne teased. "I can't imagine it being anything but wonderful."

Alessandro looked pointedly at Riordan. His expression stiffened around his eyes. "Do you 'ave a request?" Alessandro asked him.

Riordan's disdain faded microscopically. He slouched in his chair. "No," he answered. "Sing whatever you'd like."

"Don't ask me to sing!" Ian said from his perch on Bridey's lap. "I hate to sing."

"I think, because we are in such beautiful place in the sea, I sing Sorrento," Alessandro decided.

"Oh, yes!" Corinne said. "Do."

Vedi il mare come è bello!
Ispira molto sentimento.
Come te che a chi guardi
Da sveglio lo fai sognare.

Full of dinner or not, he sang as perfectly as Bridey heard him the night on the terrace in Assisi. She knew the song: Hadn't she heard it on television? It had seemed spaghetti-and-checkered-tablecloth corny then, certainly not in the same class as Alessandro's rendition. With Alessandro's voice wrapped around the song, it was lilting and sweet, like a bubble swirling and floating through the air. It carried out over the wall and across the water, toward the twinkling lights on a trio of fishing boats trolling nets in the black sea. His singing was so masculine, so full of seduction. It was in the way he stood, something from his soul that transfigured him physically. Watching him, listening, Bridey felt damp with heat; she was glad it was dark, because surely it was obvious how excited she was. She had to get him off alone tonight.

By the end of the song, everyone was sitting perched forward in their seats, even Hugh.

"Glory be to God," Maura said, almost in a whisper. "Bravo, Alessandro!"

"I told you," Corinne said.

"Excellent!" Hugh applauded. "That was absolutely brilliant."

"*Grazie,*" Alessandro said.

Bridey basked in their admiration of him. They were not people who were easily impressed, and yet they seemed genuinely bowled over. She hugged Ian with elation.

Ian squirmed in her grasp. "That was the loudest singing I've ever heard!" he declared.

Alessandro laughed. "Do you no like it, Ian?"

"I did like it," Ian admitted. "I shall just cover my ears."

"And what about you, Riordan?" Bridey asked. *So there*, she thought. "Is that payment enough?" She was the only one who caught the reluctant, you-win gaze he gave her. She also saw that he was drunk.

"I appreciate your generosity in sharing your talent with us," Riordan said to Alessandro, his tone begrudging. "Rome will be at your feet."

Alessandro was gracious, ignoring the sarcasm. "I hope you are right." He clapped his hands, rubbing them together, happy again. "I sing another, a piece of opera. One more aria. And for pretty Francesca, it sound like the lullaby. Francesca, she look very sleepy in her papa's arms."

The sweet sound of the aria floated up into the open shutter doors of the room where Tilla lay trying to sleep. The hard mattress of the bed took some getting used to. The drugs helped, but she didn't feel as knocked-out by them as she had in the last two weeks. A gentle breeze stirred the gauzy white curtains drawn across the open doors. She could hear the drone of her family's voices below in the dark. Now she listened to the voice she'd heard that night in Assisi, the voice that called to Bridey and led her darling daughter to sneak off into the night, away from her.

She rolled to her side in bed and sat up carefully. The marble floor was cool on the soles of her bare feet as she limped to the doors and parted the curtains so she could stand in the threshold of the balcony, to look down at the loggia. All she could see was the young waiter standing apart on the terrace, singing. He was backlit by the pool lights. The grove of ancient trees stood beyond, like a backdrop on stage, surrounded by the low, white wall at the steep hillside leading to the sea. The Aegean glimmered darkly, punctuated by the distant black humps of other islands in silhouette. The stars watched over them, a heavenly audience.

There was such tenderness in the music he was singing. Wistfulness. She didn't understand the words, but she knew the voice of love when she heard it. For the first time, Tilla stood in the present, not stewing over past objections; not worrying about the coming days. She rested her head against the painted blue wood of the doorway, staring out at the water, at the islands, and into her own heart.

Twenty-Eight

No chance presented itself for Bridey to be alone with Alessandro that first night. He excused himself and said goodnight like a proper gentleman. More points for Alessandro in her family's eyes, she figured.

When she woke in the morning, it was to the sound of roosters crowing in the distance. She lay in her bed marveling at how far she'd come, to be here, in a villa on a Greek island with her beautiful Alessandro.

Downstairs, Tilla and Aunt Corinne were out on the terrace, attempting to drink the nuclear-powered Greek coffee Rula poured for them. Rula coaxed Tilla with a few slices of tomatoes fried with spices, a dish of tapioca, and rolls drenched in honey.

"You eat," Rula told her. "Is good for you. I get anything you like."

Tilla took a dutiful bite of one of the honeyed rolls. She looked like a child trying to please a beloved grandparent.

"Good morning, Mumma," Bridey said, stooping to kiss Tilla on her cheek.

"Morning, sweetie," Tilla said through a mouthful.

"Where is everyone?"

Bridey plucked an orange from the bowl of fruit on a wooden table spread with a cloth embroidered with leaves and dark olives.

"Hugh's off for a walk on the beach with the twins and Aunt Maura is still asleep," Corinne reported. "Sara's not up?" She looked to Bridey for confirmation.

"Taking a bath," Bridey said. Everything in the bath was made of white marble, except for the toilet. Dark blue and white tiles covered anything that wasn't marble. It all felt very palatial, and Sara was indulging in it.

"Have you seen Alessandro?" asked Bridey.

"No," Corinne said. "And Riordan left this morning before dawn."

Corinne wore a loose red and white shift with the straps of her bathing suit beneath peeking out at the neckline. Back home when Corinne came to visit, she and Tilla would often put on their bathing suits first thing on a hot day and sit outside wearing their shorts over the suits, eating popsicles along with the kids. They'd pull their lawn chairs up to the edge of the kiddie pool and soak their feet, talking for the whole morning, until it was time to pick some tomatoes from Rob's garden and make their favorite sandwich for lunch.

"He gone," Rula said, returning from the kitchen. "Alessandro."

"Gone?" Bridey's heart jumped. "When? Where?"

"He no say. For walk. But he be back."

"Out enjoying this glorious morning," Corinne said. "How can you not?"

"Is he with Riordan?" Bridey asked.

"Riordan left for Cypress," Tilla said. "He has business there." Her statement, given so knowingly, garnered surprised looks from both her sister and her daughter.

"That's a long way away. How did he get off the island?" Bridey asked. Not that she was heartbroken to hear he was gone.

"We got boats, you know," Rula said.

Bridey shut up, spooning tapioca into her mouth. Alessandro had to be around someplace. Rula offered her coffee. When she begged off, Rula brought lemonade.

Tilla had her sunglasses pushed back on her head and her hair, now pixie short, framed her face. Freckles dotted her cheeks like tiny paint splatters. She was barefoot, wearing a pair of Maura's shorts and a sleeveless cotton blouse. She looked young enough to be one of Bridey's friends, not a mom.

The sound of a small engine grew louder as it came into the courtyard at the front of the villa.

"Alessandro, I think," Rula said from the doorway.

Bridey left her half-eaten orange and stood up. "What's he doing?"

"He got the motorbike," Rula said. She wiped her hands on her apron. "It come with the villa, but Diony, my husband, keep it at our house. I tell Alessandro, after he walk, he can pick up to use."

"Really?" Bridey's voice cracked with excitement. A motorbike! The possibilities grew by the minute.

"Sure," Rula said, as Bridey followed her through the interior of the villa to the front doors. "We got donkeys, also. Two donkeys don't carry for business no more. So we keep for rides, like for the children. Or anyone who likes." She added: "Some don't like donkeys. They afraid."

"Ian won't be," Bridey said. "And I'd love to ride a donkey."

Rula grasped the handles of the double doors in the entry and pushed them both open. The sunlight was blinding after the cool shade of the interior.

Alessandro sat outside the doors, astride the motorbike. He grinned at Bridey. "*Buon giorno!* Can you believe? Is just like my Vespa."

"Good morning," said Bridey, entwining her arms around him. "I was worried that you left me." They kissed, mindless of Rula's presence.

"Worried?" Alessandro said. "Don' you know me by now?" He nodded toward the back of the seat. "*Andiamo.* Is time to explore this beautiful island together."

Bridey straddled the seat behind him and encircled his waist. Alessandro put the bike into gear and turned in a sharp radius out of the courtyard.

Bridey glanced back at the closed, peacock blue doors of the villa, half expecting her mother to come hobbling out, yelling at her to be careful and hang on tight. But the doors remained shut.

Alessando took the high road through the little village, a collection of a small grocery, tavernas, a barren-looking shop Bridey recognized as a pharmacy, a store featuring ice, and apartments stacked like pastel boxes. Construction was going on, but at a pace that included long smoke breaks and kibitzing, so foreign to the kind of construction sites she'd seen her dad work on, where men moved over the frames and cement walls like ants.

They headed upward. The village thinned to chalky roads where separate homes stood, still square, walled, and beige. Soon the land was more expansive, windswept and rocky, sloping sharply to the beach below them. Here the homes sat far apart, kept company by scrubby, wind-stunted vineyards and patches of tomatoes and cucumber vines, or grazing goats, sheep, or donkeys. Women hung laundry in the hot, dry breeze. Dogs lazed in the shade of stone walls. There seemed to be a little church or shrine every fifty feet, always pristine white with a blue dome and doors, or an arch over bells hanging from the apex. Small crowded graveyards dotted the landscape, the rectangular low marble graves were festooned with flowers and mementoes.

Alessandro and Bridey kept climbing, until the road crested. Suddenly, the island cliffs and the sea spread out before them in one breathtaking impact. They were nearly a thousand feet above the sea, and it was as if the hand of God had taken a scoop of

Santorini, like some giant dessert, and left a frosted piece of land. They could see a large town spread out along the top of the cliff, like white icing.

The Aegean in the distance below shimmered and danced in the intense morning sun, hazy and magnetic. It was a living being, telling them its mythic dreams. Alessandro and Bridey flew along; the wind whipped Bridey's hair and made her eyes tear. Bridey was riveted by the limitless expanse of lapis blue water. She was filled with the wonderment of this love, this country, this day. The motorbike brought them freedom, but now she felt that freedom becoming a part of her being. Pure, jubilant, exhilarating joy filled her. It erupted from her in a whoop, and flowed through her hands to Alessandro's body as she held him. He slowed to a stop at the roadside and cut the engine on the bike. Without a word, the two got off and walked to the edge of the cliffside, holding hands while they stood together facing the sea, surveying the miracle of their own lives.

They spent most of the day wandering the cliffside town, climbing the stairs of its winding, narrow, cobbled streets, the worn stones made smooth and slippery by the steps of the generations before them, and exploring little shops. By noon they were both starving, and Bridey regretted not stopping to grab her tote bag on her way out. But Alessandro had drachmas in his wallet, and he purchased two pairs of sunglasses for Bridey and him. He bought her a canvas tote bag lined in a rainbow of stripes, to carry the art postcards and watercolor paintings they bought from a street artist. They came to a door framed into a little cliffside wall. The door appeared to lead into thin air, like a place in Wonderland. *Taverna Efira*, the sign on it read, with an arrow pointing down. At the bottom of a steep staircase was a terrace hanging over the sea, while the Greek flag flapped and rippled above. They ate delicious salads of sliced cucumbers, tiny tomatoes, dark olives, capers and strips of green bell pepper, topped with a thick slab of creamy feta cheese and drizzled with olive oil and spices. Bridey had never eaten anything so delicious. But it may have been the view that influenced the flavor. And the company.

Before they left the town, Alessandro purchased a small gold bracelet chain strung with round blue beads, each bead with a white circle and a black dot in the center. He fastened it on Bridey's wrist.

"I know what is this," he told her, having trouble hooking the clasp.

"Here, let me hold this end," Bridey said. "What is it?"

The bracelet dangled from her wrist, atop the gold bangles she wore. It looked mismatched, but pretty at the same time.

"Is for the Evil Eye," Alessandro said. "This eye, it keep you safe from harm." He kissed the inside of her wrist. "Is for when I am no there to do it."

"Don't talk about that now." Bridey held him and whispered against his lips. "As long as we're here, nothing can be wrong for me."

The town grew closed and quiet in the afternoon. The shopkeepers and market vendors, and most all business, shuttered away while they ate their meals and rested out of the sun, waiting to reopen in the cool of the evening. Alessandro and Bridey found their way back to the church square where they had parked the motorbike. Bridey set the tote on a low wall that circled the old church, as Alessandro reached out for her, kissing her until she felt breathless and light-headed.

"Let's go swimming when we get back," she said. "Did you bring swim trunks with you?"

"No," he said. "I never imagine I go to island. I never e'spect this. But I watch you swim..." His eyes surveyed her body. "I like to see you."

"We'll have to find you a suit," Bridey said. She returned his survey. "I'd like to see you, too."

Someone had left a bucket of thick white paint and

long-handled brushes in place beside the ornately carved church doors. A bearded, pony tailed priest in black robes walked past them with a nod and passed through the black iron gates of the church's courtyard. Bridey picked up the tote, ready to climb on the bike behind Alessandro, when she realized some of the viscous paint from the top of the wall was stuck to the bottom of the bag.

"Oh, no," she groaned, showing Alessandro. There were messy missing pieces in the formerly perfect paint job.

He laughed and revved the engine. "We better get out of here," he said. "Before they discover you take a piece of the town with you."

Ian sat cross-legged on his narrow single bed, while Francesca curled around her favorite stuffed animal. Both children were cooled from their baths, and their hair — one so fair, the other dark— twisted into just-washed curls around their faces. The shutters on the window were opened to the night breeze off the sea.

Alessandro sat on the edge of Ian's bed, while Bridey pulled a sheet over Francesca, whose lids dipped over her eyes as she struggled not to fall asleep. She pulled the stuffed toy closer, under her chin.

Ian asked for a story.

"Once upon a time, a prince live in a magic mountain," Alessandro began.

"He lived in, like inside a cave?" Ian asked.

"Sure," said Alessandro. "My English maybe is no so good for the story, so listen how you wish."

"He lived in a cave," Ian decided.

"*Si.* He live in a cave and he is very alone."

"And he was very sad?"

"Ian," Bridey warned. Given enough rope, Ian could stretch

this process far into the night.

"He is very sad because he is having only the creatures of the woods for friends," said Alessandro. "The prince, he has a spell, bad magic, from making the king very mad. The only way he can..."

Ian fixed Alessandro with the look of an attorney doing a cross-examination. "How did he make the king mad?"

"He try to ride the king's special donkey," Alessandro said, raising his eyebrows at Ian for emphasis. "The only way he can no be alone is to call a princess to his cave. And the only way to do this, is to sing."

"You're the prince!" A small hand flew up, finger pointed.

"Do I live in cave?"

Ian hunched his shoulders toward his ears, half frowning. "I don't know where you live," he said, "normally."

"In my home in Assisi, I live in my house. No more talk, okay? Or I can no tell you the story," Alessandro said. He tried to keep a straight face. The little boy squirmed with the struggle of keeping quiet. "The prince, he look for a princess, but only he find woods, and he get lonely every day. So, he sing to the animals sad songs, and songs of dreams."

Ian yawned. "But the princess hears his songs?"

"Si. One day, a princess ride the mountain on a beautiful... em.... carriage? She is making a trip. And what is this? She hear the most beautiful music! But the woods, they are very... too many trees, eh? She think: Where this music come from? Who sings this? I must find him!... The prince sing his most perfect songs for her. And, is magic! All the trees, they move from the way! Now the prince and the princess can find each other. Do you know why is this?"

"How can trees just get up and move?" asked Ian. "It would be better if he had to cut them all down."

"The trees are his friends," Alessandro said. "They don' do nothing bad."

"Who's telling this story, Ian? You or Alessandro?" Bridey said.

But she laughed as she said it. She was as enthralled as Ian, but for different reasons. Her hand patted a soft rhythm on Francesca's legs and she glanced at the little girl to see if she was also lost in the story. Francesca's breathing turned to a soft baby snore.

"So, the prince, he love this princess very much. He ask her to marry and live with him, in his cave. And the princess..." Alessandro looked at Bridey. "She say, 'yes.' Because she love him, also."

"And they lived happily ever after?" Ian asked.

"Oh, so happy! But there is more. Because they love each other, they have magic. The songs of the prince are happy now. And their love, it turn the cave into a beautiful castle."

"Were there dragons in the woods?"

Alessandro laughed. "*Finito*, my friend! Now you must sleep."

Ian reached his arms up to Alessandro. Alessandro bent to hug the little boy to him. Before he let go, Ian planted a quick kiss on Alessandro's cheek.

"Do I get one?" Bridey asked. She felt a bit jilted. She was clearly being replaced as Ian's favorite.

Ian gave her a tight hug and pursed his lips for a goodnight smooch. "I love you, Bridey," he said.

Alessandro smoothed the hair away from the sleeping Francesca's cheek. "*Buona sera, principessa*," he whispered.

This could be us, Bridey thought. *We could be like this.* She reached for his hand and led him out of the children's room. She couldn't wait another moment.

In the dark hall, Bridey was startled by the figure of her Aunt Maura. The white silk robe and negligee Maura wore, with her skin so milky in the dimness, gave her the appearance of an apparition. Bridey jumped.

"Aunt Maura," she whispered. "I'm sorry. Did I wake you?" She knew it had to be at least two in the morning. The heat from being with Alessandro still filled her.

"No," Maura said. She wrapped her thin robe around her, as if warding off a chill. "I was just on my way to the kitchen to get a drink." Her eyes glittered. "Would you like to join me?"

"I'm pretty tired." She made a move toward the bedroom door, and then reached out to give her aunt an awkward hug. "G'night."

But Maura held on to her. "Bridey."

Bridey held still. So similar in stature, they were eye to eye. Bridey could smell her aunt's perfume. Her hair was rumpled, as if she'd been asleep for a while.

"I have no doubt that you're in love with Alessandro right now," Maura said.

"Yes. I am."

"And you're old enough to decide what you want to do with that." The meaning was clear between them. "This isn't about coming in late, or how you spend your time together. I'm asking something different. Maybe you don't even know the answer right now."

"I don't know what you mean."

"Bridey, are you in love with Alessandro the person? Or are you in love with his talent?"

Before Bridey could stumble out an answer, Maura placed two fingers over her niece's lips.

"I want you to think about it, Bridey. That's all. Because it's very important to know the difference."

CHAPTER TWENTY-NINE

Twenty-Nine

In the week that passed Bridey was never so happy. Alessandro fit into her family's circle with his natural charm and sweetness. He treated Maura and Corinne like queens, entertaining them at dinner with funny stories of life in Assisi and some of the more eccentric patrons of the Hotel Windsor Savoia. He apologized to Tilla for sneaking off with Bridey to go dancing and Tilla had a hard time resisting his sincerity. Tilla just prayed Bridey would get him out of her system and chalk it up to a summer romance. Soon they'd all go back home where they belonged.

Hugh appreciated the time Alessandro spent with Ian, and liked having another male around to deflect the concentration of female hormones in the air.

With Riordan's absence, the constant vibe of judgment and condescension was gone. The room he shared with Alessandro wasn't mined territory; dinners weren't tilting grounds.

There was only one person Bridey felt the slightest twinge of jealousy over, but it was a small enough nip that she was able to push it aside. Sara. Every morning since the first at the villa, Alessandro took a walk before Bridey woke, and Sara went with him. Bridey tried not to begrudge Sara her small piece of Alessandro's time.

Besides, Alessandro's walks proved fruitful. Alessandro discovered a hideaway, a place just on the other end of the rocky hillside that formed the backdrop of the little beach store. He and Bridey had to venture out along the rocks at the waterline, to get past the hill's foot. They had to pick their way, sometimes stepping in the seawater as it filtered its way over the stony tide line. But it was worth it, because this path led to a tiny cove with high walls of stone, and in the walls of rock, someone from another time had carved a little cave, maybe as a shelter, or drop-off for fish, or for catching the octopus that slid along the deep, sheltered bottom of the cove. The water was deep enough to pull a boat up and tie it. The cave was only accessible by a slippery rock ledge, but even at night the light from the waning moon, reflected on the water, lit the way safely enough.

It was here that they found privacy, a place to strip naked and fall into each other with all the pent-up repression and appetite they hoped they concealed from her family. The cool, stone floor of the cave room felt as soft in Bridey's lust as any bed. They stared into each other's eyes and let their silence do the talking. Bridey gripped the stones behind Alessandro's head as she lifted and dropped her hips against him, and when Alessandro put her breasts to his mouth, she felt herself free-fall into a space she never expected. It was as if the cave floor dropped out from under them and her body turned to air. She let her head fall backwards and wanted to cry out. Afterward, she would lie across the stone threshold, facing the night sky, as Alessandro sat wordlessly beside her.

To Sara, it was worth waking at dawn each morning to share

her time with Alessandro. Sara brought her log with her and perched on a crumbling wall of a ruined old house, writing, while Alessandro stood on an outcrop of rock and sang strange scales, or pieces of music in Italian, Latin, French or German. He explained the story behind the songs, told her what parts he hoped to perform someday. Sometimes they spoke to each other in French; she thought that might be the best part, since only they could share that. She loved their easy companionship of two artists exercising their crafts. She doubted anyone in her family could understand.

The morning of the day it all happened, Alessandro finished practicing *Una Furtiva Lagrima*, which Sara thought was almost too pretty to be sad. Alessandro said it was difficult to reach the last high notes perfectly, so that's why he wanted to practice it.

He sat on the remains of a windowsill, twirling a stem of flowering thyme growing wild in what once may have been the kitchen. The old garden stood nearby, sprouting crimson poppies and a mound of orange trumpet vine climbing its own weathered trunk.

Alessandro looks pensive, Sara wrote. *He's been so quiet this morning. He's hardly said a word except for singing.* She chewed the pen top for a moment, stealing a look at him, and continued writing. *I can tell something is really bothering him. Is he getting bored being here? No, it doesn't look like boredom on his face. Worried, maybe. Definitely not happy.*

He saw her observing him and gave her a half-hearted smile. Then his gaze searched out over the sea. He could look like he was posing for a painting or a sculpture just by sitting still and thinking. And then, like now, people would stare at the portrait or the statue and see into it, try to interpret the thoughts or emotions they imagined it expressed.

"You look sad this morning," Sara said to him.

"Sad? No… Perhaps I think of the song."

Sara frowned, unconvinced. "It's not about what you sang."

He shook his head, reluctance written across his face. He opened his mouth to say something. No words arrived. One hand tapped knuckles lightly against his bottom lip. Thinking. Then he seemed to give in (give up?) to Sara's perceptiveness.

"I tell you secret, Sara. Do you promise you don' tell it?"

Sara set down her pen. This was so fabulous. He trusted her. "Cross my heart," she said, crossing it.

He bit his bottom lip and looked down, away from her gaze. This was serious, Sara figured. It wasn't anything like, *I'm in love with Bridey,* or, *We've been sneaking off to have sex,* stuff she already guessed. Bridey and Alessandro wandered off every night, supposedly to go into the village or walk by the beach, or they'd take off on the motorbike and go to the cliff city. But Sara heard them in the middle of one night, as they slipped into the pool and floated around wrapped up so tightly in each other they looked like a two-headed water creature. She stood by her window and the air was still, the night deep with the moon shining like a flood lamp, and heard them murmuring, breathing... It excited her and scared her all at the same time, to know what she knew.

"I am on this island, because I run away," he said finally. "I don' tell my family I come to this place. When I decide to go to Bridey, when her letter comes in Assisi, I go quick. I tell only my brother Gianni that I go to Athens. He say I am crazy to do it, but he don' tell anybody."

"He'll cover for you?"

"Because my mama and papa, they know nothing. I can no tell them, or they stop me from it. Now, I worry for it. I leave Athens. I never dream I do this, but I am here and so happy. But Gianni, he don' know I am here. Now I am gone so many days, many more days than I plan."

"Does Bridey know?"

"No. I don' want to tell her. We are so happy together. Every day, I think to tell her. But again I think, no. Not yet. One more day. And more. But all the time, I think of my family also. Do you think I am bad person? I never do nothing like this before. I think Gianni is maybe right. I am crazy a little."

Sara chewed on her pen cap, thinking. The plastic cap flattened into an oval, nicked with tooth marks. Why was he telling her? Was he asking her advice? Sara had a million questions, trying to figure it out. She'd want to write about this and she needed to know.

"Are you actually running away, or are you just, you know… taking a vacation? A break? Do you want to go back to Assisi? What about Rome? You must still want to sing opera, because you're up here practicing even when you don't have to."

Alessandro let out a yelp of frustration and tossed the limp piece of thyme toward the edge of the outcrop. It landed inside one of his shoes, left where he kicked them off when they arrived. He liked to practice in his bare feet. This was one thing Sara believed only she knew about him.

"I wan' everything to be as I wish!" he said, raking his fingers through his hair. "I wan' to go back to Assisi but I don' want to go without Bridey. I wan' to go to Rome but I don' want to leave this island where I am so happy. I wan' my mama and papa no to be worry, no to be angry with me…" He looked at her, his eyes full of resignation. "They give everything to me in my life. And I do this."

"Wow." It was all she could say. You wouldn't think someone like Alessandro would have so many problems, Sara thought. Someone like him, so gorgeous and smart and gifted, you'd think he had it made. But he looked like he was about to cry.

In the early afternoon, Hugh arranged a shopping trip to the cliffside city for Corinne, Maura, Tilla and Sara. He called for one of the two cars that picked them up at the airport and left Rula, Bridey and Alessandro with the twins.

In exchange for taking a nap, Bridey promised the twins that if they would rest first, she and Alessandro would take them to Rula and Diony's house to ride the donkeys. Ian gave them his usual protest, but since he and his sister had been playing in the swimming pool for most of the morning, it didn't take long before the two were sprawled out on their beds sound asleep.

Bridey found Rula in the dining room, polishing the etched brass that decorated the tabletop.

"Rula, Alessandro and I would like to go down to the beach for an hour while the twins are napping. Would you mind keeping an eye on them while they're sleeping? If they wake up before we get back, you could bring them down to the beach and we'll get them ready to go ride the donkeys. We're going to take the raft out," Bridey said.

"Sure, sure!" Rula said, waving Bridey along with her polishing cloth. "Go. *Yassou.*"

They launched the raft and paddled out to smoother water. Bridey wished they had the masks, fins and snorkels from the embassy's boat back in Athens. They linked hands, staring up at the first wisps of clouds they'd seen since they arrived on Santorini. From out on the water, they could see both the beach and the cove with their secret cave room. The beach was deserted, the café store closed. Bridey dared to take off her bikini top, floating bare-breasted in the water. She held onto the top by hooking it together and pulling it up over one leg. She understood why so many of the people on the island swam topless or nude, why the ancient art of the islands depicted the old culture going about their daily lives in a similar state. It was a sensuous, heady feeling, one she could only be free to experience here, on this day. It was something she would never be able to do at home.

The two floated on the raft for a half hour, drowsing and talking as the water calmed and the breeze died. They almost didn't hear the sound of a small voice calling to them.

"The twins must be up from their nap," Bridey said, lifting her head to look toward the beach. She expected to see Rula and the children standing at the shoreline. But the beach was empty. "Did you hear that?" Bridey asked Alessandro. The little voice called out again.

"*Si*, it is Ian," Alessandro answered. He turned and looked in the direction of the voice.

"But where's he calling from? I don't see him on the beach anywhere. He's not on the path, either."

It was then that Bridey realized how far they'd drifted. At the same time, she saw a child's head bobbing in the waves. Alone.

"Ian!" she screamed. He was struggling in a doggy-paddle, rising and falling, so far from them that her heart froze. Ian didn't answer. He paddled furiously toward them, like a small animal making for the other side of a river. She saw his determination dissolving to fright. He'd never make it, and now he was too far out to turn back.

"Bridey!" She heard him holler. Water slapped against his mouth and he began to choke.

"Jesus God!" Without thinking, Bridey rolled off her raft and began to swim for him.

Alessandro swam beside her. Bridey's heart hammered in terror. Ian was barely able to tread water with no pool sides to hang from, no lifeguard to call instructions. He was growing exhausted. She couldn't believe he'd made it out so far from the shore.

"Dead Man's Float!" she yelled to Ian. "Dead Man's Float, Ian! We're coming to get you!"

Ian tried to float, but he was taking in too many mouthsful of water. He began to cry, coughing out the salt water all the more. "I can't, I can't!" He sputtered. "Help me, Aless —."

He went down.

Alessandro flailed toward him and dove. Bridey powered her way to them in a stroke fueled by panic. In a horrible moment, both Alessandro and Ian disappeared from the rolling surface.

"No!" Bridey's scream carried wide over the water, bouncing back at her from the rocks that surrounded the beach. She dove underwater, her eyes wide and stinging from the salt. She could just make out Alessandro's form trying in slow motion to push Ian back up to the surface. She pulled her way downward, reaching for Ian, whose hand clamped on to her wrist as his fingernails dug in hard around her bracelets. With three strong kicks, she dragged him up through the water and lifted him to the air. Ian let out a screech of hysteria.

The raft was farther out now, skimming away with the breeze toward the direction of the cove. Damn it! She held onto Ian and tried to calm him. Where was Alessandro? *God. Help! Oh, God, please! Please.*

"Alessandro!" she called, twisting in the water to search for any sign of him. At first there was nothing, just the pitch of the waves going by. "Alessandro." It came out now as a whimper. He'd been right there near her, just a few strokes behind to the surface. The waves continued to pitch past, revealing nothing, and the water became an alien element, murky, intent on its own course toward the beach. She screamed out his name again and would have kept screaming and screaming, but he surfaced at last twenty feet from her, gasping, clawing the waves to stay up.

Ian wailed with fright. He clung to Bridey's neck. Her long legs kicked hard. "Listen, Ian," she commanded him. "Remember when we played the dolphin game? Can you play it now? Can you hold on while I swim you to shore? Don't cry, baby. I've got you. Keep your mouth closed. I've got you. Can you do it?"

He stifled his choking sobs and nodded, his long lashes clumped in wet spikes, eyes wide as a frightened fawn. Two stripes of cloudy mucus hung from his nostrils. He coughed and wretched up seawater.

She could hear Alessandro choking and breathing hard in the water. But instinct took over: the first thing she had to do was get Ian back to shore. She started a slow, steady breaststroke, using the force of the waves to help propel them toward the beach.

"Hold tight, Ian! Hold tight. Keep your mouth closed," she told the clinging child. She could feel his teeth chattering behind her ear. His fingernails dug in around her neck.

Two men ran down the path and were racing into the surf, coming to help. One of the men on the beach swam to them, the other hung back. She recognized Riordan. He cut through the water like an Olympic medalist.

"Can you make it back?" Riordan called out to her a few yards away in the water.

"Yes."

"I'm going for Alessandro, then."

Bridey spit out a mouthful of seawater and could only nod in assent. With Ian's weight on her back, she could barely keep her nose and his head above the water line. The salt burned her eyes but the sting of her tears made it unbearable. The taste of dread was metallic in her mouth, her frantic prayer a stream of sound in her head. *Please please no please help God please don't take Alessandro...* Finally she was able to touch the stony bottom. She grabbed Ian off her back and cradled him to her. Her lungs were white hot with exertion and adrenalin, muscles becoming leaden with every second. She concentrated only on making it onto the beach and setting Ian down. She didn't want to look back to see what was happening to Alessandro.

The man on the beach helped her struggle through the last few feet of surf and then ran back to stand knee-deep in it, ignoring Bridey and the little boy. He bellowed a steady stream of Italian, tearing at his hair and gesturing toward the rescue. He stumbled back with the force of a wave and continued to curse and cry out at whatever was taking place, in the sea and in heaven.

Bridey and Ian collapsed on the black sand at the water's edge. Ian puked up some of his lunch, and more sea water, which brought on a fresh bout of howling. But he was breathing and crying, he was alive and conscious and not limp at the bottom of the Aegean, and that was all that mattered to Bridey in that moment. She braced herself and sat up to see what Riordan was able to do for Alessandro. The man in the surf continued his distraught cursing. Bridey caught a view of his profile.

Gianni.

Riordan dragged Alessandro through chest deep water now, supporting him. Alessandro's arm dangled around one shoulder, and Riordan's other arm held him up at Alessandro's chest. Alessandro's eyes were closed and his head lolled backwards. He looked ashen and spent. Gianni plunged toward the men, reaching to take his brother from Riordan, enveloping Alessandro and pulling him to safety.

Riordan dragged in behind them, wiping streams of water from his face. He fell to his knees beside Bridey and Ian, catching his breath. She hadn't even noticed that he was fully dressed, except for his shoes.

"That was close," Riordan said to no one. He looked at her bare breasts, now caked in black stony sand, and unbuttoned his soaked white shirt, draping it around her shoulders.

Bridey rubbed Ian's tensed little back in agreement, too numb for words, too out of breath to feel self-conscious. Her bangle bracelets clinked together with the motion. Deep, bleeding scratches lay where Ian's nails had held to her for dear life. The salt burned and stung within them.

The bikini top floated on its way toward the cove. Somewhere out on the floor of the sea, Bridey's broken evil-eye bracelet settled on an algae-covered rock, near the lair of a female octopus.

CHAPTER THIRTY

Gianni kept up his harangue long after they'd straggled back to the villa. He alternated slapping Alessandro around the head in reproach and grabbing his brother to kiss him in relief and reunion. Riordan carried Ian and simultaneously shepherded Bridey alongside. They met Rula at the villa gate. She was wringing her polishing cloth, frantic to know that they'd found the missing child.

Riordan promptly incarcerated Ian in his room, once they knew he was okay. He changed the little boy out of his swimsuit and into dry shorts and a shirt. Ian's remorse only lasted a few minutes before he dropped off into a deep sleep, curled on his side and sucking his fingers.

Francesca pulled out a coloring book and crayons from the bedside table. "I'll stay with him," she whispered, in her best imitation of a grown-up voice. "Ian often needs looking after."

Out in the fig and olive grove, Gianni and Alessandro continued their agitated conversation. Riordan and Bridey sat inside the kitchen. Bridey felt as limp as the wet cloth she held pressed to her swollen eyes. She could hear snippets of a one-sided lecture and argument going on between the Italian brothers. She hid her tears behind the cloth, hid her guilt and regret. She should never have left the twins in the villa. They weren't Rula's responsibility. Tilla's voice raged in Bridey's head. *You've let us down again.*

"Let me see," Riordan said to her, pulling the cloth gently from her face.

Rula bent to check Bridey's eyes.

"They don't look so good," Rula pronounced. "But you be okay, I think." She brought a cup of strong tea with lemon and honey. "Drink this. It help you calm down."

Riordan's face looked blurry to Bridey. But she didn't care about her eyes. She knew they'd clear up. It was everything else that might not recover. "Thank you," Bridey said to Riordan.

He reached out and lifted her chin. He sat at the table shirtless and in bare feet, still not changed out of his damp slacks. "If I were a religious man, and I'm not, I would say that God had a hand in this," he said. "We'd just arrived and Rula was in a panic. Lucky that Ian dropped his little sunglasses on the path. It wasn't hard to figure out where he went. Another few minutes and it might have been too late."

"I thought he'd drown!" Bridey burst into tears, unable to hold back the fresh image of Ian sinking and Alessandro going down with him.

"Hey." Riordan put his arm around her and pulled her close. She laid her feverish cheek against the smooth coolness of his shoulder. "Rula, hand me a napkin, would you?" Then he wiped her nose as if she were Francesca. "He didn't drown, did he? Everyone is fine. Come on, now. Don't cry. You'll only make your eyes worse."

It felt good to rest for a moment against him. He was solid and she felt safe. A wave of homesickness hit her. She missed her dad. She needed him, needed to curl up on his lap like a little girl and feel his comfort. She still did that in her worst teary moments at home, even though it ended up making them both laugh. She was so tall and awkward and ridiculous.

Bridey put the damp cloth to her eyes again. She must look like a bulgy-eyed monster. Then something occurred to her.

"How did Gianni get here?" she asked from behind the cloth.

"I brought him back with me," said Riordan.

"I thought you went to Cyprus."

He let her go and poured himself some of Rula's tea. "I did. But on my way back, I had to stop in Athens. The Sloanes told me that an Italian man had been hanging around the hotel lobby, asking about you. The front desk confirmed it. Said he was looking for his brother who'd gone missing about a week ago, and that the brother'd told him he was headed to Athens; an American girl he was in love with was staying at the Athens Hilton with her family. No one would tell Gianni where we'd gone to, nor did they know anything about Alessandro. Gianni was beside himself when I found him." Riordan took a sip of the steaming tea and glanced toward the blue doorway as voices rose in the grove. "It seems Alessandro only told Gianni about his trip. He took all the money he'd saved to make the trip. Their parents went insane with worry, he says."

Bridey's eyes looked ravaged, lids swollen and shiny, whites turned deep pink with bloodshot, and her face had developed the hot red spots she always got from crying. "They yelled at Alessandro when he went out with me in Assisi," she told him. "They said I didn't care about his career or art, that I was just an American tourist using him for a good time."

Riordan suppressed a smile. "Isn't that your mother's line? That he's using the American?"

Bridey shook her head, unsmiling.

"Anyway," Riordan continued. "It seems Alessandro has caused quite a stir in Assisi. The whole town is buzzing and lots of people are worried about him. So I told Gianni I knew where

Alessandro was, and that he was fine and enjoying himself. I told him I'd take him to his brother and they could sort the mess out." He glanced again toward the door. "And it sounds like that's what's happening."

By the time Bridey's family arrived back at the villa after dinner, the incident with Ian had lost some of its drama. Rula went home, Gianni and Alessandro were worn out with fighting, Riordan took a long solitary dip in the pool, and Bridey put herself to bed for a while, needing to be alone, to rest, to think. Ian and Francesca were fed and bathed and ready for bed and Ian looked none the worse for wear.

Tilla became so upset after hearing that Bridey and Ian had been in danger that she dosed herself strongly with Valium, something she was trying hard to taper off. She went off to lie down and ended up passed out in her clothes on the bed.

Alessandro asked Bridey to walk with him, after things settled down at the villa for the evening. They hadn't had a chance to speak to each other alone since they'd been floating blissfully on the raft in the languid Greek afternoon. They sat on the rocky outcrop of the ruined house where he practiced every morning. The island glowed in the dark from the lights of the cliff town to the north, from its startlingly white buildings and pure blue domes, and from the light of a waning moon over the sea. Bridey's head throbbed. They sat holding hands, not looking at each other, each waiting for the other to speak first.

Somewhere beyond them in the blackness, one of the island's feral cats growled and moaned. Bridey jumped at the sound and clutched Alessandro's arm.

"Is only little cat," Alessandro said in the dark. "Nothing to be afraid. Maybe he fights for love."

They lapsed again into a silence burdened with unshared thoughts. There would be no more nights alone on the island for them, no more freedom, no more intimacy in their private cave- room. What lay ahead was as unfathomable as the Aegean in the moonlight. Decisions would have to be made, but as long as they stayed silent, neither would have to make those decisions and bring the future into reality. It might be wonderful. It might not. To remain silent preserved the present for just a bit longer, for just one more moment.

"I can no' stay here any longer," Alessandro finally said.

"Don't." The tears started up again, stinging her bloodshot eyes.

"Bridey, I must say this. Today Gianni make me know what I do. I think of myself only. I make my mama and papa crazy for worry. Gianni says they cry for me every day and they are very angry. They don' understand what make me leave them, why I run away. Many people in Assisi worry. My maestro. My friends at the hotel. They ask my family what happen. Why do I leave, do I no want to go to Rome? Nobody understand this. I don' think of nothing but me and what I want."

"That's not true! I know it's not!" Bridey argued. "You don't just think of yourself — you could have drowned trying to rescue Ian. You risked your own life! I don't believe you're as selfish as your family says you are. Selfish people take and take. What have you taken from anyone? But you give so much to everyone. Your music is your gift to anyone who hears it. You don't keep that for yourself. You're giving your life to something the whole world can share. But there's so much more to you than music, Alessandro! So much more. Maybe that's why you ran away to find me, because you know in your heart there's more to you than your career. There has to be a reason why you're here, instead of back home."

She let go of his arm. It hurt to touch him, to feel the flesh and muscle that she made love to only yesterday.

He turned toward her. "Is because I love you! Is the only reason. I can think of nothing else. I read your letter and I know if I don' come, you forget me. You dance with Riordan and you are lost for me. I want nothing but to be with you, to touch you, to make love with you. Never am I so happy, these days with you on this island. Never I am so free. You are my Miss America, no?" He stroked her hair over and over, as if petting their mutual anxiety away. "The first time I am with you, I know God send you to me. I tell you, at my church of San Damiano, I do something big to be with you again. You tell me I must do something 'spectacular' for you. You remember your words to me?"

"Of course I remember. But I don't even know what I meant then. Is this all my fault? Am I some kind of career-wrecker?"

"I don' wreck my career," he said. He sounded surprised that she would say that. His hand dropped away from her hair and fell to his thigh. "I go to Rome. This I know I must do. Bridey, I can' no run away from my singing. I can never do it. It come from my spirit. It come from God. He give my voice to me. Is what I work for, what I dream, and my family dream, and the people of Assisi dream when I win the competition. Only one thing make me more happy from being with you, is when I sing."

Bridey buried her face in her hands and sobbed. She felt again her own shame and guilt for her own selfishness, for shoving Ian and Francesca off onto Rula, for almost causing Ian to drown, for how close she came to leaving Alessandro to fend for himself in the water. Maybe it was all a punishment for using her mother's illness to do what she wanted, for being glad it had worked out that way. If it hadn't been for Riordan... Alessandro should have told her he wasn't a good swimmer, they wouldn't have gone so far out on the raft. But she could forgive his embarrassment. Gianni couldn't swim at all; he was afraid of the water. It could have all been different tonight. A terrible kind of different. Alessandro's voice would have been silenced forever and she would have been responsible. She could have lost Ian. It was a miracle to be sitting with Alessandro tonight. Now it was time to face facts. The miracle happened for a reason. Alessandro and she couldn't stay on the island forever, no matter how hard she fantasized or pretended. He didn't belong to her. He never did.

Alessandro slid down onto his knees in front of her. He wiped tears from her cheeks. "Shh. Shh, *mi amore*," he whispered.

"I love you," she said. She swiped at her nose. It was hot and running. Her head hurt. Her muscles ached. Everything about her felt pain.

"This is why I ask. Come with me to Assisi. For my wife, the mother of my children."

It sunk in what he was asking. "When? How?"

"Now," he said. "I leave with Gianni in the morning. I must go back to Assisi. Come with me."

"Tomorrow! I can't do that. It's not possible. I thought you meant... someday."

"You say you love me," he objected. "Why is no possible?"

"I do love you, Alessandro, but it's not ..." It's not that kind of love, she realized. Not immense enough to make her elope, to dump her own family and the hopes they had for her. The dreams she had for herself. It was a first love, the kind you never get over, no matter how it ends up. It was the love of a dream. Not the kind of love that could survive committing your life to someone you only knew, so far, in pieces. Is this what Aunt Maura was talking about? Love being confusing?

He gripped her hands. "Is not what?"

"It's not that simple. I can't come to Assisi now. Your family hates me, for one thing. They blame me for everything."

"Come to Rome," he urged her. "I leave my family in Assisi. In Rome we can be together alone. My family don' know you the way I do. When they see what I see, they love you also."

"And do what in Rome? You'll have enough to do there, without worrying about me. I don't even speak the language."

"You can learn Italian. I teach you."

"And I have school to go through, remember? The university? That's three weeks away. I should have been home by now, getting ready."

He sat back up beside her. "For what do you need the school?

If we marry, I care for you, and our children."

"I need school!" she said. "I'm only eighteen. I need an education. I have plans. And ambitions! And what about my family? They expect me to do things, too. I love them."

But here was the divide. "Bridey, you share with me your wish to be in the world. I give to you that opportunity. If you are with me and I am success in the opera, we travel to other countries — to London, maybe to New York and you see your family there. If we put our dreams together, there are many more the chance they come true."

If.

It was a mighty word. Just two letters, yet it had so much power. Alessandro was poised on the cliff of risk, ready to fall forward and spread his wings, believing he would catch the updraft and soar. But Bridey wasn't as confident, not fledged enough yet, and the precipice was steep, the unknown too full of jagged points. She needed more time to take flight.

She would have to let him go. If she followed him now, that is all she would be able to do, perhaps forever. She might never soar on her own. She looked into his eyes and her heart dissolved into them, bags packed and ready to go. But her head, her voice, said something different.

"I can't. If I did it now, it would be a disaster."

"You are saying no?" Alessandro dropped his voice.

"I'm not ready for it all," she said. "Right now."

He hunched forward, resting his arms on his thighs, gripping his hands, and stared down at the ground. They could smell the scent of thyme and rosemary mixed with the sea air. He said nothing. A cat appeared, walking the line of the house's crumbled wall, eyes flashing in reflected light. It jumped down to vanish into the dark.

"I do love you," Bridey repeated. "You're the most perfect man I've ever met. You've given me so much, Alessandro. You're everything I could want for a husband. It's just not the right time."

"Bridey," he said finally. "Is something maybe you don' think about."

"What's that?"

"When we, we make love, we don'... take care. You know? We don' stop before -—. So, maybe you are no ready, but maybe my baby start inside you an' you don' know this for now. Do you never think of this? If you are no ready, why do you do it?"

Why did she do it? The truth was she liked the danger of it. The potential. It gave him an aura of potency she couldn't explain, and knowing she kept a part of him inside her afterward made the sex all the more secret and powerful. It was like a piece of his gift to absorb, so that it became a part of her, too. A piece no audience could ever share.

Like so many of the good girls of Providence, she opted to play Russian roulette with her fertility. This time, the wheel spun in her favor. In her bath that morning, a small plume of red had drifted out of her and swirled up to the surface. She could feel the faint warning stripes of cramping, flashes of distant heat lightning within her. "No," she said.

"You don' think of this?"

"I'm not pregnant, I mean. I'm sure. You don't have to worry."

"I worry," Alessandro said. "You can be sure? Because, if there is a baby, what do you do?"

"There won't be."

"If it is so," he repeated, staring into her eyes, "what do you do?"

Did he want it to happen? She could see desperate hope there in his eyes, a last chance to open a door to a future with him. His own future. If the unimaginable did happen, could she accept that it was meant to be? Could she shelve her life for his, before hers even started?

"If there was a baby," she said, "I would tell you. We'd deal with it. I would never do anything without you." The look in his eyes was killing her. This was no path she was prepared to take.

To try to lighten things, she said: "If there was a baby, we'd have to have the funeral of my entire family. Because they would all drop dead from shock." It was a lousy joke. She regretted it the moment it escaped from her.

His voice was full of reproach. "I don' joke. All I say to you is the truth. I go tomorrow. If you don' come, we don' see each other for long time. I am afraid for it, Bridey. Maybe I never see you again." His voice faltered with tears. "And I... I don' know what I do without you. You are the muse. My love."

She wrapped her arms around him and her own tears seeped onto his shoulder. This was really happening. It was really ending. "Oh God," said Bridey, "I don't want you to go! I just want to stay here. I want time in this place to last forever. But I want more time, to know what I'm meant to do." She kissed his neck, the hollow of his beautiful throat. His temple. His lips. "Couldn't you stay with me? Couldn't you come to America and audition? You could live in New York. I could come up from Washington on the shuttle to see you while I'm in school. Aunt Corinne would be there. And Sara. You wouldn't be alone. They love you! Everyone loves you, Alessandro. Ian loves you. I love you." She was babbling. Bereft, and wildly hoping he would listen and decide to make a U-turn in his plan.

But he didn't.

"I go to Rome," he said, his voice firm, though he was crying. "Is my fortune. My reward. I work so hard, all my life. If I am success in Europe, I come to New York someday. But for now, I must go back to Italy."

There wasn't anything left to say. *For now*, he said. It was something. A piece of hope between them.

Riordan drove them to the island ferry early the next morning. Gianni rode in the front seat with Riordan, relieved to have his younger brother safely in tow, anxious to get away. Gianni avoided looking at Bridey. Clearly, to Gianni, this disaster was her fault. Bridey curled up against Alessandro in the back, holding hands and saying nothing, staring out from behind her dark glasses through the open windows at the dramatic, windswept landscape of Santorini. They were mute with the agony of saying goodbye. She could have stayed at the villa and avoided the sight of him standing on the deck as the ferry pulled away, but she savored every minute she had left with him.

Riordan shifted gears, descending a series of steep switchbacks barely wide enough to make it past an oncoming truck, until they pulled into the harbor landing. They parked and Riordan bought tickets for the Athens ferry. Hugh insisted on paying the fare, including their airline tickets back to Rome and the train fare north to Assisi. He was grateful for Alessandro's attempt at saving his son without regard for his own safety.

The ferry ride would take eight hours. The brothers were booked on a late night flight to Rome and the train would have them back in Assisi the next day. The ferry was already docked and ready to depart.

Paros, Naxos, Mykonos, Athens, the sign read.

In the end, words didn't come. Their goodbye was said in the tears in their eyes and the last clinging link of hands, until they had to let go. Bridey watched in misery as Alessandro boarded and turned to face her from the aft deck of the ferry. He was a silent, unwaving figure growing smaller and smaller as the boat pulled away and churned out to sea. She stood rooted to the spot until all that was left were the last waves of the ferry's wake, slapping against the dock.

Thirty-One

Bridey watched the ferry as it headed out toward the horizon. The early morning sun was already beating on her shoulders from a clear sky the color of wild cornflowers. The clouds of yesterday afternoon were already long gone. A curious flatness filled her. Last night she felt as if being without Alessandro would be like missing a piece of her flesh, with the same sort of raw, needle-like pain no bandage could relieve. Now, she stood staring blankly out to sea, as still as one of the ancient paintings on a wall in the island's buried ruins of Akrotiri. Her stillness intrigued a pelican sitting on a nearby post. He turned his doleful, long-beaked face to survey her with one eye, then extended his wings and folded them again, shrugging: What are you going to do? That's life. Terns and gulls wheeled in the air above, filtering down their own shrill comments.

Riordan came up behind her. He'd stood a respectful distance back while Bridey said goodbye and Alessandro and Gianni boarded the ferry. He put his hand on her shoulder. "I could do with some coffee," he said. "How about you?"

She startled, as if asleep on her feet. "Sure."

He maneuvered the old Citroen back up the mountainside, one tanned arm casually resting on the window frame. Bridey sat beside him in the passenger seat, her chin propped on her hand. She yawned from the hangover of crying spells and emotion in the last twenty-four hours. She hid her eyes behind her sunglasses, but she caught Riordan glancing at her as he drove. He reached the top road and shifted gears, picking up speed as they wound alongside the cliff's barren walls of sharp stone layers. The Aegean spread before them in a gleaming panorama, deep sapphire against the brilliant sky. Already they could see the varied wakes of ships and small fishing boats that traversed the expanse below. One of them might be the ferry.

"This is quite a place, isn't it?" Riordan said after a time.

She kept her face turned to the view, the wind thrashing her hair around her throat, whipping her cheeks. "I love it here," she said.

"Better than Athens? More than dancing the night away?" He smiled at her, trying to prompt a smile in return.

Bridey had no smile to give him.

He weaved the car though the narrow tangle of streets in the cliffside town, parked outside a post office, led her along the maze of alleys and stairs and finally into a two-story café' that perched at the tip of the island. He asked for a table on the open top level and they were given one at the wall with a view of windmills and the islands in a haze to the north.

"I suppose bringing Gianni here to fetch Alessandro put the nail in the coffin of any chance for friendship between us," he said quietly, after they'd been served. "But I couldn't leave Gianni staking out the Hilton and asking questions." He traced the square of the pattern in the tablecloth over and over with the end of his spoon, as if funneling his thoughts into geometry. "Still, I don't like to see you so flattened. Like the light's gone out of you.

It's between Alessandro and his family, Bridey. You have no part in it."

She sighed, so tired and low it felt like an effort to move her mouth to speak. "He had to go back sometime and face his family. He knew that. He told Sara as much." She watched him trace angles. They were both silent for a few moments. "You know," she said, "I wonder if Alessandro accepted Uncle Hugh's offer to come here with us because it put off having to admit to his parents what he'd done, leaving for Athens. He escaped all that pressure and work for awhile."

"I thought it was because he was following a wild love affair." He said it without sarcasm. She could almost hear sympathy.

Bridey finally smiled a little. Alessandro did love her. She wasn't wrong about that.

Her tea was hot and sweet. There was about a half-inch layer of honey and sugar in the bottom of the cup. She picked up a sticky pastry covered in cinnamon and crushed almonds. "As for you and I being friends," she said, "I can never thank you enough for what you did yesterday. You were a hero. I was never so happy to see anybody in my whole life, when I saw it was you swimming for us." She looked into his eyes. "If you hadn't come then, Alessandro might be dead today."

Her gratitude seemed to surprise him. "Thank you," he said softly. "But don't discount what you did yourself. We can all see the self-flagellation you've been doing. Ian can be a basket of trouble, Bridey, even when he isn't inspired by adulation for someone and spoiled by indulgence, however loving. You had no way to know he'd try to come after you. It's his willfulness and lack of fear that got him into trouble out there. He's too little and innocent to know his own limits. I'm afraid it won't be the last time he'll bite off more than he can chew."

"I guess I just feel so guilty about Alessandro."

"Why? You're right, you couldn't have done it. You were frightened and exhausted. You both might have ended up drowning."

"It's about more than that," she said.

"Ah." He shifted in his chair and folded his arms, faking an Irish accent. "Would you want to be tellin' Father Clarke about it now?"

I want to tell somebody, she thought. She stared at the pastry in her hand.

"I can keep a confidence," he assured her. "You have no idea."

She met his eyes. Secrets. She was sharing hers. Now was the time to ask. "What do you do at the Embassy, exactly? Sara and I have been trying to figure that out since Athens. Are you a bodyguard?"

He sat silent for a moment and Bridey knew he was gauging her. "I suppose, in a sense, you could say I'm a bodyguard. Your uncle does very important work and there are a lot of people who would like to do him harm. Have him out of the way. I keep an eye out, officially." He tapped out a drum rhythm with the spoon on the edge of the table before speaking again, hesitating. "And unofficially, he's been very good to me. He's my superior, but he takes a personal interest. And he needs a vacation. A bit like Alessandro needs a vacation, but more political." He paused again, drumming. "I have a confession to make. I've made it part of my job to watch out for you as well. As you may have noticed." His smile was embarrassed. But he grew serious again. "That night Alessandro sang at the villa, well, I got a bit plastered. When I went to bed, I woke Alessandro up. Told him if he did anything to hurt you, if he wasn't absolutely straight up with you, he'd have to answer to me. I'd raise him up an octave, to castrato."

Bridey couldn't help smiling at the idea of Riordan being protective and jealous. "What did he say?"

More geometrics traced on the table. Riordan stared downward. "He told me he was almost afraid of how much he loved you. Never felt anything like it. And that he would do nearly anything to make you happy. Then he told me to back off, that I was drunk and needed some sleep." Riordan looked up at Bridey. "I know how to spot liars in my line of work. He wasn't one of them. I think with Alessandro, what you see is what you get."

Bridey nodded, watching his eyes. "And you don't let anyone see anything."

"Never mind that," he said, breaking away from her glance. "You've cleverly veered away from the subject."

"What subject?"

"The one you brought up. Your guilt."

So she told him about Alessandro the waiter, about play-acting in front of her family, and the fact that it had gone into something far more serious. She didn't tell him any details about what went on in Assisi and in the cave room, because she could tell by the way he watched her that he knew. He filled in the blanks.

"Last night when we went off to talk, he asked me to elope with him, to go back to Assisi, or at least come to Rome. I told you the first night in Athens, when we were dancing, that it was serious. Remember?"

"I do remember," he said, his voice softening. "I remember all of it. I thought my duty there was going to be dead boring. And then you were added to the mix. Full of piss and vinegar about Alessandro." He studied her. "And yet, you're still here. You had your chance and you didn't take it."

"I couldn't do it," she admitted. "The thought of running off to Italy and following Alessandro around, not knowing anyone but him; and he kept talking about being married, and having a baby, and I can barely take care of myself! I'm not ready for any of that. And I miss my dad. My little brothers. My dog. I miss home." For the first time in weeks, the pull of home felt like gravity.

The waiter came to check if they wanted more coffee. Bridey let him fill her cup just to get him to leave them alone. In a few more days, Alessandro would be back to filling cups of tea and serving people again, she expected. Back to the Hotel Windsor

Savoia for a few more weeks.

Riordan leaned forward on the table. "Bridey, I take back everything I said once, about you being better off marrying and having babies. I was a complete ass to say that. But you've proved your mettle. And you're right to have dreams and big plans for yourself. You thank me for jumping in the water yesterday, but I only finished off what you were in the middle of. And I have to tell you…" He reached out, asking to take her hand. She gave it. His eyes were intent. "I think you're bloody magnificent. You're strong and smart and you're brave. You've got all the makings of someone who'll go far in the world. And there's a lot of world left for you to see."

She ducked her head, shy from the compliment. He said she was magnificent… And to be thought so by the imperious Riordan Clarke! Damn. She'd done it at last. He held onto her hand and she made no move to pull it away. There was peace between them finally, the kind of respect survivors share, the sort of feelings that open doors.

"Perhaps you'll make another trip one day," he said. "And we'll meet again in some part of the world. Only this time, we'll start as real friends. I'd like that, Bridey. I'd like to see what world you'll conquer next."

When Bridey arrived back at the villa, Corinne, Sara and Maura were sunning by the pool. It was almost too quiet. They looked at Bridey with sympathy, like mourners at a wake. Riordan had dropped her off at the front courtyard and gone to arrange for cars to take them and their belongings to the plane in a few days. This time the donkeys would precede them to the airport. Diony would see to that.

"Where're Uncle Hugh and the twins?" Bridey asked. She was afraid there might be something wrong with Ian.

"He took them to ride the donkeys," Corinne said.

"How are your eyes today?" Maura asked.

Bridey took off her sunglasses. Her eyes still felt as if they were lined with the sand from the sea floor. The swelling was down, although she felt tender inside, bruised with feeling.

"Ouch," said Sara. "They're really red."

"Those are some nasty scratches," Corinne said, pointing out her wrist and neck. "Did you put anything on them?"

Bridey got the feeling they were making small talk. She examined her wrist. The most painful thing about it was the missing bracelet. She didn't even have that left of Alessandro. All she had was the tote bag he bought her, with the paint cemented to the bottom. "Rula put some herb salve on them," she answered, touching her neck where the thin sore scratches marked Ian's panic. "Where's my mom?"

"She's upstairs in her room," Maura said. "She'd like to see you now you're back."

Bridey felt her heart drop. She headed up to the room Tilla shared with Corinne.

Tilla was lying on her bed, toying with a set of onyx and silver worry beads, a present from Rula. She hadn't really smoked a full cigarette since their ride into Rome three weeks ago. She figured it was a good start on quitting. The worry beads gave her something to do with her hands.

"Hey, Mumma." Bridey greeted her softly, somewhat warily. "Aunt Maura said you wanted to see me. Is everything okay? Are you feeling all right?"

Her mother looked up from her pillows. She was dressed, lying on top of the spread, resting. She held her arms out to Bridey. "Hello, my sweetheart girl," she said, just like she had done since Bridey was a child. "I know you're having a bad day today. I thought you might need a hug."

Bridey's face crumpled and she crawled wordlessly onto the bed. She rested her head on Tilla's chest and was enfolded in her arms, back beneath her wings. Tilla smoothed Bridey's hair and kissed the top of her head. They stayed that way for a while, quiet and alone. Bridey breathed in her mother's scent, the fragrance of unconditional love and security. Tears slid from her eyes, and Tilla brushed them from her cheek.

"I didn't want you to hurt this much," Tilla said to her. "But someone once told me, the deeper the pain, the greater the capacity we gain for happiness and love. It stretches our souls. Makes them bigger. It doesn't seem like a very fair bargain sometimes."

"It isn't fair," Bridey said. "I saw so much joy in Alessandro. I felt it with him and I..." She broke down. "I didn't want to let him go."

Her mother's arms tightened around her. "Oh, Dolly, I know. I know that feeling. You're my joy and I don't want to let you go. But I know if I never did, eventually you'd lose your own joy. It's taken me a while to figure that out. And it hurts. But now I know. If you try to hold on to someone, or hold them back, you'll only end up crushing the thing that makes you love them in the first place."

It would be years before Bridey would tell her mother that Alessandro wanted her to leave with him or that he'd asked her to marry him. For the moment, she wanted only to rest in her mother's embrace, to feel at peace with her again, to close her eyes and know that no matter where she went or for how long, being held by her mother would always be a way of coming home.

Maura, Corinne and Sara hesitated in the doorway.

"Come on in," Tilla told them. "It's okay."

Her family settled around them, sitting on the double bed.

"We're all going to miss him," Corinne said. She patted her niece. "I'm sorry he left the way he did. But if you ran away, I imagine we'd turn things ass over tea kettle to find you, too."

"He didn't want you to know, Bridey," Sara told her. "He didn't want to ruin things for you. You should have seen him yesterday morning, talking about it. He was almost crying. He was really tortured about what to do. I'm sure you'll see him again, someday. He loves you. You know it was love at first sight."

Maura crossed her long legs and picked up Bridey's limp hand in hers. "Ian was in tears this morning, when he found out Alessandro was gone," she said. "We all loved having him here. But he wasn't here for us. He was here for you. Came to claim you. Though, Bridey, when I heard him sing, the picture changed. He's headed for a place I'm not sure you'd want to go. And no, I don't mean Rome, Corinne." She glanced at her sister, warning her not to make light of what she was about to say. "Alessandro has the chance— a chance, not a guarantee — to reach the top of his profession. It will mean being on a lot of stages, singing in lots of spotlights, getting attention from all sorts of people, good and bad. It will mean giving up a normal life. And living like that can ruin some people. He's willing to risk that. He's willing to do whatever it takes. But I can tell you that anyone who is in love with him, or marries him, will have to take second place at best. Music is his passion, Bridey, and it will be his mistress. Even if he manages to keep an even keel, have a wife and a family, that mistress will be demanding. No matter who he loves, she'll always have to stand aside in the wings, because that mistress will demand it. And that can be a lonelier and lonelier place as the thrill wears off."

Bridey sniffed back her tears. "I know what you're saying," she said.

"No," said Maura. "I don't think you do. When you're eighteen, you think you know all you need to. What you don't know now is that you're still in the thrill of what it's like to love. Just at the beginning. And that's fine. But as time goes on, you'll see more clearly. There's so much more to it."

They stayed in the bedroom talking. Bridey sat up against the headboard of the bed, listening to her mother and aunts fall into the easy chatter of sisters. Sara stared across them and gave Bridey a sad little smile. She would miss Alessandro, too, as all young girls do with the first man who treats them as if they're not fourteen, caught in childhood and still in a chrysalis, but soon to be a butterfly drying her wings.

Bridey winked back at her. They had each other. They'd be okay.

The big board in Heathrow flipped its individual bars with the names of airlines and flights arriving and departing.

So Bridey wouldn't see London after all. No meeting with her pen pal, no pilgrimage to Carnaby Street this time. Bridey stood in the airport, free at last. Corinne linked arms with shaky Tilla as they searched the board overhead for their British European Airways flight AZ632 into JFK.

"Gate 43A," Sara said. "It's right there. I can see it, just down the concourse." She pointed left.

The board flipped again and Bridey watched as BOAC listed its next flight to Rome, now boarding. Gate 40B, two gates down to the right. She stared off in that direction.

Sara looked from Bridey to the board and back again. Bridey turned to her with a smile. She shifted the canvas tote with the pieces of Santorini stuck to its bottom and put her arm around Sara's shoulder. They followed their mothers slowly down the concourse.

Maybe, if her miracle lasted, if it flew with her, she'd visit Alessandro in Rome next summer. She had a standing invitation to come to Amman when things settled down. The world was a much smaller place than when she left weeks ago, and a thousand times more beautiful to her. She could go anywhere from here. But for the time being, she was finished with this itinerary. In a few weeks, a new one would start in Washington. For now, just for now, she'd come far enough.

• • •

Although this book is a work of fiction, it does contain some real situations in Europe and the Middle East during the historic summer of 1967.

The character of Hugh Nowell is based on my late uncle, Jack O'Connell, who was known as a CIA "legend." My uncle was the Middle East Chief of Station for the CIA during the 1960s and into the early 1970s. He was a spy, a very big and important spy, but his own children didn't know what he did until they saw one of the CIA directors on the cover of *Time* magazine when they were teens, and asked their dad, "Why is 'Uncle So & So' on this magazine?" My uncle told them then what he did while they grew up in Beirut and Jordan. He was out of the CIA by that time, working in international law and serving as U.S. legal counsel to His Majesty King Hussein and the country of Jordan. My aunt knew he was CIA, of course. She was with him from the start in Pakistan, Lebanon and Jordan. Sadly, she died suddenly right after they finally came home to the United States. Her death led to my uncle leaving the CIA to be able to care for their children left motherless.

When the Six Day Arab-Israeli War of 1967 started, all British and American dependents were evacuated out of Israel, Jordan, and other countries. Dependents stationed in Jordan were sent to Greece.

My Uncle Jack remained a close friend and advisor to King Hussein right up to the King's death in 1999. Hussein asked my uncle to write the unknown story of Hussein's life-long desire for peace in the Middle East and the King's behind-the-scenes, repeated efforts to bring peace about. My uncle was involved in all the peace processes over a 40-year period, both as a CIA intelligence officer and in his international law practice. He fulfilled his promise to Hussein when he wrote *King's Counsel: A Memoir of War, Espionage, and Diplomacy in the Middle East* (W.W.Norton & Company) with veteran Washington journalist Vernon Loeb. The book was OK'd by the CIA but it was not published until after my uncle's death in 2008.

About five years before my uncle died, he asked me to help him with a novel he was writing. Over the next six months working on the book, I learned the most fascinating things about espionage. He finished the book but it remains unpublished. Helping my uncle with his book finally felt like being at "the grown-ups table" with him.

DISCUSSION QUESTIONS

1.) The story takes place in the summer of 1967, often called "The Summer of Love." How were things different then? How are they the same today?

2.) Bridey turns 18 in Venice on her tour. How is she different from the eighteen-year-olds of today? In what way is she similar?

3.) Was Bridey right to defend her mother, aunt and cousin from the man in Ulm? Did she overreact?

4.) Was Bridey right or naïve to go off with Alessandro? What would you have done?

5.) Would Bridey's story be different if Father Clement wasn't a part of the tour?

6.) Corinne is often at odds with Tilla over Bridey. Do you think sisters can have rivalries over their children?

7.) Who do you think Hugh Nowell is?

8.) Discuss Bridey's relationship with Riordan Clarke.

9.) Tilla is prescribed some very heavy pain medications and anti-anxiety drugs by two doctors. Many women received the same drugs for a variety of illnesses and conditions during that time. What do you think happened to Tilla after she returned home?

10.) What would your answer be to Maura's question? Was Bridey in love with Alessandro's talent, or with him as a person? Can the two be separated?

11.) Do you think Bridey made the right choice in the end?

CPSIA information can be obtained at www.ICGtesting.com
Printed in the USA
BVOW03s1559050515

398953BV00004B/9/P